COX

After serving in the army for eight years, Kate Lace has found the best way to deal with testosterone-filled men is to point a gun at them; it certainly helped in getting her husband up the aisle. Since that momentous, if slightly controversial, day, she has had three children and finds the same tactic works on them. However, now that she's a full-time writer, she has had to come up with more subtle ways of keeping her characters under control as pointing a gun at her own head has not proved productive. She has written six books including *Gypsy Wedding*.

Other books by Kate Lace

Gypsy Wedding

COX

KATE LACE

arrow books

Published by Arrow Books 2012

2 4 6 8 10 9 7 5 3 1

Copyright © Kate Lace, 2012

Kate Lace has asserted her right under the Copyright,
Designs and Patents Act 1988 to be identified as the author of this work.

First published in Great Britain in 2012 by
Arrow Books
Random House, 20 Vauxhall Bridge Road,
London SW1V 2SA

www.randomhouse.co.uk

Addresses for companies within The Random House Group Limited
can be found at: www.randomhouse.co.uk/offices.htm

The Random House Group Limited Reg. No. 954009

A CIP catalogue record for this book
is available from the British Library

ISBN 9780099570820

The Random House Group Limited supports The Forest Stewardship
Council (FSC®), the leading international forest certification organisation.
Our books carrying the FSC label are printed on FSC® certified paper. FSC
is the only forest certification scheme endorsed by the leading environmental
organisations, including Greenpeace. Our paper procurement policy can be
found at www.randomhouse.co.uk/environment

Typeset by SX Composing DTP, Rayleigh, Essex SS6 7XF
Printed and bound by
CPI Group (UK) Ltd, Croydon, CR0 4YY

For Ian, with love

Acknowledgements

The real Oxford Boat Race crew in 2011 did not include either Dan Quantick or Rollo Lyndon-Forster but for the purposes of fiction I supplanted two of the crew with these fictional characters. I apologise unreservedly to the real crew and coach for this.

I have also done the real GB Rowing Team's Women's Eight a huge disservice in this book for which I also give a grovelling apology but for my narrative I needed to make our national rowers much less brilliant than they are in real life. As I write, both our men and women rowers top the world ranking tables – no mean feat. There are also certain events that dominate the annual rowing calendar and which I may have jiggled about. The trouble is I am writing a work of fiction and for fictional reasons I needed things to work differently. It is not the fault of those who advised me that I mucked around with reality. So, this is all made up with just the background of the sport of rowing itself (and none of the people involved) featuring.

I need to thank a number of people in the rowing world, Henry Pelly who was patient beyond compare, who lent me books and answered endless questions, Diana and George Pelly for inviting me to Henley so I could see proper rowers in action, Ben Lewis the head coach at East Molesey Boat Club who took me out on the water so I could see rowing 'up close', Neil Hussey who told me about sports injuries and how to treat them, Richard Boulton who told me about the training and Mark Perkins who gave me some really key material about coxing.

Besides the rowing experts I need to thank my family, poor dears, who lived with me while I wrote this, my agent Laura Longrigg for being supportive and encouraging and above all these people I need to thank Gillian Holmes for holding my hand and making sure I wrote the best book I could.

There is nothing – absolutely nothing –
half so much worth doing as simply messing about in boats.

Kenneth Grahame – *The Wind in the Willows*

PART I

1

Henley-on-Thames
July 2010

Rollo Lyndon-Forster lounged in a plastic garden chair in a hidden corner at the back of the vast blue and white marquee where all the boats were stored between races. It was quiet here in this little-frequented spot and Rollo felt utterly relaxed as he leaned back, his legs splayed, a happy smile lighting up his extremely handsome face as a curly blonde head bobbed up and down in his lap. Maybe this wasn't the best blow job he'd ever had but still, it was pretty damn good. He could feel the girl's tongue (What *was* her name? Bella . . . Beatrice . . . Becca? Something beginning with 'B' anyway) swirling around his cock as her mouth moved up and down. He shut his eyes as the swell of an orgasm began to build. Just a few more—

'Rollo!'

The girl kneeling at his feet jumped so suddenly he felt her teeth graze the skin at the tip of his penis. Shit, he thought, if I'm going to get circumcised I want an anaesthetic first.

He snapped open his eyes but he already knew exactly who had interrupted them. 'Fuck off, Dan.' He stared coldly at the six foot four athlete towering above him.

The girl, magenta with embarrassment, wiped her mouth and scrambled awkwardly to her feet, catching her heels in the hem of her dress, and fled.

Rollo watched her go. He didn't think, given her apparently low embarrassment threshold, he'd be able to persuade her to finish what she'd started. It was only his assurances that no one ever came to this corner of the boat tent that had enabled him to get her to go this far in the first place. Never mind, plenty more fish in the sea. Somewhere at Henley was bound to be another girl who might be up for a good time.

'What the fuck do you think you're doing?' said Dan.

Rollo tucked his now flaccid penis into his lycra shorts and pulled them up. 'I would have thought that even you might have managed to work that out.' Rollo stood, his height matching Dan's almost exactly but whereas Dan was dark, with dark brown eyes, Rollo was fair and blue-eyed. 'Please don't tell me I've got to spell it out to you. Didn't Mummy tell you the facts of life?'

Dan gave him a cold stare and shook his head, ignoring the barb. 'You haven't registered at the admin tent. Chuck told me to tell you to get your arse in gear and do it now.'

Shit, he hadn't either. He'd been on his way to do it when Blondie or Barbie or whatever her name was had distracted him. He shrugged as he glanced at his watch. He still had a few minutes but he was cutting it fine. Oops. He began to walk past the racks of boats towards open side of the tent.

'And start focusing on the race,' yelled Dan after him. 'I want to win even if you don't.'

Rollo ignored him. As if a quick blow job was going to spoil their chances. Dan really ought to lighten up a bit. He really was a bore. After all, half the girls came to Henley hoping to pull a rower but Dan never took advantage. More fool him. Still, thought Rollo, all the more for me.

'This is the life,' said Amy.

She looked around at the scene, at the July sunshine sparkling off the water, at the crowds that thronged the banks of the Thames at Henley: the buff bodies of the rowers in their tight lycra rowing shorts and T-shirts or all-in-ones, the ladies in their high heels, frocks and fabulous hats and the men in their colourful blazers and boaters. It was almost like some sort of Seurat painting brought to life. In the distance a jazz band was playing a jolly ragtime melody, the smell of crushed grass filled the air along with vowels that could cut glass and the occasional smattering of applause as the spectators stopped socialising and acknowledged the rowing. 'Cor,' she said in a low voice to her friend Ellie, 'I wouldn't push him out of bed.' She eyed a hunk in a Harvard rowing blazer as he strolled past.

'Amy, sweetie,' said Ellie, 'you say that about almost every man you clap eyes on.'

'You make me sound like some sort of hussy. There's no harm in looking, you know.'

Ellie agreed. 'Although you probably don't have a chance; he looks the sort to have taken a vow of chastity. It's very fashionable in America these days.'

7

'Really! Why would anyone do that?'

'It may be hard for you to believe this but some people don't believe in sex before marriage.'

'Then they're mad. No test drive? No try before you buy?'

'*Some* people have standards.'

'Hey!' Amy gave Ellie a friendly punch on the arm. 'What are you implying?'

'Nothing, nothing, I swear. Don't get your knickers in a twist.' Ellie smiled down at her diminutive friend who was the cox in the Bath women's eight of which Ellie was stroke. Ellie was nearly six foot of honed muscle; she was tanned, athletic and Titian-haired and was a complete contrast to Amy's five foot three of soft curves, blonde curls and deceptively innocent-looking blue eyes.

It never failed to amaze Amy how attractive men seemed to find her. She was perfectly aware what she looked like; didn't she stare at her own reflection in the bathroom mirror ever morning as she combed her hair, slicked on some lip gloss and brushed her mascara wand over her long but pale eyelashes? Unremarkable – that summed her up. What she didn't realise was that her face *was* unremarkable in repose but the instant it became animated, the second she smiled – and she smiled a lot – her smile lit her up, her face transformed and she became irresistibly lovely.

Ellie changed the subject. 'Aren't you nervous? I mean, supposing we don't just lose but lose horribly?' She sighed and jiggled her bottle of mineral water to ease some of the tension she was feeling.

8

'Then we relax, have a blinding time, party till we pull – or drop – and then go home.' Amy smiled up at Ellie finding the possibility of the outcome she'd just described quite attractive.

Ellie sighed. 'But supposing we lose by miles. How humiliating would that be?'

Realistically, it was a possibility. They'd both seen the draw and their first-round race was against a women's eight from Brown University in the States; the crew that had every chance of winning the Ladies' Challenge Plate and a crew that boasted a couple of really serious contenders for the American Olympic rowing squad.

'We won't,' Amy said reassuringly. 'I mean, we may lose, but not by miles.'

'How can you be so sure?'

'Because I'm your cox and I know what you're capable of. We may not win but we're not going to be thrashed.'

'I suppose,' said Ellie, grudgingly. 'But—'

'But nothing. Look, I've trained with you for months and months, I've looked after your injuries, I've done your physio—'

'Physio?' said a voice behind them.

Ellie turned round and squinted up into the sun at the man, taller even than her, who had asked the question.

'Oh, it's you. Might have guessed you'd come sniffing around at some point. Hello, Rollo.'

Amy followed her gaze. *Bloody hell, wow!* she thought as she clapped eyes on a blond, bronzed hunk with the body of a gladiator and the face of a film star. Oh, and dark blue eyes framed by even darker lashes, she noticed as her eyes met his.

'And I'm *not* sniffing around, as you so rudely put it.'
He spoke to Ellie but smiled at Amy. 'Aren't you going to introduce me?'

'If I must.' Ellie sounded surprisingly sulky. 'Amy, Rollo. Rollo, Amy.'

It was an intro of sorts, Amy supposed, but she decided to ignore Ellie's lack of grace.

Amy stuck her hand out and shook Rollo's. 'Hello.' She flashed her very best and brightest smile at him.

Stuff the rower from Harvard, this was the rower to try to pull. She didn't think she stood the slightest chance but, heck, there was no harm in trying.

'And hello, Amy,' he drawled back at her, increasing the volume of his smile to give her the benefit of his dazzling even teeth. Amy's insides instantly did flick-flacks before dissolving into mush. 'So, you're a physio? How interesting. I could do with a consultation.'

'Only just,' said Amy. 'I only graduated recently.'

'And she's *our* physio,' interrupted Ellie. 'She's here to do the physio for *us*.'

I could moonlight, thought Amy, hopefully.

'I'm sure you could spare her for just a few minutes,' said Rollo.

'I'm not busy,' said Amy, avoiding the evil look that Ellie shot at her.

'I'd be very grateful,' said Rollo.

'Yeah, and we all know what *that* means,' snapped Ellie.

Amy thought she knew what it meant too, and she reckoned that a very grateful Rollo was a deeply attractive prospect. Although, to judge from the way Ellie was glowering at Rollo, Amy decided it might be best to keep that opinion to herself.

'What's the problem?' Amy asked Rollo.

Rollo rubbed his left shoulder. 'An old injury is giving me a bit of grief.'

'I could give you a massage,' said Amy, having to battle to keep her voice from squeaking with excitement at the thought of getting up close and personal with him. 'Maybe help with some stretches.'

'Perfect. And I'm sure Ellie can spare you. Can't you?' he said, challenging Ellie to contradict him.

'Briefly,' said Ellie. 'We're racing later.'

'What have you entered?' Rollo asked. 'The coxless four?'

Did he just emphasise the word 'coxless'? Amy thought. Unable to help herself she glanced at his rowing shorts. Well, he certainly wasn't that!

'We've got an eight entered. Amy's cox.'

'Really?' he said taking Amy's hand. 'Well, I promise I'll get her back to you in good time for your race, and all in one piece.'

Why did that innocent comment sound incredibly dangerous coming from Rollo, wondered Amy? And why did she hope he'd send her back in tatters?

'Just make sure you do,' said Ellie coldly.

Amy wasn't sure if Ellie was cross with her for agreeing to go with Rollo or angry with Rollo for suggesting it. But she didn't care; she had the undivided attention of a sex-god.

'How did you get into coxing?' asked Rollo as he guided her into the boat tent and through the racks and racks of boats and blades piled high there. There were hundreds of rowing boats – single sculls, double sculls, quads, eights – all stacked waiting to be taken out and raced.

'I was allocated a room in digs next to Ellie when I first went to Bath. She'd rowed at school and one day she persuaded me to have a go at coxing because she thought I was the right size. The weather was nice, the river was beautiful and I got the hang of what they wanted me to do quite fast. Actually,' added Amy, 'it was the coxing that made me want to get into sports physio rather than the general stuff that I'd planned to do. Somehow, dealing with athletes' bodies is just so much more rewarding.' She glanced across at Rollo. Dealing with his body certainly would be.

'But you are a proper, *qualified* physio.'

'Oh yes,' she said cheerfully. 'Graduated last month. Of course I haven't had a huge amount of hands-on experience yet but—'

'I'm sure we can change all that,' said Rollo with a straight face but a wicked twinkle in his eye. 'I'm happy to give you all the hands-on experience you could want.'

Oh, yes please!

They'd reached the rear of the tent. Here the air was completely still and rather muggy and smelt of crushed grass.

'No one will trip over us here,' said Rollo.

Trip over? So he was planning on lying down? Better and better. Although, as Amy glanced about her, there wasn't an awful lot of cover if anyone should wander past.

Rollo sat on the grass and Amy hunkered down beside him.

'So what was the original injury and what treatment have you had?' she asked, trying to sound professional and cool. He's a patient, she told herself, even if he is a fitty.

Rollo explained just exactly what was wrong with his shoulder. 'So just a bit of massage should help,' he said. 'Loosen me up before my race. Should I take my T-shirt off?'

Yes he should, although it wasn't going to help her blood pressure, but realistically Amy couldn't work on him if he was all covered up. She swallowed in anticipation of getting a look at his buff body. 'If you don't mind,' she replied.

Rollo stripped off, revealing a perfect six-pack and a tanned torso. Shit, he was gorgeous through and through! Amy's heart rate went ballistic.

'You'd better lie down,' she said, hoping that Rollo wouldn't realise the astounding effect he was having on her.

Rollo lay on his stomach as Amy knelt beside him and got to work manipulating his muscles.

'Oh that's good,' he mumbled. 'Wonderful. So, Amy, have you got a job lined up?'

'Yes, at the John Radcliffe in Oxford.'

'You don't say.'

'Why?'

'Guess where I'm doing my master's.'

'Oh.' Oh my God, more chances to cop off with this guy. 'So do you row for Oxford?'

'Not yet, but I'm going to. I've rowed in the Isis boat.'

At Amy's enquiring look, Rollo elaborated. 'That's the

13

reserve Oxford rowing crew, we race against the Cambridge reserves before the actual boat race.'

The Boat Race wasn't for months and Amy didn't know much about rowing at Oxford but she was pretty certain no one could ever be sure of their seat in the Blue Boat, even if they had rowed for Isis, until it was almost race day. But Rollo was obviously in no doubt. After a beat she said, 'How can you be so sure?'

'Because I always get what I want.'

'Do you now?'

Rollo rolled over onto his side, propped himself on his elbow and looked at her. 'I do, especially if it's something I really want.'

If Amy's heart had had a rev counter attached it would have been in the danger zone. But he was a bit of a cheeky git assuming she would fall at his feet, just like that. She brought herself up short: *falling at his feet* was exactly what she was doing. Maybe she should play at being just a little harder to get than she had – she didn't want to look too easy.

Coolly, or as coolly as she could, she returned his stare with a raised eyebrow and said, 'And you think I'm impressed by that?'

But Rollo just returned the look. 'Aren't you?'

Damn – he knew she was lying. She changed tack. 'Do you want this massage or not?'

Rollo nodded.

'Then lie down,' she ordered.

Rollo pouted but did as he was told. Silence fell as she worked but she found she wasn't able to get the right pressure on Rollo's shoulder. If he were lying on a proper massage table it would be easier but this makeshift arrangement, him lying on the grass, wasn't allowing her to dig her fingers into where they needed to be. She sighed heavily and stopped.

'Don't stop,' muttered Rollo. 'This is heaven.'

'It's no good, it's not working.'

If he was enjoying her massage it most certainly wasn't. The whole idea of a sports injury massage was to break down the scarring of the old injury so the muscle could heal again in the correct way. And breaking down the old scar was a painful business.

'Who cares?'

Amy did. 'I need . . .' Amy stopped. What did she need to be able to really get to grips with Rollo's muscles? 'I need a better angle to work at.'

'So?'

'So . . .' The trouble was Amy had pretty much worked out how she could achieve that angle but she wasn't sure she wanted to.

'Come on. "A problem shared is a problem halved", as my nanny used to say,' said Rollo.

'Nanny?' Then she realised that Rollo was exactly the sort to have that kind of background.

'Of course. Didn't you have one?' said Rollo. He rolled over onto his side and propped his head up using his right hand again.

Amy shook her head. Jesus, what was this guy like?

'Anyway, leaving Nanny out of it, what's your problem?' said Rollo.

'I need to sit on you, to get the right angle and pressure.'

'Sit on me?'

'Yes. Roll over again.'

Rollo did as he was told and once he was lying face down on the grass again Amy straddled him so that her knees were either side of his ribs and her bum rested on his. She got to work.

Once again Dan was searching out Rollo. Their race was in forty minutes, they had to get their boat rigged, on the water and paddle downstream to the start. If they weren't there and ready at the allotted time then the other team would be awarded the race and their trip to Henley would be a complete waste of time. What, thought Dan angrily, does Rollo not understand about that simple fact? Really, the guy is such a flake sometimes. So he'd checked the loos, checked the riverbank, checked that Rollo hadn't been eyeing up the girls queuing to get into the Stewards' Enclosure and had finally run into a fellow rower who'd told him he'd seen Rollo going into the boat tent with a blonde in tow.

Not again. Rollo had sneaked off to finish off what Dan had interrupted earlier. For God's sake couldn't he, just for once, focus on his rowing and not on his dick?

Dan strode through the tent, heading for the corner where Rollo had holed up before. He rounded the barrier formed by a stack of boats and there was Rollo on the floor with a blonde on top of him.

'Oh, for fuck's sake, I might have known it,' he yelled at his rowing partner.

'Known what, Dan?' said Rollo, not even looking at him.

Dan's temper boiled over. Like Rollo didn't know exactly what he was talking about. 'Just for once,' he thundered, 'just for one fucking time, can't you leave off screwing for a few minutes. And right before a race. Today of all days.'

'Shut up, Dan,' said Rollo nonchalantly, not reacting in the slightest to Dan's diatribe.

Dan looked at the girl, noticed her properly and instantly spotted several things. This girl was in shorts and a T-shirt and not a floaty dress. Her hair colour was a completely different blonde, and she was sitting on Rollo's back so whatever else they were doing, they weren't actually screwing. Finally he noticed that he'd made her extremely angry.

'Excuse me,' she snapped, her very pretty blue eyes narrowed in rage. 'What's your problem?' She stared at him belligerently, waiting for his answer.

'I thought . . .'

'Yes?'

Dan shook his head. 'Never mind. I thought Rollo was finishing off some business he'd started earlier.'

'Business?' The blonde raised her eyebrows and then she looked at Rollo. 'Business?' she repeated as she climbed off and knelt on the grass.

Rollo gave her a lazy grin. 'It was nothing. A groupie.'

'Really.' Her voice was larded with sarcasm. 'Then no wonder your friend jumped to conclusions.'

'Danny-boy does that a lot,' said Rollo, rolling over and sitting up. 'Don't you Danny-boy?'

Amy stood up and looked from one to another as she assessed the pair. The animosity between them crackled like static. 'For your information,' she said to Dan, 'I am a trained physiotherapist and I am giving your . . .' she hesitated, '. . . your *colleague* some treatment.'

'Oh,' said Dan.

Well, that made sense, now he thought about it. But he refused to feel guilty about jumping to conclusions. Given Rollo's track record it had been perfectly justifiable.

'"Oh" indeed, Danny-boy,' said Rollo with a sneer of superiority. He shook his head as if in complete horror at Dan's crass behaviour. 'Thanks for the massage, Amy.'

She took it as her cue to leave. 'Your shoulder should be a bit looser. And I really have to go and join my crew shortly. We're racing too.'

Rollo put a hand on her arm to stop her from leaving while he had another dig at Dan. 'Tut, tut. I think you owe Amy here an apology.' Dan didn't offer one so Rollo continued. 'One of these days, Danny-boy, someone'll take exception to your off-colour comments and knock you down. And it'll be no more than you deserve.'

Dan gave Rollo a cold stare and breathed out slowly and deliberately. 'Our race starts in forty minutes,' he said evenly, battling not to lose his temper completely. 'We need to get the boat rigged and on the water.'

'Whatever you say, Danny-boy. I'll be with you in two ticks. Run along while I say thank you to the lovely Amy.'

Dan stared at Rollo, a muscle ticking at the corner of his mouth, but he didn't leave.

'Run along, Dan. I *said*,' Rollo's voice hardened, 'I'll be with you in two ticks.'

Dan stormed off, knowing that if he didn't go he really would lose his temper.

Amy stared at his departing back as Rollo chuckled. 'So easy to wind up, it isn't really a sport at all.'

But Amy barely heard him. She'd thought Rollo was a sensational-looking man but then Dan had appeared on the scene. And while Rollo was a blond Adonis Dan was Heathcliff on steroids: dark, brooding, intense, tall, hunky . . .

'Amy?' said Rollo.

'Sorry,' said Amy returning her attention back to him.

'I was saying how easy it is to wind up Dan,' Rollo repeated a tad sulkily.

'Then you shouldn't,' said Amy, feeling some sympathy for Dan. Rollo had treated him appallingly.

'He'll get over it. Besides he shouldn't be such a dreadful oik. Now then, before you disappear, follow me.'

As she trotted through the boat tent, following Rollo and trying to keep up with his long legs, she wondered for a second why she was obeying him. He was such a bastard calling Dan an 'oik', but she still fancied him. Although, if it came to a choice between the two (she should be so lucky) she'd definitely go for Dan. Towards the Lysander Club end of the boat tent Rollo stopped and bent down to reach under one of the racks. He pulled out a large padlocked plastic case. He deftly twiddled the combination on the lock and then flipped open the lid. Inside were a rowing blazer, white flannels and a rowing cap along with sundry other personal possessions. He pulled out his blazer and rummaged in the inside pocket.

'Here.' He handed her a card.

Rollo Lyndon-Forster, she read. Marford House, Marford, Berkshire. In one corner was his mobile number and in the other his email. Even Amy, who suspected that in Rollo's social circles she too might be considered an 'oik', knew that an address like his meant that Marford House was probably a big ancestral pile. It was more than likely that the village had been named after the house, not the other way round. Which might explain the business about the nanny.

'Give me a call when you're up at Oxford.' He smiled his lazy, slow-burn smile at her and, once again, Amy's insides went into party mode, quite contrarily to the way her head was behaving. 'Ciao and thanks for the massage. Maybe we'll see each other after the racing but if not . . .' And he leaned forward and gave her a peck on the cheek. Her insides went berserk.

And then he was gone.

Slightly dazed, Amy wandered back out into the sunshine to find Ellie.

'You're back,' said Ellie. 'You've been a while.' Her voice was unmistakably chilly.

'I only gave him a massage,' said Amy defensively.

'Really.'

'Yes, really.'

'So he didn't pounce.'

'No.'

'Probably only because he's got to get his shit together and get to the start for his race,' said Ellie, gesturing at their programme.

'Yes, his rowing partner said something of the sort

when I was sorting out his shoulder.'

'Saved by the bell then.'

Amy nodded. 'So, has he pounced on you? Is that how you know him?'

'No.' Ellie sounded both emphatic and disdainful. 'But everyone in rowing knows everyone, and more especially, everyone in rowing knows Rollo, probably because he's loaded and is always buying people drinks or just flashing obscene amounts of cash. And that probably explains why most of the women rowers seem to know him in the biblical sense.'

'So is that why you don't like him,' asked Amy shrewdly, 'because he hasn't made a pass at you?'

'No, you're wrong and he did. I turned him down. I don't like the way he breaks hearts.'

'He won't break mine.' Amy closed her eyes and imagined Rollo with no clothes on. She opened them again when she heard Ellie's snort of disgust.

'And I don't like the way he's screwing around,' said Ellie, 'when he's supposed to be getting married to another rower called Tanya.'

'Married? But he can only be our age.'

'Look, I don't know the details,' said Ellie. 'But it's fairly common knowledge.'

'And does this Tanya know how he behaves?'

'I don't know. I've never met her, but I can't imagine she's thrilled if she does know, can you?'

'Maybe she thinks that it's worth putting up with everything because of his dosh.'

'From what I've heard, her family is just as loaded. And that said,' Ellie paused before saying, 'I've heard she's a bit of a goer too. Sleeps around a lot – bit of a slapper really. So maybe the ruling classes just do things differently. Who knows . . . or cares?'

But Amy did care because, whatever Ellie said, Rollo was the fittest bloke, in every sense of the word, to have crossed her path in a long time . . . or he would have been if she hadn't met Dan too. Him and Dan – what a pair.

2

Dan and Rollo sculled lazily downstream towards Temple Island and the start. To their left two eights, racing for a place in the next stage, thundered past, the coxes yelling at their crews to inspire them to dig deeper for resources of energy to beat the other team, the blades slicing into the water with hypnotic rhythm, the boats surging forward with each straining pull, the crews performing as a single powerful engine. Behind puttered a sleek launch with the umpire standing in the bow, his signal flag at the ready to indicate to the crews if they were failing to hold the racing line. And then came the V of the wash spreading behind the three vessels, slapping against the banks of the river and rocking Dan and Rollo's little craft. They steered their boat around behind Temple Island and its wonderfully elegant folly and approached the start. On either side rose the tree-covered hills of the Thames valley, with the occasional clearing in which stood individual houses of breath-taking grandeur commanding fabulous views and even more fabulous price-tags. George Harrison had lived here, Dan knew, and now it was presumably the natural habitat for merchant bankers, Premiership footballers and others in the 'filthy-rich' bracket.

Dan, in the bow seat, stared at Rollo's back, trying to keep his emotions under control. Why, he wondered, considering how little we have in common, how much we loathe and despise each other, should we be so compatible in a boat? One of life's sick jokes, he concluded.

Paddling gently and using a combination of their oars and the tiny rudder hidden under the hull, they manoeuvred their craft between the two pontoons and brought the stern to rest neatly against the front of the Buckinghamshire station one where a young lad, lying on it face down, grasped it to hold it in position. Looking over Rollo's shoulder and between the two pontoons Dan could see the umpire's launch and, beyond, the wooded banks of the Thames as it stretched downstream towards Marlow and then London. Next to them on the Berkshire station was a pair of Australian scullers, dressed in green and gold vests and with green and gold blades; the Davies twins. Identical in every way and so perfectly matched as a pair.

Dan began to focus on the race. He was brimming with energy and tension and his legs jiggled involuntarily as they waited to be given the signal to go. From the back, Rollo looked relatively calm but Dan knew his jaw would be working, almost as if he were chewing gum. The twins would be hard to beat but he and Rollo weighed more than a stone more than their opponents. But would the extra drag caused by their weight be counterbalanced by the added power it ought to bring them? Theoretically it should but . . . but it was only theory. The reality was just about to be played out. And if they lost that was them out of the competition. Each race at Henley was a tussle between two crews with only the winner going forward to the next round. With no heats and no repêchage – where boats that have failed to qualify by a small margin get a second chance – it was instant death.

The umpire called out to check both pairs were ready. Dan and Rollo both slid their seats as far forward as they could go, their blades buried in the water behind them, ready for the moment they would thrust themselves backwards, pushing their feet against the stretcher in an explosive surge to drive the boat through the water.

'Attention, go!' yelled the umpire.

Rollo and Dan drove themselves backwards at full force, shooting the boat away from the pontoon. At the limit of their stroke they both then hauled their bodies on their sliding seats back into an almost foetal position ready to repeat the process.

With each surge they began to draw away from Australia, inch by exhausting inch, as their blades swept through the water on either side of them, a lesson in technical brilliance as they cut cleanly in and out of the water, dipping and flashing. On the towpath to their right the crowds hollered and yelled for the home team, on their left a crowd of corporate types out junketing on a paddle steamer added to the roar of noise as they raced the mile and a third to the finish.

By Fawley, the halfway point, Dan's muscles were screaming but he drove himself on relentlessly, as did Rollo in front of him. The Australians were starting to inch back again. Their blades were almost level and in danger of touching. The umpire shouted at them to keep to their own stations and Rollo must have touched the rudder pedal a smidge as they moved slightly over to the Buckinghamshire bank.

On they raced, neck and neck down the river, the crowds yelling encouragement and the temple, on its eponymous island, grew smaller and smaller as they hammered down the straight course. They flashed past the burger joints, bars and shops, past the picnickers and campsites that lined the towpath until the cheerful melee of the public area began to morph into the gracious lawned enclosures reserved for the rich, the aficionados and the connected. The finish was almost upon them.

In, out, forwards, back, Rollo and Dan swung their oars in absolute synchronicity. Dan risked a glance at the opposition. Dead level.

'Come on,' he roared at Rollo. They increased the rate from thirty-seven to thirty-eight, their bodies screamed in protest, but it was only for a few more seconds. They inched ahead by a canvas as they passed the Fawley Stand but the Aussies weren't giving up. They were coming back. Once again their blades were dead level and then two strokes later the twins' oars were a fraction ahead. Dan and Rollo had peaked too soon.

Dan knew he had nothing left to give; he'd pressed the accelerator as hard as he could and as they swooshed past the Stewards' Enclosure to the finish the positions didn't change.

The hooter blipped to indicate the Australians had won just a split second before Dan and Rollo passed the line.

Dan couldn't believe it. All that pain, all that work and they'd lost. In front of him he saw Rollo's shoulders slump and knew his teammate felt the same way. Fuck!

Wearily they returned the Australians' three cheers and then rowed to the jetties in front of the boat tent. Bringing the boat alongside they undid the gates and then, with their oars released, they pushed their sculls onto the wooden decking, steadied the boat and climbed back onto dry land. Neither said a word, partly because they didn't have spare breath, but also because there was nothing to say. They'd lost: their time at Henley was over. They might as well park their boat, get changed and then go and find a bar to drown their sorrows in.

Amy and Ellie moved away from the riverbank and back into the crowds of people milling about on the grass in front of the boat tents.

'They shouldn't have lost,' said Ellie.

'They only just lost,' said Amy loyally.

'A canvas. They should have managed to hold them. Rollo won't be pleased.' As she said this the two boys stamped past carrying their boat, both wearing thunderous expressions on their faces.

'It was all your fault, you stupid fucker,' snarled Rollo over his shoulder to Dan.

'Because we weren't as fit as them?' countered Dan. 'Because you haven't trained enough? Because you didn't have your eye on the ball?'

'Because you made us push for the finish too soon. If it hadn't have been for you, we'd have won that.'

'Maybe you should have focused before the race instead of trying to pull half the women here.'

'Maybe you should mind your own business.'

Dan didn't reply but his face was dark with anger. God, thought Amy, he did look masterful and dangerous when he was cross. The two men and their boat disappeared into the boat tent.

'I think I'll keep out of their way for the foreseeable future,' said Ellie. She glanced at the big clock outside the main administration tents. 'I suppose we'd better round up the crew and get ready to row. We're on in thirty minutes ourselves. Then we can go and find some tea or something.'

Amy snorted. 'You can have tea. I'm going to sink some Pimm's.'

Ellie shook her head. 'I won't risk it unless we lose.' She sighed as she remembered who they were up against. 'So I will be able to join you, now I think about it.'

'Don't be defeatist.'

Ellie pulled her phone from where she'd tucked it into the lightweight jacket she had slung over her rowing kit. She deftly texted a message and sent it.

'I told the crew to meet us here,' she said. 'Oh look, here come some of them already.'

Three striking women wearing the same coloured all-in-ones as Ellie appeared from out of the regatta shop and waved. They came over and joined their teammates.

'Saved by the text,' said Yolande who had the number three seat. 'I was getting sorely tempted by some of the kit in there.'

A couple of others rolled up. And then the final two of the crew arrived.

'Right, time for a gentle warm-up,' directed Ellie. The eight women began to do a series of stretches and exercises to get their muscles moving before Ellie led them away from the boat tent and off on a jog around the car park behind it. While they did that Amy made herself useful by carrying their blades down to the water's edge in several trips. When they returned they checked over their boat, packed surplus clothing and kit away in lockable boxes, ditched their trainers and then, bare-footed, carried their boat down to the pontoons and dropped it gently into the water.

With the skill and assurance of the accomplished rowers they were, they stepped into the craft, laced their bare feet into the shoes attached to the foot-stretchers, got their blades into the riggers and screwed tight the gates. As soon as her crew was settled and ready Amy gave them directions to push away from the jetty and then, plugging her mike into the cox-box at her feet, started steering them away from the jetties into the middle of the Thames and then up towards the start.

'Okay,' said Amy into her head-mike as they neared Temple Island. 'We've got tough opposition but let's give this our best shot.'

Ellie, sitting facing her cox in the stroke seat rolled her eyes and mouthed 'no chance'.

'You are a great crew,' said Amy, ignoring her friend, 'you've trained hard and you deserve to win.' She glanced over to where their opposition were on the water as they waited, like the Bath crew, to go to the start. Shit, they were huge. And their muscles . . .

A few minutes later the Bath eight were positioned like Rollo and Dan had been earlier that afternoon, being held against start point and waiting for the flag to drop.

'Attention, go.'

They were off. And in half a dozen strokes the Brown team was pulling away and by the quarter-mile point they were a full length in front. Amy tried every trick at her disposal to motivate her crew, to get them to dig for resources, to try to catch up, but even when the Brown eight appeared to be coasting for a few hundred yards at Fawley, Amy knew that her girls wouldn't be able to make the difference. To be put against one of the top-seeded teams seemed unfair, but it was the luck of the draw. That was how Henley worked.

But even though they knew they were destined to lose they were still determined to put in a good time so Amy's crew rowed their hardest. They crossed the line two lengths behind but gee'd up by the knowledge that their time had been perfectly respectable and if they'd been drawn against almost any other crew they'd have progressed further.

'At least we can go and get pissed now,' said Amy as they got the boat back out of the water; a sentiment that cheered everyone up, despite their disappointment.

Half an hour later, showered, changed and looking glamorous, the crew sallied forth from the changing rooms behind the boat tent and headed behind the Stewards' Enclosure to the towpath and one of the dozens of tented, temporary bars set out along the length of the river.

They stopped at one of the first they came to. It was late in the afternoon, the crowds were starting to thin out, the last few races were taking place and the sun was dipping towards the horizon so the bars and restaurants weren't nearly as packed as they had been just a couple of hours earlier. The girls found a table and Amy, feeling mellow now her job was done and tired from their early start from Bath, slumped into a chair and turned her face to the sun. Ellie pottered off to order a couple of jugs of Pimm's and the rest of the eight began to dissect their race, almost stroke by stroke. Warmed by the sun, relaxing now that she could, Amy felt herself drifting off.

'Sorry.' A man's voice, right by her ear, shocked her into wakefulness

'Wha—?' She turned to see who was talking to her. For a second she didn't recognise this tall, dark-haired guy wearing a blue and orange striped blazer and a panama hat. Then the penny dropped: it was the bloke who'd accused her and Rollo of having sex. What had Rollo called him? Oh yes, Dan. 'Hello.'

'I'm sorry.'

What for – being obnoxious? Or for being utterly drop-dead gorgeous? Even more gorgeous if that were possible now he was all spruced up. 'Really?'

'I was out of order for saying what I did earlier. It's just . . . well, Rollo . . . I jumped to the wrong conclusion but it was an honest mistake. And Rollo was right, I do need to apologise to you.'

His apology seemed genuine and Amy thawed a little and gave him the benefit of the doubt. 'A mistake, you say? Based on his previous performance? His unfinished business?'

Dan nodded. 'That's my excuse. Anyway, I'd like to buy you a drink, to show there's no hard feelings.'

Amy noticed the crew had stopped chatting and were blatantly eavesdropping. She stood up. 'Thanks. Tell you what, I'll come to the bar with you,' she said, not sure she wanted an audience or competition, and her crew could certainly prove to be either.

On their way into the bar tent Amy passed Ellie who gave her a curious stare. Amy suspected Ellie would want to know how she'd managed to pull not only Rollo but his rowing partner in a matter of a few hours.

'What can I get you?' said Dan.

Amy opted for Pimm's and then stood in silence as the barmaid took the order and then Dan's money. Once they got their drinks, Amy plonked herself down in a chair in the corner of the tent.

She raised her glass. 'Apology accepted,' she said.

'Good. You sort of got in the firing line.'

Amy shrugged. 'Shit happens. My mate Ellie says Rollo's got a reputation a mile wide.'

Dan nodded.

'And that he's loaded.'

Dan nodded again. 'His family would make Croesus look like he was on state benefits.'

'Lucky old Rollo.' Amy sucked on her straw again and tried to stop herself from staring shamelessly into Dan's dark brown eyes that were fringed with the kind of thick black lashes that most women would kill for. And at his skin that was beautifully tanned without being swarthy.

It was completely unfair that a bloke could be so fanciable. 'So,' she said clearing her throat. 'Are you at the same college as Rollo?'

Dan nodded. 'Why?'

'Oh, it's just I'm moving to Oxford in September. Got a job at the John Radcliffe.'

'Really?'

Amy waited expectantly for the 'we must get together for a drink' line. Nothing. 'Yes,' she said. 'I'm looking forward to it. Not that I know anyone there. Well, no one except you and Rollo.' Hint hint.

'I expect you'll soon make friends.'

Oh. How obvious does a girl have to get? *Very*, apparently. 'Maybe you could show me some nice bars, show me around the city?'

'I'm probably the worst person in the world to ask for information about any sort of social life. By the time I've done the academic stuff, and my rowing training and the part-time job, my free time is almost non-existent. I'm probably about the most anti-social guy in the entire university.'

'Oh.' Well, there was always Rollo she supposed, but fanciable as he was Dan was just as gorgeous and some - how so much nicer, especially as he'd apologised for his earlier faux pas. She tried another tack. 'You mentioned rowing training . . . could I join your boat club?'

Dan shook his head. 'Not really, it's a college club for college members.'

Jeez – another knock-back. 'That's a pity. The Bath club think I'm quite a useful cox,' she wheedled.

'There are loads of rowing clubs around Oxford

though. I'm sure you'll find one who'll welcome you with open arms.'

But I want to be at your club, Dan, I want to be able to ogle you. Amy sighed.

A shadow fell across them and they both looked up. Staring at Amy with curiosity was a woman in jeans, a skimpy T-shirt and blue and orange hair.

Dan struggled out of the deckchair and stood up. 'Karen! You found us. Love the hair.'

'Got it done to match the college colours.' Karen stood on tiptoe and planted a kiss on his cheek.

So who's this? Amy wondered. A girlfriend? Maybe that was why he was so off-hand about showing her around Oxford.

'Nice one,' said Dan as Karen did a twirl so he could admire the full impact of the dye.

Karen stopped spinning and stared at Amy. 'And this is?' she asked, one eyebrow raised.

'Oh, Amy. Let me introduce you then I'll get you a drink.'

Dan did all the social niceties and then left the girls to chat while he went off on his errand.

'You known Dan long?' asked Karen.

'All of about a couple of hours,' said Amy honestly. Karen seemed to relax as she explained about her encounter with Rollo and how she'd first met Dan.

'Rollo's a shit,' said Karen with feeling.

Another member of the Rollo Lyndon-Forster fan club. 'So you're not charmed by him either.'

'What do you think? I can't stand the way he treats Dan. Just because Dan has to work his way through uni doesn't make him a lesser person. He's got twice the brains of bloody Rollo but what with having to train for the Blue Boat, working and studying he has to graft for every crumb he gets, while Rollo just chucks money at his problems.'

Dan returned with Karen's drink.

'Shame you lost,' said Karen turning her attention to Dan. 'I bet Rollo went off on one.'

Dan nodded.

'Twat. Of course it won't be his fault. Never is. Did he blame you?'

Dan shrugged and Amy remembered that Rollo had indeed blamed Dan. Karen turned to Amy. 'So what's your connection with rowing?'

'I cox a crew from Bath. And I'm working as their physio for the next few weeks.'

'Rollo got her to give him a massage,' said Dan.

Karen rolled her eyes. 'So she said. I wouldn't have touched him if I had a vat of disinfectant on standby and was wearing a bio-hazard suit.' She sipped her drink again and gazed at the crowds of people around them. Then she said, 'I don't believe it.' Her eyes narrowed at whoever it was that she'd seen in the crowd.

The other two followed her gaze across the grass. Standing about twenty yards from them, also in the blue and orange striped blazer and surrounded by a group of glamorous girls including half of Amy's crew, was Rollo. And as they looked, he turned and saw them.

'Jolly good,' he called. 'Danny-boy, be a good chap and fetch me a couple of jugs of Pimm's and a dozen glasses.' He waved a fifty-pound note at Dan. 'Come on, chop-chop.'

Dan shook his head and turned away from Rollo. The girls around Rollo giggled and egged him on, except Ellie who, Amy noticed, was looking disgusted.

Rollo pushed his fingers through his heavy blond fringe, and patted one of the women on her bottom before moving over the grass towards Dan's table. He put the money on it and leaned on the wooden surface.

'Come on, Dan. You're the waiter amongst us, crack on.' He pushed the note right towards Dan.

Dan stood up, eyed the big denomination note with contempt, a look he transferred to Rollo, and then, in a flash, drew his fist back and landed a punch squarely on Rollo's nose. The thwack was sickening and there was a split second of silence before Rollo yelled in pain and blood spurted down the front of his garish blazer. All the witnesses standing around them cried out in either horror or surprise. Ellie applauded.

Amy knew she oughtn't to approve but that little display of machismo was deeply impressive. Go, Dan. Good-looking, clever, fit *and* assertive. Quite a package. And Rollo had deserved it.

A tall elegant girl from Rollo's group raced forward, grabbing a bunch of tissues from out of her handbag. 'Get some ice,' she ordered the others in the sort of cut-glass voice that carries for miles as she moved to Rollo's side. She held the tissues under his nose to staunch the flow of blood while one of Rollo's other admirers raced to the bar.

About half a minute later the other woman returned. 'Here's the ice, Tanya.' She handed Tanya an ice bucket full of the stuff and a tea towel.

Amy began to take a surreptitious interest. Tanya? It had to be one and the same. She assessed Rollo's girlfriend. Very groomed, very confident, very glossy and a body to die for.

Tanya applied ice wrapped up in the tea towel to the bridge of Rollo's nose and made soothing noises as she did so. The group surrounding them began to chatter again as it became obvious that no lasting damage had been done – except to Rollo's pride. Rollo looked in pain as Tanya dabbed and wiped and cleaned his face up while making sympathetic noises.

'There, there, baby. How do you feel?' she murmured as Rollo leaned against her and lapped up the attention.

To Amy, they seemed pretty much a couple under these circumstances. Except from what Ellie had said their relationship was only for show. Well, if Tanya didn't mind Rollo playing away from home, why should Amy worry?

Tanya finished mopping up Rollo. She took a good look at his face before dropping a kiss on his forehead. 'You'll live,' she announced.

'Doesn't feel like it,' said Rollo thickly, his nose blocked with drying blood. He put his hand up to feel how bad the damage was but Tanya knocked it away.

'Don't, you'll just make it bleed again.'

'You don't think it's broken?'

Tanya peered at him. 'Worried it'll spoil your pretty looks?'

'Worried that I ought to go to A & E,' countered Rollo.

'You'll be fine,' she said. 'Stop being such a drama queen.'

'But he hit me,' said Rollo.

'And you wound him up.'

'Only because he's an oik.'

Tanya stared at Rollo. God, he could be a bastard but there had to be something about him to compensate for all those good looks and money. Anyway, she could hardly criticise him too much because she knew she could be a bitch. But the way Rollo constantly goaded Dan was getting tedious. Frankly, she'd be glad when they both graduated and moved on.

Maybe Rollo had seen a look of disapproval on her face. 'Let's not talk about Dan,' he said. 'Let's go back to my digs here and then go out to dinner. I need something to take my mind off my nose.'

Tanya understood exactly what Rollo was offering. Did she fancy a shag? Might as well, there was fuck all else to do.

3

Oxford
September, 2010

'So what are your digs like?' asked Ellie over the phone.

'Not too bad. Quite a nice bedsit in St Clement's,' replied Amy, sitting on her unmade bed, surrounded by boxes and cases. Most of them were half-unpacked with clothes and kit spilling out onto the floor in untidy heaps. Outside the window the throb of a bus engine waiting at the traffic lights could be heard. Amy imagined she'd get used to the endless traffic noise in no time.

'Erm . . . which is where?'

'Oh, not too far from the centre of Oxford and not a million miles to the hospital.'

'A nice healthy walk each day to get there.'

Amy spluttered. '"Not a million miles" doesn't mean it's walkable. Besides, the hospital is halfway up a hill that's like the north face of the Eiger. I think I'll be getting the bus.' And she was undeniably handy for the bus routes as another one pulled up with a squeal of brakes.

'Wimp.'

'Just because you're into masochism and pain doesn't mean the rest of the British population are perverts.'

There was a brief silence from Ellie ending in a sigh that neatly expressed her disapproval of Amy's aversion to exercise. 'As a health professional you really ought to take more interest in a healthy lifestyle.'

'Fuck off,' said Amy amiably. 'When are you going to come and visit and check out the scene here?'

'I dunno, Ames. I've got training to do at weekends and a job to hold down, which means there isn't a lot of free time.'

'You still set on making the British squad?'

There was a deep and heartfelt sigh. 'It's a long shot, Ames. But you've got to try. If I can get picked for the club team and qualify for a development grant then I'm home free but until that magic moment . . . well, you just have to keep trying, don't you? Anyway, have you found a rowing club yet?'

'Give me a chance, Ellie. I haven't even unpacked.'

'Just asking. Remember there's going to be a whole load of keen students rocking in any minute now and if you want to bag a seat as a cox you need to get on with it.'

Ellie was right. So maybe it was an excuse to fish out Rollo's card and give him a ring?

'Okay, I'll work on it.'

'When you're straight, why don't you come over to me? I'm only at Reading. Shit, Amy, there's even a direct rail link from Oxford to Reading.'

'Is there?' But Amy knew exactly what a weekend with Ellie would consist of and most of it would be watching Ellie train. 'We'll see,' she said. 'Now I've got to go. I need to find a cheap place to grab a bite. I haven't unpacked anything to eat off or with, so I think fish and chips beckons or a pub snack.'

'Another healthy choice?' said Ellie.

'I'll eat salad for the rest of the week but right now,' said Amy, looking at the piles of unpacking still to do, 'I need fuel.'

The girls bade each other farewell and then Amy fished around in her wallet for Rollo's card. She tapped it against her thigh for a couple of seconds while she worked out quite what her opening gambit would be, then she dialled.

'You have reached my voicemail,' said Rollo's voice. 'Leave me a message and your number and I'll get back to you – promise.'

'Hi,' said Amy, feeling self-conscious in a way that answering machines always made her feel. 'We met at Henley. I'm Amy, I gave you a massage.' She stopped, she was in danger of rambling. 'Anyway, I've arrived in Oxford.' She left her number. 'You said to call, so I have,' she finished, feeling a bit lame. She disconnected then made her way down the three flights of stairs from her top-floor flat and out onto the main road.

To her left was Headington Hill and to her right were Magdalene Bridge and the High. She headed towards the High Street and the city centre as that seemed the most likely place to find somewhere to eat.

She passed a couple of pubs, a Thai restaurant, a couple of Indian takeaways, and a pizzeria but nothing that reached out to her and her limited funds and said 'eat here'. She wandered on, getting closer to the centre,

41

enjoying the buzz of the early evening in a vibrant city with a large student population.

Her gaze lit on a sign indicating that down a narrow side street was a bistro offering a deal on a drink and a main course for a fiver. Her sort of price and furthermore a delicious smell of onions and herbs seemed to be wafting towards her. Her tummy rumbled loudly. That decided her; if she didn't get some nourishment soon she'd fade away.

The alley leading to the bistro was narrow but decorated with some brightly coloured hanging baskets and it was clean and didn't smell of wee. Amy approached the entrance, a low door down a couple of steps so the restaurant was sunk below ground level. The door was propped wide open and inside was a flagstone floor that had been polished to a deep shine by generations of feet passing over it. This place had obviously been built back in the days when Oxford's idea of an afternoon's entertainment had been burning a few martyrs at the stake. Amy went in.

The tables were covered with bright gingham tablecloths in a multitude of colours, Edith Piaf was providing quiet background ambience and unusually there were no fruit machines or TV screens, just several groups of people chatting, laughing and eating in a great atmosphere. The smell of whatever was on the menu was sensational.

Amy checked out the specials on the blackboard and caught the barmaid's eye. 'Omelette, salad and a glass of red please,' she said.

'Off the Pimm's?' came the reply.

Amy was utterly perplexed. 'Sorry?'

'I thought you liked Pimm's.'

'I have been known to drink it but . . .?'

'So you don't remember me then?'

Amy stared at the woman smiling at her over the bar. The voice wasn't unfamiliar; that slight country burr and flat vowels rang a vague bell, but she couldn't place it. Amy shook her head. 'I'm really sorry but I haven't a clue.'

'Maybe if my hair was blue and orange,' said the barmaid as she poured Amy's drink.

'Oh my God. Henley. When Dan punched Rollo! You're Caroline?'

'Karen.'

'Karen, I'm sorry. It's just I didn't expect to meet you here. To be honest, I didn't expect to meet anyone here. I only moved to the area today and I don't know a soul.'

'Well, you know me.'

'I do. Blimey, this is like that film *Casablanca*. Of all the gin joints . . .'

'. . . in all the world . . .' added Karen.

'. . . you have to walk into mine,' they chorused in unison.

'Want to share the joke with me?' said a male voice behind Amy.

She span round and saw a waiter in an almost floor-length black apron and a T-shirt with the bistro's logo on the chest. 'Dan! Still rowing?' she said. 'Or have you taken up boxing?'

'Rollo deserved it,' said Dan evenly.

'Maybe.'

'Trust me, he did,' said Karen. 'In fact, he's had it coming for about the past ten years.'

Amy shrugged. Whatever was going on between Dan and Rollo was none of her business and she certainly didn't want to get involved or take sides.

'Anyway,' said Dan, 'I really can't chat, I'm supposed to be working.' And he disappeared off into the kitchens.

Amy sighed. It looked as though her chances of getting to know Dan better were slimmer than ever. Why was the bloke she fancied the most, by a country mile, proving to be so hard to pull? You're losing your grip, Ames, she told herself.

She picked up her wine and some brochures lying on the bar about things to do in Oxford and moved across to a table set for two at the edge of the room. Sitting down, tucked right into a corner, she opened a couple of the pamphlets and started reading about what was on offer. Quite a lot, apparently, but nothing was mentioned about rowing clubs. Maybe finding someone to cox for was going to be harder than she anticipated.

Around the bistro a few of the other tables had been taken by some other diners but the place was hardly packed, although Dan seemed quite busy to-ing and fro-ing with baskets of bread, menus and drinks and he certainly didn't seem to have time to stop and chat to her.

Before Amy knew it, her glass of wine appeared to have evaporated. Surely she couldn't have sipped it that fast? She checked out her funds and reckoned she could afford to buy herself another one. Picking up her wallet she was about to head to the bar when the door to the bistro crashed open and a whole gang of twenty-somethings rocked in, like a flock of exotic birds suddenly swooping down to land.

The noise level went through the ceiling as the big group, all chatting and laughing, seemed to take over the whole place. Without a word to the staff they began moving tables so they could all sit together, arranging chairs noisily and grabbing menus off the bar. They didn't seem to notice that they were inconveniencing the other diners or that the way they'd placed their newly formed table was half-blocking the access to the loos.

It was only when they had settled down that any sort of order was restored. A lad with his back to her caught Dan's eye, raised his hand, clicked his fingers and said, 'Jump to it, Danny-boy. Champagne all round. Three bottles of your finest, and glasses too, and don't let any of these wasters get their paws on the bill. This is my treat.'

The crowd around the lad laughed and cheered as he acknowledged their gratitude with a gracious nod of his head.

Amy might not have recognised Karen straight off but she knew the new arrival's voice and gestures all right. Rollo.

'And make sure the champers is properly chilled, Dan. I don't want to have to complain to the management about you a second time now, do I?'

Those around Rollo made sounds of agreement and Amy could see Dan's eyes narrowing as he took the comments on the chin.

Just as soon as she'd taken her place, Tanya spotted Amy sitting in the corner and recognised her instantly:

that girl at Henley, the one who'd been with Dan when he smacked Rollo, the girl with the massage skills, Rollo had told her later. Massage skills? Tanya could imagine what sort. So what the fuck was she doing here? For a mad second Tanya wondered if Amy was stalking Rollo before she realised she was completely overreacting. Henley and Oxford weren't a million miles apart – in the same county, in fact. No, it was just plain old coincidence. She noted that Rollo hadn't seen her as he was sitting with his back to that side of the room. Good. Not that Tanya cared that much if Rollo had a fling with her but the trail of broken-hearted undergrads that seemed to be cluttering up Oxford these days was getting boring. And looking around the group, she could see he might be planning to add another couple of names to the list because at the end of the table, gazing at Rollo as if he was a God, were two fresh-from-the-factory first years.

Still, apart from them, all the usual suspects were present, which was nice: Seb, the army officer now being sponsored by his regiment to do a degree; Maddy, a second year with enviably thick chestnut hair who followed Seb around like a dog although, to Tanya's knowledge, he'd never once noticed her or spoken to her; Angus, who trained like a demon at rowing but had limited technique, relying instead on brute force to get the boat to go through the water; Angus's girlfriend Susie; and Christina and Stevie, the lesbians.

Such a waste, thought Tanya, not for the first time, as she stared at the two women: they made Kate Moss and Erin O'Connor look like frumps. Rollo was always making off-colour comments about joining in or converting them, but if anyone was going to be converted, thought Tanya, they might manage it with her. Fuck, they were beautiful. And, past them were the two newbies, looking a bit bewildered at the company they found themselves in. So if Rollo was planning on a threesome tonight with those two freshers, Tanya needed to find a partner to keep herself amused.

She looked around the table to see who might be available. As there were only three men present her choice was rather limited. Rollo probably had his own sordid plans, Angus was making eyes at Susie, so he was no good, Christina and Stevie might just be considered a possibility but they probably didn't fancy her, which left Seb. He'd do.

Amy, sitting at her table, watched the interaction amongst the group, fascinated by the camaraderie and glamour they seemed to exude, except for two girls at the end who really didn't seem to belong. They were like a pair of sparrows in a cage full of birds of paradise.

Karen brought over Amy's meal and plonked it down on the table along with her cutlery and a table napkin. 'Don't take any notice of them,' she said quietly. 'Rollo only comes here so he can get Dan to run around after him.'

'I would have thought he comes here because it's a nice place with good food,' said Amy, trying to steer a middle course. She only knew three people in Oxford and she wanted to be friends with all of them.

'Maybe,' Karen conceded, but made an expression that

looked as if she strongly disagreed. 'Can I get you anything else?'

'Another glass of wine, please,' requested Amy.

'I'll bring it right over.'

'Thanks.' Amy picked up her knife and fork and tucked in, pretending to be engrossed in her food, while watching everything going on at the other table from under her lashes.

Much as she wanted to get to know Rollo better, much better, she wasn't sure she would fit in with this sort of social set. They were so confident and loud and brash – way out of the league of a physio from the sticks. Maybe she would be more compatible with Dan. But when her wine arrived, delivered by Dan, and she flashed him a smile he shot off to clear one of the other tables and pretty much ignored her. That went well.

She carried on watching the dynamics of the other table as she ate her omelette and salad.

Tanya, Rollo's supposed girlfriend, had her hand firmly wedged between the thighs of another bloke. It seemed like what Ellie had said about the way she carried on was true. And the girl with the thick chestnut hair sitting opposite the couple was shooting looks of sheer venom at Tanya when she wasn't making sheep's eyes at the object of her rival's attention. Someone wasn't happy, deduced Amy. Poor kid, and she didn't look like she was a match for the likes of Tanya. Amy reckoned few would be.

Tanya, unaware that she was being observed and assessed, fondled the bulge in Seb's trousers as she gave him the benefit of her brown-eyed stare. When she'd first touched him there he jumped like he'd been stung and had looked horrified.

'Don't you like it?' she'd whispered, leaning into him.

'Er . . . yes,' he'd croaked.

'Good.' She'd smiled at him and he'd smiled back, before he'd glanced nervously down the table to where Rollo was sitting.

'Oh, don't mind him,' said Tanya, lightly.

Seb's eyebrows had collided with his hairline. 'But—'

'But nothing. How I spend my free time is my business and my business alone.'

'I suppose.' As he assimilated just what Tanya was saying – and what she was doing – he began to respond in the way Tanya had hoped and she felt his erection grow until he'd had to shift uncomfortably in his seat.

'Want to follow me into the lavs?' she whispered again.'

'What, here? Now?!'

'Why not.' She gave him a smouldering look. But the champagne and the glasses arrived and the moment of opportunity passed. By the time the fizz had been poured and passed around Tanya knew she'd have to start all over again with Seb and she wasn't sure she could be bothered. And then she saw the look on Maddy's face and thought, what the hell, just for the sheer devilry of it.

'So how's the training going?' she cooed at Seb, putting her hand back on his crotch again. Not that she was particularly interested in anyone's training except her own but when talking to a rower, it was always a good gambit.

'Fine,' said Seb. He launched into his latest times on

the ergo machine, how he'd done at the Chester Head and the other regattas and races he'd entered over the few months since Henley.

Tanya stifled a yawn. She wanted Seb to talk *to* her, not *at* her – there was a difference. Her gaze slipped past his face and landed on Maddy who looked like she was about to cry. Diddums, she thought. If Maddy didn't have the gumption to grab the bloke then why should everyone else have to be equally pathetic? Maddy sensed Tanya was staring at her and returned her gaze. Tanya gave her a look of triumph.

Maddy fled to the loos.

4

In her corner Amy had watched what had been going on at the other table and although she didn't know any of the occupants, bar Rollo – and Tanya by reputation – her heart went out to Tanya's victim. Leaving her omelette half-eaten, she followed Maddy to the ladies'.

Behind a cubicle door Amy heard someone snuffling. She waited quietly. After a couple of minutes the girl, puffy-eyed, emerged and gave Amy a wary look.

'Are you okay?' asked Amy.

The girl shrugged but didn't reply.

'Is that your boyfriend Tanya was making a pass at?'

The girl gave her a wide-eyed stare. 'You know Tanya?'

'No, but I know of her. And I met Rollo, back in the summer.'

'She's a bitch.'

Amy nodded. 'That's sort of what I've heard too. I'm Amy by the way.'

'Maddy,' said Maddy. 'And it wasn't my boyfriend she was trying to cop off with but I fancy him like mad and I'm sure she knows and was just doing it deliberately.'

Amy frowned. Maddy sighed and shook her head. 'Maybe I'm being too hard on her. Maybe . . .' she shrugged. 'Maybe I'm overreacting. It's been a long day and I got a lousy mark for an essay I thought was good and I joined the rowing club last year so Seb would notice me but I'm a rubbish rower and he still hasn't . . .' she tailed off. 'Why am I telling you this?'

'Because I'm here?' suggested Amy.

'I'm sorry.'

'Don't be. Has it helped?'

Maddy nodded. 'A bit.' She grabbed a paper towel and blew her nose vigorously then turned and had a quick check of her mascara. 'So, do you know Rollo through rowing?' she asked as she removed a black smear under one eye with the corner of the towel.

'We met at Henley. A mutual friend introduced us.'

'He's okay. Bit of a ladies' man, though.'

'So everyone says,' said Amy. 'Aren't he and Tanya . . .?'

'That's the rumour. Can't say it makes any sense, though. Not when you consider how she carries on.' Maddy looked crestfallen again. 'Sorry, Tanya's a sore point. Are you studying here?'

'No, working. Or I will when I start tomorrow. I've got a job at the John Radcliffe. Which also means I need to finish my supper and get on home. I need to be on my best behaviour tomorrow. First impressions and all that.'

'Thanks,' said Maddy as Amy headed for the door.

'It was nothing,' said Amy. She slipped back to her table and was thankful her food hadn't been cleared away.

Rollo's group were in full swing and had ordered yet more bottles of champagne when Amy went to the bar to pay her bill. She made sure she positioned herself well out of Rollo's line of sight. Sure she still fancied him but here and now was neither the time or the place for a reacquaintance – that could wait till he picked up her voicemail.

'So now what do you think of Rollo's gang?' asked Karen nodding in the party's direction as she rang up Amy's bill.

'They're okay. They seem like lots of fun.'

'And they don't care how Rollo treats Dan.'

What was Karen's problem? She was acting like his mum when Dan could obviously handle himself with Rollo. 'So? Dan seems to rise above it.'

'He does, but he shouldn't have to.'

'If you ask me, the way Dan ignores Rollo's jibes does more to annoy Rollo than what Rollo does to Dan.'

'What if I told you that Dan was a scholarship boy at Rollo's posh public school?'

'I'd say, well done him.'

'And what if I also told you his mum was the dinner lady there?'

'Oh.' Well, that put things in a different light. Even Amy who'd only gone to a comp could see that might be tricky.

'Oh, exactly. The poor boy at the toffs' school. Can you imagine how miserable some of them made his life, Rollo especially?'

'So why didn't Dan report them? There are rules against bullying – even posh schools have those.'

Karen handed Amy her bill. 'If that's what you want to think.'

Amy had no reply to this and scrabbled about in her purse to find the money which she handed over after a few seconds. 'Thanks, that was a great meal. Keep the change.'

'See you around,' said Karen.

Amy rather doubted it; she couldn't afford to eat out often, if at all. She turned to leave the bar just as Rollo got to his feet and left his table in search of the loo. As he turned to avoid another table he came face to face with Amy. His eyes widened in surprise.

'Well, he-*llo*,' he drawled

'Hi,' said Amy. And whoosh, her insides went into free-fall.

'You look like you're about to leave.'

Amy nodded. 'I am.'

'Correction, you *were*.'

'No, I—' All her earlier resolve about this not being the time or the place shot straight out of the window as Rollo took her arm and led her back to his table and pushed her down onto his seat. Screw being sensible, screw the early night . . . Actually – just screw. No! She absolutely had to get some sleep tonight. 'Don't let her run away,' he instructed his followers as he disappeared off to the loo.

She smiled vaguely at her new drinking companions as a clean champagne glass was brought to her by Dan and someone filled it to the brim with fizz.

'Budge up.' Rollo was back and was trying to shoe - horn yet another chair into the group around the

54

overcrowded table. It was hopeless. No matter how much the others tried to make a space it wasn't going to work. Rollo shoved his chair out of the way and before Amy realised what was going on or managed to protest, he'd lifted her bodily out of the chair, sat down himself and swung her onto his lap. Amy flung a look of helplessness at Tanya who just shrugged and turned to talk to someone else. Tanya really didn't seem to care, so why should she?

'Shall we talk about the first thing that comes up?' Rollo asked Amy, a picture of wide-eyed innocence. The crowd around the table hooted with laughter but under her buttocks Amy felt his cock stirring and knew her face had gone crimson. She made to ease herself off Rollo's lap but he had his arm around her waist and she felt it tense, holding her firm.

'Don't go,' he said quietly in her ear. 'Aren't you enjoying yourself? I know I am.'

What the hell! She allowed herself to relax against him, but then she glanced across the bar and saw Karen and Dan raising their eyebrows. Well, so what?

The banter and conversation rolled around her. She was introduced to the group, discovered they were all rowers with Dan and Rollo at St George's Boat Club and discovered that Angus and Susie were an item. She met Seb, who seemed nice but she couldn't work out why Maddy was quite so besotted with him, was introduced to Christina and Stevie, who were so impossibly glamorous, clever and sophisticated that Amy felt quite intimidated, and she found out what they were all studying and because Rollo's lap was comfy, after a while she didn't care that her plans for a sensible early night had gone to pot. The chat and the drink flowed and the minutes flew by.

'What do you think?' asked Rollo.

'Huh?' She'd been busy gossiping with Angus and Susie about the latest series of *The X Factor*.

'About going on somewhere else? A club or somewhere.'

'Oh.' Amy glanced at her watch. Jesus, it was almost half eleven. She hadn't finished unpacking, her first day of work at the hospital was the next morning, and before she went to bed she had to find and press her work clothes, locate her bed linen and make up her bed. No way could she spend the night on the tiles. In fact, she ought to have been home at her digs hours ago. 'Can't, sorry. Things to do, places to be.' She went to stand up again and again Rollo tightened his grip. 'I mean it this time, Rollo. Gotta go.'

'Don't be a spoilsport.'

Amy wondered if his voice sounded just a touch slurry. But then maybe hers did too. There were an awful lot of empty bottles on the table.

'I've got to go to work tomorrow,' she explained.

'And you've got training, Rollo.' Dan was standing by the table. 'As have I, and most of the rest of you. And when you lot have gone I can close up.'

'Don't be such a wet blanket, Dan,' Rollo said dismissively.

Some of the others were now glancing sheepishly at their watches and nodding in agreement with Dan. Rollo pushed Amy off his lap and patted her bottom. 'Well, that's another evening ruined.' He glared at Dan who completely ignored him and returned behind the bar carrying several empty champagne bottles with him as he went. As the party began to gather up their belongings and get ready to leave Amy saw Karen give Dan a peck on the cheek. She was surprised by the little stab of jealousy that she felt, and was cross with herself for feeling that way. She might fancy Dan wildly but she hadn't got anywhere with him and it looked like he was taken.

'If I wasn't so mad about Angus I'd give him one,' said Susie, following Amy's gaze.

Amy felt herself blushing.

'He's gorgeous, isn't he,' the other girl added. 'The only trouble is I don't think he's ever dated anyone here, and trust me: it isn't for lack of girls trying to interest him.'

Amy remembered he'd said something at Henley about being seriously anti-social, but it also looked like he might be with Karen, which would explain why he hadn't dated anyone else. She'd have to wait and see how things turned out. Because if he wasn't with Karen, then maybe she could be in with a chance.

She was just leaving the bistro when Rollo stopped her.

'You left a message on my phone, I see. You were keen to get hold of me, weren't you? And then the fates made sure you did.' He raised his eyebrows and gave her a suggestive smile.

'Serendipity,' said Amy. 'Actually, I wanted to ask you about rowing here in Oxford, but it's a bit late in the evening now.'

'I'll ring you tomorrow. Maybe arrange for you to come over to the boat club. There's a load of experts there who can tell you all you need to know.'

'Thanks, Rollo. Really.'

Rollo leaned forwards and gave her a hard kiss on the lips. 'My pleasure.' And he was gone, leaving Amy feeling slightly breathless.

Dan wearily shut and locked the door after the last of Rollo's party had left. He slumped against the doorjamb.

'You're knackered,' said Karen. 'You head off, I'll clear up.'

Dan shook his head. 'That's not fair.'

'It's perfectly fair. I don't have to be up at five for a three-hour training session.'

'I'll grab a nap during the day. It's Thursday tomorrow, I've got the day off here and I've only got one lecture later in the afternoon.'

'I don't know how you do it. Before I start on this,' Karen gestured to the remaining debris littering some of the tables, 'I'm going out for a ciggie. Want to come and talk to me?'

Dan shook his head, grabbed a tray and began clearing the rest of the mess from Rollo's tables. He plonked the bottles and trays of glasses on the bar for Karen to deal with while he moved the furniture back to how it should be and whipped off the dirty tablecloths to go in the washing machine.

The chef called goodbye to him from the kitchen door and silence settled. Not for the first time in his life Dan wondered what it would be like not to be scraping around for money and to have the sort of wealth and privilege that Rollo had been born into.

He remembered his first day at public school, the day he'd first met Rollo, the day that he thought his luck might have changed for ever and then discovered that it hadn't. They were all new boys, they were all eyeing each other up and down, working out who might be worth knowing, who might be brainy, who might be sporty, who might be a future Prime Minister, because, as the school's literature boasted, they counted many amongst their alumni.

Dan had known he was indistinguishable from all the others in his uniform. There was nothing to mark him out as the scholarship boy. All he had to do was talk properly, keep his head down, work hard and all would be well. There had been plenty of scholarship boys who had done just as well and often better than their privileged peers whose parents were spending thousands on their children's education. So why, his Housemaster had said, would it be any different for Dan? Dan wasn't to worry, Mr Curtis had assured him. Generations of scholarship boys had slotted in seamlessly. And Dan had believed him.

He was in the Westminster House common room about a week after the start of his first term when Rollo swaggered in. Dan had seen Rollo at a distance but had had no reason to associate with the boy who was in the year above. And anyway, as a Remove he was so junior it was as if he were diseased. 'Don't speak until you're spoken to' was a given, so Removes pressed themselves against corridor walls when any of the older boys went past, gave up their seats in the common rooms and tried to attract as little attention as possible.

'Have you noticed,' said Rollo to the little gang of boys that always seemed to hang around him, 'that the Remove's scholarship boy this year is called Quantick? An uncommon name I think you'll agree.'

Dan felt his face flare. Shit, was Lyndon-Forster going to talk to him? He desperately hoped not. He squirmed in the battered armchair, sinking lower into the cushions and wishing he could dematerialise like the Tardis. But Rollo moved closer to him.

'And have you also noticed that one of our very own dinner ladies is also called Quantick? And,' continued Rollo, 'this is the really interesting part, there's only one Quantick listed in the local phone book.' He strode over to Dan. 'So, Danny-boy, is our lovely Mrs Quantick your mother?' Rollo smiled at Dan disarmingly.

'Well, my mother is lovely and I'm proud of her cooking.' Pleased that this demi-god was acknowledging his mother's talent in the kitchen he owned up to the connection.

The group of half a dozen lads instantly fell about, whooping with laugher. They roared, they honked, they guffawed. Tears streamed down their faces, they clung to each other, sobbing with mirth, gasping for breath.

'See,' said Rollo, wheezing and wiping his eyes. 'I told you so.'

And leaving Dan feeling as though he'd been knocked to the floor by a prizefighter, Rollo and his toadies left the common room to spread the news and the joke around the school.

'What doesn't kill you makes you stronger,' his mother said, giving him a big hug when he recounted the awful story later in their cosy kitchen. But from then on Dan felt as though Rollo's revelation *was* killing him. The concept of 'death by a thousand cuts' made perfect sense to Dan as, day by day, Rollo never failed to miss an opportunity to take a poke at his victim, intimating that the fact that his mum cooked their meals meant she was worthless because she worked for a living and hadn't inherited pots of wealth. It didn't matter that Dan was the brightest boy in his year by far; no one cared. All they cared about was that his mother worked in the school kitchens.

'Penny for them,' said Karen quietly.

Dan sighed. 'Not worth that.'

'You were miles away.'

'Not really,' said Dan truthfully because his old school wasn't so very far from Oxford and his tormentor, now at the same college as Dan while he studied for his master's, lived in the corridor beneath him. No, the past he'd tried to get away from was all very local these days, thought Dan, but it was too late at night to go into explanations.

'So I see that Amy was taken in by Rollo. If he gets many more notches on his bedpost there'll be nothing left of it.'

'It's a free country,' said Dan evenly. 'I just thought she had better taste.'

'Me too.'

Dan sighed.

Karen spotted the wistful look on Dan's face. 'You don't fancy her, do you?' she said accusingly.

61

'No. No, of course not.' But there was something about Amy, something about her eyes and the way she smiled that haunted him. And he suddenly realised that he was jealous of the fact she'd been sitting on Rollo's lap and not his.

The pair finished tidying up the bistro. They put the takings in the safe, made sure the place was secure, all the gas taps in the kitchen and lights everywhere were off and then exited by the main door into the alley.

'Want to come back to mine?' said Karen.

Dan weighed up her offer briefly – he knew what else she was offering – and a friendly fuck would be nice after a shit day, but he was bushed. He shook his head and kissed her on the nose. 'Early training. Another time.'

'Okay, well, you're always welcome, you know that.'

They parted company on the High; Karen getting a late bus back to Blackbird Leys and Dan walking back to his college, thinking as he walked about why Amy had made such an impact on him. Obviously she was a complete babe but there were loads of those around Oxford and he'd been immune so far. And more worryingly he fancied a bird that Rollo did too; as a general rule anything or anyone that Rollo wanted or admired made Dan instantly loathe it or them. So why Amy? But Dan didn't have time to think further on the subject as he'd reached his college. He passed through the fifteenth-century arch that guarded the entrance to St George's College, went past the porters' lodge, acknowledged the greeting from the duty porter, and made his way across the quadrangle to his rooms.

Dan paused on the ancient steps outside his door and

Amy crowded in on his thoughts again. He swatted her away. He didn't have time for a girlfriend so he wasn't interested in her. Right? Right.

The next morning, down at the St George's College boathouse, on the appropriately named Boathouse Island, Dan and Rollo were working on the ergo machines. They'd already done a couple of three-thousand-metre pieces on the river and a run along the towpath and now, after a warm-down and a rest they were working out in the gym on the rowing machines. The swoosh and thwack of their seats racing back and forth on the sliders, the whirr of the fans and the sound of their panting breaths dominated the ground-floor gym. A slight tang of body odour hung in the air along with the smell of sweaty trainers and damp towels.

In many respects the gym at the boat club resembled any gym, anywhere in the world except for one difference: in front of the two men was a huge plate-glass window with a stunning view across the Isis to the opposite bank. As they worked out on the ergos, scullers, rowers and punters took their craft up and down the river. The low, early morning autumn sun beamed and glistened on the water and across on the other bank a massive ride-on mower was cutting the grass of a cricket pitch. Not that Dan or Rollo were aware of the view spread in front of them; their attention was fixed on the digital read-outs telling them how fast they would be covering two thousand metres were they rowing for real on water instead hauling away on a rope on a simulator.

'Come on, put some beef into it,' urged their coach, Chuck Hanson, in his heavy American accent that always reminded Dan of John Wayne's. He was standing behind them, watching the figures clicking over on their displays. An ex-Olympic rower himself he knew exactly what was required to make the grade to move up to the elite end of the rowing spectrum. And even though he hadn't rowed competitively for some years due to injury, his mid-thirties body didn't carry an ounce of spare flesh, his skin was tanned and his hair still as dark as when he'd picked up a gold at the World Championships just before his injury.

The two men had no spare energy or breath to answer but acknowledged the spur by digging deeper and hauling on the handle to spin the fan faster and to increase the rate.

Slowly the distance left to row flicked down to zero, first for Dan and then ten seconds later, for Rollo. They both collapsed panting, sweat pouring from their brows and down their backs and chests, their legs trembling with exertion.

Chuck leaned forward to make sure he was reading the displays right. 'Five minutes fifty-three for you,' he said to Dan. 'Excellent.' He peered at Rollo's. 'And six minutes four point five for you. Not good enough. Not good enough if you're going to try out for the Blue Boat.'

He walked between the machines and then turned and faced the two men. Dan and Rollo looked up, squinting against the light shining through the big window.

'So what you been up to, Rollo? Late night?'

Rollo looked the picture of innocence. 'No, Chuck, honest.'

Chuck rolled his eyes. 'Rollo, I may only be the goddamned coach but I ain't stupid. I have eyes and ears. My eyes tell me you look hung-over and my ears have been hearing stuff that backs that up. Stuff about you drinking champagne like it was beer, stuff about you hanging around with girls, stuff about late nights.' He glared at Rollo, daring him to contradict him. 'Well? Because if it's true I am not going to waste my time coaching you any more. You can kiss goodbye to your chances of a place in the Blue Boat. They won't want you if you can't, or won't, knuckle down and make a few sacrifices.'

Rollo sighed. 'You're mistaken. I'm as fit as anyone.'

Dan stared ahead. He knew he could drop Rollo right in it. He could tell Chuck about the previous night, about the number of champagne bottles he'd put in the recycling bin and that would be Rollo screwed. He knew Rollo wanted to be selected to be a Blue, and if Rollo didn't make it, then his own chances went up a notch. But could he?

In the picture window he could see Rollo's reflection, as clearly as if it were a mirror. He saw Rollo's eyes flick guiltily towards his across the glass and a look that asked him to back up his rival. Would he? Dan stared back at Rollo, making him sweat. He narrowed his eyes as he considered how he might play this, saw Rollo swallow and then dropped his gaze. He gave Rollo the merest hint of a nod of his head.

'I've got a bit of an injury,' said Rollo.

'Oh yeah?' Chuck didn't sound convinced.

'Shoulder. I really pulled a muscle a while back. Didn't I, Dan?'

Dan nodded. 'It probably caused us to lose to the Davies twins at Henley.'

'Really. So why haven't you had it sorted out?' growled Chuck.

'I thought it was getting better.' Rollo rubbed it theatrically. 'I'll make an appointment with Marcus.' Marcus was the club's physio.

'You haven't heard?' said Chuck.

'What?' said Rollo.

'He's gone down with glandular fever. Out of action for at least a month. Apart from anything else we don't want him spreading it around.'

Rollo snorted. 'Whatever else you've heard about me, Chuck, I am *not* going to be kissing Marcus.'

Chuck's brow furrowed. 'What? I don't get you.'

'Glandular fever is known as kissing disease over here,' Dan explained evenly. 'It's reputedly how it's spread.'

'Is that so?' Chuck sounded supremely sceptical. 'Just as well it isn't called "screwing-around disease" or I imagine you would have a terminal bout of it.' Rollo looked livid but he had the sense to keep quiet. 'But whatever glandular fever is or isn't called it still doesn't solve our problem. And because we'll have to pay Marcus sick pay we can't afford another physio so you'll have to make your own arrangements. I expect you can afford it, though.'

'I'm sure there's someone in Harley Street,' said Dan, 'who would give you a consultation.'

Rollo shot him a look. 'Actually, I was thinking of asking little Amy to help. She wants to join a rowing club and she's a physio. It seems like a perfect solution to me.'

'She's got a job,' interrupted Dan. 'So she doesn't need another one.'

'But she wants to belong to a rowing club. If she was our physio . . . I mean, I know she's not studying at St George's but maybe, as an employee, she could get out on the water with some of our crews, be a sort of honorary member. I think she'd like that.'

'Hang on, hang on,' said Chuck. 'Just who the hell is *little Amy?*'

'A physio. She graduated in the summer, she works at the JR but she's a cox in her spare time and she wants to row here in Oxford. Don't you see, this is the perfect solution for all of us.'

'Is she any good?'

Dan was expecting some lewd answer from Rollo like 'she's sensational' and was a little surprised when Rollo just shrugged and said, 'She had a go at sorting out my shoulder at Henley and seemed to do a reason - able job.'

'And you lost,' Chuck pointed out. 'That's not much of a recommendation.'

'We might have lost by more if she hadn't,' argued Rollo.

Chuck sighed. 'She'll be better than nothing I suppose.

It's only for the short term. Get hold of her, ask her if she can help.'

'Isn't it handy that Rollo's already got her number?' said Dan.

'Why doesn't that surprise me?' said Chuck, rolling his eyes. 'I assumed you'd be getting a few early nights now the long vac is over. So what's with this new broad on your radar?'

'Amy is not a *broad*,' said Rollo.

'Whatever.'

'Amy and I are just friends,' insisted Rollo.

'Make sure it stays that way,' said Chuck. He left the two men to continue their training session and went upstairs to the coach's office to deal with paperwork, regatta applications and the day-to-day minutiae that went with running a boat club.

Dan and Rollo got busy with the weights to carry on their training.

'You shouldn't lie to Chuck about your late nights,' said Dan.

'Piss off. You're not my keeper.'

'No, but I'm part of the St George's team – as are you – and I care about the team's performance. I don't like to see the rest of the crew being let down by a weak link.'

'Seb and Angus were there too.'

'But not drinking themselves stupid.'

'I did not.'

'No?'

'No.'

'Do you want me to mention to Chuck what your bar bill was last night?' said Dan.

Rollo got up from the lateral pull-down machine and moved to exercise his abductors. 'He wouldn't believe you,' he said as he adjusted the weights with the big steel pin.

'He'd believe the MasterCard slip.'

'You're a shit, Dan.'

'I don't think so. I could have dropped you in it earlier. I think a bit of gratitude is called for.'

'So what are you after?' sneered Rollo. 'Money?'

'Don't judge me by your standards,' said Dan. He got up and picked up the free weights to begin some straight-arm raises. 'I just want you to back off with the smart-arse comments.'

'I doubt if I can change the habit of a lifetime, Danny-boy.'

'I'd try if I were you.'

'Does Chuck know about the punch you threw at Henley?'

'If he did, he'd cheer.'

'I doubt it. I think if he knew, he'd find another rower to scull with me. He's an American – all Uncle Sam, apple-pie and political correctness. And that includes not condoning violence. So if he knew he'd have to take disciplinary action and you'd be off the team. It's quits, Danny-boy. Stalemate.' Rollo raised an eyebrow. He got off the machine. 'See, you lost again.' And he sauntered out of the gym leaving Dan fuming.

As Amy left the hospital after a long, long day of finding her feet and meeting new colleagues, she switched on her mobile phone. She glanced at the screen: three missed

70

calls and all from the same number – a number that wasn't coming up as one already programmed into her phone. As she sauntered down the hill to Marston to catch the bus back towards the city centre, she wondered who it might be. Whoever it was, they were persistent. That word, *persistent*, made her reach into her handbag to rummage around for Rollo's card. She compared the numbers. Eureka.

Her stomach gave a little flip as she hit the dial button. Rollo answered on the second ring.

'Amy,' he said.

So he'd programmed her number into his phone then. Good sign.

'Amy?' he repeated when she didn't answer immediately. 'You there?'

'Yes, yes of course. What can I do for you?'

She heard a low chuckle as an answer before Rollo said, 'Actually, I think we can be of mutual benefit to each other.'

'Really?' Better and better.

'Would you like some extra hands-on experience?' he said.

'I beg your pardon?' And of course she did but she was hoping for dinner or a date first.

Rollo chuckled again. 'You've got a dirty mind, Amy. I'm talking about physiotherapy.'

'Oh.' Not what she had in mind at all, which left her feeling rather foolish. 'I don't know. I've got a job with the hospital so I'm getting plenty.' She heard that chuckle again. 'Experience,' she added icily.

'Well, I'm offering you some extra. At the rowing club.

71

You said you wanted to get back into rowing so this could be a win–win situation. You want to row; we're in temporary need of a physio. There is a drawback though – we can't pay you. But on the plus side, if you do this, we won't charge you the membership fee. How about it, what do you say?'

It seemed too good to be true. She hesitated as she thought about the offer.

'A couple of hours,' elaborated Rollo, 'two or three evenings a week.'

'So where's the club? I don't have any transport except buses and my own two feet.'

Rollo gave her directions as to how to reach the club.

'But that's easy. I can jump on a bus.'

'Then it's meant to happen, isn't it? You'll do the job?'

'I need to check with the JR first. That's the day job and I daren't piss them off by moonlighting. I need to earn a proper living, remember.'

'Okay. Just let me know as soon as you get the nod. Or not. If it's a "no" we need to look elsewhere. Now, what are you doing this evening?'

Her hopes rose again. 'Unpacking.'

'Sounds dull.'

Amy had reached her bus stop and tucked her mobile under her chin while she ran her finger round the timetable attached to the shelter. One due in just a few minutes. 'It's got to be done.'

'Sack it. Come out instead.'

She was sorely tempted but . . . 'No, really. I've got a lot of stuff to do and besides I'm knackered. It was a late night, last night.'

'I wasn't suggesting boozing. I was going to take you to the boat club, introduce you to a few people. If you see what a nice bunch they are there it might help you make up your mind.'

'Oh.' Sheesh, she must stop assuming he was about to offer her a date. If she carried on like this she'd wind up looking sad and desperate. 'But didn't I meet a load of them last night?'

'The club has a lot more members than that and you ought to meet Chuck, the coach. You'll be working for him if everything pans out. Say yes, please.'

Amy wavered.

'I'll pick you up and have you back home in under an hour.'

'Okay.' She saw her bus approaching. 'Look gotta go. I'll text you my address. I'll be ready about eight, is that okay?'

'Cool. See you then.'

Amy severed the connection just as her bus hissed to a stop beside her. She dropped her phone in her bag and jumped on.

Amy had just finished unpacking yet another suitcase when her phone trilled to indicate an incoming text.

Can u w8 on pavement with u in 5 mins

Shit, was that the time?

Amy dragged a comb through her hair, grabbed her handbag and door key, abandoned the clothes she'd been about to hang up in her wardrobe and raced down the stairs. A couple of minutes after the front door slammed behind her a sleek red sports car slid to a halt.

'Jump in,' instructed Rollo.

Amy didn't need asking twice as already, behind Rollo, a tail of traffic was building up. She clambered in and, because she didn't realise quite how low the car was, her entry was embarrassingly short of elegant.

She was trying to regain her composure when Rollo, ignoring the hoots from other frustrated road-users, managed to piss off the drivers on both lanes by executing a nifty three-point turn. With an airy wave out of the window he left the angry drivers behind him as he shot off back down St Clem's to the Magdalene Bridge. They headed down the High before turning off down a back street. Expertly he nipped along the road, squeezing his vehicle between the parked cars and the oncoming traffic, then diving down further side streets until he reached a dead-end. On the way he impressed upon Amy that all she had to do was to convince the coach about her credentials as a physio and her potential as a cox.

'There *may* be some money we can spare you, but I doubt it. But what you will be getting is club membership and our undying gratitude. But you've got to get past Chuck first. He wasn't completely persuaded when I suggested this to him.'

'Right,' said Amy. She tried to sound positive but it was all too good to be true. And, in her limited experience, people like her just didn't get this lucky. Rollo switched of the engine and pulled on the handbrake.

'Shanks's pony from here,' he apologised.

'That's all right,' said Amy scrabbling for the door handle so she could get herself out of the car before Rollo could do anything chivalrous like giving her a hand. If she was going to be ungainly and inelegant she wanted to do it without a witness. Looking like Bambi on ice, legs all over the place and not a shred of dignity, Amy hauled herself upright and was looking reasonably together by the time Rollo eased his way past the long sleek bonnet to get to her side.

'I'll just lock this baby up,' he said, plipping the key before taking Amy down a path that led through trees and hedges and away from houses and civilisation. It was quite dark but the path was flat and it wasn't too tricky to see their way as it led over a small river by way of a footbridge and onto a small triangular island formed by the confluence of sections of the fragmented Isis and Cherwell. The path led to the back of a row of boathouses that fronted onto the main stream of the river. They picked their way along the hardstanding in front of around a dozen boat clubs. The area between the buildings and the jetties was littered with boat racks, bikes and trailers, and young men and women were standing around chatting about the finer points of rowing, training and the work, life and play balance.

'Here we are,' said Rollo taking Amy's arm and steering her through a pair of large double doors. On either side were yet more racks of boats of every size and beyond them Amy could see changing rooms. To the left was a gym and she could hear the clang of weights machines and the grunts of the men and women working out. In the corner was a steep staircase. Rollo headed for that and the pair went up to the first floor and the clubroom. She thought she recognised Seb and Angus but Rollo swept her onwards, past battered sofas and across a threadbare rug, into a small office space with a sloping ceiling and a wide window that looked out, under the eaves, to the Isis below.

'Aha, Chuck,' said Rollo as strode towards the man seated at the desk there. An attack of nerves made Amy's heart rate take off. Chuck – the man who had the power to give her access to a club where she could not only carry on coxing but which would also provide her with an instant social life.

In the corner, at a desk near the big window sat a burly man in a loud checked jacket. Amy reckoned he must be in his mid-thirties. Behind him the glass with the night behind it reflected the warm glow of the clubroom, the lights from the bar in the opposite corner and the shadowy shapes of the members. The hum of conversation had begun again, interspersed now and again by a burst of laughter, but Amy ignored everything and focused on Chuck. He didn't look ferocious, she decided, quite pleasant really, with lots of smile-creases round his eyes. She didn't think working for him would be a hardship – assuming she was offered the job and the JR didn't object.

Chuck looked up.

'Hi Rollo,' he said. 'And this must be Amy, right?' He stood and extended his hand. Nervously Amy offered hers. She tried not to yelp as Chuck crunched her fingers and seemed to try to yank her forearm from her elbow.

'So Rollo tells me you're a physio.'

Amy nodded as she flexed her fingers. 'I qualified in the summer.'

'Excellent. And you're keen on rowing.'

'Well, coxing, yes.'

'You know we can't pay you. And you know that you won't be able to compete with our crews as you're not studying at the college?'

Amy nodded. 'Rollo said he thought money might be an issue but I don't mind or about the competitions, honestly. It'd just be nice to keep my hand in.'

'You sure about that?'

'If you'll have me, and if my proper employer has no objections. I mean, I can't see it being a problem. What I do here won't affect the day job but I just need to get official approval.'

'I'm sure they'll be cool. So, assuming that, how about Monday, Wednesday and Friday evenings? From around eight?'

Amy nodded. It sounded reasonable. 'I don't want to sound cheeky, but when the proper physio returns, will I still be allowed to be a member?'

Chuck nodded. 'I'm sure we can work something out.'

'Then it's a deal,' she said happily.

Chuck turned to the room. 'Hey guys,' Silence fell. 'Hey, this here lady is Amy. She's standing in for Marcus till he gets better. If you have any physiotherapy require - ments then ask her.' While he still held the rowers' attention he explained what Amy's consultation times would be. 'And she's got a day job so you're not to pester her outside of these times. And she's also a cox, if any of you need one to fill in when training, especially you lady rowers.'

'Tanya's got more cox than she can handle,' someone heckled.

Then another voice, which sounded suspiciously like Seb's, said, 'She can give me a massage any time.'

'Cox and a massage expert – sounds like a marriage made in heaven,' said another voice – not one Amy recognised. She rolled her eyes and then caught sight of Maddy. She grinned at the familiar and friendly face and then saw Susie who waved her fingers at her. Despite the ribald comments, or maybe because of them, Amy felt relaxed and at home. Working here could be fun.

'Knock if off,' said Chuck. 'Any more comments like that and I'll double your training schedules.'

There were mutters and a few groans but no more smutty innuendoes.

'Follow me,' growled Chuck to Amy. He led her back downstairs and through the gym where he unlocked a door at the back. He pushed it open and switched on the light. Once the neon strip had stopped buzzing and flicking on and off a small consulting room was revealed complete with a massage table.

'This is where you'll work when you're here. You come and get the key from me. If I'm not here whoever is running the bar will be able to let you have it.'

'Okay. And you think some of the crews may want me to cox?'

'Sure, why not. We've got a couple of coxes already but I'm sure there'll be plenty of call for another one.'

'Good,' said Amy happily.

'I'll leave you to it, let you have a look around and get your bearings.'

Chuck disappeared and Amy stared around her new empire. A counter with cupboards and drawers underneath, a sink and the massage table. She opened a couple of the drawers and found the usual stuff: tissues, latex gloves, a roll of bin liners, tubes of antiseptic cream, tubular bandages, sticky tape . . . She shut the drawers again and looked in the cupboards; empty apart from one that concealed a bin and another that concealed a small freezer stocked with ice-packs. So that was that.

She wondered if she was supposed to start offering physio sessions this evening or if she was free to go back home to finish her unpacking. Chuck had said she was expected to turn up on Mondays, Wednesdays and Fridays but she was here now so she might as well stay. Rollo had lured her out with the promise that she'd only be out for an hour, but heck, who was she kidding that she was going to carry on unpacking tonight? She might as well make herself useful.

Amy clipped the door back and sat on the chair beside the counter trying to look professional and as if she was expecting her next patient. To keep herself occupied she got out her phone and checked her texts.

'It seems as if our paths are destined to cross on an almost daily basis.'

Amy glanced up. 'Dan!'

'So you're the new Marcus?'

'Apparently, although I'm not sure how much good I'll be able to do.'

'I'm sure if Rollo was happy with the services you provided then everyone else will be too.'

Amy ignored the slight innuendo there and instead stared at Dan. Here he was in lycra again. There were, she knew from coxing at Bath, some men who really weren't designed for lycra all-in-ones but Dan certainly was. Every sculpted muscle, every inch of his toned body, every bit of him, and she meant *every* bit, was enhanced by his skin-tight kit. Amy could feel a wave of lust start to ripple up her from her toes to her scalp as she forced her eyes to return to Dan's face. What she would give to provide Dan with some services! Rollo was gorgeous but undeniably bad news, but Dan . . . Dan was something altogether different.

'We'll see if the members are satisfied once I've started work properly,' she said as lightly as she could to mask the heat that was thundering through her veins. 'Do you want any physio?'

Dan shook his head but he didn't go. He leaned against the doorjamb. 'Not at the moment, thanks. But then, I expect Rollo's already booked you solid for the foreseeable future.'

Amy shook her head. 'No.'

'But I thought he had an old injury.'

'He might but nothing that he's asked me to work on specifically.'

'So he's not planning on monopolising you.'

'Me? Good Lord no. I'm here for the benefit of all of you, not just him.'

'Really?' Dan sounded quite heartened.

'Of course. I think Chuck would have something to say, don't you, if I only treated Rollo?'

'Probably,' he conceded. 'Anyway, I just came by to see that you've begun to settle in, make sure you have everything you need, that sort of thing.'

'Thanks, it's all fine.'

Dan glanced at his watch.

'Don't let me keep you,' said Amy. 'Wouldn't like you to be late for a date or anything.'

Dan frowned. 'Date?'

'Well, whatever you've got next on the agenda.'

'Essay writing.'

'Lucky you.'

'It's got to be done. No doubt I'll see you around.'

Amy nodded. 'Look, if you see Rollo, tell him that if he wants his shoulder worked on, I'm happy to see him now. Got nothing else to do so I might as well make myself useful.'

'If I see him I'll tell him.'

Amy was left in peace for a few minutes till Seb wandered in. He asked her a few questions about some stretches and then disappeared. Amy wasn't sure if he really needed the information or if he was checking out the new physio to reassure himself that she really did know her stuff. Amy longed to tell him that rather than checking on her he'd be better off giving Maddy a bit of attention but didn't think it was really her place to interfere. Not yet anyway.

Two minutes after Seb left Rollo rocked up.

'Dan said you wanted to give me a thorough going over.' He raised his eyebrows suggestively.

Amy suspected Dan had said nothing of the sort. 'I heard your shoulder is still playing up.'

'On and off.'

'Let's see if I can make it more off than on,' said Amy. 'Hop on the table and lie on your front. And take your top off.'

'Just my top?'

Amy didn't bother to reply, just rubbed some oil on her hands while Rollo settled himself into position.

'So it's the left shoulder?'

'Yes,' said Rollo, his voice slightly muffled by the towel he was lying on.

Amy got to work. She heard a hiss of breath from Rollo. 'That hurt?'

'A bit.'

She worked harder on that specific area for a couple of minutes. 'That should help,' she said as she stopped the massage. 'It may feel a bit bruised for a day or two and I want you to ease off the upper body training for a week or so. No reason why you can't maintain your overall fitness level with plenty of running and gym work on your legs, but lay off the ergo and the weights for a few days. I'll tell Chuck, if you like.'

'No, it's okay, I'll do it.'

Rollo rolled over on the table and then sat up. He was directly in front of Amy and before she realised what was going on he grabbed her round the waist and pulled her against him, clamping her hips with his legs so she was completely trapped. Then he reached up his left arm, pulled her head forwards and kissed her hard on the lips. Although surprised by his assault, it was exciting and erotic and it wasn't at all unpleasant being up close and personal with a semi-naked sex-god. Amy didn't resist, leaned into him and parted her lips to allow Rollo's tongue to stab into her mouth. As she did so she felt her legs begin to weaken and a pool of liquid heat seemed to form deep inside her. She responded with her tongue, rubbing it against his, exploring his mouth, tasting him, her fingers entwined in his thick hair as Rollo pulled her harder against him.

She could feel his erection grow swiftly and impressively against her stomach.

'Look what you've done to me,' said Rollo pulling back, panting slightly.

She looked down at the large tent in his shorts. So he thought she'd drop her knickers just like that? It was about time Mr Lyndon-Forster learned that he couldn't have every girl in Oxford that easily.

'That's a nasty swelling,' she said, in a low voice. 'I think it's going to need special treatment.'

Rollo's eyes darkened with lust. 'Are you going to suck the poison out?'

'Something like that. I certainly have the perfect remedy. Lie down, big boy, and Nurse Amy will make it all better.'

With a groan of anticipation, Rollo did as he was told and laid on his back expectantly with his eyes shut, a smile playing over his lips and his cock straining against the fabric of his shorts.

Amy reached into one of the cupboards to get what she needed and then returned to Rollo's side. Deftly she lifted the elastic at the waist. As she did so she saw him hold his breath. In one swift movement she stuffed an ice-pack right down the front.

It took Rollo a second to register what was going on.

With a yelp he sat bolt upright while simultaneously hauling out the ice-pack, then he leapt off the table looking thunderous, while Amy giggled helplessly.

'What the fuck . . .?' he roared throwing the pack down behind him on to the table.

'Yup, that did the trick. The swelling's all better,' said Amy, still laughing as she looked at the front of his shorts, now back to their normal shape.

'But why? I thought you were up for a quickie.' Rollo sounded sulky and annoyed.

'Not in my treatment room. And if I ever find you contemplating using it for anything like this again I'll think of something even more unpleasant to do to you. Understand?'

Coolly she picked up the ice-pack and returned it to the freezer while Rollo stormed off, livid.

Amy folded up the towel from the treatment table, switched the light off and shut the door. She didn't think she'd have any more takers for treatment, so she went up the stairs to the bar, cosy with its low lighting despite it occupying the entire top floor of the club. She bought herself a Diet Coke and sat down on a saggy, battered leather sofa to wait for Rollo to offer her a lift home, although, given the way she'd treated him she wouldn't be surprised if she was out of luck. She stared into her drink, wondering whether she ought to resign herself to walking back when she felt the sofa bounce as someone else sat on it.

'Hiya, Amy.'

She glanced across. 'Maddy.'

'You don't mind me joining you?'

'Be my guest.'

'Fancy running into you again.'

'Rowing seems to be a small world. It's down to Rollo that I've got the job here. It's quite nice to think that I've got a ready-made set of friends, even though I'm new to the area.'

'Friends, with Rollo?' said Maddy incredulously. 'I can't imagine him wanting things to stay at that level for long.'

'So I've heard,' said Amy. 'In fact . . .' She was about to tell Maddy about what had gone on in the treatment room when she was interrupted.

'Hello,' said another voice. 'Budge up you two.' It was Susie, Angus's girlfriend. She plopped down into the space in the middle. 'So,' she said, looking first at Maddy and then at Amy, 'who are you talking about? Any juicy gossip that I should know about?'

'Well,' said Amy. She looked around, checking if anyone else was in earshot and then, to be doubly sure she was only going to be confiding the information to the two girls she bent her head towards them. 'You'll never guess what's just happened in my treatment room.' She gave them a detailed account.

'But that's priceless,' said Susie, shaking with sup - pressed laughter.

Maddy shook her head in disbelief before she too began to giggle.

'His face must have been a picture,' spluttered Susie.

Amy nodded. 'Mind you, I think I'll have to walk back to my flat. Can't see him wanting to give me a lift home now.'

'Don't worry. I can give you a lift,' said Maddy.

'And I'm going to buy you a drink,' said Susie.

'I've got one, but thanks.' Amy picked up her Coke and took a slug of it.

'Sure? I'm getting one for myself.' But Amy was happy with her Coke and Maddy declined too. Susie came back a minute later with an Archers and soda and squeezed back between them.

'Now, where were we? Oh yes, hearing how Rollo got frozen out. Of course, you're not the first one here to resist his charms. He made a really big mistake when he joined the club by trying it on with Christina and Stevie.'

Susie nodded across at two women standing at the bar, both drinking mineral water and wearing tracksuits that, with their height, looks and figures, they made look like Paris couture. Amy remembered them from the bistro the night before.

'Well, I can see they'd be right up Rollo's street.'

'Yes, except they're both on the other bus.'

'What?'

'They bat for the other team,' elaborated Susie.

'You mean . . . Oh, I see,' said Amy.

'Of course Rollo is convinced that they'd only have to spend a night with him – preferably as a threesome – for them to realise the error of their ways, but frankly, I can't see it myself. Why would they want Rollo, given what they've already got?'

Amy nodded. She understood exactly what Susie meant.

'I'm going to stick at trying to interest Seb, thanks all the same,' said Maddy. She stared across at him, on the other side of the room, where he was chatting to a group of rowers. She sighed. 'I expect you two think I'm a sad loser.'

Amy could see the attraction but for all that he wasn't her sort. Maddy saw the look on her new friend's face.

'I know, I'm obsessed. Probably certifiable.'

Amy laughed. 'I don't think that I'd go that far. After all, aren't women programmed to try to select the man they consider the best from the available gene pool to procreate with? So if you're wildly attracted to Seb it's because you're biologically programmed that way.'

Maddy's eyes lit up. 'So my ambition to sleep with Seb is in my DNA?' She pumped her fist in the air. 'Yesss!' She jumped up and kissed Amy on the cheek, so startling her she almost spilled her drink. 'Oh my God, this is so perfect. I knew there had to be a reason why I'm completely smitten by the man, even though . . . well, it doesn't matter. Hooray, so my desire is legit, all out of my control and part of my physical make-up. All I need now is to get him to notice me.'

'Instead of Tanya,' said Susie.

Maddy's face crumpled at the memory of the previous evening and she nodded again. 'She does it because she can. Pulling blokes is just a game to her. How can I compete with her? She's just so . . . oh, never mind.' Maddy looked close to tears.

'If it's a game she'll get bored soon,' said Amy reassuringly.

'Maybe, but she didn't have to pull Seb, in the first place, now did she.' Maddy looked stricken.

'Perhaps not. But he's a grown-up and has a mind of his own.'

Maddy nodded sadly. 'Maybe I'll get a chance when she spits him out again.'

6

'How's it going?' drawled Chuck from the door of Amy's cubbyhole. 'How's your first couple of weeks been?'

Amy was working on Seb who, she now knew, was one of Chuck's hopefuls for the Blue Boat. Not only had Seb rowed for St George's but had also rowed for the army before the military had decided it would be worth their while to sponsor him to do a degree in electronic engineering. Amy had wondered about confiding to him that he had a secret admirer in the club but had decided that it really wasn't her place to interfere. Much as she was tempted to try a spot of matchmaking she felt that if she dabbled she might end up making things worse rather than better.

'Fine,' she said as she pushed against Seb's flexed foot making him grimace in pain.

'Ouch,' he muttered.

'And relax,' said Amy lowering his leg back onto the table.

'She's a sadist,' said Seb to Chuck.

'And did I ask for your opinion?' said his coach.

'Then be grateful you're getting it for free,' said Seb.

'And you should feel the same way about this treat-ment,' countered Chuck.

Amy stood back. 'I'm done,' she said to Seb. 'Go and get changed and go for a run but take it easy. Don't over do it, okay. Just a jog for about a mile.'

'Yes, miss,' he said with a grin.

'And I'm sorry I hurt you.'

'No, you're not.'

'You're right, I couldn't care less.'

Seb left, closing the door behind him.

'You're a hit with the guys,' said Chuck.

'And the girls?'

'They're not such a tough market, less critical.'

'And far more used to having their health looked after by a member of the opposite sex.'

'Exactly,' said Chuck with a slow smile, which Amy returned.

She liked Chuck. She'd decided after her first couple of visits that he was a sincerely nice guy, hard-working and charming but not prone to flannel. Just straight-forward and straight-dealing and she knew that if she didn't cock up, working for him would earn her a decent reference and maybe get her another step close to being a professional sports physio as opposed to just a physio. Yes, taking the gig here had been a good move even if she was working as a volunteer.

There was a knock on the door. 'Looks like I've got another client,' said Amy.

Chuck nodded. 'Keep up the good work, sweetheart.'

Amy smiled, pleased to have his approval.

Chuck left and in strolled a tall brunette with endless

legs, the sort of glossy hair you only saw advertising shampoo and a walk that would have looked perfect on a fashion-show runway. Amy recognised her instantly, even though their paths hadn't crossed since that night at the bistro. Tanya.

She sashayed over to a chair sat down and crossed her elegant legs.

'I've heard you're doing a good job here,' said Tanya. 'And I've also heard you've done a bit of coxing.'

Amy had done a lot more than 'a bit' of coxing but she wasn't the sort who bragged. 'Some, yes,' she answered carefully.

'For Bath.'

'Yes.'

'Hmmm.'

And they'd done bloody brilliantly – won loads of Heads, and regattas but Amy wasn't going to rise.

'The thing is,' said Tanya, 'the eight I row with has a perfectly good cox, but she's a med student and the pressure of work is insane. Well, isn't it for all of us?' She stared at Amy. 'Oh, of course you're not studying here.'

'No, I just loaf around all day at the JR.' Fuck, she'd risen!

Tanya smiled, smugly. 'As I was saying, we have a cox already but I need someone else who might be more available at the weekends than Hannah. Given that you want to cox, I wondered if you'd like to accept my offer. It wouldn't be every weekend, obviously.'

Jeez, Tanya sounded more like she was bestowing a knighthood on a peasant than giving Amy a chance to have even more of her free time whittled away. But it was a tempting offer – she missed coxing.

'When do you train?' she asked.

'Saturdays at eight for a couple of hours and then Sunday afternoons.'

Amy considered the hours. What else did she have to do?

'Fine.'

'Good.' Tanya got up to go. 'Just one other thing. I don't suppose you'd like to help me organise the boat club Christmas ball, would you?'

Amy was taken aback. 'Me?'

'Why not?'

'Because I don't know the first thing about balls,' replied Amy flatly.

'You don't need to know about balls,' said Tanya. 'You just need to be reasonably efficient.' She stared at Amy. 'It's only stuff like helping me allocate tables, choose the menu, sending out the tickets. All basic admin stuff, no special skills required. And if you do it you get to choose which table you sit on – assuming you want to come – so you end up with all your favourite people. You can manage a spreadsheet, can't you?'

Amy nodded.

'How's your handwriting?'

'Okay,' she said cautiously.

'Because I need someone to write the names on the tickets and I don't want it to look as if I've given the job to someone who's barely literate.'

'I think you'll find I don't fall into that category.'

'Good,' said Tanya with a sniff. 'Then I'm sure you'll

do fine.' She swept off, leaving Amy feeling battered.

'Can I come in?' said Dan, standing in the doorway.

Amy looked up. 'Hi, Dan. Yes, of course, what can I do for you?'

'I saw Tanya leaving. I came to check you're still in one piece.'

'Just about. She's quite something, isn't she?'

Dan nodded.

'She wants me to help her run the Christmas ball.'

'I think that's a compliment.'

'And to cox for her eight at weekends sometimes.'

'That's certainly a compliment.'

'Best I don't let her down. I don't think I want to make an enemy of her.'

'It might be easier having her as a friend than not,' advised Dan.

'The trouble is, I didn't actually say "yes" to helping her with the ball and yet she's taken it for granted that I've agreed and even worse, I've got a feeling that Tanya wants a lackey rather than a colleague.'

Dan laughed.

God, he was so gorgeous when he lightened up. 'I thought you worked on Wednesday evenings,' she said, wanting to keep his attention for just a little longer.

'I do but not all of them. The manager is pretty good about me having time off for training. There's no shortage of students wanting part-time jobs around here. As long as I sort it out with the other employees he's pretty laid back. Although if I get selected for training for the Blue Boat I'll have to give up the job altogether.' Dan gave a heavy sigh.

'But isn't making the Blue Boat what you all want?' Amy was fully conscious that all the serious college rowers had the one ambition: to be selected to row against Cambridge in the Boat Race.

'I do, I do, but I need the cash.'

'I can imagine.'

'Still, if I get picked up for the Oxford crew and if I get a shot at selection for the national team then I might become eligible for a development grant.'

'I don't want to be a bucket of cold water but there seem to be a lot of *ifs* there.'

Dan nodded ruefully. 'I don't suppose you fancy coming to watch a race next month?'

'I suppose. Where is it?'

'Chiswick – we're entering a coxless four in the Fours Head.'

She'd assumed it was going to be on the Isis or the Cherwell, but Chiswick! 'Dan, I'd love to come and watch but I've a real problem with transport.'

'Maddy's coming along, she'll give you a lift.'

Amy was tempted. Maybe Dan saw her wavering. 'There's masses to do, loads of teams enter, hundreds. There's a real party atmosphere on the riverbank. It'd be nice to have another friendly face supporting us.'

'You'll have heaps of supporters.'

'Well, I imagine Rollo will have his own private fan club there –'

'Naturally.'

'– and Susie will be supporting Angus and I know Maddy's coming along so you'll have some mates from the boat club to keep you company while we're on the water.'

'Is Seb rowing?'

Dan nodded. So that explained why Maddy would be there. Amy wondered if Dan had twigged how besotted Maddy was with him.

'It's a great day out,' insisted Dan. He gave her a winning smile and Amy was won over. He really was a lovely bloke. Not boyfriend material, obviously – he was too taken up with his degree and rowing and his job to be any use in that department – but so long as she could find out whether he was with Karen or not, it was worth a try. And if going to Chiswick to support him was going to help make it happen, then it was a no-brainer.

'Why not? You've convinced me.' She gave him a smile.

'Thanks. Maddy's got all the details. Go and have a word with her.'

'Okay, I'll go and find her and sort it out.'

Amy shut up her little treatment room and went upstairs to the bar in search of Maddy. Unsurprisingly, she had positioned herself so she had an uninterrupted view of Seb, although, as usual, he seemed unaware of her presence. She looked a bit miserable, thought Amy. Poor old Mads. Maybe things would change at the Fours Head.

Amy flopped onto the sofa beside her friend.

'Hiya,' she said.

Maddy looked across at her and her face lit up with a smile.

'Hi, Ames. Finished torturing rowers for the evening?'

'Yup. And I've come to see you because I've got a bit of a favour to ask you.'

95

'Shoot.'

'Dan says you're going to the Fours Head.'

Maddy nodded.

'He's persuaded me to come along for the day too.'

'Fantastic,' said Maddy with enthusiasm.

'The trouble is, I've got no wheels.'

'But I can give you a lift.'

'That's what I was hoping you'd say.'

'So,' said Rollo, right by Amy's ear. She swivelled on the sofa and saw him leaning on the back of it, eavesdropping unashamedly. 'Danny-boy's got himself a date,' he sneered.

'It's nothing of the sort,' countered Amy. And then regretted her words. 'I mean,' she elaborated, 'he asked me to come along to support the crew, said it'd be a fun day out, and I agreed.'

'Glad to hear that's all it is. Don't want to see a nice girl like you ending up horribly disappointed. You're way too good for him.' He strolled off over to the bar.'

'You know, if he wasn't so utterly irresistible he'd be such a complete bastard,' said Amy.

'He doesn't do it for me,' said Maddy.

'No, hon, but that's because you don't have eyes for anyone but Seb. And we're going to have to come up with a strategy to make it a two-way street. We can start the process at Chiswick if we can't make it happen before then.'

The Saturday of the Fours Head dawned overcast but dry. Maddy picked up Amy from her flat at seven thirty which, she had assured Amy the night before, was essential if they were going to find somewhere to park and get a good pitch on the towpath.

'And we don't want to be stuck any old where. We need to get to where St George's are boating from. It's daft going all that way to support them and then being nowhere near the team.'

'But seven thirty?' Amy had protested.

'They've got an early draw so they'll be going off before midday.'

'But that gives us hours.'

'It may seem like it but trust me I think the time will be tight. Besides, it's probably going to take us half the morning to find a parking space. In fact, it might be an idea if we park well away from the river and then walk. Wear comfy shoes.'

So when Maddy had picked up Amy in her battered little 2CV she was pleased to see that Amy had paid attention and was wearing her Uggs.

'You look nice,' said Amy as she clambered into the car.

'Thanks,' said Maddy. 'I'm really hoping Seb might notice me today. I mean, it shows some commitment to travel all that way just to see them hurtle past in a matter of a few seconds. Surely he'll notice the effort we've made.'

'I'm sure the crew will appreciate it.'

'But it's Seb I want to appreciate it, not the others.'

'Do you know who else is going up to support them? Tanya?'

'Didn't you know?' said Maddy. 'She's rowing with Christina, Stevie and Susie. And the best thing is, they're boating from another boat club so they won't be around at all, all day.'

Amy glanced across the car to Maddy. 'Then at least you don't have her to distract Seb.'

Maddy nodded and smiled. 'I honestly feel I might get lucky today. Oh God, Ames, I'm so excited I can hardly think straight.'

'Well, please try,' said Amy. 'I really don't fancy you driving us along the M40 in a total daze.'

'It was just a figure of speech. Although I do have butterflies.'

They drove along the road for a few minutes, in companionable silence. Amy was looking forward to the day ahead; Maddy was thinking – as she so often did – of Seb.

'What do you think their chances are?' she asked Amy. 'I so want Seb to win, well and the others of course.'

Amy shrugged. 'I'm no expert but they certainly train hard enough.'

'So which of them do you think is the fittest?'

'Fittest in looks or most buff body?'

Maddy giggled. 'No contest. Seb on both counts, but then I am horribly biased.'

'And don't I know it.'

Maddy laughed. 'I can't help being obsessed. But who do you fancy the most? Who would be your pin-up?'

'Well, Dan for buffest body and Rollo for looks.'

'What's wrong with Seb?'

Amy rolled her eyes. What was Maddy like? 'Nothing, hon. Honest. He's lovely but he's not my type.'

'You're just saying that because you know how I feel.'

Amy shuffled in her seat. 'No, I'm not. Truly. And I'm not sure Rollo is my type either, not as a person because I think he's a bit too much of a bastard. But you have to admit he's a very pretty boy and I wouldn't kick him out of my bed if I ever managed to haul him into it.'

Maddy shook her head. 'Really?' She sounded astounded. 'Not struck on blond blokes, me.'

'Then isn't it just as well we're all different. Wouldn't it be insanc if we all went after the same type?'

Maddy switched the conversation to the Christmas ball, sharing with Amy everything she'd heard about the previous ones. Allegedly St George's was rated one of the best.

'Did you hear about Angus and Susie last year?'

'No, why?'

'Well, the evening was well under way, and the staff at the Randolph were setting up the table for the breakfast buffet which was going to be served at around two and a bunch of us noticed that the whole table was shaking. The orange juice was slopping out of the jugs and everything. It was like there was some sort of earthquake.' Maddy giggled at the memory.

'Go on,' said Amy.

'So Rollo goes and lifts up the tablecloth and there they are, at it like rabbits. Her dress up, his trousers down, and Susie looks at Rollo cool as a cucumber and says, "Give us a bit of privacy, there's a love" and goes back to having her brains shagged out. And I don't think Angus even noticed!'

'Bloody hell.'

'I know, it was a hoot.' Maddy stopped chatting while she negotiated the merging of the dual carriageway with the main section of the M40 and accelerated past a couple of trucks in the slow lane. 'Anyway, do you think Seb will come in mess kit?

'I suppose he might.'

'He'll look so dashing. Maybe if I catch his eye today I'll be able to cop off with him there.'

'I'm sure,' replied Amy.

Maddy let herself revel in a fantasy which involved Seb in uniform, on horseback, riding to her rescue, which lasted all the way until she came off the motorway. Amy didn't do anything to interrupt the silence and enjoyed the peace and quiet. Maddy didn't chat much on their way into London as she had to concentrate on finding her way through the suburbs to the southern bank of the Thames and an area that was close enough to where St George's was based that they could walk the last leg of the journey.

'This'll do,' said Maddy finally, swinging her car into a near-empty car park.

Amy took in her surroundings. 'But you can't park here, it's a school.'

'And today is Saturday. Just how many of the little darlings are going to be pitching up for lessons today?'

'Yeah, but they'll still have rules about unauthorised parking, won't they?'

'Let's risk it, shall we?'

'It's your car,' mumbled Amy.

'And I'll pay the fine if we get clamped.'

Amy gave her a look which said, pretty eloquently 'too right you will' before she clambered out of the car.

Maddy grabbed her backpack off the rear sear of the little car, locked it up and then the pair set off towards the river. As they walked Maddy hauled her *London A–Z* out of her backpack. She flicked through the pages until she found the correct one.

'Not far,' she said cheerily, flipping the book shut and chucking it back into her bag.

It was obvious the river was close; there was a smell of wet mud and above them seagulls called to each other with a raucous yark-yark cry. Overhead, the sky was milky with high, thin cloud and the temperature had a real edge to it with a brisk breeze making sure that any exposed skin got a real chilling. A brighter silver disc in the sky showed the position of the sun but its watery, dilute rays didn't have the energy to break through the clouds. Maddy set off at a lick to keep their circulation moving.

'Where are we going?' asked Amy, panting ever so

slightly as she struggled to keep up. Maddy kept forgetting how much fitter her rowing had made her since she'd taken it up.

'The boathouse. St Edmund's School has their boathouse on the tideway and it's where the boys are boating from. Them and about another fifty or so crews.'

'Fifty?'

Maddy nodded. 'This event is just mad. You've no idea. There are going to be over five hundred fours thundering downstream all trying to catch the crew in front.'

'And do they?'

'Oh yes. Well, some do, it depends on how good the teams are. The idea is that the fastest teams set off first, but of course, it's like handicapping in golf; it doesn't always work like that and sometimes outsiders can really surprise everyone. That's what makes it so fun. Anyway, it's not all about overtaking, it's about being the fastest.'

Maddy wove her way along a couple of side streets with Amy belting along beside her until they suddenly turned onto the Thames towpath.

'Not far now,' she said cheerily.

'That's what you said a mile ago,' protested Amy. Now she was really puffing. But then she stopped dead as she saw what was happening on the river. The whole of the tideway was thick with fours and quads.

'Crikey,' she puffed. 'There's thousands of them.'

'Told you.'

The towpath widened out and they had suddenly arrived in the midst of a scene of total chaos. Or that's what it appeared to be at first sight. Everywhere, over the hardstanding and slipway between a boathouse and the river were trailers loaded up with boats, men and women manoeuvring boats into the water, people carrying blades, rowers warming up, rowers chatting, trainers and coaches haranguing. Bedlam.

The two women stopped in their tracks as they sought to keep out of the way of the activity and also try to work out where the team they had come to support might be.

After a few minutes of fruitlessly trying to spot the guys Amy got out her phone.

'I suppose,' she said as she pressed its buttons, 'that Rollo will have his with him.'

'I would imagine so,' said Maddy. 'He's never one to miss a social opportunity.'

Amy found Rollo's number and hit the call button. She listened for a few seconds, then slid her phone shut. 'Voicemail.'

'Oh well,' said Maddy, 'nice try.'

'Don't you have any of the crew's numbers?'

'No.'

'Not even Seb's?' Amy's sheer astonishment was clear.

Maddy felt stupid. 'I haven't really had the opportunity to ask for it,' she explained.

Amy looked stunned. 'What?'

Maddy shook her head. 'I've never really spoken to him,' she said sadly. 'I'm so terrified he'll tell me to bugger off I haven't dared risk it.'

'How come you've never told me that before? Oh, Maddy, that's the worst case of unrequited love I've come across.'

'I told you I am a sad loser. I'm completely in love with him and we've never even had a conversation.'

'No you're absolutely not.' Amy gave Maddy a hug.

'Ahem, sorry if I'm interrupting something.'

The girls span round. 'Rollo!'

'You've decided to join Christina and Stevie's camp have you?'

Any rolled her eyes. 'Do you have to bring sex into everything?'

Rollo nodded. 'And why not, I say?'

'We were just looking for you,' said Amy, deciding that she didn't fancy a conversation with Rollo about sex right this moment.

He changed tack. 'I saw I missed a call from you and imagined it meant you'd either arrived or were stuck in traffic. But I assumed it was the former and thought I'd come looking for you.'

'Thanks, Rollo,' said Maddy. 'It's mad here, isn't it.'

'Quieter round the back. It's where we've set up camp.' He linked arms with the girls and led them along the river frontage and then into a large sports field. Beside the entrance was a sign proclaiming that this was St Edmund's School Boat and Cricket Club and trespassers would be prosecuted. Maddy took in the amount of prime real estate that the two facilities occupied, the smart pavilion and the swanky boathouse, and wondered how enormous the fees must be to fund this level of sporting amenities. However, it was obvious that no cricket was going to be played in the near future as the outfield was covered in trailers, tents, boats, portaloos and towing vehicles. Rollo might have thought it was quieter but the bedlam looked much the same as it had been on the towpath. The whole scene was bewildering. How on earth did the crews remember which boat was theirs? Or which tent? It all seemed completely disorganised and chaotic, in fact, it reminded her of Glastonbury – only with less music. And, at the moment, less mud.

Rollo stuck two fingers in his mouth and let rip a piercing whistle. Over the trailers and heads of the rowers they saw a distant arm waving. Someone, belonging to the arm, was jumping up and down in an attempt to see over the intervening heads.

'Seb,' breathed Maddy. She felt her insides clench and the colour rose in her face. Please God she just looked warm from their trek and not like some love-struck twit. She felt Amy's gaze on her and looked away, embarrassed. The last thing she wanted to look like was a twelve-year-old girl coming face to face with Justin Bieber. Cool was the look she wanted, not pathetically infatuated – even if that was the case.

They reached the team's camp. Chuck was bustling around checking the rigging of the boat. Dan and Angus were lolling on green collapsible camp chairs while Seb was wandering around, eating cold beans out of a tin. Maddy's innards did a set of flick-flacks – even shovelling food into his mouth he was irresistible. Around the group were supporters, fans, hangers-on – all of whom seemed to be women. Probably Rollo's exes, thought Maddy. And no Tanya since she and her crew were based somewhere else on the river.

'Hiya Amy, Maddy,' Chuck said, stopping what he was

doing and coming over to give the two girls a hug. 'I'm really pleased you've taken the trouble to come and support the boys. It's a great morale boost for them to see familiar faces from the club.' He wrapped his arms around the pair of them and gave them a squeeze. 'Hey, put them down,' said Rollo.

Chuck let the girls go and as soon as he did Rollo draped an arm over Amy's shoulders in a faintly proprietorial manner.

Maddy looked about her, wanting to see where Seb was. If she could just catch his eye maybe she could give him some indication that she'd come here to support him rather than the whole crew. But he'd finished his beans and was now crouching in front of Dan and Angus chatting to them with his back to her. Oh, this was hopeless.

Then Angus stood up and ambled over to Amy. And then Seb followed. A feeling of total exhilaration swept through Maddy as he approached.

Maddy edged closer to Amy so she was standing right beside her. Come on Amy, get me into a conversation with Seb now.

Amy grabbed her arm and pulled her right into the middle of the group. 'Yes, it's all thanks to Maddy that I'm here. She gave me a lift up so I could watch the action. Didn't you, Maddy?'

Thank you Amy, I love you.

'All right, Maddy? Aren't you rowing today, then?' said Angus.

'No, because I'm crap,' she said, honestly. 'I love rowing but my technique stinks, so I just do it for pleasure.'

Seb looked at the empty tin, still clutched in his huge hand and cast about for somewhere to get rid of it. He spotted a bin nearby and lobbed the can with devastating accuracy right into it.

'Blimey,' said Maddy, impressed.

'Grenade training has its uses,' he said, actually turn - ing and noticing her properly.

Dear God, grenade training. How macho is that! 'Hi Seb,' said Maddy, hoping against hope she sounded normal and not like some sort of crazed, bunny-boiling groupie.

'Hi Maddy.' He kissed her cheek. Maddy felt electricity jolt through her – a real, thrilling shock. Had he felt it? Was it just her?

'Sweet of you to come and support us.'

'Amy and I felt it was the least we could do.'

Apparently it was just her who had felt the electricity, as Seb began to talk to Angus about the Head and their chances and Maddy was back out of the loop once again. Seb and Angus were discussing possible tactics and rowing technicalities, most of which went straight over Maddy's head. She tried to look interested and like she understood if only so she could spend more time in Seb's company. She hoped to goodness he didn't ask her any questions about rowing because she knew she'd make a complete twat of herself if he did.

She glanced across at Amy who had Rollo's arm around her waist. If only Seb would do that to her.

'Seb's right,' said Rollo to Amy. 'It is sweet of you girls to come along here today.'

'Yes, well,' said Amy. 'It passes an otherwise dull Saturday.'

107

Rollo leaned into Amy and whispered something in her ear. Instantly, Amy unwrapped his arm from around her. Maddy was no expert at lip-reading but even she tell that Amy had just told Rollo to fuck off. Rollo had obviously suggested other things to do with a dull Saturday.

Dan moseyed over to join the group.

'Oh, look,' said Rollo. 'It's Mr Congeniality.'

'Piss off, Rollo,' said Dan, in a bored voice.

Rollo snaked his arm around Amy's waist again. Maddy, who had spent endless hours observing the members of the boat club from her favourite corner of the sofa, knew he was doing it to wind up Dan – after all it had been Dan who'd asked Amy along to support him. Typical bloody Rollo, she thought. He never missed an opportunity to needle Dan even though they were going to be rowing together in just a short while. Dan, as usual, seemed to rise above Rollo's schoolboyish baiting and ignored Rollo entirely. At least Seb was an easy-going sort and got on with everyone, thought Maddy. It was just a crying shame he wasn't getting it on with her.

'Good journey here?' Dan asked Amy, ignoring Rollo.

'Pretty painless. Bit of a schlep from where we parked the car, though wasn't it, Mads?'

'A couple of miles,' she admitted, dragging her eyes off Seb to look at Dan as she spoke to him.

Chuck joined the group. 'It's getting time for you boys to start thinking about warming up,' he said. He looked at Rollo. 'You haven't even changed. Chop, chop, as you Limeys would say.'

Rollo released Amy and went off towards their vehicle to grab his sports bag and then to their tent.

Dan moved to be closer to Amy. 'Rollo's ego is quite big enough, without you encouraging him.'

'I did not encourage him. You know what he's like.'

'I thought you came to support me.'

'Of course I did but doesn't that mean supporting the whole team? And while we're here we'll also cheer on Tanya and her crew, won't we, Maddy?'

Maddy forced her attention away from Seb once again. 'Oh yes, in fact almost any crew from Oxford as long as they don't look like beating you guys.' She smiled at Seb, who smiled back.

Chuck tapped his watch. 'Time for a few stretches and a jog to warm up and then we need to get your boat in the river and up to the marshalling area. Sorry to break up the party, girls, but the lads here have work to do.'

Maddy and Amy stood back as the boys moved off. As they began loosening up and stretching out their shoulders and legs they were joined by Rollo who now looked like he was ready to row. After a few minutes they moved off at a steady lope to jog around the edge of the sports field. Maddy watched Seb's every move, noting the effortless rhythm of his movements. And then it was time for them to collect their upside-down boat off the rack on the trailer and lug it to the water's edge. In a neat and precise move they turned it over and then lowered it into the water. Chuck had followed them carrying their blades. One by one they climbed into the narrow craft, took their oars from Chuck, fitted them into the riggers and screwed the gates shut.

'Good luck,' called the girls as they pushed off. The guys waved and smiled at them. Maddy analysed Seb's:

had his smile been aimed specifically at her, had it rested on her longer? Or was she just fantasising? They watched the boat drift away from the bank until the current began to take it and the crew started to paddle upstream to the start at Mortlake.

'You might need this,' said Chuck handing them a programme. 'If you're to make any sense of how they're doing, that is.'

Amy took the booklet and opened it.

'This is the order the crews start in,' explained Chuck, 'and each boat has to display its race number on the bow,' he turned a page or two, 'so this is the lads' start number and they start after the Oxford Brookes third crew but hopefully, by the time they pass here our boys will be ahead.'

'Or maybe ahead of Newcastle,' said Maddy.

'Indeed.'

'So it's a bit like Formula One racing,' said Amy, remembering the explanation that Maddy had given her. 'The fastest start at the front and everyone else is trying like buggery to overtake everyone else.'

'Exactly,' said Chuck, clapping Amy on the shoulder. 'But it'll be a while before our guys come past. I suggest you go and grab a coffee and enjoy the atmosphere.' Chuck wandered off, leaving the two girls and the now rapidly emptying towpath as more and more boats and crews took to the water. The supporters and spectators, knowing there was some time before the first boats to start came past wandered off to find better vantage points or to grab a bite to eat from one of the concessions with a pitch in the vicinity.

'So?' said Amy.

'So?'

'So how was Seb?'

Maddy sighed. 'Lovely.'

'What did you talk about?'

'Nothing really. He mostly spoke to Angus about rowing.'

'And what did you say to him?' said Amy, trying to keep her impatience under control.

'Nothing much.'

'What? I push you together and you don't grab him and run off with him into the bushes?'

'But he was talking to Angus about rowing and I didn't want to interrupt. I don't want him to think I'm mad, or clingy or . . .' She shrugged and looked a bit doleful before she brightened. 'But he did notice me and he did give me a kiss and he did say I was sweet.'

'So now we have to work on that. I think we need to get him and you paired off for the Christmas ball.'

Maddy was astounded. 'You could do that?'

'What is the point of me helping Tanya organise the wretched thing if I can't act like a fairy godmother at the same time? You've bought a ticket, Seb's bought a ticket, neither of you is bringing a partner, so all I have to do is seat you next to him. If you can't pull him under those circumstances, Maddy Brownlow, I give up!'

'You think I could?'

'For God's sake, of course you can. You'll be looking a million dollars and he's a bloke with a pulse and urges. If that isn't a done deal I don't know what is.'

8

The crew of four were in position at Mortlake ready to begin. They were rowing steadily downstream to Chiswick Bridge and the starter. On the towpaths on each side of the riverbank they could see the crowds that lined the Thames, cheering on their teams. The elite crews had set off long since and the four from St George's were waiting to row with the other senior-level fours and were beginning to feel the damp chill air penetrate through their tops. They were all getting restless, as were the crews they could see lined up further upstream. Everyone wanted to be off, to be rowing the classic University Boat Race course, albeit in the reverse direction, travelling the easy way, with the current. But four and a half miles was still a long way and all the rowers knew it was going to be a terrific test of stamina.

Rollo, at stroke, swivelled round to address his crew. 'I didn't tell you earlier but Chuck says the coach and his assistant from the National Squad are here. Apart from the fact that if we do really well here, if we get spotted for the GB Rowing Team it increases our chances of a placc in the Blue Boat. This would make me, for one, very happy. So let's not fuck up, eh?'

His tone was light but his crew knew what his subtext was. *Make me look good.*

Dan stared at the back of Angus in the number two seat. He didn't want to look at Rollo. He knew his disgust at Rollo's selfishness would be completely obvious. Clearly Rollo believed he was the only one in the crew who mattered. Never mind about the others wanting a seat in the Blue Boat too, Rollo was only thinking of himself – as usual. It was a shame, thought Dan, that he wanted a seat as badly as Rollo. Because if that hadn't been the case he'd have been tempted to throw the race. He sighed heavily.

'Nervous?' said Angus, feeling the gust of breath on the back of his neck.

'Only the usual pre-race jitters.' He glanced at his watch and then grabbed a look downstream to see how many of the previous cvent's boats were still waiting to go through the start. Just a couple.

'I think it's about time,' he said. As he spoke the sound of an air horn reverberated across the water. The four men in the boat stripped off their tops and passed them down the boat to Rollo who shoved them in the stern. The line of boats began moving further downstream to pass under the Chiswick Bridge where they would each, in turn, take a flying start past the university stone from where their time would be taken. The clock for each crew would be stopped again as they raced past the other university stone at Putney.

As they neared the bridge the cheers of the crowds

lining the parapets above them crashed down onto the water. There was no time for their nerves to worsen as they almost instantly drew level with the marshal who read their number and then gave them the order to go.

The four men, a perfectly attuned team, began rowing in earnest so when they passed the actual start line they were at a rate of thirty-four and already gaining on the next boat. The rhythm of the splash of their blades and the thwack of their sliding seats became hypnotic as they shot down the river. Rollo, steering with his foot, nudged the boat minimally towards the Middlesex bank to clip a yard or two off the bend before straightening the boat out to shoot between the two central piers of Barnes Bridge. In the gloom under the wide bridge the shouts of the race spectators echoed weirdly and the chill air became even danker. And then in another stroke they were out again in the light and the Oxford Brookes team were theirs for the taking.

'One down,' muttered Dan as they forged past in a couple of dozen strokes. But were they rowing especially fast or were the opposition rowing slowly? If they caught the next boat they'd begin to get an idea. He risked a glance over his shoulder. The next boat was, in terms relative to its start position with the Brookes boat, in much the same place. Our boat must be flying, he thought. If we can just keep this up.

But Dan was aware of his thigh muscles starting to burn and a deep ache settling in his shoulder and there were still miles to row. He concentrated on his technique, trying to make each stroke perfect, to get the blade in the water at exactly the right angle, to get as much thrust behind each stroke as possible, to get the oar cleanly out again, to feather it perfectly and then to repeat the whole process again and again. Dan forgot his tiredness, he forgot the ache in his thighs, he forgot the strain on his shoulders, and he bent his mind to rowing as perfectly as he knew how.

In his line of vision he could see the distance between them and the Brookes boat growing. He glanced quickly over his shoulder. Newcastle's crew were only yards away. The rules stated that they mustn't impede an overtaking crew but would they get out of the way?

'Newcastle coming up,' he yelled between puffs of breath to Rollo.

Rollo's response, as stroke, was to nudge the rate up a notch.

A marshal in a safety boat near the bank blared an order, through a megaphone, for the Newcastle boat to move over. Out of the corner of his eye Dan saw them respond as they moved towards the Surrey bank, leaving clear water for the St George's boat. A dozen strokes and they were past.

'Two down,' muttered Dan.

By the time they got to the Hammersmith Bridge they'd also hunted down a crew from Reading University and one from Southampton. They had to be in with a chance of a prize.

They swooshed past the St Edmund's boathouse.

'Come on St George's, come on, Dan,' he heard Amy shriek across the water. Other voices joined in the clamour, urging the crew to do their best.

'Go, St George's, go,' yelled a chorus of female voices.

'Come on, Seb,' another voice shouted.

Other girls shouted encouragement to Rollo and Angus. From his position in the bow seat Dan could see the effect the fan club had on his teammates; shoulders straightened, backs stiffened and the mood of the crew went up exponentially.

By the time they crossed the finish line they'd passed two more crews and Dan knew they'd done well. He was sure the coach of the Oxford University Boat Club would be taking a keen interest now in this particular crew but would he take all of them for the final squad? Rollo was probably a shoo-in, having already rowed for the Isis team the previous year, but the others? After this performance, surely he too had to be in with a chance of becoming a Blue. It was a thought that kept him going even though his body was screaming with exhaustion and they had to paddle miles back upstream, back to the boathouse.

But when they got there, the elation of their supporters made the cramps, the numbing chill from being on the water for over three hours, the sheer knackering tiredness, all worthwhile. And best of all was when Amy came rushing over to him and planted a big kiss on his cheek. Out of the corner of his eye he saw Maddy throw her arms around Seb. All around them the St George's supporters were cheering and clapping; the atmosphere was amazing.

'Chuck says you did brilliantly,' Amy told Dan, her eyes shining with happiness. 'He reckons you had to have won your race. He's got the time that you passed the finish so if you set off on time, you must have done fantastically. I'm so glad I came and watched.'

116

Dan felt all his symptoms of exhaustion just vanish.

'And me, was I splendid too?' asked Rollo, muscling in on the conversation.

'Yes, you were. All of you were. Look,' she said turning back to Dan, 'I'm about to head back to Oxford with Maddy in her car. And you lot will be going back in the minibus, but why don't we meet for a celebratory drink somewhere this evening? I owe you that much at least.'

'You owe me?'

Amy nodded. 'I've had a great time here today and I wouldn't have dreamed of coming if you hadn't persuaded me. So thanks.' She stood on tiptoe and gave him another kiss on the cheek.

'Oh, okay.'

'What's your mobile number?' Amy pulled her phone out of her pocket and got it ready to programme his into it, then she gave him hers. 'So where shall we meet tonight? It's got to be somewhere central, I haven't got any wheels.'

'You and me both. How about the Angel and Greyhound? That central enough for you?'

'Perfect. I live almost opposite! See you there about eight.'

Dan watched her walk away and wondered why he felt so attracted to Amy. Was it that she was always so upbeat and optimistic? Was it that she was kind? Was it that she was undeniably pretty? Karen was a good mate and didn't seem to be looking for commitment any more than he was, but Amy . . . Amy was in a different league. He wondered what she'd be like in bed.

9

The pub was rammed when Amy got there and she had to fight her way to the bar through throngs of noisy students. She had no idea how she was going to spot Dan so she rang his mobile. She could tell from the racket in the background when he answered that he'd already arrived.

'Where are you?'

'Right behind you!'

Amy grinned and turned round as she severed the connection. 'Hiya. How are you feeling?'

'Knackered, still elated, still buzzing . . .'

'Good. Well, not good that you're knackered, but I'm glad you're feeling happy.'

'Very. And happier now you're here.'

'Why, did you think I wouldn't turn up?'

'No, of course not.'

But Amy could tell from the look on his face that he had had doubts. 'Good, because you ought to understand I'm not the sort to stand a guy up. Now what are you drinking?'

'I can't let you buy me a drink.'

'Why on earth not? I asked you out, remember.'

Amy heard him mutter something about it not being right.

'Bollocks to that,' she said and elbowed her way to the bar. 'I'm getting you a pint,' she called to Dan. 'What sort?'

He capitulated. 'Best bitter please. And I'll see if I can get us a table.'

Amy got their drinks and then squeezed back through the crowd to where Dan had managed to find a couple of unoccupied stools crammed into a corner with no table to go with them. Still, it was better than standing, which was the alternative.

'Cheers,' she said, handing Dan his and plopping down next to him. They both took a long slurp of their drinks.

'And congratulations,' said Amy.

'Thanks. It was a great win.' He looked at her. 'I was so glad you enjoyed it.'

'Well, I wouldn't have done if I hadn't known people rowing. That makes all the difference, you know.'

Dan rested his pint mug on his knee. 'Would you have come along if it had been Rollo who'd invited you?'

'Now there's a question.' Amy considered her answer. 'Why?'

'Because for some perverse reason I want to know what you think about him. I really don't like the way he acts around you.'

For a second Amy was irritated by Dan's attitude but then she realised that he had her best interests at heart. 'Dan, I *am* a grown-up. I really can look after myself. And

119

Rollo's not that bad. I'm sure half of what people seem to say about him is just urban myth.'

Dan rolled his eyes. 'Even if only a quarter of what people say is true it still makes him the biggest serial shagger since Casanova.'

Amy laughed. 'So, are you jealous?'

Dan, who'd been mid-gulp, almost choked. 'Jealous?!' he spluttered. 'Jealous of that wanker?'

Amy lowered her drink and said with a completely straight face, 'Given how much shagging he's supposed to get I don't think "wanker" is an appropriate description.'

Dan had the good grace to grin. 'Well, you know what I mean.'

'Anyway, I want you to tell me all about you, and all about rowing and how you got into it.' Amy rested her drink on her thigh and looked at Dan expectantly.

'You're not really interested, are you?'

Amy nodded. 'Yes I am. So come on, tell.'

'Okay, but you're a sucker for punishment. Tell me when you've had enough and I'll stop.'

'Deal.'

So Dan told how he'd taken up rowing at Belvedere because it was an escape, how rowing on the lake gave him a place where he could get away from the boys who called him names because his mum was the dinner lady there and how it was an escape from Rollo's incessant bullying. 'Of course, I spent so much time on the water I suppose it was inevitable that I got reasonable.'

'Is that code for *fucking good*?' asked Amy.

Dan grinned. 'Maybe. Anyway after that I was entered

into all sorts of inter-schools rowing events and I began to win a rather embarrassing amount of trophies. Because of that other boys began to take an interest – rowing had been seen as a bit of a second-rate sport up in Belvedere till then because the school hadn't done well in regattas and races for some years – and suddenly we had a pretty decent squad. And that was when Rollo and I got paired together.' Dan gave a rueful laugh. 'How ironic. I took up rowing to get away from him and that was the very thing that pushed us closer together than ever before.'

Amy made sympathetic noises and they both took another swig of their drinks as they considered the unfairness of life.

'Hey, your drink's almost empty,' said Dan. 'My round.'

He drained his drink and shouldered his way through to he bar, returning a few minutes later with another pint for himself and another glass of wine for Amy.

'So,' said Amy, taking the glass from him, 'why on earth did you go for a place at the same college as Rollo?'

'I didn't. I applied to St George's knowing that Rollo was at Balliol. The last thing I was expecting him to do was carry on to study for a master's and come to St George's to do it.'

'Knowing Rollo he probably did it to spite you.'

'That's not even funny.' There was a lull in the conversation. 'So tell me about you.'

'Nothing out of the ordinary,' said Amy. 'Ordinary comp, then a chance of escaping to uni where I dis - covered sex and drugs and rock and roll.'

'You're kidding me.'

'Only about the rock and roll.' She giggled. 'Nah, not really. I did smoke a couple of spliffs but they always gave me the most awful headaches so I never bothered again. And then a mate in Halls persuaded me to try coxing and well, that's about it.'

'Life on the edge, eh?' said Dan.

'Indeed. And, ooh look.' Amy turned her empty glass upside down. 'My round, drink up.'

'Is this wise?' asked Dan.

'I live life on the edge, remember. Besides, you need to wind down and celebrate after everything today. I think we deserve to get a bit wrecked, don't you?'

Amy grabbed Dan's glass and made her way to the bar again. By the time Amy's watch showed ten – or, at least, Amy thought it did, only she had to close one eye and really concentrate to get the hands in focus – they were both fairly mellow.

'One for the road?' said Amy enunciating with studied care.

Dan shook his head. 'There a limit to what even I can drink.'

'Spoilsport. Coffee?'

'Nah,' said Dan. 'I think it's time to call it a day.'

'Oh.' Amy felt a little thump of disappointment land in the pit of her stomach.

'Come on,' said Dan, 'I'll walk you home.'

Amy got to her feet and lurched. 'Whoops.' Dan grabbed her by the arm, removed her wine glass from her hand, which he dumped on the bar, and steered her out of the pub.

The air inside had been warm and fuggy and the air outside was sharp and bracing. And it hit Amy like an express train, causing the best part of a bottle of wine to go straight to her head. Her knees began to buckle and if it hadn't been for Dan's steadying hand she'd have fallen over.

'So where's home?' said Dan when Amy didn't seem to want to move from her spot on the pavement.

'Other side of the road,' said Amy, indistinctly.

Dan checked for traffic and then half dragged, half carried Amy across. 'Now where?'

Amy pointed to a tall terraced villa further down the road. 'That one.'

'Keys?' asked Dan when they got to the front door.

Amy leaned against the door as she rummaged in her bag. 'They're in here somewhere,' she said peering in. Dan gently removed the bag from her hand and found them in seconds. He opened the door for her.

'There,' he said, 'home safe and sound.'

Amy turned to go in, tripped over the step and fell flat on her face, measuring her length on the hall floor. She lay there giggling. 'Ooops,' she said.

'Are you okay?' asked Dan, worriedly.

'Just fine.' She smiled up at him lazily.

Dan sighed. 'Which floor.'

'The third.' Which for some odd reason set Amy off again. Dan bent down and grasped her hand but Amy was completely uncooperative and tugged on his hand hard which meant Dan, taken unawares, lost his balance too and ended up falling over beside her. At this point he got the giggles as well and they both lay there, convulsed with laughter. Eventually they calmed down and Dan staggered to his feet.

'Come on, Amy. Let's get you up these stairs.' He was just sober enough himself to realise that giving Amy a fireman's lift – easy enough given his strength and her size – probably wasn't the best idea. One false step, one trip and they could both take a tumble that could end up with truly awful consequences. Equally, sweeping her up in his arms was off limits for the same reason. The only way to get Amy to the top of these stairs would be to get his arm round her waist and try and propel her physically. He looked at Amy and at the gradient of the stairs, squared his shoulders and hauled her upright.

Amy had stopped laughing and was doing her best to be helpful but it still took some minutes to get her to her front door. Dan propped her against a wall as he found the right key and let the pair of them in.

Amy managed to totter through the door under her own steam and flop onto the shabby armchair under the window. Yellow light from the street streamed into the room until it was banished by Dan switching on a table lamp.

'You'll be all right now, won't you?' he asked.

'Am I very pissed?' said Amy.

Dan nodded. 'You ought to drink lots of water before you go to bed.'

Amy nodded seriously, but she didn't move.

Dan looked at her. Would she do as he'd suggested? He made his way into the tiny kitchen, barely bigger than a wardrobe and opened the cupboard doors until he found the one containing her meagre supply of crockery and glasses. He pulled out the biggest tumbler he could find, filled it with cold water and brought it over to her. 'Drink this,' he ordered.

Obediently Amy took the glass and gulped the water down. Dan returned to the kitchen and refilled the tumbler and again Amy glugged the lot. She lay back in the chair.

'Thank you, Dan.' She looked very vulnerable.

Dan sat opposite her, on the edge of the bed. The room was so small that their knees were touching. 'You sure you're going to be all right?'

'I think so. I'm sorry,' she said, her eyes starting to fill with tears.

'What on earth are you sorry for?' Dan was genuinely bemused.

'For wrecking a nice evening.'

'You didn't.'

Amy turned a tear-stained face in his direction. 'I didn't?'

'Don't be such a numpty, of course you didn't.' He leaned forwards to reassure her, taking her hands in his, and suddenly, although neither of them seemed to take the initiative, they were kissing. After a couple of minutes Dan drew back.

'I must go,' he said.

'Please don't,' said Amy, shuffling forwards in her seat and nuzzling his neck.

'Amy, this wouldn't be right. You're a bit pissed and it wouldn't be fair.'

'I'm not so pissed I don't know what I'm saying,' said

Amy, taking his earlobe in her teeth and nibbling it very gently.

Dan groaned.

Amy moved over to the bed so they could cuddle up even closer.

'You don't have to take advantage of me right now,' she whispered. 'We could just snuggle and then in the morning . . .'

Given the amount he'd had to drink he probably wasn't good for much tonight himself, but her offer for the morning was more than tempting and she was very attractive. Not that he'd jump on her if she changed her mind. A squall of rain spattered against the glass like gravel. Dan considered his options: stay in the warmth of Amy's flat or walk home in that shower.

'Are you sure?' Dan asked.

'I've never been more sure in my life.'

Amy awoke slowly and as her senses began to kick in, so did certain realisations.

Something had crapped in her mouth. Yuck.

Someone had ground sand in her eyes. Ouch.

Someone had hit her over the head with a mallet. Groan.

That's right, she'd been out with Dan, hadn't she. Fragments of memory of a pleasant evening came back – and memories of rather too much wine.

She felt a movement beside her. Someone was asleep next to her. What-the-fuck?

Ignoring the pain in her head Amy flipped over in bed and stared at the body. Dan? Double what-the-fuck?

She lay back on her pillow and tried to piece together the end of the evening and she had to admit, eventually, that she couldn't actually remember returning home. So had she invited Dan or had he invited himself and had they . . .? Oh please God, they hadn't. Not, thought Amy, that shagging Dan was that bad a prospect, far from it, but an off-your-face, drunken shag really was horribly slutty. Her mother would be horrified. Actually, never mind her mother, Amy was pretty disgusted with herself too.

She turned her head to look at Dan. Was he the sort of bloke to take advantage of her in that state? Despite the grittiness of her eyes, she forced herself to stare at him as she made the evaluation. He was a bloke, he was loaded with testosterone, so yes . . . but on the other hand he was nice, he was a gentleman, so maybe no. Whatever else Dan was she was pretty sure he wasn't someone who would take advantage of an open goal, so to speak. She sighed and looked at the ceiling again.

She didn't feel as if she'd had sex. She rolled back to look at Dan and found herself staring directly into his eyes.

'Morning,' he said.

'Morning,' croaked Amy.

'How are you feeling?'

'Rough.'

Dan chuckled. 'Can't say I'm surprised.'

'Was I horribly pissed?' whispered Amy, feeling a flush of shame creep through her.

'You were pissed but not horrible. You're a very jolly drunk.'

'Is that good?'

'Better than the snotty, maudlin sort, yes.' Dan propped himself up on an elbow so he could look at Amy better. 'Although you did worry that you'd ruined things by getting off your face. You got a bit tearful then.' He brushed a curl off her forehead.

Amy tried to ignore the tingle that zipped down her from head to toe. 'Err . . . Dan. Did we . . . you know . . .'

'You mean you can't remember?' Dan stretched lazily. 'Well, let me put your mind at rest, drunk or sober you are sensational. I mean, where *did* you learn those tricks.'

Tricks?! Amy tried to keep her head. She'd never done tricks in her life. Shit. She must have been very drunk indeed.

Dan chuckled again. 'Don't worry, I'm teasing. Although I'm on a promise for this morning.'

'Really?' Amy tried to sound casual. She swallowed. Well, if she'd promised him a shag she'd look a bit of a lying cheat if she didn't follow through. And, all things considered, it might be quite nice. But as chat-up lines went, being told by your prospective partner that he was 'on a promise' left something to be desired.

'But it's all right,' said Dan. 'I won't demand that you deliver. I mean, you were very drunk when you made the promise and it wouldn't be fair. Although, in my defence you did tell me that you *weren't* so drunk you didn't know what you were saying. I think your words were we could snuggle overnight and then in the morning . . .' Dan grinned and gave her a wink. 'But, maybe, in the cold light of day, you don't think it's such a good idea.'

Amy felt ridiculously disappointed. 'Oh.'

Perfect – a hangover *and* a rejection. She threw back the covers, sat up and instantly regretted the sudden movement. Her stomach lurched and a wave of nausea flooded through her. She sat stock-still waiting for it to pass.

'You all right?' asked Dan with concern. 'You've gone as white as a sheet.'

For a few moments Amy didn't trust herself to speak. Slowly she felt less grim until finally the fear that she was going to hurl ebbed away. She wiped the sweat off her top lip.

'Just as well I made you drink about a pint of water last night,' said Dan, still looking worried. Although whether he was worried for Amy or worried he might have to deal with vomit wasn't obvious.

'Thank you. That's probably why I can function *at all* this morning.'

'You lie down. I'll make you a nice cup of tea and possibly some dry toast.'

Amy felt enormously grateful. She lay down gingerly and shut her eyes. She felt marginally less vile. Then she realised that she was in her pyjamas. Had she managed to change into them? Had Dan got her ready for bed? Had he seen her naked?

'Dan?'

'Yes.'

'Who . . . I mean . . . did I undress myself?'

'Not entirely. Is that a problem?'

Amy wondered whether it was.

'If you're wondering,' said Dan, 'you've got one of the nicest bods I've seen in a long time.'

129

'Oh.' She was surprised by how little embarrassment she felt that he'd seen her naked. Maybe it was because he'd been complimentary about her.

Dan got out of bed and wandered into the tiny kitchen. From under her eyelids, Amy watched the movement of his buttock muscles under the cotton fabric of his boxers. *Nice arse.*

She heard him filling the kettle, banging open the cupboard doors as he searched for stuff. For a second she contemplated getting out of bed to go and help him but as even the thought made her feel crap again, she decided to lie still. She wasn't entirely sure she was going to be able to manage tea and toast but if she was going to be sick, it would be better to have something to be sick on than retching on an empty stomach. She listened to the hiss of the kettle, the clunk of toast going into the toaster, the sound of her fridge door opening and shutting. It was nice being looked after. That was the downside of living away from home – no one to molly-coddle you when you were below par. Except, right now she did have someone. The lovely Dan was doing his best to act as head nurse.

Dan came back into the room carrying two mugs of tea and a plate of toast. Normally Amy loved the smell of toast but it wasn't really helping her hangover this morning.

'Just the tea please,' she muttered, swallowing.

Dan put her mug on the chair by the bed. 'I put sugar in it. It might help.'

Very carefully and slowly Amy sat up. This time she didn't feel quite so ill as the previous time. She reached out and grabbed her mug then cradled it. Dan tucked into the toast with gusto.

'Don't you have a hangover?' she asked.

'Nope. But given I probably weigh twice what you do I probably drank the equivalent of about half what you did.'

'Why didn't you stop me?' said Amy taking a sip of her tea.

'I did try. You weren't interested.'

'Ah.' She took another sip. She decided she ought to make light of her drunken offer the night before. She didn't want Dan to think she was the sort of girl who did that sort of thing all the time. 'Right, well, unless you want to hold me to that silly promise, when you've finished your toast you'd better get off.'

'Why? I don't think it was a silly promise at all. Of course if you'd rather not, I understand, but I was rather hoping that it wasn't just the wine talking.'

'What?' squeaked Amy, almost slopping her tea. Her shock at his request must have been written large across her face. 'No, of course it wasn't.'

'That's good, because last night you did seem quite keen.' He smiled at her lazily.

His smile unlocked something inside her. God, he was irresistible. 'I still am,' she admitted.

'Me too.' Dan flipped back the duvet and pushed down the elastic of his boxers to reveal a startlingly large erection.

'Oooh, you certainly are.' Amy put down her mug, her hangover muscled out of her consciousness by lust, and rolled over and snuggled up next to Dan. She wrapped

131

her fingers around his cock and began to move them up and down. 'Is that nice?' she asked staring into Dan's eyes.

'I think you know the answer to that,' he said gently.

'Just want to be sure I'm not losing my touch.'

'And what a touch,' said Dan with a groan. He pulled her against his chest, wrapping his strong arms around her and kissed her face all over before his mouth moved onto hers and his tongue parted her willing lips.

Amy felt her pelvic muscles clench in a delicious spasm as lust, desire and sheer wantonness coursed through every nerve. She let Dan's tongue thrust wickedly in and out. In response she increased the speed her fingers slid up and down his velvety skin.

Dan's mouth left hers and he slowly unbuttoned her pyjama top and began to move slowly down her body, kissing first her neck then her shoulders and then, oh the delicious ecstasy, her breasts. It was Amy's turn to groan as Dan slipped his hand between her legs and his finger stroked her clitoris.

'Is that nice?' he asked, staring deep into her eyes.

'Fabulous,' whispered back Amy as a myriad of wonderful sensations flooded through her. They kissed again as their caresses became more urgent and intense.

Dan drew back from her. 'I think we'd both better stop before one of us explodes, don't you?'

Amy sighed. 'Must we?'

'I think we can find something else to do we'll both enjoy as much.'

Dan flopped back against the pillows and Amy stared at his wonderful cock. Then she ripped off her pyjamas and climbed on top of him in a fluid movement, strad -

dling him, rubbing her clitoris against his foreskin and kissing him deeply. He reached up and delicately pinched her nipples. Amy arched her back in ecstasy and gave a little whimper.

'Hang on,' Dan pulled away with a sigh. 'Not just yet, honey.'

'What?' She couldn't believe he wasn't ready, she was almost beside herself with desire and anticipation.

'Protection, sweetie. I think we've got far too carried away as it is.'

Amy knew he was right but she still pouted with disappointment.

Dan tipped her off and got out of bed, pulling off his boxers as he did so, then, with his glorious penis waving in front of him like a conductor's baton, he strode across the room. In seconds he'd extracted a little packet from his wallet and was back in bed.

'Will you do the honours?' He lay back on the mattress and watched as Amy slowly rolled it down his erection, rubbing his soft skin as she did so. It was Dan's turn to arch and moan.

'Come here,' he said as soon as she had finished. With one strong arm he lifted her on top of him and with the other hand he held his penis, ready to guide her onto it.

Amy gasped as she felt him enter her before she let her body sink deeply onto him, impaling herself till she felt a hard pressure so deep inside her it almost hurt. She stared deep into Dan's eyes as she began to lift herself up and down, supporting herself with one hand on his shoulder while his fingers toyed with her nipples. The rhythm was slow as she moved, tantalising both of them with the promise of more. She ran the fingers of her other hand through the whorls of hair on his chest, feeling their roughness, smelling his masculinity, revelling in the sensations of him moving inside her. Each one of her senses was engaged as she kept the slow sensuous rhythm going.

Then Dan grasped her hips, lifted her a few inches and took control. He began thrusting into her himself, quicker and more urgently, harder and more powerful, using his strength and length relentlessly until Amy felt the heat build in her and the wave of an orgasm crashed over her and rolled through her, and then again and again. She collapsed against Dan's chest as he arched and shuddered and came too.

'Wow,' said Amy softly when she'd recovered her breath.

'Wow,' echoed Dan. He dropped a kiss on Amy's forehead as she rolled off him, still panting, her body slicked with sweat. 'That was sensational. The perfect end to a perfect weekend.'

'End? You don't have to go, do you?'

'I should. I've got an essay to finish.'

'I understand,' Amy said, hoping she'd managed to mask her disappointment. 'I know you're busy.'

'On the other hand, I don't have training today. Chuck gave us the time off because we did so well yesterday. So I suppose . . .'

'Yes?'

'How about I stand you a nice breakfast and then we see if we can find something to do with the rest of the morning. I'm sure my essay can wait a few hours.'

'You sure?'

'There's nothing I'd like to do better.'

'There's just one thing though.'

'Yes?'

'I'm not sure about the breakfast, maybe just tea and toast for me. But I'm sure I'll be able to manage afters.'

In the end they went to a greasy spoon where Amy found she could manage a fry-up after all, then, revived, they rushed back to work off the enormous quantity of calories they'd both eaten, and to talk some more. It felt to Amy as if she'd known him for ever. A small voice inside her head told her to ask about Karen, but she couldn't bring herself to say anything. She couldn't imagine that Dan was the sort to two-time a girl, he just seemed too decent.

Dan finally dragged himself reluctantly back to his rooms and his essay at around midday. Amy understood that he had no choice but still felt bereft when he'd gone. To fill the void she got busy with the list of ball-related jobs Tanya had given her to do. Besides, she knew full well that she'd get quizzed about her progress the next time they met, which was bound to be next evening when Amy was due to work at the boat club again. But it was hard to concentrate when she could still feel his hands on her body, still taste him in her mouth, still smell him on her clothes. Waking up with him in her bed had been a most unexpected pleasure, and Amy couldn't wait until he was with her again.

10

'There's a party at my place, and I'd like you to come,' said Rollo to Amy. She'd just arrived at the boat club for her evening stint of providing physio cover and had hardly taken her coat off. 'Please.'

'That sounds like fun. In your rooms?'

'No, my parents' house.'

Not so convenient but a party was a party when all was said and done. 'Okay, when?'

'This Saturday. House party, so you can stay the whole weekend.'

She remembered he lived in Berkshire. 'I dunno, Rollo, it's a long way on a bike,' she joked, but the reality was that her pay as a physio wasn't wonderful, the rent on her flat was exorbitant and an expensive train fare wasn't in her budget.

'Tanya'll give you a lift. Or Maddy. Or anyone from the club with a car.'

The thought of spending a couple of hours in an enclosed space with Tanya didn't make the prospect any more enticing. But if Maddy was going . . .

'So how many are you inviting?' said Amy, intrigued by

the throw-away 'or anyone' line.

'About thirty people.'

'And they're all staying!?'

Rollo nodded. 'Big house.'

Ah yes, she remembered, the house that had a village named after it. 'I don't want to sound like I'm putting you off but I need to check my diary.' Find out what Dan's doing. 'I'll let you know on Wednesday when I'm here next, is that okay?'

Rollo nodded and wandered off.

Amy picked up her coat from where she'd dumped it on the massage table and hung it on the hook behind the door. She had to jump back to avoid being hit by it as someone barged in.

'Watch it,' said Amy grumpily, emerging. 'Oh, hi Dan.' Her attitude changed completely when she saw it was him. 'Social call or something more serious?' She gave him a peck on the cheek.

'You get a lot of social calls then?'

'No.' She wasn't going to mention Rollo's visit; she didn't think for a minute that Rollo would be inviting Dan to his house party so if he was free that weekend she'd decline his invitation. It would be fun to see the sort of pad Rollo called home but it would be much more fun to spend time with Dan.

'It's my wrist,' said Dan. 'I think I strained it racing on Saturday. I didn't notice it hurt Sunday morning – I had other things on my mind.' He gave her a wicked grin. 'It was only when I began writing my essay that I realised how sore it was. I strapped it but it's still sore today and it's making training a bit of a bugger.'

'Sit on the table and I'll have a look.'

Dan heaved himself up onto the black PVC surface and held his hand out to Amy. She began manipulating it. 'Does this hurt?' she said as she flexed it. The hiss of breath from Dan was all the answer she needed. 'And this?' Another hiss. She carried on for a few minutes trying to work out just what the problem might be before she let go.

'I can strap it for you so you don't make it worse. But if you want to carry on training you're going to need some painkillers.'

Dan bit his lip. 'You're right. I'm just scared of my performance slipping. The Oxford coach has called me up for one of the two Trial Eights to race the Boat Race course.'

'Oh Dan, that's fantastic,' said Amy, genuinely pleased.

'It's not just me. He wants the four of us – me, Rollo, Angus and Seb.'

'Because you won the Fours Head?'

Dan nodded. 'I think that must have had a lot to do with it. And our time was fantastic. Just a few seconds over nineteen minutes.' Amy nodded as if she under - stood how impressive this was. 'And he's asked Chuck to help him with the training. It's brilliant for St George's, of course; it makes the college the one to apply to if you're into serious rowing.'

'That's great.'

'It is, but having a knackered wrist couldn't come at a worse time. I'm sure the coach won't take all of us . . .' He paused, looking completely despondent. 'And as Rollo and Angus rowed for the Isis team last year they've a much better chance than me. It's rare for the Blue Boat to take someone who hasn't trodden that path first.'

'But you want it really badly.'

Dan nodded again. 'Of course, everyone in the frame does. We all have ambition beyond what is normal.' He shrugged. 'I'm just one of a whole bunch of hopefuls but just because I want it so much it makes my head spin it doesn't give me any advantage over anyone else.'

'Well, I'll strap it up for you for the time being and I'll pop in tomorrow and check it again if you'd like.'

'I'm working tomorrow at the bistro.'

'Then I'll pop into the bistro.'

'Would you?' He sounded completely stunned that she'd take the time to help him.

'Of course. It's what friends do.'

'You're a star,' said Dan. He leaned forwards and kissed her. Amy felt her insides go to mush so she pulled back.

'First things first,' she said. Dan raised an eyebrow as she got some bandages out and started to strap up Dan's sore wrist. 'So when's the trial?' she asked as she cut some lengths of tape to secure her handiwork.

'A week on Thursday.'

'You'll be fine. I'm sure there's a seat in that boat with your name on it.' She patted his wrist and then deftly wrapped the tape around it.

'We'll see.'

'So what are you doing on Saturday?'

'Sorry, Ames, I've got to lock myself away during the day to write two other essays I am completely behind on and Friday night and Saturday night I'm working at the bistro.'

'Oh well,' she sighed. 'Now, I mean it about not using your wrist too much and that means no wanking,' she said firmly.

'Won't need to if you're around,' said Dan. He kissed her tenderly. 'But I wish it was otherwise, honestly, but I really have to focus and much as I'd like you to distract me, I simply can't afford it. Maybe when these essays are delivered . . .'

'You let me know when you want that distraction and I'll make sure I'm around to do it. In fact,' Amy glanced at the door and then her watch. 'I don't think I'll be required for any more consultations tonight. We could try out some distraction therapy right now. What do you say?'

Dan kissed her again. 'I can't think of anything I'd like better.'

She grabbed hold of the end of the treatment table and began to manoeuvre it towards the door. 'Don't want anyone barging in. If I got caught breaking my own rules I can just imagine the can of worms that would be opened.'

'Really?'

'I told Rollo that if he even thought about having sex in here I'd have his gonads on toast. No, actually, the last bit's a bit of an exaggeration but the message was the same and I wouldn't mind betting he's told half the boat club.'

'So why the change of heart?' Dan said as he helped Amy shunt the table across the door.

140

'My treatment room, my rules, my goalposts. And I've just moved them.' She reached under her white work overall, whipped off her knickers and then lifted herself onto the treatment table where she sat on the edge revealing a tantalising amount of thigh.

'Now, Mr Quantick,' she said with a wicked grin, 'I need a deep heat massage to solve my particular problem.'

'Do you?' Dan slowly unzipped his trousers. 'Is this the massage tool you have in mind?' He dropped his trousers just enough to reveal his throbbing penis.

'It most certainly is.' Amy's voice was husky with pent-up lust. She wriggled to the edge of the table and spread her knees.

Dan slicked his fingers over her labia and then pushed them deep into her. 'God, you feel good.' He moved forwards, held her steady with his arm around her waist and entered her hard and fast. Amy gasped and pressed her head against his shoulder as he began pumping. With astonishing rapidity her orgasm began to build. She deliberately clenched her muscles around him and it tipped her over the edge. Shuddering and gasping she smothered her yips and squeaks in Dan's chest as he carried on relentlessly. At the point when it was getting too intense and she would have to beg him to stop, she felt him arch and give a final, almost brutal thrust as he came too.

Amy leant against Dan, as he supported himself on trembling, shaking arms against the table.

'Fuck me,' breathed Amy.

'I think I just have,' said Dan.

141

They leaned together, giggling, until they felt strong enough to pull apart.

'So, you were asking about next Saturday,' said Dan, after he'd zipped himself up again and thrown Amy her knickers which she caught deftly. 'Was there something special you wanted to do?'

'Not really,' she answered as slid off the table and stepped into her cotton briefs. 'Another time, maybe.'

'I'll make it up to you after the Boat Race, or before, if I don't make the squad.'

Amy gave him another kiss. 'I know.' But she wished he'd find more time for her now.They moved the table back to its normal position, then Dan left to get on with some extra training, promising he'd not use the ergo machine but hit the treadmill instead. Amy tidied up her treatment room, removing any traces of what had just happened, and then made sure all her kit was ready for her next session at the club. While she did it she decided that Rollo's invitation sounded fun. Just because Dan was going to be occupied all weekend didn't mean she had to miss out on a perfectly good party. Inwardly Amy was rather pleased and flattered to have been invited and she wondered if she'd get to meet some of Rollo's other friends – the ones whom she imagined that when they talked about 'estates' they meant grouse moors and acres of rolling countryside whereas, when her friends did, they meant cheek-by-jowl houses.

A knock startled her.

'Yes,' she called as she glanced at her watch. A bit bloody late for treatment.

'Good,' said Tanya, 'you're still here. Can I come in?'

She strolled in looking lean, athletic and stunning, as usual.

'Of course. And congratulations on the Fours Head. Chuck tells me you got second place in your competition.'

'Thanks. But the boys did even better; first, which was really something for them to crow about, especially as they had some tough opposition.'

Amy nodded. 'And I hear they're being looked at as serious Blue Boat possibles.'

'Me too, for the women's race.'

'Well done you.'

'Look, I'll come to the point. I've got a big favour to ask. Can you cox for me at Saturday's training session?'

'Oh.' No, she couldn't, not if she was going away with Maddy.

'Got plans?'

'I have, rather – Rollo's house party. I need to cadge a lift off Maddy or someone though.'

'He's invited you two, has he?' Tanya sounded surprised and more than a little condescending.

Amy wasn't sure how to respond so she just said 'Yes.'

'You only need to get there in time for lunch and our session should be over by nine. Even given the state of Maddy's car that should be possible.'

So Tanya wasn't offering her a lift in her own snazzy runabout. Not that Amy would have accepted.

'So will you do it?' Tanya pressed. 'Eight o'clock here for just an hour. If you bring your kit for Rollo's party with you, Maddy can pick you up from here and you can be on your way shortly after nine.'

It seemed Tanya was determined to have her own way. Amy gave in. 'Okay,' she agreed. She hadn't done any coxing for ages and it would be nice to get back on the water, even if it was with Tanya.

'Good. Now have you banked the latest ticket money and finished those envelopes?'

'Yes, all sorted.'

'I'll have another little list of things for you shortly. I'll give you that when I see you on Saturday.'

No 'thank you' for the tasks she'd already done, noted Amy wryly. That would be too much to expect.

Tanya swept out with a breezy 'be sure you're not late', leaving Amy feeling as if she'd been done over. Or was that the result of that wicked shag with Dan? Either way, she locked up her room and crawled up the stairs to the bar in desperate need of a drink.

11

Terrified of being late for Tanya, Amy was a good fifteen minutes early at the boat club. The eight was there already, getting changed into their rowing kit, checking the riggers, adjusting their sliding seats and doing some light stretches. Amy was glad of her thick hoodie and gloves as the air was damp and chill and the stiff breeze lowered the temperature several notches when it gusted past. It was barely light and Amy questioned her sanity as she could have been enjoying a hot shower and a leisurely breakfast before heading off to Rollo's, instead of tramping around on a slipway in the perishing cold.

Ten minutes later the boat was launched, Amy was plugged into the cox-box and was giving instructions into her head-mike to the bow and stroke sides alternately to get the craft away from the shore and into the middle of the Isis. Once safely in mid-stream she allowed the crew to paddle gently downstream at a rate set by Tanya. Every now and again she tugged on one or other of the lines that controlled the rudder to tweak the course. Other rowers were out on the river, scullers, pairs, quads – even another eight swept past at full tilt – and Amy kept a sharp lookout in the winter gloom for the hazards they presented.

Tanya, as stroke, sat directly in front of Amy, swooshing back and forth on her sliding seat with a slow rhythm.

'When we get back,' said Tanya, between each drive, 'remind me,' thwack, slide, 'to give you a list,' thwack, slide, 'of florists to get quotes from.' She paused for a couple of strokes. Then continued, 'And final numbers to the caterers,' pause, 'by next weekend.'

Amy nodded.

'I've written it all down,' thwack, slide, 'along with some other stuff.' Pause. 'Let me know how you get on.'

Amy was tempted to salute and say 'Aye, aye, sir,' but she restricted herself to nodding.

They reached the point on the Isis where they would begin their two-kilometre row back to the boathouse. Amy had already had instructions from Tanya as to how she wanted the distance rowed so once the boat had been turned through one hundred and eighty degrees, Amy's job as cox started in earnest.

'Attention, go,' she yelled imitating an official regatta start. 'And drive, drive, drive,' she called to get the crew rowing both in perfect unison and at the correct rate. She glanced at the cox-box and saw the rate was exactly what Tanya had ordered: thirty-seven.

In front of her the crew was straining against their oars, their thighs driving against the footstretchers, their arms and shoulders hauling against the heavy resistance of the water on their blades.

'And push,' called Amy encouragingly. 'This is great.

146

Concentrate on technique, ladies. And drive, drive, drive.'

The craft skimmed upstream, whooshing past serious and amateur rowers alike. In the meadows and on the towpath dog walkers and pedestrians watched the crew in admiration at their unfaltering stroke and perfect rhythm. Amy allowed the crew to slacken off in the third five-hundred-metre section ready for the final, lung-bursting surge to the finish line at the boathouse.

'Keep those legs working,' called Amy. She could see Tanya gritting her teeth, her forehead beaded with perspiration, as she upped the rate for the last section. 'Just twenty more strokes,' she said. 'And nineteen, eighteen, seventeen,' she counted down in time to the strokes. 'Almost there. Fifteen, fourteen, drive, drive, drive for the finish.'

The eight collapsed over their oars, gasping and panting as Amy said 'plip' to imitate a finish-line hooter.

'Brilliant effort. Fantastic, well done.' She checked the cox-box. The girls' time was excellent. Maybe not Olympic standard but certainly good enough to be in with a chance at Henley.

'Thanks, Amy,' gasped Tanya. 'You were so much better than I expected.'

Gee, thanks Tanya. Damn me with faint praise, why don't you. 'I'm glad I came up to scratch.'

'It's a shame you're not studying at the college, or I'd replace Hannah with you.'

'Well, I'm not so you can't.' Amy felt sorry for poor old Hannah, the med student and regular cox. She was obviously going to be told to up her game by Tanya. But

Hannah's performance wasn't Amy's concern and it wasn't her fault if she was better, although it was good for her morale.

Amy steered the eight back to the slipway and then helped carry some of the blades back to the racks while the others got the boat out of the water. Job done, she went into the changing room, got out of her thick tracksuit and hoodie and into a pair of jeans and a flattering top. Then while Tanya and the others were in the showers she skipped off up to the bar to wait for Maddy. Not that she could go until she'd been given her tasks for the ball from Tanya but at least she could warm up in comfort and maybe scrounge a cup of tea off Chuck if he was about.

Maddy was already there. 'Ready to go?'

Amy explained about having to wait for her directives from Tanya.

'Can't she give you the lists at Rollo's?'

'Apparently not. And I don't want to risk upsetting her.'

Maddy made a moue of understanding. 'Too right you don't.'

Christina and Stevie arrived, pink from the training session on the river and their subsequent shower.

'Fantastic coxing,' said Stevie. 'Really impressive.'

'Thanks,' said Amy, pleased that they'd noticed her ability. She checked it was still just them in the bar and Tanya hadn't yet walked in. 'Tanya just said that I was better than she expected.'

'That's Tanya for you,' said Christina, snuggling next to Stevie on the sofa. 'You going to Rollo's?'

Maddy nodded. 'We're just waiting for Tanya to give Amy more jobs to do for the ball and we're off.'

'How's it going?' Stevie asked Amy.

Amy shrugged. 'Fine, I think. We'll find out on the night, won't we?'

'It'll be a blast,' said Christina, reassuringly. 'The Randolph does these events all the time. Tanya makes a big production out of organising it.'

'Tell me about it,' said Amy ruefully.

Twenty minutes later Maddy's little car was bowling down the dual-carriageway, laden with the girls' suitcases filled with clothes for the weekend, the radio blaring out pop favourites, the heater going full blast and the wipers battling with the dank winter rain and the filth being sprayed off the road by the other traffic.

'I must give you some money for the petrol,' said Amy.

'Don't be daft. Besides, it's nice to have the company. And I don't think I'd have accepted Rollo's invite if you hadn't.'

'I know what you mean. Blimey, a *house party*? It's like something out of an Agatha Christie novel. But it doesn't alter the fact that this is the second lift I've bummed off you.'

'No, it really doesn't matter. I'm sure one day I'll need a favour from you. Things have a way of evening up.'

Amy nodded. 'I'm sure.'

Amy thought about the ball later that month. She'd repay her then by making sure Maddy was sitting next to Seb. 'Did Rollo invite Seb?' she asked innocently.

'I don't know. I couldn't bear to find out.'

'I'm sure he has, they row together. Although I know Dan's not going. Got other commitments.'

'Or Rollo blanked him.'

'Probably.'

Maddy shook her head. 'Well, given their history . . . sheesh.'

'You know about it? Dan just said he and Rollo went to the same school where his mum was the dinner lady. I haven't liked to pry too much, I think some things still rankle. I don't like to pick at scabs. I nearly turned the invite down though.'

'Why?'

'I felt a bit mean taking Rollo up on his offer when Dan's having to work this weekend.'

'What? What's the point of both of you being miserable? You don't get any brownie points for passing up an opportunity like this. Rollo's parties are legendary. Anyway, you aren't dating Dan are you?'

'Sort of.'

'Sort of? But isn't he with Karen? Are you his guilty bit on the side?'

Amy's stomach clenched. No! 'But he doesn't have time for a proper girlfriend. Everyone says so – even Dan.'

'Not what I'd heard. Last I heard he spends a lot of nights at her place.'

'Oh.' She felt as if she'd just been kicked. 'Maybe I got the wrong end of the stick,' she said dully. Or maybe Dan lied to me.

A thought that was confirmed by Maddy saying, 'Or maybe he fancies you and doesn't want you to think there are any obstacles in the way. Like another girlfriend.'

Surely Dan wouldn't pull a trick like that. Amy felt sick at the possibility. She really liked him, and from the way he'd been behaving she'd thought he felt the same. What made it worse was that she liked Karen too. She'd met her again when she'd gone over to the bistro to sort out Dan's bandages and they'd got on really well again. Amy had finished re-strapping up Dan's wrist and had stayed on for a drink and a chat. She and Karen had had a good laugh about work and life, and Dan, in quiet moments between customers, had joined in. She hadn't noticed any body language between them, but then they'd been at work, so that didn't really mean anything.

'No,' Maddy prattled on, cheerfully taking Amy's silence for prurient curiosity, 'I think you'll find Dan and Karen have definitely got something going.'

The sat nav told them to turn off the main road. Amy peered at the screen, glad of any excuse to occupy her mind with something other than Dan.

'It says we're almost there,' she told Maddy.

'Jolly good. I want a pee and a cuppa. It seems a long while since breakfast.'

A speed restriction slowed Maddy down and then they passed a sign saying they were entering Marford. 'So where's Marford House?' said Maddy as she drove along the pretty main street.

'Turn left,' said the computerised voice. 'Then you have reached your destination.'

The two girls looked left. A long straight avenue, lined with massive silver-trunked beech trees stretched up a hill and disappeared over its crest.

Amy gasped. 'You don't think this is his front drive do you?'

Maddy nodded, her eyes popping. She turned onto the road and headed up the hill. At the crest the drive continued into the grey murk until visibility ceased.

'Fuck me,' said Amy. 'This is some approach. What the hell is at the other end?'

Maddy drove on until—

'Shit,' said both girls in unison. About half a mile ahead, appearing out of the dreary, lowering drizzle was an enormous house, built from pale stone and complete with mullioned windows and battlements, and to go with it was a lake and a stable block.

'Should we park up and get changed before we get there?' said Maddy.

The girls looked at their jeans and Primark tops and sweaters. 'Into what?' said Amy. 'I left my Paris originals back in my flat.'

'We'll have to do,' said Maddy. Then she added. 'There's going to be *staff* isn't there.'

'There's got to be.'

'Do you think they've got a butler?'

By now the car was scrunching across the huge gravel sweep, almost the size of Horse Guards Parade, in the front of the house. Maddy drew up beside a flight of steps that led to the vast double front doors. She hauled on the handbrake and turned to face Amy. The pair of them burst into nervous giggles, and the giggles grew till they were both honking and rocking with laughter.

'Oh my God, flunkies,' said Amy, finally drawing breath and wiping her eyes, which set them both off again.

There was a knock on Amy's window. It was Rollo in cords, check shirt and cravat holding a large black umbrella. The surprise sobered them up in an instant. Wiping her eyes yet again, Amy pressed the button to lower the window.

'Rollo! Hi.'

'I just wondered if there was a problem, only I saw you draw up a few minutes ago.'

'No, no problem.' Amy gulped down another burst of laughter that threatened to escape. 'We were just . . .' she glanced at Maddy.

'We were just admiring the house,' said Maddy smoothly, leaning across Amy and giving Rollo an innocent smile.

'Then come along and see the inside. I'm freezing here.'

The girls clambered out of the car, stretched and then went to the back to get their bags.

'Leave those,' said Rollo. 'Someone'll come and sort that out for you and then park the car. Just leave the keys in the ignition.'

Amy and Maddy both made a conscious effort not to catch the other's eye as they trailed beside Rollo while he did his best to keep them dry. Scrunching over the gravel and pattering up the steps to the vast front doors, they looked at the grounds, the roof, the crenellations, any - thing but each other.

'Come on in and welcome,' he said, standing back to let them through first and shaking the drops off the big brolly before parking it in a stand made from an elephant's foot.

'Blimey,' said Amy as she clapped eyes on the interior.

The vast, double-height hall was dominated by a huge staircase that led up to a gallery running around all four sides with doors and corridors leading off it. The walls were covered with ancestral portraits interspersed with the odd animal head or set of antlers. The floor was black and white chequered marble tiles and hanging from the ceiling were two of the biggest chandeliers Amy had ever seen. She half expected to see a couple of blokes in period costume duelling to the death while a damsel in distress looked on from behind the balustrade.

'It's lovely, isn't it,' said Rollo.

'It's big,' said Amy honestly.

'So which bank did you rob to buy this?' asked Maddy, bluntly.

Rollo smiled. 'We didn't *rob* one; we founded one. A bit like the Rothschilds. Anyway, follow me.' He led the way across the hall and through another pair of double doors. Behind them was a large but relatively cosy room, decorated in pale blue with cheerful fires burning in grates at either end. It was full of people, about half of whom Amy recognised. The ones she didn't, Maddy informed her in a whisper, were mostly undergrads from St George's – but obviously not ones who rowed or Amy would have met them. They were all lounging about the huge drawing room, chatting, drinking coffee and eating biscuits that were being handed round by a couple of maids in black skirts and white blouses.

'Downton Abbey,' whispered Maddy to Amy, who promptly had to suck in her cheeks to keep herself under control.

'I think you know lots of people, don't you,' said Rollo.

The assembled guests waved at the two girls and the boys stood up. Obviously their posh surroundings brought on a show of manners that they wouldn't have displayed in the confines of the boathouse. The girls looked at his guests. Yup, they certainly did.

'And I'm sure you'll get to know everyone else over the course of the weekend,' added Rollo.

'No Seb,' said Maddy.

'I'm sure he'll be here shortly,' said Amy reassuringly.

Christina, Stevie and Tanya must have passed them somewhere en route as they'd already arrived. Not that it came as a great surprise they'd beaten them to it, given that Maddy's little car struggled to reach seventy miles per hour unless it was travelling downhill with a following wind.

'So,' said Rollo. 'Coffee, or would you like to see your rooms?'

Maddy, who was bursting for a pee said. 'Room, please.'

'Yup, that's good for me too, Rollo.'

'Back in a minute,' he said to his guests as he led Amy and Maddy back through the hall, up the stairs and down a couple of corridors. Amy noticed how thick the carpets were and how warm the air. This might be an ancient monument of a building but it certainly had all modern amenities – or it seemed to. Amy hoped the plumbing would be the same standard as the central heating and the soft furnishings.

'Okay,' said Rollo opening a door. 'This is you, Maddy,

and Amy, you're here.' And he turned around and opened the door on the other side of the corridor.

'Can you find your way back to the drawing room?'

Amy thought she could.

'Just one thing before you go, Rollo?' asked Maddy. 'The nearest bathroom?'

'Your room is en suite.'

Of course, in a place like this with the sort of funds that seemed to be available, what else.

'I'll leave you to settle in. Join us for coffee when you're ready.'

Rollo disappeared and Amy went into her room, leaving Maddy to dash into hers.

As rooms went it was pretty big. In fact Amy reckoned she could get her entire flat in it. Opposite the door was the tall window with leaded lights and a window seat beneath it. The bed was vast and covered in a daffodil-yellow damask counterpane – completely impractical, thought Amy, definitely dry-clean only. On the dressing table was a vase of fresh freesias that filled the room with their scent and beside the bed was a pile of fashion mags and half a dozen novels. Someone had gone to a lot of trouble to make her feel at home. Amy shook her head in amazement. There was entertaining and *entertaining*. As a lesson in how it should be done, this was breath-taking.

She checked out her bathroom – huge roll-top bath, big fluffy towels, towelling bathrobe, slippers and an armchair. An armchair? In the bathroom?!

A discreet knock at the door interrupted her before she had a chance to check out the toiletries on the counter.

'Come in,' she yelled, expecting it to be Maddy. Instead a fit young man in black trousers, white shirt and maroon tie pushed open the door with her case under one arm and Maddy's at his feet.

'Your luggage, miss,' he said deferentially. 'Shall I arrange for someone to unpack for you?'

'Good God no,' said Amy aghast at the thought of a stranger finding her less-than-new knickers and her second-best bra.

'I took the liberty of hanging your coat in the garden room along with the others, miss. I hope that is satisfactory.'

Amy nodded. *The garden room?* 'Yes, fine,' she said weakly. She thought about her own parents' semi in a village about ten miles from Taunton; two receptions, three bedrooms, kitchen and bathroom and it had seemed perfectly spacious and nice. How the other half live!

She waited until she'd heard Maddy's case being delivered and the flunky had departed before she launched herself across the corridor. Maddy was slack-jawed with astonishment, both at the size of her accommodation and the hunkiness of the footman – or whatever his title was.

'And fit or what?' said Maddy. 'Do you think it's bad form to shag the staff?'

'Hang on,' said Amy. 'I thought you were after Seb.'

'Yeah, but a girl can window shop and fantasise.'

She had a point. And given that Dan had turned out to be no better than Rollo, she was free to do a lot more than that, if she fancied it. 'Look, Maddy,' said Amy. 'Just

157

look at this room. Apart from anything else, what about the size of the bed? If you can't manage to pull Seb here then frankly, you don't deserve him. So forget the flunky and concentrate on Seb!'

'Just because you fancy the flunky too,' grumbled Maddy before she conceded that Amy had a point.

They returned to the drawing room without mishap and joined in the general chatter as they sipped their coffee and munched home-made biscuits. Suddenly Maddy gave a little squeak.

Amy looked at her questioningly.

'Seb's here,' she whispered. Amy looked over her shoulder. Lucky old Maddy, but it just served to make her feel even more alone and unloved. Bloody Dan.

A couple of minutes later Rollo clapped his hands.

'Okay, folks, a few house rules. Enjoying yourselves is mandatory. I don't want to see any long faces on any of your ugly mugs. Obviously, I am only referring to the guys' ugly mugs here.' There was general jeering at this point and someone threw a half-eaten biscuit at him. When the catcalling died down, Rollo resumed. 'The girls, of course, are as sensationally beautiful as always. Now then, downstairs there's a games room for fun and games.' Lewd whistles greeted that statement and Amy wondered how many in the room noticed his wink in her direction. Rollo ignored the heckling and carried on. 'I've laid on some clay pigeon shooting after lunch, for those of you who fancy having a go at that. As it involves giving the order "pull" I've no doubt some of you will be more than happy to participate. There's a swimming pool in the basement if any of you fancy having a dip.

And girls, don't worry if you haven't brought your cossies, no one is going to mind if you skinny dip.' Rollo looked around the room, waggling his eyebrows expressively while Tanya, Christina and Susie all told him in pretty graphic terms what he could do with his suggestion. 'Spoilsports,' said Rollo with a disappointed shrug. 'And if none of that appeals then there are horses in the stables or walks in the country. Lunch will be at one but I thought we'd have a few champagne cocktails first, just to get into the swing of things. So, in the meantime, go away, find something or *someone* to do and we'll meet back here at half twelve for drinkies.'

'Now's your chance,' Amy whispered to her friend. 'Dragging Seb off into the undergrowth and banging his brains out is almost compulsory – your host has virtually said so.'

'But supposing Seb doesn't want to be dragged?'

'Are you kidding me? He's a bloke, since when has any bloke turned down a chance of a shag?' Dan hadn't, she thought miserably.

'Exactly, that's my point. How lame would I look if he did?'

'Oh, Maddy, of course he won't.'

'No? Just look at the way Tanya's gazing at him. How can I compete with her?'

Amy looked at Tanya who was eyeing Seb up like a hungry lioness might view a straggling wildebeest. She didn't hold out much hope for Maddy's chances at this rate, but she couldn't tell her that. 'I'm sure you and Seb can get it together. You've just got to make an effort. Which means that you've got to make sure that if Seb decides to have a go with any of those activities Rollo's laid on, you do too.'

Maddy nodded at the wisdom of Amy's advice. 'Mind you,' she said, cheering up slightly, 'doesn't it all strike you as showing off just a bit?'

'Strikes me he's acting more like a redcoat from Butlin's. It'll be a knobbly knees contest next!'

Maddy giggled. 'It does make you wonder what he's trying to prove. And do you feel ever so slightly patronised?'

Amy gave Maddy a nudge to stop her saying anything else as Rollo wandered across the room to join them

'How are your rooms?' he asked.

'Just lovely, but of course you knew that.'

Rollo shrugged. 'I'm pleased to think that standards aren't slipping.'

'So,' said Amy. 'What's the excuse for all this?' She gestured to the other guests lounging on the sofas and chairs ranged around the room.

'My parents are away in Mauritius for a month. You can't waste a free house, now, can you?'

Apparently not. And even more so if you've got staff to do all the organising for you, thought Amy. 'Even though Blue Boat selection is so close?'

'I think that even if I take my foot off the gas for one weekend I've still got every chance of making the grade.'

Amy was astounded by his confidence – but then, she reasoned, she shouldn't be. She'd seen it displayed before. 'Dan doesn't think he should.'

'Well, just because Dan knows he might fail,' said Rollo with a hint of a sneer, 'doesn't mean we're all panicked into non-stop training.'

'Don't be so horrible,' said Amy sharply.

Rollo raised an eyebrow. 'No? Anyway, he can spend the weekend consoling himself with his rowing and the lovely Karen instead.' And Rollo walked away.

'Told you,' said Maddy.

'What?'

'Dan and Karen.'

Amy nodded, not trusting herself to speak. Why did the thought of Dan and Karen together hurt so much?

Across the room Tanya eyed up the two new arrivals. Fish out of water, the pair of them. It was quite sweet the way they gawped every time a member of staff passed by. She wondered how they were going to cope with mealtimes because Rollo liked showing the plebs how it was done properly. There were bound to be half a dozen courses and different wines to be drunk with each and every one. She flicked over a page of *Vogue* with an elegant finger, glanced at the fashion plates on the new page before she looked up again and saw Rollo standing just a little too close to Amy. Why did Rollo have to sniff round that Jones girl like she was a bitch on heat? He obviously wanted her. Tanya wondered why he didn't just seduce her and get it out of his system and then she and he could get back to normal. It was the chase and the conquest he liked but once he'd scored he couldn't be bothered with a woman after that – with the exception of herself, but then she and Rollo had an understanding about that. So the sooner Rollo got Amy into bed the happier she'd be. And this weekend might provide the ideal opportunity.

And then there was Maddy and Seb. She watched

161

Maddy gaze longingly across the room at Seb. Tanya sighed. Dear God, hadn't that girl copped off with him yet? The expression on her face certainly suggested that she hadn't. Why didn't Maddy just tell him she wanted a shag? It never failed.

She contemplated Seb. Whatever other failings Maddy had, Tanya couldn't fault her taste – Seb certainly came up to snuff in the looks department. His conversational skills were lacking, she remembered, but you didn't have to screw *and* talk. Maybe if Maddy couldn't be bothered to get her arse in gear and make a move on Seb then she would. And that would leave the way clear for Rollo to make a move on Amy.

Well, that's a plan, thought Tanya, as she returned to her magazine.

After lunch the weather cheered up so Amy, along with most of the party, went out onto the lawn to try their hand at shooting clays. A couple of the men had already had experience of firing twelve bores and they, Rollo and a lackey or two helped teach the others. Amy soon got the hang of jamming the gun hard into her shoulder so that when she pulled the trigger the recoil didn't almost knock her off her feet, and then she had a go at firing at actual targets.

'Pull,' she shouted and, from below the ha-ha, a clay was launched like a Frisbee into the overcast sky. Amy missed the first half dozen but then she fired and bits of the target scattered over the landscape. She felt ridiculously elated and it made up for how miserable she felt about Dan, although she was trying put a brave face on it. She didn't want Maddy to notice and ask awkward questions.

She yelled 'pull' again, this time imagining it was Dan she was aiming at. And the clay shattered. Yesss. She fired another half dozen shots, each time mentally taking a pot at Dan and ended up hitting more than she missed. She rested the stock of the gun on the ground, her arms aching and her shoulder slightly bruised but feeling much better. Shooting, she decided, was very therapeutic for getting things out of your system.

Angus was standing behind her. 'Want a go?' she asked.

He nodded eagerly. 'Have you finished?'

'I don't think my shoulder can cope with much more of a battering.' She handed the unloaded twelve-bore to Angus.

'Have you done this before?' he asked her.

Amy shook her head.

'Then you're not bad for a beginner.'

'Thanks. How about you?'

'I've been out on few shoots in Scotland. Grouse, pheasant, that sort of thing.'

'Oh.' Shooting at clays was one thing, killing little defenceless critters, was another. 'Don't tell me,' she said, 'it's sport and the birds actually enjoy it.'

'I doubt it,' said Angus evenly, 'but I expect it beats being packed into a lorry and being killed in an abattoir. Birds in the wild don't know what's hit them – no pun intended – and they have a lovely, free-range life right up until that moment. I think most chickens would happily swap places.'

163

Amy couldn't be bothered to argue the toss so she left Angus to slaughter his ration of clays and wandered back to the house. She was cold and the thought of toasting her toes in front of one of the fires in the drawing room held a lot of appeal.

She went in through the garden-room entrance, which was a vast paved room with hooks for coats, racks for wellingtons and outdoor shoes, to say nothing of a huge Belfast sink, shelves full of vases of every size and masses of flower-arranging paraphernalia. It was an upper-class glory hole. She dumped her coat on a nearby peg, wiping her shoes on the big coir mat that covered several square metres of floor as she did so.

She slipped along the corridors towards the main hall and her destination. The house seemed deserted although she knew it couldn't be. For a start, somewhere there had to be a couple of dozen staff all beavering away, clearing up the last meal and getting ready for the next. She concentrated on finding her way back to the main rooms of the house, making sure she didn't get lost in the warren of corridors but amused herself as she went by looking at the pictures and portraits she passed, wondering about the previous inhabitants of this grand pile.

Rollo saw Amy leave the rest of the party and head towards the house. As he watched her go, Tanya wandered over to him.

'Go on,' she murmured in his ear, 'you know you want to.'

Rollo knew exactly what she was alluding to and put his arm around her. 'You are incorrigible,' he said.

'Pots and kettles.'

'So what have you got planned?'

'I thought Seb might make an interesting conquest.'

Rollo chuckled. 'You'll have get past Maddy first.'

'Pah, no contest.' Tanya clicked her fingers. 'She's a wuss and if she can't make the effort to get what she wants I don't see why I should hold back.'

Rollo gave her a squeeze. 'I'm glad I'm not a woman; you are utterly ruthless. I wouldn't want to have to compete against you.'

'I'm glad you're not a woman too,' said Tanya. She leaned in and gave Rollo a quick, hard but probing kiss. She then leaned into him and felt his crotch. Impressive. 'Much as I'd fancy making use of that I suggest you don't waste it. I'd go after her if I were you. Tell me what she's like. I bet that under that "I'm a medical professional" exterior she's a fox.'

Rollo patted Tanya's bottom and left her heading towards Seb. Her kiss had got him completely aroused and fucking Amy would be a good way of getting his rocks off.

He ran across the grass and went in to the house via the garden room. Amy's coat was hanging on the peg so she'd definitely come into the house and not gone for a walk around the grounds. Excellent. He'd already decided on a gambit that was guaranteed to lure her into bed. It was one he'd used before and it had never let him down yet. He left the garden room and headed towards the main part of the house. Would she go to the drawing room or the comfort of her bedroom? He hurried along the corridors, looking for his quarry.

Amy jumped out of her skin when she heard her name.

'Rollo! Don't do that,' she snapped as she regained her composure and saw who'd scared the daylights out of her.

He held his hand up. 'I'm sorry. It wasn't my intention. Honest.'

'Okay, I believe you.'

'Didn't you like the shooting?'

Amy nodded. 'It was fine; I'm just cold. I came back in to warm up.

Rollo took her hands. 'Oh, you are. Frozen.' He rubbed her hands between his and then let her hands go and held her face instead. 'Your face is frozen too,' he said quietly. 'Chilled to the bone.'

Amy felt a thrill run through her as he brushed her cheek with the ball of his thumb. And then he dipped forwards and kissed her hard on the mouth. His hand had left her face and held her close against him, pressing her firmly against his body. The combination of a very obvious erection, money, power and looks was almost more than Amy could resist. But, despite the fact that she was turned on by him, she was turned off by the way he'd just *assumed* he could have her, like he had some sort of *droit de seigneur*? She got her hands against his chest and gave him a shove.

Rollo drew back, startled. 'What was that for?'

'You could ask, nicely you know, before you snog me like that. How about saying "please"? You can't go around kissing people, just because they're staying at your house,' she said.

'Why not? Come on, admit it, you liked it.'

'No, I didn't,' she lied.

Rollo raised an eyebrow, his disbelief obvious. 'That's a shame. It would rather mean this whole weekend has been wasted if you really meant that.'

'Why? You could always try someone else.'

'Come on, Amy. You're not stupid. This . . . this party . . . this whole shenanigan. It's all for your benefit.'

Jesus! Did he really think she was stupid enough to fall for a line like that? She might have fallen for Dan's 'I'm-too-busy-for-a-girlfriend' crap, but she wasn't dumb enough to fall for Rollo's lies too.

The thought of Dan made her furious, and suddenly screwing his arch-rival seemed like a very good way to get him back. And she could play Rollo at his own game at the same time.

'Oh Rollo,' she said, hoping to goodness she sounded genuine. 'I had no idea. Gosh, how flattering.' She stopped. Now she was laying it on too thick. She looked up at Rollo from under her lashes and gave him a weak smile.

Rollo put his hands on Amy's shoulders and looked into her eyes. 'I wanted to get you here, to this house. I knew if I asked you, on your own, you'd find endless excuses not to come. But I thought if I made it a party, got Maddy and a load of your other friends to come along too . . . well, you see it worked. Here you are. I was in bits all morning, waiting for you and Maddy to arrive. That's why I was watching for the car. I wouldn't normally bother. That's the advantage of having staff.'

'Really? You mean, all this, was just to get *me* here? To

Marford House? Oh Rollo.' Shit, was that last bit too much?

Rollo nodded. 'Yes.'

'But why?'

'Because I want to make love to you.'

'Me?!' Amy was quite pleased at her acting. She thought she got just the right amount of surprise into that one syllable.

'Yes, you.'

'But what about Tanya?' Her concern here was genuine. If Tanya took offence and it came to a catfight, Amy knew she'd be toast! Six foot of toned Amazon against five foot three of less-than-fit female . . . the words 'blood' and 'carpets' sprang to mind.

'Tanya?'

'Your *fiancée*?'

'No, she's not.'

'But everyone says the pair of you are getting married.'

'Probably, yes, eventually. It's sort of a done deal, but we're not engaged or anything, not yet anyway.'

'Really?'

'Amy, I think I'd know if I'd popped the question, don't you?'

'I suppose.'

'So let's leave Tanya out of this. She doesn't have anything to do with how I feel about you.'

Amy sighed. 'Look, Rollo, don't think I'm not flattered. I am. Really. But if you've got Tanya waiting to trot down the aisle with you, why are you bothering with me?' Amy was genuinely perplexed. She really didn't see herself as others saw her.

'Because I can't get you out of my head. I've fancied you from that moment at Henley when you sat on me. I want you, have done for months.'

Amy still wasn't quite sure why Rollo had picked on her, considering the other women staying that weekend and her curiosity was aroused. 'But I'm a million miles from Tanya's league.' Which was undeniably true. 'Tanya's beautiful. She's a . . . a . . . a gazelle. I'm more of a . . . a koala.'

Rollo spluttered. 'A koala?'

'Well,' said Amy defensively, 'little, kind of cute, and cuddly. But no way would I be in a contest for the world's most beautiful animal and Tanya, the gazelle, would. Simple.'

Footsteps clattered across the hall at the end of the corridor. Rollo grabbed Amy's hand. 'Come on, we can't talk here. This is ridiculous.' And before she could snatch her hand back he dragged her towards the main stairs. She was thankful to see that as they crossed the expanse of chequered tiles whoever had passed through the hall had gone and there was no one to witness her being towed behind her host like a reluctant dog being taken for a walk.

He took the stairs two at a time, Amy panting behind him, and then he shot along the gallery and in through a door, slamming it behind him before Amy quite realised what was going on. But with the door shut she came to her senses. She was in Rollo's bedroom.

'Now look,' said Rollo, grabbing her shoulders and pushing her towards a large cheval glass in the corner of the room. 'I do not see a koala.'

'No,' she said. 'But I do see a short woman with a big bust and a bad haircut.'

Rollo laughed.

'Piss off,' said Amy crossly.

'I love it when you talk dirty.'

Amy was about to retort something even more profane when she realised this would only encourage him. 'Well, thanks for the natural history lesson and everything but I need to get back to the others.'

'Why?'

'Because I do.' She turned round to face Rollo and took in the enormous room, the vast four-poster bed, the book-lined walls, the big, curved bay window . . . and the double bed was so huge you'd need a tracking device and sat nav to find your partner in it. Not for the first time since she'd arrived in the house Amy wondered why people felt they needed so much space in the first place. What was wrong with 'cosy' as a concept?

'But I would like you to stay here.'

'I don't think so.'

'What do I have to say to convince you?'

Amy shook her head and as she did so Rollo pounced, caught her in his arms and kissed her again. Amy knew she ought to fight him off but her heart didn't obey her head. Her legs felt shaky and her pulse began to accelerate. Breathlessly she clung to him. In response his hand moved up from the small of her back to the nape of her neck and his kiss deepened.

Rollo drew back; his pupils were so dilated that his deep blue eyes were almost black. 'Now tell me you don't want me.'

And Amy couldn't.

Rollo scooped her up and carried her over to the four-poster, dropping kisses on her forehead as he walked across the room. Amy knew she oughtn't to be allowing this, she knew it wasn't right, but it didn't feel wrong either. Gently, Rollo laid her on the red silk counterpane and then climbed onto the bed to lie beside her. He propped himself up on his right elbow and caressed her shoulder with his left hand, then stroked her face, her neck before slowly undoing the buttons of her top. He peeled away the stripy fabric revealing her pale skin and lacy bra, then his head lowered towards her and he was kissing her collarbone, her jawline, her earlobe before he moved to her mouth and kissed her hard.

Amy let her lips part in response and the kiss deepened. It was slow and languorous and utterly sensational. All through her a slow fire was starting to burn and it was as if sparks flew off it when Rollo traced his finger across the edge of the lace of her bra and then rubbed his thumb over her nipple. Amy moved her hands to Rollo's chest and began to undo his buttons then she slipped her fingers under the material and ran them over the hard muscles that lay beneath. His skin was deliciously soft and smooth and his chest had just a smattering of golden hair, the perfect amount, in Amy's opinion; enough to be manly, not enough to be a mat. She twirled her fingertips through it, revelling in the sensation. All her senses were heightened and the feeling of the slightly wiry hair under her hands was sheer delight and only intensified her arousal.

His hands slipped around to her back and she felt her

bra being unclipped. She rolled away from him and threw off her shirt and bra, then she unzipped her jeans, lifted her hips and slid out of her trousers and pants. She shivered, partly because she was naked but partly because she was almost wild with lust and anticipation.

Rollo jumped off the bed and stripped out of his clothes in seconds, then threw back the bedclothes and climbed in, reaching into a bedside drawer as he did so for a small foil packet. Amy dived in under the covers too, snuggled up next to him and nestled in the crook of his arm. She could smell clean bed linen and the warm musk of his body and she could feel his hand curl round her body, pressing her close to him as his thumb rubbed the skin on her waist before it moved down to the top of her thigh and her buttocks.

'You have such delicious curves,' he whispered to her as he ripped open the packet with his teeth and extracted a condom.

'Koala curves.'

'No, perfect curves. Now, make yourself useful.' He handed her the rubber sheath.

Amy slipped it over his cock, rubbing the warm velvety skin as she drew it along its length. Rollo sighed gently then he kissed her again, pushing her onto her back and running his fingers lightly over her tummy and then up to her breasts, which he fondled and caressed before moving down to kiss them. Amy arched involuntarily as an exquisite bolt of pleasure pierced right through her.

Rollo's hand moved down to her groin before his fingers slipped between her legs. 'Christ, you're wet,' he murmured.

And in one fluid movement he was above her and in her and Amy moaned in pleasure at the moment.

Rhythmically he slid forwards and back as Amy edged closer and closer to a climax. She could feel the blood pounding through her even as Rollo pounded into her, his urgency and desire matching hers. She felt her orgasm building and building until it burst, like a firework and she bucked and arched until with a shudder he came too.

Panting, he collapsed beside her, staring at her as she gazed lazily back. 'You were sensational,' he said, brushing a strand of her damp hair off her forehead.

Amy smiled, a slow, post-coital smile and sighed. 'Thank you. And you were a fab fuck too.'

Rollo squeezed her nipple. 'I told you, I love it when you talk dirty.'

Amy chuckled. 'At least I'm warm now.'

'You're red-hot and you know it.' He glanced at his watch.

Was he checking out his time, like his ergo score? Was it a personal best? If so, thanks very much, thought Amy. Dan might be a shit but at least he'd got manners and doesn't check out his performance quite so obviously.

'I don't want to be a party-pooper but I'd better go and find my other guests,' said Rollo.

Nor did Dan fuck off immediately afterwards.

'I can't lie here all day,' said Rollo. He slid out of bed and gathered up his clothes. 'But you can stay as long as you like.'

In his bed, on her own? No thanks, but she was going to make sure she sounded just as indifferent. 'I'd better put in an appearance too. Before Maddy starts asking awkward questions.'

'I doubt if she's noticed. She's only got eyes for Seb.'

Rollo moved to a door in the corner of the room, and Amy watched the way his muscles rippled in his taut buttocks and thighs. Not an ounce of spare flesh, she thought. All muscle. Just like Dan.

She sighed. What the fuck was she doing thinking about Dan again? Dan was with Karen. She had to forget about him. In the meantime, she could console herself with fantastic sex with Rollo.

She could hear the sound of a shower running. She ought to have one herself before she went back into polite company. She scrambled across the huge bed, retrieving bits of her clothing as she went, and then followed Rollo into his bathroom. If she'd thought her bathroom was big, this one was vast. And all tiled in shiny black marble, with a stone floor. Although there was obviously underfloor heating installed as the flags were toasty.

The shower itself was on a scale with the rest of the bathroom and there was plenty of room for two. Silly to waste water, thought Amy as she dumped her clothes on a chair and slipped in beside Rollo. But this was no ordinary cubicle as apart from the showerhead itself there was jets of water that thundered out of the walls at all angles. It was like being in some sort of upright jacuzzi but so much more exhilarating.

'Seconds?' he asked as water dripped down his face.

Amy shook her head as piping hot water sluiced over her shoulders. 'I don't want to be greedy. And you haven't got any protection.'

'Spoilsport,' he answered as he bent to kiss her on the mouth while his hand dived between her thighs. Amy's legs almost gave way as Rollo expertly rubbed her clitoris, while hot water poured over them. Suddenly Rollo whipped the showerhead off the wall and let the powerful jet massage her in place of his fingers. He twisted the head to alter the spray from normal to high pressure. The force of the water was almost painful but utterly sensational at the same time. She writhed slightly so the jet pounded directly onto her clitoris. Dear God . . . the intensity of the feelings in her groin just grew and grew until she was almost sobbing with anticipation.

'Jesus,' whimpered Amy as Rollo kept the jet playing between her legs and massaged her nipples with his free hand. She felt her knees begin to tremble as the relentless force of the water drove her over the edge. The sound of the splashing drowned out her yelps as she clung to Rollo's slick body for support as she came again.

Rollo flicked the power shower off and grabbed two huge towels, one of which he wrapped around Amy. 'You owe me one,' he said with a wicked grin as he tucked his own towel around his waist.

'I won't forget.'

'I'm going to hold you to that. Is it a promise?'

Amy promised.

'Excellent. I can't wait to collect.' He dried himself and dressed, gave her a peck on the nose and left, leaving Amy feeling a tingle of anticipation about paying him back.

175

12

Maddy came into Amy's room at about seven. 'Where
have you been? I wanted to talk to you.

'I got cold, I came indoors.' And I came in Rollo's bed
and in his shower . . . 'Why?'

'Because I saw that bitch Tanya making eyes at Seb
again.'

'Oh, Maddy.'

'Why does she do it, Ames? Why, when she's got Rollo?
Why does she make a play for Seb too?'

'Because she can. And, let's be honest, you and Seb
aren't—'

'We might be,' interrupted Maddy, 'if Tanya didn't
interfere.'

'But you can't blame her. She can't be accused of
breaking you two up when you haven't got together.'

Maddy's eyes glistened suspiciously. 'And we won't get
it together if Seb thinks he's in with a chance with her.'

'But surely he knows that he isn't really.'

'He's a man,' said Maddy grimly. 'If it's offered on a
plate he'll take it.'

Well, thought Amy a bit guiltily, it's not just men . . .

'But that doesn't mean he won't ever look at you, does it? And why don't you take a leaf out of Tanya's book? Maybe you ought to be a bit more obvious.'

'You think?'

'I do. For fuck's sake, Maddy, do you want to get it together with Seb or not?' Amy was getting a bit exasperated with her friend. Why couldn't she see that pussy-footing around was getting her nowhere and just chuck herself at him? She softened her tone. 'I dunno, Mads. But if it's any consolation I wouldn't have thought that, even if Seb does go with Tanya, it would stop him from getting it on with you. I don't think Tanya is so sensational in the sack that blokes feel they can never go with anyone else – *shag Tanya and die* doesn't seem to be how it works; if it were, there'd be no men left alive in Oxford, not if half what I've heard is true.'

'I suppose.' Maddy gave a deep sigh. 'I just wish he'd notice me, not her.'

'He will. Maybe tonight.'

'Are you changing for dinner?'

Thank God, a change of subject. Amy loved Maddy but she was getting a little tired of the constant updates on the Seb situation. Especially as Maddy didn't seem pre - pared grab to the bull by the horns – or even Seb by *his* horn.

'I've got a dress with me and it'll have to do. Although I feel I should find some grand gown and a tiara.'

Maddy nodded. 'I know what you mean.'

'So?'

Maddy's brow creased. 'So?'

'So, what are you planning to wear to wow Seb?'

Maddy sighed. 'I've got a dress that suits me – I think.'

'Great. Tell you what, I'll help you do your make-up if you like.'

'That'd be fabulous. I always manage to cock up my eyeliner and end up looking like a panda on drugs.'

Amy laughed. 'Well I think I can make you look a bit better than that.'

'Maybe I'll have another go at chatting him up this evening. See if I can wrestle him away from Tanya. Make him notice me for a change.' She glanced at her watch. 'I think I'll go and have a nice long soak with loads of smellies and then make myself irresistible.'

'You do that, Mads.'

Amy and Maddy swanned into the drawing room, both looking stunning, Amy in an emerald green maxi dress and Maddy in an animal print shift with floaty sleeves. But as they looked around their friends already gathered there they noticed that all the women did. Even Christina and Stevie had decided to glam up and were wearing sparkly tops and very fetching and flattering cocktail trousers instead of their usual, rather severe look. Maddy and Amy each took a glass of champagne offered to them by a member of Rollo's staff and wandered over to join them and Susie who, for once, wasn't hanging on Angus's arm.

'Hiya,' said Amy as she insinuated herself into the group and therefore nearer the blazing log fire. 'Have any of you tried out the pool?'

'It's just fab-u-lous,' drawled Susie. 'I mean,' she lowered her voice, 'gold mosaic dolphins and a bar might be a bit OTT but bloody hell, if you've got it, flaunt it!'

And Rollo's certainly got it, thought Amy as her mind drifted back to how she'd spent the afternoon. 'Talking of flaunting it,' she said sipping her fizz, 'have you managed to find dresses for the ball? It's not long now.'

Susie nodded enthusiastically. 'I went to that place up near where you live. They've got some stunning stuff you can hire. Although Angus offered to buy me something but I can't see me going to lots of posh do's once I've left here. How about you, Ames?'

Amy was about to reply when she heard Maddy give a little squeak. She knew that squeak; without a doubt it heralded the arrival of Seb.

'Look!' breathed Maddy. Amy clocked the look on her face then turned and followed Maddy's besotted gaze. And Amy could see why Maddy was even more smitten – as if that could be possible – because Seb had turned up in full mess kit. In a room full of black and white penguins Seb was a fully fledged peacock.

Even Christina and Stevie were impressed. 'Now that's what I call an outfit,' said Christina. She turned to Stevie. 'You'd look fab in that – that red is so you! Ask Seb how you get hold of a uniform like that.'

'Isn't it a crime to impersonate an army officer?' said Maddy, still gazing at Seb.

'It's a crime that Stevie isn't in that cute jacket,' retorted Christina with a grin, and giving her partner a hug.

Dinner was an elaborate affair with enough cutlery and glasses in front of each guest to bamboozle those not used to formal dining. Amy noticed with exasperation that while Seb and Maddy were sitting next to each other, Tanya was on Seb's other side. Shit, thought Amy. Exactly what Maddy didn't need.

Amy herself was sitting between Angus and Chuck, who were pleasant enough company when they weren't talking about seat racing, technique and obscure boat clubs Amy had never heard of. They did try to include her in their conversation but Amy wanted a break from rowing so in the end the two men chatted across her, which suited Amy just fine and left her to watch the triangle of Maddy, Seb and Tanya. To her dismay it looked like it was getting fraught – or at least fraught for Maddy. Across the acres of polished mahogany Amy could only watch as Tanya monopolised Seb and Maddy consoled herself with an endless supply of alcohol. She could only hope that Maddy's capacity for wine was better than her own – Amy had learned her lesson about over-doing it the evening after the Fours Head and was taking it steady.

Watching Maddy knock back the booze and Tanya flirt was so frustrating that Amy distracted herself from the awfulness of Maddy's dreams unravelling by watching what else was going on. Furthest away from Rollo, Christina and Stevie were feeding each other morsels of fillet steak and giggling at some private joke. Next to them Susie was chatting to one of the single scullers and to judge by the looks she kept flicking at Angus she was trying to make him jealous and lure him away from his conversation with Chuck. Some of the unknown non-rowing undergrads, whose alcohol intake wasn't restricted by punishing rowing training schedules, were being extremely boisterous and noisy and the whole dinner was getting quite Bacchanalian.

As Amy's gaze swept up the crowded table towards Rollo she noticed Seb jump and his eyes widen in shock. Then she saw the curve on Tanya's lips. What was going on there? She shoved her napkin off her lap, dived after it and had a gander under the table.

Wow! Down here was a whole different set of manners. For a start, Amy could see exactly why Seb had looked so startled. Tanya had opened his flies and was now gently massaging his cock with her right hand while Amy knew for a fact she was nibbling on game chips with her left. She had to give Tanya full marks for multi-tasking, although Amy wished it was Maddy who was showing such initiative. Maybe she'd get the chance to tell Maddy how to play the game. She'd have to find some reason to excuse herself from the table and whisper in Maddy's ear.

Amy looked along the rows of lower limbs and saw a number of shoes off and toes being run up and down other people's legs. She tried to work out which belonged to whom when Angus appeared beside her.

'Lost something?' he inquired jovially.

Hastily Amy grabbed her napkin. 'Just looking for this.'

'Good God.' Angus had caught sight of the action going on opposite. 'She's a minx. Wish I was sitting next to her.'

'Well, thanks very much,' said Amy.

'Oh, sorry. I don't mean . . .' Even in the low light level Amy could see that Angus was blushing furiously. 'You're not the sort . . . I mean . . .'

Amy put her hand on Angus's arm. 'Sweetie, relax. I know what you mean. Tanya's a one-off.' She scrambled out from under the table. A second later, still brick-red, Angus emerged. Rollo looked at her then Angus and a frown of anger creasing his brow. Amy rolled her eyes. Uh-oh, she could guess what was going through Rollo's mind. She shook her head at him, but he looked daggers back. She wished she'd played more games of Charades. What was the mime for no-I-haven't-given-Angus-a-quick-blow?

The staff came in to clear the plates and top up the wine glasses, although to judge by the raucous racket, most people had had plenty. Actually, thought Amy, her rowing mates probably hadn't had that much but as they rarely drank anything but soft drinks just a glass or two was enough to get them drunk. The other undergrads though were completely pissed.

A number of the guests used the break between courses for a trip to the loo.

Maddy got to her feet and wove a slightly unsteady course to the door. Amy seized the opportunity to follow her to tell her to be a bit more like Tanya.

'Maddy, wait,' she hissed once they were in the relative cool and peace of the vast hallway. She grabbed Maddy's arm and dragged her into the drawing room.

'This had better be quick, Ames. I'm busting for a pee.'

Amy began to tell Maddy what she needed to do to attract Seb's attention but instead of inspiring Maddy to get a grip – literally – and do something, it just made her start sobbing. Big snotty drunken sobs.

'How could she?' she wailed. 'And how could Seb let

182

her?' She wrenched her arm out of Amy's grip and fled to the loo. Dejectedly, Amy followed her and waited by the locked door until Maddy emerged.

'Fight fire with fire,' said Amy, handing Maddy another tissue. Maddy blew her nose and when she'd finished mopping herself up Amy did a quick running repair on the smudged mascara under her friend's eyes.

'What's the point?' wailed Maddy.

'You mustn't give up. Faint heart never won fit bloke – or something. I'm sure if you gave Seb the least encouragement he'd leap at the chance. Tanya's got a reputation a mile wide and I honestly don't think he wants to be gobbled up by a maneater like her.'

'And I bet she's an expert at that too,' said Maddy, refusing to be cheered up.

'What?'

'Gobbling,' said Maddy.

'I don't think Seb is going to judge you on how good you are at giving him a blow.'

'No?'

'No.'

Maddy sighed heavily. 'The trouble is, I can't do what Tanya just did. I just know I can't.'

Amy nearly shook her friend in frustration. 'Then just put your hand on his thigh. Bat your eyelashes at him, suggest you go for a moonlight walk around the grounds . . . For heaven's sake, Maddy, stop being so defeatist.'

Maddy looked like she might cry again so Amy decided she ought to leave her to it before she said something to ruin a perfectly good friendship.

Cross with Maddy, and herself for not being more

sympathetic, Amy stomped back into the dining room. As she passed the head of the table Rollo snaked out an arm and pulled Amy against him.

'What were you and Angus up to?'

'Nothing.'

'Didn't look like nothing to me.'

'Yeah, well it was and I think we've established that you have a dirty mind.'

'If you hang around after dinner, I can show you just how dirty it is.'

Amy shook her head. 'God, you're a randy bugger, Rollo.'

'Now, that's an idea.' He made a lewd gesture.

'No – absolutely not.'

'Spoilsport.' He slapped her bottom as she left his side and returned to her seat.

Maddy was already back in her place and appeared to be trying as hard as she could to drown her sorrows, knocking back the wine in her glass by the gulp and then holding it out for the staff to refill. Amy watched her and wondered if she ought to intervene, but given how badly she'd handled things only a few minutes previously she decided that on balance she was better leaving well alone.

'Amy . . . Amy?'

'Sorry, how rude, I was miles away.'

'You're being offered coffee,' said Chuck.

She accepted a tiny demi-tasse of black coffee and played with the handle while she tried to ignore the way Maddy was hoovering up wine and instead listen to Chuck's predictions for the Isis winter league. Thankfully, before she fell into a coma, Rollo stood up, signalling the end of the meal and suggested everyone should move into the drawing room and more comfortable seats.

For a moment Amy thought Maddy had succeeded in getting Seb's attention, then she realised that he was being a gent and supporting her as she left the room, but maybe that was no bad thing. At least he was noticing her now and had his arm around her. Satisfyingly, Tanya looked completely miffed. But, unsatisfyingly, Maddy looked like she might pass out at any second. Yes, she was pissed as a fart.

'Amy,' said Rollo in her ear as she moved out of the dining room. He must have been waiting for her outside the door. Despite her better instincts, she felt a slow burn of lust spark into life deep inside her. 'Meet me in the garden room in about ten minutes. I've got some entertainment laid on which should allow us to slip away unnoticed.'

Amy wondered what Rollo had planned and shivered with anticipation. But once again, in typical Rollo-style, he was taking her for granted and forgetting about any wooing, unless that was next on the menu. While Rollo's flunkies handed round more drinks and coffee, Rollo drew back the heavy, dark blue silk curtains that hid the two huge French windows.

'Okay, you bunch of piss-heads, go and grab your coats – it's fireworks time. And, yes,' he said in answer to a question from Angus, 'of course, you can take your drinks with you, like you haven't nearly drunk my dad's cellar dry!'

'If you want so see sparks fly,' said someone, 'just

switch the lights out. There are so many bodies rubbing together, someone'll burst into flames.'

There was an outburst of smutty laughter before Rollo's house guests began to stream from the room, Amy amongst them.

She was collecting her jacket when Rollo murmured, 'Let the others go. Stay here.'

She turned and frowned at him. 'But you said there'd be fireworks.'

'And I think I can offer you something much more explosive than that. You'll see.'

Slowly the guests grabbed their outer clothing, and disappeared back to the drawing room and then the terrace. In a few minutes she and Rollo were alone.

The most enormous, thundering crash reverberated overhead. Amy jumped out of her skin.

'That'll be the fireworks, then,' said Rollo, putting a comforting arm around her and then drawing her to him for a deep, spine-tingling kiss. 'But who needs pyro - technics when we've got each other.'

You can say that again, thought Amy as her insides fizzed and sparkled, like a Roman candle.

Rollo drew back. 'Come on,' he said. He took Amy's hand and led her to a bank of cupboard doors on the back wall. He wanted to shag in a kitchen cupboard?

Utterly bewildered, Amy followed but everything fell into place when Rollo opened one of the doors and revealed a narrow staircase.

'The back stairs – or one flight of them. The house is riddled with them. In the old days we didn't want the guests tripping over the maids carrying hods of coal or buckets of hot water. That would have been dreadful. Had to keep the guests thinking it all happened by magic.'

'Besides, you didn't want them meeting the working classes.'

'It would never have done. Their stay would have been ruined.'

Rollo switched on the light on the stairs and they began to climb the steep steps. After two flights Amy guessed they were on a level with the guest bedrooms. She was panting quite heavily and wondering how on earth the poor little underpaid and overworked maids of the past managed to climb these stairs and lug coal and water. They obviously bred 'em tough in those days.

'Here we are,' said Rollo. He pushed open a door and led Amy through.

'But it's my room?' she said, astounded.

'Precisely.'

The only light came from the glimmer of a dim bulb on the back stairs and the flickering bursts of strange incandescence from the fireworks overhead.

'So why couldn't you just use the main stairs like everyone else?'

'Because this is more fun.' He smiled wickedly. 'Come on, admit it, you were intrigued.'

Amy agreed that she had been, but then she had a thought. 'Am I in this room because of these stairs, so you can slip in here with no one spotting you?'

Rollo smiled a slow smile. 'It might have something to do with it.'

'So why the need for secrecy?'

'Do you really want everyone knowing what you're getting up to?'

'I don't care one bit and why should I? I think *you* don't want the others to know what *you're* getting up to. Too many jibes about too many notches?'

'No, that's not it at all.' Rollo looked hurt. 'Anyway, if it was all about notches, I've already collected another one, haven't I?' He grinned lasciviously. 'No, it's all about you. You're irresistible, Amy. Why else would I have done all this . . .' he waved a hand in the general direction of the fireworks '. . . for you.'

She decided to test out her theory. 'But you could have said the same to any girl here. Come on, admit it,' she goaded.

Rollo looked petulant. 'But I didn't.'

Amy raised her eyebrows. 'Really?'

Rollo's temper flashed with almost the same intensity as a rocket exploding outside the window. 'No, I fucking didn't,' he snapped.

'Ooh, temper,' she said. 'I reckon if I hadn't come across you this afternoon you'd have tried the same line on one of the others.'

'Don't be ridiculous.'

'Come off it, Rollo, this is your party, you wanted to be sure of having a good time and everyone knows what that means as far as you're concerned.'

'I wanted you to have a good time. Don't deny you didn't.'

'It was okay.'

'Just okay?' Rollo's eyes narrowed in annoyance.

'You surely don't think you were the best ever, do you?'

Rollo's face darkened and a muscle in his jaw twitched. She'd scored a hit, maybe she'd even gone a bit too far. Suddenly Amy was bored of playing games and Rollo's arrogant assumption that he could just snap his fingers and she'd fall at his feet, swooning again, was really pissing her off. Well, he could shove it. He was spoilt and big-headed and the instant she'd shown the least bit of resistance he'd gone off on one. She couldn't imagine what she'd ever seen in him, the twat.

But, before she had a chance to tell him what she really thought about his childish strop, Rollo had turned and was already heading back down the hidden stairs. Amy listened to his footsteps clattering into the distance before she moved to the bed, switched on the bedside lamp and sat on the edge. She'd pissed off her host, that was for sure, for daring to say 'no'. She had a nasty feeling Rollo wasn't going to leave it there.

Feeling suddenly weary and completely fed up, Amy decided to go downstairs, put in an appearance for a few minutes, just in case anyone had noticed she'd been missing, and then go to bed. The light on the back stairs clicked off, which reminded Amy that the funny little door was still open. She slid off the bed and went to close it. Just for good measure she moved an armchair and wedged it against the now invisible opening. Switching off the light in her room, Amy groped her way in near darkness to the main door to the corridor. She blinked when the brightness of the landing lights hit her. She made her way down the grand staircase and across the deserted hall. The crashes, shrieks and bangs of Rollo's pyrotechnics were still enthralling everyone – even the staff, if the lack of activity in the house was anything to judge by. She scuttled across the chequered tiles and into the drawing room, eager to get to the safety of the rest of the party.

'And where have you been?' Chuck peered around the side of a big armchair as she passed.

Amy yelped, her guilty conscience making her jump. Fuck, her absence had been noticed after all.

'My room. Why?'

'You and Rollo both absent? At the same time?' Chuck raised an eyebrow at her.

'Were we?' She tried to look innocent.

'Amy, he's trouble. He's a bloody good rower but he's bad news when it comes to anything off the water.'

'So?' Amy felt a little ripple of annoyance. What business was it of his? 'Chuck, I'm over twenty-one. I think what I do – or don't do – is my business, don't you?

'I know, but I care about you, Amy, and Rollo's a shit when it comes to women. As long as you haven't fallen for the "I arranged this house party just for you" trick, which is how he's managed to score with half the female undergrads in Oxford.' Chuck paused and gave Amy a significant look. She surprised herself by being able to hold his gaze steadily. 'Anyway,' continued Chuck, 'I wouldn't have noticed your absence but for the fact that your mate Maddy needs a hand and I thought you were the person to help her. When I tried to find you to tell you, you were nowhere to be found. And then I noticed our host was missing too.'

Amy knew she was blushing. But never apologise, never explain, wasn't that the maxim the aristocracy used when they got caught out? She cleared her throat. 'So, Maddy . . .?'

'Seb's had to take her up to her room. I think she needed to lie down before she fell down.'

'Oh dear.' Amy sighed. Behaviour like that wasn't going to help her quest to pull Seb.

The cacophony outside reached epic levels and then gave way to sudden silence. There followed whistles of approval and applause and then the house guests began drifting back into the room bringing with them the scent of cordite and smoke and cold winter air. Amongst them was Rollo, Amy noticed. He must have nipped around the back of the house via the garden-room door. As the guests filled the drawing room, slapping their hands and stamping their feet, Amy slipped back out again to go and play Nurse Nightingale.

Maddy was lying on her side, out for the count. Seb was hovering beside her.

'Thank God you're here,' he said to Amy. 'I think she ought to be undressed and put to bed properly but . . .'

'So?'

Seb shuffled awkwardly.

'But you're not comfortable about doing it yourself.'

Seb nodded. 'Besides, if she's sick, I will be too. I may be good in a firefight, I may be able to beat off the enemy with nothing more than my bare hands, but I can't cope with other people's bodily functions.'

Typical man. 'Tell you what, you go and find me a basin or a bucket and I'll sort Maddy out.'

Seb gave Amy a look of gratitude as he raced off to run the errand. Amy got busy, slipping off Maddy's shoes, unzipping her dress and hauling her out of it. She was knackered by the time she'd got Maddy down to her underwear and under the covers. For someone who looked as slim as Maddy, she weighed a surprising amount.

Seb returned a few minutes later with a large, shallow, decorated bowl that looked more suitable for arranging flowers in than for being used as a sick bucket.

Amy looked at him enquiringly, her brow furrowed.

'I could only think of stuff I'd spotted in the garden room,' he explained. 'I didn't want to involve the staff.'

'It'll have to do.' Amy made sure Maddy was wedged into the recovery position with a couple of pillows, placed the bowl on the floor directly below Maddy's face (more in hope than expectation that her patient would hit the target) and made sure her temperature and pulse seemed normal.

'She will be okay, won't she?' asked Seb, a note of real concern in his voice.

'Apart from a vile hangover, yes, I think she'll be fine.'

'You sure?'

'Fairly. In fact, if it'll reassure you, I'll stay here tonight. This bed is big enough for both of us.' And if Rollo comes looking for me in my bed, he won't find me there.

Seb looked relieved. He smiled and said, 'Thanks Amy. Night night.'

'So, how have you got on?' said Tanya, sidling up to Rollo

as the house party trooped back into the drawing room.

Rollo licked his index finger and drew a tick in the air. 'Scored,' he said. 'You?'

'Not yet. Seb was too busy wanting to play with guns for me to have a go at him this afternoon and then that silly tart Maddy got off her face at dinner and Seb insisted on playing the knight errant. He's probably holding a bucket for her right this minute.' Tanya looked around. 'So have you left little Amy panting for more?'

'Little Amy has just blown me out,' said Rollo sharply.

'You do mean *out* and not *off*,' said Tanya.

'Ha ha,' said Rollo mirthlessly. 'I had her this afternoon but I fancied seconds. She wouldn't come across.'

'But isn't that your modus operandi – date 'em and dump 'em?'

'Yeah, that's *my* modus operandi. I don't like anyone else nicking it. With you being the exception.' He gave her a kiss on her forehead. 'Anyway, I mustn't keep you, you've got an army officer to seduce. He's in the green bedroom, by the way, if you want him.'

'I might just,' said Tanya. 'Unfinished business bores me.'

With the fireworks over and the wine and fresh air now taking its toll on Rollo's house guests who were lolling on the drawing-room chairs in various stages of inebriation, Tanya made her way to the main stairs. Behind her was the sound of the party getting more and more rowdy. Any minute now someone was bound to suggest some stupid game like getting around the room without touching the floor, and those sorts of drunken high-jinks bored Tanya even more than unfinished business.

She made her way to the green bedroom and opened the door. As she expected, Seb wasn't around. She undressed carefully leaving a trail of lacy lingerie across the floor of the bedroom from the door to the bed. As she draped a sheer stocking over the edge of the bed, she hoped that Seb didn't reel up to bed completely off his face. Still, if he couldn't perform tonight she'd have him in the morning. She went into the bathroom and checked her appearance. Sizzling, was her opinion. Seb wasn't going to have a chance. She had a quick rummage in the bathroom cabinet. Good old Rollo, he always thought of everything his guests might want or desire. There, on the middle shelf, was a cornucopia of sizes, styles and flavours of condoms. Choices, choices. She selected a raspberry-flavoured ribbed one and returned to the room and assumed her best wanton pose on the bed. Hurry up, Seb.

Fifteen minutes later, when she was actively considering hauling Seb bodily upstairs herself, the door crashed open.

There was a pause while Seb took in the situation, his mouth formed into a perfect 'O' – not unlike one on a blow-up doll, though Tanya.

'Fuck me,' said Seb, finally.

'Seb, darling, that's *exactly* what I'm here to do.'

Seb's eyes actually boggled. She licked her finger and began to circle one of her nipples which stiffened obligingly. 'Come on, honey, I'm ready. Get out of those tight trousers.'

Seb didn't need telling twice. Despite the complexity of getting out of his mess overalls, boots, bum-freezer jacket and spurs, Seb managed the operation in record time. His penis, as he approached the bed was agreeably rigid, noticed Tanya, and startlingly large. Impressive. Tanya stretched out her arm and grasped the thick organ.

'Come here, Big Boy,' she whispered seductively, as she pulled Seb towards her. Seb stumbled slightly as he almost fell onto the bed. He gazed at Tanya as she put the corner of the little foil packet in her teeth and then ripped it open.

'And now for my party trick.' She wedged the thick rubber circle against her teeth and using her tongue and some puffs of air she unrolled the first inch. Then she bent forward, her arms extended theatrically to underline the fact she was just using her mouth, and rolled it onto Seb's cock.

'There you go, Big Boy,' she said as she sat back and admired her handiwork and his erection. Poor little Maddy, she thought wickedly. Missing out on *all* this.

She flopped back on her bed, and raised her knees to her chest. 'Come on, babe, I'm ready if you are.'

Seb rolled off the bed, stood up, grabbed her hips and pulled her across the emerald counterpane towards him. Holding her legs apart and staring down at her he guided himself into position and then entered her with one smooth thrust.

Tanya whimpered. 'Shit, Seb.' He wasn't just big . . .

He grinned at her wickedly. 'I'm not known as Seb the Stallion for nothing.'

He pushed back and forth getting as deep as was

physically possible and then some. Tanya writhed in front of him, staring at him, willing him on, enjoying the feeling of the slow burn building inside her, thrilling at the way Seb stretched her, filled her, hammered into her, until, oh God, oh God, oh God . . .

Seb, excited by her orgasm raced for his relentlessly, ignoring Tanya's whimpers and quiet shrieks, part pleasure, part pain, until he collapsed forward onto his elbows, his chest slick with perspiration resting on her breasts, his mouth meeting hers in a tender kiss.

Tanya could feel his heart hammering against her. What a fuck! One of the best ever. Although she wondered if she'd be able to walk in the morning, because just as soon as Seb had got his breath back she was having some more and then some more and more . . . She was going to drain Seb dry.

Rollo's guests had finally found their way to their own rooms – or someone else's – and he left the staff to clear up the myriad empty glasses and bottles, tidy the rooms and secure the house for the night. Here he was, Billy No-Mates at his own party. He was the one without a bedfellow. He'd set his heart on banging little Amy's brains out and now . . . nothing.

He wondered if Tanya had finished with Seb and was back in her room. Only one way to find out. He went up the stairs to the suite Tanya always used when she came to stay and opened the door. It was in dark-ness so he flicked on the light. Bugger, the bed was empty and still made up. He could hardly go to the green bedroom and haul her and Seb apart – assuming that's where she was. Not the done thing at all.

Feeling immensely frustrated, he angrily slammed the door and stormed off to Amy's room. 'Ready or not I'm coming,' he snarled under his breath. 'And you are too.' But when he barged into her room that was also vacant.

Livid, he stamped across the house to his own quarters. His house party, his guests and everyone was getting their rocks off but him. Un-fucking-acceptable. He'd give Tanya a bloody good seeing-to the next time he got her into bed. Teach her to go off with sodding Seb. The trouble was, the harder he fucked her the more she enjoyed it, so it would only serve to encourage her and she'd get more out of the punishment than he would. Pah!

Dan and Karen were finishing clearing up the bistro. Already, most of the glasses had gone through the industrial dishwasher, the tablecloths had been piled into linen bags ready for the laundry, the pot-boy had scoured all the pans and the candles and night-lights had been blown out. Now the main lights were on and the atmosphere of cosy French provincial dining was destroyed. Dan took off his ankle-length black apron and stuffed it in a bag on top of the tablecloths.

'You off on the river first thing?' asked Karen.

Dan shook his head. 'No rowing for a bit. Amy's orders.' He waved his strapped wrist at his co-worker to prove his point.

'So no early start. A possible lie-in, even.'

Dan nodded before he realised quite what Karen was offering.

'So . . .?' she said, stroking his arm.

It was tempting but then a vision of Amy, her big blue eyes and her tousled hair, flickered through his head. A quickie with Karen or do the decent thing and save himself for Amy? No contest. He was fond of Karen, he was, but Amy was special and the last thing he wanted to do was jeopardise the relationship he'd managed to forge there.

He gave Karen a kiss. 'Hon, there's nothing I'd like more but I've got essays to write, as well as the training to fit in. Much as I'd love to come back to yours I'm so short of time this weekend I just can't spare a moment. Not even doing something just for the sheer pleasure of it.'

'Okay,' said Karen, but Dan could tell from her voice that she was hiding her disappointment.

'Another time,' he lied.

'Yeah, sure.'

She knows, thought Dan. How do women do that? But he turned and left the bar anyway.

It seemed like a very long night to Amy as she set her phone to wake her every hour to make sure Maddy hadn't managed to roll out of the recovery position. By the time morning came around she was dead on her feet but she forced herself to go across the corridor to her own room, shower, dress and then put in an appearance at breakfast. As she left her room she looked longingly at her own bed. Maybe, now she knew Maddy was sleeping soundly and not in a drunken coma, she could have a quick snooze. But she decided against the idea. If she gave in she'd sleep until lunchtime; better just to man up and keep going. Regretfully but stoically she left her room and made her way to the dining room.

Chuck was already down and tucking into bacon and eggs but he was on his own. The others had all presumably made a night of it.

'How's Maddy?' he asked, after they'd exchanged greetings.

'Sober now, I think. Well, not drunk. Not *as* drunk,' she corrected. And she recounted her efforts to make sure Maddy had come to no harm.

'You're a good friend,' said Chuck.

Amy helped herself to bacon, eggs and grilled mush - rooms that were piled up in silver chafing dishes on the sideboard, before grabbing a Sunday paper and sitting down opposite Chuck. She'd decided that Chuck would be more suspicious about her absence the previous evening if she didn't mention it than if she did. Now was as good a moment to put him off the scent as any.

'So,' she said before she tucked into her meal, 'last night, why did you worry about what I got up to with Rollo?'

'Because I like you. You're a good kid and I don't want to see you get hurt by the likes of him.'

'Well, no reason to worry about that,' she said as lightly as she could. 'Honest.' Indeed, no point in worrying because his advice had come too late.

In reply Chuck just gave her a long stare.

'Where are the others?' she asked, changing the subject.

'Sobering up like Maddy, I would imagine. It was one helluva party and there was a lot of drink around. You

199

probably had a lucky escape when you went off to look after Maddy. If any of the St George's squad think I'm going to take it easy with them tomorrow they're in for a nasty shock. I don't mind Rollo's other friends going on a bender but not his rowing buddies. No sir-ee.'

More of the revellers drifted in as Amy ate her break - fast and then helped herself to toast and marmalade. Unlike the dinner the night before when the noise level had been deafening, almost the only sound at breakfast was the rustle of papers and the occasional subdued request for butter or salt. There were clearly a lot of sore heads around. Amy was thankful hers wasn't one of them.

She finished eating, grabbed a cup of coffee and a glass of orange, which she took up to Maddy's bedroom. She opened the door and crept in, not wishing to wake the invalid if she was still sleeping. But on hearing the click of the door Maddy rolled over and gazed at Amy, ashen-faced.

'How are you feeling?' Amy said.

'Shit,' said Maddy truthfully and almost inaudibly. 'Was I very drunk?'

'Utterly. I brought you this.' Amy put the orange and the coffee on the bedside table.

Maddy groaned and turned her head away. 'How bad?'

'Well, you didn't hurl over anyone. But you really did miss an opportunity; Seb carried you up to bed just before you passed out.'

Maddy's eyes glistened with tears. 'Oh no.'

'Sorry.'

Maddy looked at her dress and shoes in a heap on the floor. 'Tell me he didn't have to undress me too.'

'No, I did that.'

'Oh Amy, he's going to be so disgusted by me. That's it, I've blown it, he's never going to look at me again. Tanya's won.'

'No, she hasn't. Anyway, she doesn't want him, not really. I think she's just playing games with him.' Like Rollo probably is with me. 'He seemed quite concerned about you last night.'

'Oh, Amy!' wailed Maddy. 'I've ruined everything. *Everything*.'

It was Monday evening and Dan was sitting on Amy's treatment table as she strapped his wrist up yet again.

'You overdid the training at the weekend, didn't you?' she said sternly. She was still angry with him for lying about his relationship with Karen. But since she'd gone with Rollo at the weekend she was hardly in a position to cast the first stone.

'A bit,' he admitted. 'But I want this seat so much. Still, I'm in better nick than the others. Did you hear about Chuck bawling them out today?'

Amy shook her head. 'Did he?' she said feigning innocence. She wasn't going to tell him voluntarily where she'd been at the weekend. She knew how he'd react – not that he had any sort of right to make a comment about her behaviour, but she didn't think that would stop him. And given how bruised she felt about the weekend and how foolish she felt, she didn't need Dan sticking his oar in too. 'What was it about?' she asked, still playing the innocent.

'It seems Rollo took advantage of his parents being away in Mauritius to have some sort of giant sleepover. You can just imagine the sort of losers he invited to go.'

Amy nodded, keeping her eyes on Dan's wrist and praying to God her face wasn't flaring.

'Really,' she murmured non-committally. 'So who went?' Please say you don't know.

Dan sighed. 'I don't know and I don't care. And I'm not going to give Rollo the satisfaction of showing any sort of curiosity about it. All I know is that Chuck was there—'

'You don't think he's a loser do you?'

Dan frowned and shook his head. 'Of course not. Rollo probably just wanted to cosy up to him – you know what he's like. Anyway, Chuck saw the sort of shenanigans they got up to and wasn't best pleased. Called them a bunch of drunken layabouts and told them that unless they get their shit together they can forget about him busting a gut to get them up to the right level. Which pisses me off because I'm getting the fallout too and I spent the week-end upright, sober and not shagging myself senseless.'

God, what if he found out about her and Rollo? She shouldn't care, but she did, damn him.

'You really don't like Rollo, do you?' she said, wanting to deflect Dan away from the subject of shagging.

Dan shook his head. 'I don't mind him having more money than sense, but I resent the fact that he thinks that makes him superior.'

'It's going to be tough if you keep getting put in the same crew as him.'

'If I make it to the Blue Boat I've got a chance of making the National Squad. And if I do that . . .' He stopped.

'Go on.'

'No, it's a mad idea.'

'Tell me.'

'I haven't even told my mum.'

'Oh.' Amy sighed.

'I want to win gold at the Olympics.'

Dan said it so quietly Amy wasn't sure she'd heard it right. 'What?'

'A gold medal. That's what I want.'

'Blimey.'

'And I want to win it myself. I don't want to be part of a crew.'

'You mean you don't want Rollo to have any part of it.'

Dan nodded. 'Precisely. Single sculls. Then it's just me, my medal, no one else to take the credit.'

Outside the door to the treatment room Rollo moved away quietly. He'd been going to surprise Amy. He didn't like the fact she'd had the last word and he was determined he was going to have her a second time and in her treatment room whether she liked it or not. It was a point of principle now. But Rollo's interest in sex and making his point went out of the window when he heard what Dan had to say about his rowing and the fact that he was planning to dump his partner. Which was a bit of a bugger because Rollo knew he'd never find another partner like Dan in the double sculls, and he was relying on Dan to give him his own shot at a medal.

Still, he thought, forewarned is forearmed and all that. Change of tactics – that was what was required. Thoughtfully Rollo went on his way.

After Amy had finished sorting Dan out she drifted up the stairs to the bar area. She felt out of sorts, cross with Dan, cross with Rollo and cross with herself. The boathouse was relatively quiet as most of the men were out on the river, trying to prove to Chuck that they weren't losers, layabouts and drunks. The members of St George's College who were hoping to be in the Boat Race squad were putting in an extra training session to try to restore the damage wrought by the weekend. As usual, Maddy was curled up in the corner of one of the battered sofas, mucking about with her phone.

'How's tricks?' asked Amy.

'Dunno.' She sounded really down.

'That bad?'

Maddy shrugged. 'I haven't seen Seb so I don't know if he thinks I'm a twat or a slag for getting so pissed.'

'Oh, Maddy, I'm sure he doesn't. And I expect you haven't seen him because like all the others he's trying to make it up to Chuck.'

'You think? Nope, I think I'm in the doghouse, to be honest.'

Amy hoped it was a kennel big enough for two because if other members of the rowing club found out about her own behaviour at the party, she was going to be joining her.

She decided to change the subject. 'Getting excited about the ball? Now that'll be a good moment to try and pull Seb. Just don't get wasted.' She put on her stern face.

'No I won't, but I don't stand a chance do I? I *had* hoped that I might get a dance or two with Seb. Fat chance now.'

'Don't be like that. I'm doing the seating plan. You are going to be seated next to him again. Honestly Mads, getting you off with Seb has become my mission in life. I'm going to get you into his bed if it's the last thing I do.'

'Won't do any good,' said Maddy refusing to be lifted by the news.

'You don't know that. You don't know just how worried he was about you on Saturday night.'

'Was he?' A small glimmer of hope crossed Maddy's face.

'He was. In fact, if I hadn't volunteered to sleep beside you I think he might have done.'

'Really?'

Amy remembered how nervous Seb was about the thought of Maddy hurling. 'Actually, no, probably not. Seb's a proper gent.' She thought that Maddy would prefer that as an excuse to him being repelled by the thought of vomit.

Maddy's face fell again. 'And proper gents want to go out with proper ladies. And that's the last thing I was.'

'That's so not true.'

'Proper ladies, don't get off their faces on red wine. Anyway, thanks for your efforts, Ames. Shame it was all wasted, just like I was.' And with that she slumped back into misery.

*

The next Saturday, just two days after the Blue Boat trials and a week after Rollo's party, the boat club bar was packed and the noise was deafening. For once Chuck wasn't the least bit worried about anyone drinking and the champagne corks were popping. The boat club had something to celebrate and they were doing it in style. Seb was filling glasses with fizz as fast as was possible; Christina and Stevie were acting as waitresses and passing trays of bubbly to anyone who wanted one – which seemed to be just about everyone. Susie was hanging off Angus's arm and gazing at him like he was a Greek God, a superhero and an 'A' list movie star combined. Rollo looked predictably smug and suave at the same time, Seb was bouncing about like Tigger on speed and even Dan managed to look really genuinely happy and was beaming out hundred-watt smiles.

'Isn't it wonderful?' said Maddy, jumping up and down and clapping her hands.

Amy had to lean in to catch her words. 'Fan-bloody-tastic,' she hollered back. 'The boys must be so thrilled.'

'I mean, it's no guarantee that they'll actually row in the Boat Race but it's a step nearer.'

'And look at Chuck. I've never seen him smile so much.'

'Not even when they won the Fours Head,' Maddy agreed.

A tray of brimming champagne glasses carried by Stevie came within grabbing distance and Maddy and

Amy helped themselves to one each. Then Chuck banged an empty bottle on the bar and silence fell.

'It's not often I am moved to make a speech but I think that the fact that four of our rowers have definitely made it into pre-term training camp for Blue Boat shows something about the dedication, motivation, professionalism and—'

'—sadism of the coach,' yelled a heckler from the back.

'Yes, that too,' said Chuck after the laughter had died down. 'So I'd like you to raise your glasses to Dan, Rollo, Seb and Angus.'

A huge cheer erupted as everyone toasted the St George's College rowers.

'I think,' said Amy to Maddy, 'that you ought to go over to Seb and give him a big celebratory snog.'

Maddy's face flared with colour. 'I couldn't. Not after . . . you know.'

But Amy grabbed her by the arm and yanked her across the room. 'Yes, you can,' she hissed and then she shoved Maddy hard so she fetch up right under Seb's nose.

'Maddy's got something to say to you,' said Amy. She turned round to leave Maddy and Seb together and cannoned into Dan.

'Whoops,' she said as her drink slopped over her hand. She licked the champagne off her skin.

'And haven't you got something to say to me?'

'Err . . . congratulations?' said Amy rather stonily, because what she really wanted to do was give him a piece of her mind about lying to her about Karen.

'Is that all?'

'Huge congratulations?' she offered, still without any warmth.

'How about *I'm a loser for going to Rollo's house party*?'

It was the turn of Amy's face to colour. 'How . . . I mean . . . who told . . .' She was mortified with embarrassment. And worse, did he know more about the weekend than just that she'd been a guest?

'Maddy told me. I don't think she meant to, she let slip what a pal you'd been when she got off her face there. I don't think you could have helped her if you'd been in Oxford.' Amy didn't reply. 'Why didn't you tell me?'

Amy shrugged. 'Because you despised everyone who'd taken Rollo up on the offer.'

'Chuck was there. I don't despise him.'

'I'm not your coach.' She nearly added, I'm not your anything, but decided that sounded hideously self-pitying. And why did she care? This is ridiculous, she told herself.

'I wouldn't despise you for going to Rollo's,' said Dan. 'Honestly. It's a free country and I expect his hospitality was terrific.'

'Yes, well . . .' And the least said about that the better. Moving on . . . 'Are you looking forward to the boat club ball?'

Dan shrugged. 'Not really.'

'Oh? It should be a good evening, shouldn't it?'

'I suppose.'

'You don't sound convinced.'

'I haven't got anyone to go with. These do's are always a bit lame if you're on your own.'

'But I thought Karen . . .?'

'Not her sort of thing at all.' Dan stared at her. 'I don't suppose . . .' He left the question hanging. 'I mean, if you've not got a better offer.'

Oh. But then the real reason for his invitation hit her. You haven't got anyone to go with so I'm better than nothing. Go alone or go with Dan? She forced a smile. 'If you're asking me to go to the ball with you then I'd love to.'

Dan smiled broadly.

'But,' added Amy, carefully. 'Just as friends.' She didn't want to risk getting hurt again.

'What?' said Dan, baffled.

'I know how busy you are at the mo. I know rowing is your priority.' She didn't notice Dan's smile fade somewhat.

'But I thought you and I . . .'

'Look, Dan, what with one thing and another,' and Karen, 'you've got a lot on your plate. You don't need more complications.' Like running around with two women. 'So that's settled then,' she finished, cheerily. Keep it light, don't let him know what a fool you've made of yourself over him and Rollo. 'And I am pleased you've made the squad for the Blue Boat, I really am.'

'Thanks,' said Dan. 'I'm pleased too although it really complicates life. The job has to go, for starters. Chuck says he can get me some funding so I should be okay, but then there's the training we're expected to do and somehow I've got to finish my degree. God knows when I'll find the time – at night, I suppose.'

Amy put her hand on Dan's arm. 'Oh, Dan, I'm sure you'll manage.'

Dan gave her a wry smile. 'Yeah. Besides, who needs sleep?'

'A much over-rated pastime.'

13

Amy supposed the ballroom would be ready in time but she really couldn't see how and she wasn't soothed by the fact that the Randolph's events manager seemed calm enough and Tanya was utterly cool. She could understand the man from the Randolph's attitude – he must have overseen dozens, if not hundreds, of big swanky parties – but Tanya? How did Tanya stay so calm? Maybe, underneath, she was panicking like Amy was.

She looked about the room again and saw a scene that looked more like a tsunami had just washed through than a big, glitzy social event was about to take place. Huge rounds of wood were being rolled across the floor by the hotel staff and put on stark metal trestles, stacks of banqueting chairs stood around higgledy-piggledy, the flower-arranger's foliage was in vast buckets and there were step-ladders and decorations strewn everywhere, adding to the chaos. When the tables were bare it seemed impossible they'd be transformed into anything suitable for a ball but then, when the staff had flung over circles of crisp white damask, the tables suddenly looked very swanky. At the far end of the room, some of them were already having the candelabra and cutlery arranged on them and piles of little gold chairs were being dragged across the carpet ready to be tucked in under the tables. In the corner a florist was producing the first of three large pedestals, at one end of the room the band was setting up and at the other the DJ was plugging in his decks and checking his records, CDs and lights.

'Amy,' called Tanya. Amy hurried over. Tanya handed over a printed floor plan of the room with each table numbered. 'As soon as the staff put the numbers on the tables to match this floor plan, you're to go round and put out the place cards. And while you're doing it,' Tanya handed Amy a file of papers and a couple of packets of sticky dots, 'can you check the names on the cards against their dietary requirements and give the veggies green dots and black ones for anything else. Understand?'

Amy was tempted to point out that she already had a 2:1 which made her officially 'not stupid' but thought better of it. Likewise about saying, 'yes miss', and tugging her forelock.

The scene was utterly transformed into a fairy tale by the time Amy got back at just a little after half six to be sure of being there before any of the guests arrived. The cutlery and glassware glittered in the soft candlelight, the flowers were fabulous and the room looked perfect.

Forty-five minutes later the ballroom at the Randolph was packed, as was the bar area next to it. The sound of glasses clinking, people talking and music playing gave the area a fabulous atmosphere that was enhanced by the three beautiful chandeliers that dangled from the high ceiling. A Christmas tree in one corner made the mood festive and reminded everyone that the Michaelmas term was drawing to a close.

'I love it when a plan comes together,' said Tanya, who was looking utterly ravishing in a deep red silk sheath dress that was so simple even Amy knew it had to have cost a fortune. Dresses that fell and draped liked Tanya's didn't come off the peg at Debenhams. Amy, for her part, was wearing a gold lurex cocktail dress that she'd found in a charity shop. It had cost her thirty quid, which she knew was pricey for Oxfam, but it looked like it had cost ten times that. Obviously she was completely outshone by Tanya but Amy was pleased with her own appearance all the same.

The two women were standing near the entrance behind a table covered in a white cloth, checking the tickets of the guests as they arrived.

'I take my hat off to you, Tanya, this is fantastic,' said Amy during a lull.

'You helped.'

'I worked out seating plans and sent out tickets – hardly tough jobs. You organised the menu, the band, you booked the room, got the raffle prizes . . . You've worked like a Trojan.'

'Not really.'

'Pah. You made it all look so easy.'

'I knew what I was doing. I've got previous. I've done a lot of this sort of thing for Mummy.'

Amy suppressed a smile. Now why aren't I surprised? 'Really?' she said innocently.

'Ya, Mummy runs all sorts of good causes. She says

213

because we're privileged we have certain duties. So we hold charity balls and all sorts at our place. Once you've organised one . . .'

'You've organised them all.'

Tanya smiled at her as though Amy empathised completely about running a charity ball in her own home. Obviously a three-bed semi was the perfect venue.

'Ya. We've got this place in Buckinghamshire – actually it's not far from Rollo's – well, the estates are adjacent but it's a fucking long way to walk, even if you cut across country and don't go down one drive and up the other.'

Amy had to look away, scared she was going to crack up laughing. She'd been brought up on an estate herself – but not one like Tanya's, obviously. She got herself under control.

'So, given that you've probably got an inheritance coming to you at some time, why the hell do you put yourself through it with rowing? I mean, it's not the easiest sport in the world, is it?'

Tanya looked at Amy with an expression of undiluted astonishment. 'You don't know?'

Amy looked mystified.

'You mean you've never tried it? But you cox.'

'And I'm not the right build.'

'You could enter the lightweight class.'

'But look at me.' She stretched out her arms. 'Look, little levers. I could never compete. The lightweight women might be smaller than you are but they still have gazelle-like limbs.' She couldn't bring herself to add 'not koala ones'. That was her private joke with Rollo.

Tanya didn't contradict her. 'But that reminds me, it's about time we got you out on the river again. You were so good the morning before Rollo's party.'

I was pretty good *at* Rollo's party, she thought. Or at least that's what your fiancé said. 'Thanks.'

'But you were. In fact the eight have been saying we ought ditch Hannah and take you on instead.'

Amy shook her head. What? No way. And how completely unfair it would be to Hannah. 'You can't. I'm not part of the college,' she declined. 'Sorry,' she added as a sop.

Tanya looked at her and sighed. 'The day job. Of course.'

Why, Amy wondered, had Tanya made her feel she'd owned up to having tertiary syphilis and not just a need to earn her keep?

'Excuse me, ladies, but is this a private conversation or can anyone join in?' Dan stood by their table, a bottle of champagne in one hand and three glasses in the other.

'As you've come bearing gifts it is most certainly an open conversation,' replied Tanya. 'Although Rollo should be bringing me a drink, not you.'

'Hey, Rollo isn't the only guy who knows how to look after the ladies. Or in your case, women.' He grinned.

'You'll get a slap, if you're not careful Dan,' said Amy, taking two glasses out of his hand and passing one to Tanya. 'And I think that Tanya meant that as she's come as Rollo's guest it should be him supplying her with drink, not you.'

'Well, if I'm honest, this is really Rollo's fizz. He's put

a dozen bottles on our table and I didn't see why you girls should miss out just because you're working.'

'A dozen!' said Amy.

'Oh, you know Rollo, never one to hold back when it comes to generosity,' said Tanya.

'Never one to hold back when it comes to showing off,' said Dan sotto voce to Amy.

'Now, now,' she whispered back. 'Just be thankful we're not having to pay the booze bill.'

Dan filled their glasses and promised to come back to refill them if they got stuck there for much longer but it was only a matter of minutes before the last of the guests arrived and were ticked off the list. Then Tanya organised the hotel staff to remove the admin table and they were able to join everyone else in the main ballroom. Some couples were already dancing to the band, which was playing cover versions of popular hits, while everyone else was chatting and networking and getting increasingly raucous as the drink flowed.

Amy sat down, thankful to take the weight of her stilettos. They were killing her already and it was only eight thirty. What state were her feet going to be in by the time the ball ended at two? To take her mind of her aching toes she looked around the table. All very satisfactory. She'd even managed to place herself diametrically opposite Rollo, and the huge floral arrangement in the centre meant that there was no way they could talk to each other. Dan was placed next to her, then on his right it was Maddy, then Seb, once again in his mess kit, and then Tanya and Rollo. On Amy's left were Chuck and Hannah, Angus and Susie.

Then Seb got up and walked to a small podium at the edge of the room. He banged on the lectern.

'Can I have your attention please, ladies and gentlemen?' Nothing happened. He tried again slightly louder. Still nothing. He gave it a couple of seconds then bawled 'Shut up,' at full volume. Instant silence fell. The band stopped playing and the dancing couples scuttled back to their tables.

'Well, I'm glad learning to shout orders across a parade square at Sandhurst has proved useful for something. Now then, as the boat club captain, despite the fact I'm only a lieutenant, I'd like to welcome you all to our eighty-seventh annual Christmas ball. And before I go any further I want a huge round of applause for Tanya and Amy for organising it all.'

As the clapping started, Amy felt her face blaze with embarrassment. She wasn't used to this sort of praise. But Tanya, poised and confident, was on her feet nodding in acknowledgement. Dan pulled Amy's chair out and forced her to her feet.

'I know how much you've done; don't let Tanya hog the limelight,' he told her. Beaten, Amy smiled at the partygoers before she sat down again as swiftly as she could.

'Now,' continued Seb, 'although you'll need no encouragement, this is a great opportunity to celebrate this year's rowing successes, which are too numerous to detail—' more heckling, shouts of 'false modesty' and thunderous, appreciative applause, '—and I expect you to pay suitable tribute by eating, drinking and making merry. For those of us with commitments in the spring—'

217

'That'll be the Boat Race will it, Seb? Thought you'd drop that in,' bawled a voice.

'—this'll be our last opportunity for a booze-up, so I expect the full support of everyone at St George's in our endeavours. So,' he raised his glass to the partygoers, 'let battle commence!'

Rapturous applause broke out for a third time, the crowd's enthusiasm probably having quite a lot to do with the amount of champagne already consumed. Maddy's was especially ecstatic but that had nothing to do with bubbly as, so far, all she'd drunk was sparkling water. No way was she going to make the same mistake twice.

Seb returned to the table, drawn it, seemed, by Maddy's besotted gaze. Amy wondered if it worked like some sort of Trekkie tractor beam – once she'd locked it on to Seb he was powerless to go anywhere else.

Amy looked around the room and decided that this was quite the swankiest party she'd ever been to. Looking at the table decorations, the flowers and the band Amy couldn't believe that the eighty-pound tickets covered anything like the price of all those extras, to say nothing of the cost of a three-course dinner as well. Amy suspected that Tanya had bank-rolled some of the expenses. But if she had, she was much more subtle about her largesse than Rollo ever was.

Suddenly, the waiters, marshalled like troops on parade, appeared with the first course and the dinner part of the evening was under way. Amy noticed approvingly that Maddy was still hardly touching her wine. Maybe this was going to be her lucky night.

'So,' said Amy to Dan as she tucked into her warm goat's cheese tartlet, 'what are your plans for Christmas?' She knew it was a lame conversational gambit but it was preferable to silence.

'Training, writing essays, more training, more essays,' said Dan. 'Going home to Mum's for a great feed. The cooks in college are good but home cooking . . .'

'Home cooking is the best. But aren't you going to take a break over the hols?'

'How?' asked Dan. 'When?' he added.

'But *you* wanted the place at Oxford *and* the place in the Blue Boat squad. If you don't want it you can always donate it to someone else.'

Dan fiddled with his bread roll, breaking it up into small pieces. 'I'm sorry. I'm just feeling the pressure.'

'And I'm sorry for not being more sympathetic,' conceded Amy taking another mouthful. 'I know how much your rowing means to you.'

Dan turned to her with a light in his eyes that was almost messianic. 'It's everything. To make the national squad, to row at the Olympics . . .' He stopped. 'Sorry, I'll get boring.' He gulped down a huge mouthful and washed it down with a swig of wine.

'No, not at all. I think it's admirable to have such an amazing ambition.'

'Karen doesn't think so. She thinks I'm mad.'

Amy felt as if she'd been knifed. Bloody Karen. Here I am, dolled up to the nines, and you're thinking about her. 'Well, she said brightly, 'not everyone is interested in sport.'

'No, and it doesn't matter. I don't mind. Her father

was into pigeon racing apparently, and I can't say it's something I've taken even the remotest interest in.'

'Although it would be nice to have a shared interest wouldn't it?'

'Why?' Dan looked genuinely bemused.

Amy didn't like the thought that he and Karen were too busy shagging to talk. She laid her knife and fork together on her plate and decided it would be less painful to talk to Chuck during dinner. At least, she thought, casting a glance in Maddy's direction, she and Seb seemed to be getting it together. If nothing else Maddy had her hand on his forearm and was leaning into him so she could talk directly into his ear. Seb was smiling and looking into her eyes. If that body language didn't lead to something, thought Amy, she'd eat one of the flower arrangements.

It wasn't just Amy who was watching the others at the table; Tanya was taking an interest in the other guests too, in particular, Amy and Dan. There was something going on there but she couldn't put her finger on it. When he had walked through the door Dan had approached their table looking like a Labrador bringing a stick back to his master – all eager and expecting praise, and Amy had visibly brightened at his arrival. And now she had a face like wet weekend. Tanya was riveted to know what Dan had said to upset her. Maybe he'd found out about Rollo and Amy at that over-the-top house party. As far as she was aware, she was the only person, other than Rollo and Amy themselves, who knew about what they had got up to while the others had all been busy slaughtering clays. Not that she'd let on – she had better manners than that. Besides, she quite liked Amy; she'd been pretty helpful with the ball arrangements and she was a startlingly good cox. No, Tanya didn't want to piss her off by wrecking anything that was going on between her and Dan. The lower classes, she felt, were very narrow-minded about sex. She didn't think that, if Dan had designs on Amy, he'd be pleased to know his arch-rival had got there too. Even though it would be terribly amusing to see the look on Dan's face, she really wasn't that cruel.

The plates were cleared and roast guinea fowl was served followed by a fabulous orange and chocolate pudding. Thanks to Rollo there was no shortage of wine on the table – the fact that Maddy was hardly touching hers meant each bottle stretched that wee bit further.

As the last morsels of pudding were scraped from the plates, the band struck up again and couples surged back onto the dance floor. Dan grabbed Amy's arm.

'Come on, I love this one,' he said as the band struck up with a very good version of 'Somebody Told Me' by the Killers.

Amy allowed herself to be dragged onto the floor humming along to the lyrics and was surprised when Dan took her into his arms and began to do a proper ballroom dance. He towered over her by a foot so she was pressed against his chest as he swept her around. She breathed in his clean, wholesome smell. No aftershave, nothing fake, just a faint muskiness and soap. She shut her eyes and allowed herself to recall what it had been like to rest her head against his chest without the encumbrance of clothes.

Dan was a surprisingly good dancer and because he was so strong Amy found it incredibly easy to follow his steps.

She looked up at him. 'You're good.'

'One of the advantages of going to a posh school. They expected us to learn a lot of social graces. I haven't had the chance to do it much since. So a bit of practice now and again helps keep the skill trudging on for a few more years, but it's a rare opportunity.'

'Won't Karen let you dance?'

'What's Karen got to do with this?'

'Don't you take her dancing?'

Dan shook his head. 'I don't think it's her sort of thing. She's more into *EastEnders* and *Hello!* magazine and lying on the sofa than clubbing and partying.'

'I suppose because she's on her feet a lot and working evenings.'

'Maybe.'

Amy let the subject drop. Karen wasn't here and she was, and enjoying the dance. The Killers number ended, the band segued into Oasis's 'Live Forever' and Dan carried on dancing.

'Anyway,' said Dan, bending down to put his mouth close to her ear, 'why are you so interested in Karen?'

'No reason,' she lied.

Dan's hand, resting on the small of her back, relaxed the pressure and Amy drew back slightly so she could look at his face.

'Really?' He tipped his head to one side. 'You *do* know

that Karen and I really are just good friends, don't you? That's *all* it is.'

'Are you? That's not what I heard. Everyone has said you're an item.'

'Well, we're not.'

'Oh.'

'And I think I should know, don't you.'

'You could be lying your arse off.'

'I'm not lying you know,' he said. 'Yes, I don't deny Karen and I have had a certain amount to do with each other but it's never been serious.'

'Fuck buddies?'

Dan nodded. 'Beautifully put, Miss Jones. But abso - lutely, totally, nothing else. Promise.'

The pressure of his hand resumed on her back, pulling her hard against his body, so hard that the buttons on his dinner jacket dug into her ribs. Not that she was going to complain. She wasn't going to do any- thing to spoil the moment. She thought back over a couple of previous conversations. Maybe she'd been so convinced that Dan was with Karen she'd missed the signs that he wasn't; the way he'd looked after her after the Fours Head, the way he'd cared she'd gone to Rollo's, the way he'd confided his ambition for Olympic gold to her and not even to his mum, the way he was dancing with her right now. Dear God, how could she have been so dim? She snuggled closer, revelling in this perfect moment. She wanted it to go on for ever.

Across the room, Seb was literally sweeping Maddy off her feet. He'd picked her up like a baby and had carried her onto the dance floor where, to whoops and whistles from many of the partygoers, he was holding her close against his chest, twirling around on the parquet floor. The smile on Maddy's face was a picture. Amy had never seen anyone look happier.

She looked up at Dan. 'Have you seen those two?' she said. 'That's a good match if ever I saw one.'

Dan grinned. 'Someone's on a promise.'

Dear God, yes please, thought Amy. Please let Maddy make it into bed with Seb. And, she added as a little coda to her prayer, if you could see me right with Dan, I'll be nice to Karen for the rest of my life.

A shriek, a shout and an enormous crash of cutlery and crockery brought the moment to a screeching halt. The band's playing came to a ragged and discordant halt and the silence was shattering. Everyone turned to see the source of the commotion. A complete table had been tipped over and lying in the middle of the debris of broken glasses, a destroyed flower arrangement, scattered cutlery and a couple of over-turned chairs for good measure, was Seb and beside him in a sprawl of blue beaded silk, was Maddy.

And behind them, revealed by the collapsed table, were Angus and Susie, his trousers down and her skirt round her waist, caught in mid-shag.

'Who says history never repeats itself?' said Dan drily, before releasing Amy and striding over to see how Seb was.

'My fucking spurs. I caught my fucking spurs on something and went arse over tit,' said Seb to his hushed and shocked audience. Behind him, looking amazingly nonchalant, Susie and Angus were getting to their feet,

224

rearranging their clothing and taking an ironic bow in response to an even more ironic handclap.

'Well,' said Susie, unabashed. 'We thought we ought to start a tradition. Make it an annual event.' Now decent, she and Angus acted as if they'd been caught having a crafty fag behind a potted palm, not in flagrante delicto in the middle of a ballroom.

Maddy was lying by Seb quietly while Seb was pale and moaning. She looks okay, thought Dan, maybe her fall has been cushioned by Seb. For his part, Seb didn't look too clever.

'Here, give us your hand,' said Dan, striding over and holding out his.

Seb went to move and winced. 'Shit.' He lay back in the chaos, his face ashen.

'Problem?' asked Dan.

'My shoulder,' he hissed, his face contorted.

Without regard to the knees of his dinner suit Dan knelt down in the mess. 'We've got to get you upright somehow. You can't stay here.'

'Just give me a mo,' said Seb. Around him the party had gathered out of concern and curiosity. Behind them the waiters hovered, wanting to restore order as soon as they could. Dan bent forward and took Seb's good arm and used his considerable strength to lift Seb out of the disaster scene. By the time Seb was fully upright his face wasn't just white but covered in a sheen of sweat. Maddy took this moment to pass out cold.

Dan dumped Seb on a chair and turned his attention to Maddy, whipping off his DJ and making it into a pillow to support her head.

'Amy,' he ordered, 'check to see if she's got any tight clothing that should be loosened and then ring for an ambulance.'

Amy got busy loosening the zip at the side of Maddy tight gown.

'I've already phoned,' said Tanya. 'They're on their way.'

'I think Seb's bust his collarbone,' said Dan. 'Did anyone see what happened to Maddy?'

'I think she might have hit her head on the edge of the table as Seb slipped,' said Chuck. 'But it all happened so quickly, I can't be sure.'

On the floor Maddy was starting to stir again. Amy put a restraining hand on her shoulder. 'You keep still,' she ordered her friend.

Maddy groaned.

'We think you've had a bang on the head.'

Maddy tried to move again.'

'Lie still, an ambulance is on its way.'

'Wha . . .?'

'Just lie still and keep quiet.'

The sound of distant two-tones penetrated the subdued ballroom. Around them, the waiters had rocked into action, carting away the flowers and then gathering all the debris into the middle of the tablecloth and lifting the whole bundle out of the way and off behind the scenes. The table was righted and another member of staff brought a clean cloth. By the time the ambulance crew had arrived with their bags of kit the evidence of the accident, apart from the two casualties, had all but disappeared.

226

Maddy opened her eyed and looked up at Amy. 'How's Seb?' she mumbled.

'Dan thinks he's bust his collarbone. But let's not worry about him, eh?'

'One minute he was dancing with me in his arms,' she whispered, a little smile on her lips, 'and the next, wallop. Poor old Seb. It's going to scupper his chances of rowing in the Boat Race. Even if his shoulder heals in time his training's going to take a hit.'

'Don't you worry about him,' said Amy. She moved out of the way to let the ambulance crew check her friend over. She went to stand by Dan again.

'I've told the crew I'll go with them to the hospital,' he said to her. 'Then if they need to stay in I can get their kit.'

'Poor old Mads,' said Amy. 'I reckon she and Seb were going to get together this evening. Fat chance now.' She didn't add that her chances were equally wrecked if Dan was going to the JR too. She knew how long it would take to get this pair through casualty on a Friday night in a city stuffed with students. Hours and hours.

As the two casualties were carted off on ambulance trolleys accompanied by Dan, the band struck up again but Amy's heart wasn't in further drinking and dancing. She collected her coat, called a taxi and went home, alone.

14

Amy was in the stern of the boat as Tanya's eight rowed gently to the start of their two-thousand-metre piece.

'Good ball, last weekend,' said Amy to Tanya, who was thrusting forward and back on her sliding seat.

'I thought so. And thanks for your help.'

'I didn't do that much.'

Tanya shrugged. 'You pulled your weight and you didn't let me down. You left early though. Didn't you fancy the breakfast?'

'Well, Dan had gone with Maddy and Seb and I just felt a bit flat what with the accident and everything.'

Tanya gave her a look that Amy interpreted as 'you wuss'. But she didn't offer a shred of sympathy that Amy's night had been ruined.

Amy kept schtum. She could get her own back so easily and she would. The rate back was going to be punishing. Instead she said, 'I hear Seb's on the mend.'

'He is, but he's bitching about his training regimen going to pot and Maddy is having a high old time acting as Florence Nightingale.'

That sounded hopeful, thought Amy. Maddy nursing

Seb? Just because Seb had a broken collarbone didn't mean that he and Maddy couldn't get it on, did it? All it would take was a bit of ingenuity, assuming Maddy had the gumption to take advantage of the situation.

They reached the point on the river that marked two kilometres back to the boathouse. Steered by Amy and with directions to the stroke and bow sides the boat was turned tidily.

'Ready for some hard work?' said Amy, shooting Tanya a grin.

'Of course.'

'Good.' You are going to be *so* sweaty by the time I've finished with you! 'Attention, go,' she said into the head-mike. 'And drive . . . drive . . . drive . . .' She glanced at the cox-box. Thirty-eight. That'd do to be going on with. She'd see if she could get them a bit higher for the final sprint but she wasn't going to let this lot drop the rate in the third piece. This wasn't just getting her own back on Tanya; she wanted to see how much she could push them. She was sure this eight was capable of more than they'd been achieving since she'd been associated with St George's.

The eight rowers were almost sobbing when Amy let them rest on their oars outside the boathouse. Stevie leaned over the side of the boat and threw up her early morning tea. The scum was quickly whisked away by the current.

'Jesus, Amy,' panted Tanya, when she could get her breath. 'What was that about?'

'Just wanted to see what you could do. And "more than you have been" is the answer.'

229

Tanya flexed her aching shoulders and mopped her brow with the sweatbands on her wrists. 'Hannah isn't such a slave driver.'

'Then she should be. She should be wringing every last drop out of you. Tell her. If you've got a chance of making the Oxford women's crew then you need her to push you.'

Amy could almost see Tanya's cogs turning. 'I don't suppose . . .' She stopped and sighed. 'But you've got a day job and you're not in college, so it's a no.'

'Sorry,' she said automatically.

Amy pottered into the boathouse while the crew dragged in the boat and their weary bodies behind her. She told Chuck what their time was.

'Jeez, Amy, what did you use on them – a cattle prod?'

'I just pushed them a bit.'

'More than a bit, Amy, that time was fantastic and you know it.'

Amy shuffled her foot. 'But it's the crew's time, Chuck. They just need motivating.'

Tanya stood beside her, then bent double, her hands resting on her knees as she recovered from more than six minutes of hideous physical hell.

'And she knows how to motivate, Chuck,' she panted. 'Isn't there any way we can bend the rules so she can cox for us all the time?'

'It's impossible, Tanya. She isn't even a student any - where in Oxford. We can't bring people we just happen to have dragged off the street into the team.'

'And anyway, I can't,' said Amy wanting to get away from the vision of being dragged off the street like a hooker or a stray dog. 'The day job.'

'Yeah, yeah, the day job, Amy,' said Tanya, crossly. 'We can get round that. I'll pay you the equivalent, okay.'

Oh. Silence reigned as Amy and Chuck both took in what was on the table.

'It's still gotta be a "no",' said Chuck before Amy had a chance to open her mouth. 'She doesn't study here; she's the volunteer physio. And not even that for much longer.' He turned to her. 'Amy, I'm sorry, but I came over to tell you Marcus is better.'

Amy had been pulling off her hoodie and stopped, her arm half in and half out of a sleeve. 'Oh.' She knew she was only required as the physio as long as Marcus was ill, but she'd got used to her voluntary work and had grown to love it. 'Does this mean you'll be letting me go?'

'It's hardly that. It isn't as if we're paying you.'

'No, I know, but . . .' She finished hauling off her top and folded it up, holding it against herself like a security blanket. Suddenly she felt quite bereft. What was she going to do in the evenings? Sitting alone in her flat watching TV didn't have much appeal and her wages didn't stretch at anything much more exotic. She could come down to the club but without a reason to be there, without a purpose, she just be some sort of sad groupie.

Chuck heard the hesitation and sadness in her voice. 'You mean you want to stay on?'

Amy nodded. 'I like it here. This place is my social life. I like the people. Besides, there was a suggestion, when I got this job, that Marcus might just let me work as his assistant. I could do with learning from his experience.'

'I see. Well, I can't see that being a problem. Besides, I'd quite like it if you stayed on.'

231

'Why?'

'I like having you around,' he said sincerely.

Tanya, tired and having lost her argument about having Amy cox full-time, went off into the clubhouse to take a shower.

'Could you ask Marcus what he thinks?' said Amy when she'd gone. 'He may not want me hanging on.'

'Tell you what, how about I tell Marcus what *I* think – that he's missing a trick if he doesn't.'

'Would you? Really?' Amy stood on tiptoe and planted a smacker on Chuck's cheek.

'Buy me a drink, if my plan works, and we'll call it quits. How about that?'

'You're on.'

For Dan, Angus and Rollo the joys of messing about in boats were wearing quite thin. Training for the Blue Boat squad was tough. It had begun pre-term, up on the Tideway where for two weeks they had flogged up and down the Thames in eights, fours and in single sculls to get used to the conditions, the currents and the weather. They suffered gales, blizzards and intense cold as they battled their way up and down the water or thundered along the towpath on gruelling training runs. For six hours a day they trained with breaks for meals and to allow their bodies recovery time but even with the rest periods the training was relentless. It was during this fortnight that Angus was told that he wasn't going to make the final eight. His strength was phenomenal but it wasn't enough to compensate for his crap technique. Devastated, he'd sloped back to Oxford and his studies, leaving just Dan and Rollo to uphold the honour of St George's.

At weekends there was no let-up, with races organised against some of the best other crews around; crews that were based on the Tideway and who knew all the advantages that were to be wrung out of the eddies and swirls, the currents and vagaries of the tides. In the pre-term training fortnight there had been no chance for them to get back to their rooms or digs in Oxford and they were all accommodated in friends' and relations' houses around Putney, cycling to the boathouse at Putney or sometimes getting a lift in a mate's car. Chuck, and the chief coach, Mike, swapped the crew around. At one point Rollo was stroke, but then it was decided that a rower from another college should have the honour.

Seb, unable to take part because of his knackered collarbone, helped out the two coaches in the gym by urging the crew to greater and greater feats on the ergo machines. As a mentor and unofficial third coach he was an inspiration to the crew when spirits were flagging or the motivation dipped.

Dan, for his part, seemed to do nothing but row, eat and sleep. His studies had taken a back seat, although his tutor was hugely supportive of him and helped him where possible to keep up to speed with his academic work. They both knew that as soon as the Boat Race was over he would have to get his head down and really graft but until that first weekend in April they agreed his rowing was his priority. In fact, rowing took up so much of his time he lost touch with all his old Oxford buddies, including Karen and Amy.

Once term started, their training moved back to the University Boat Club near Oxford with endless sessions on the ergo, every afternoon spent on the water and more time spent in the gym in the evening. Their diet and sleep were regulated, they were weighed and measured, their hearts monitored, their oxygen uptake quantified: it was as if they had become rowing robots.

With Seb out of action and using the opportunity to catch up on his academic work and even Rollo having to curtail his social life, Tanya and Maddy found themselves a bit adrift at the boat club.

Tanya, feeling abandoned and not having made the final cut for the women's eight – for which she blamed Amy for not having taken up her offer – had taken to hanging around the clubhouse even more than usual, almost as much as Maddy.

'God,' she said, one evening, throwing an out-of-date copy of *Hello!* back onto the table in front of the battered old sofa. 'I am so bored. I am so bored I could scream.'

Maddy looked up from her iPhone that she was always fiddling with. 'So why now, suddenly?'

Tanya slumped back on the tobacco-coloured leather. 'I don't know. I haven't seen anyone for weeks. No one is going out; no one is having any fun.'

Maddy sighed. 'You're right. The last fun I had was Rollo's house party and the ball. And those were both ages ago. Last year even.'

'Rollo's party was good, wasn't it?'

Maddy looked at Tanya. She was tempted to tell Tanya that it would have been a whole lot better if she'd kept away from Seb. But maybe Tanya dallied with the hearts of so many men she didn't even remember them as individuals. 'It was all right,' she conceded.

'I thought it was sensational.' There was a few seconds before she added, naughtily, 'How's Seb?'

Maddy glanced up. She never quite trusted Tanya. Was there something cryptic in that last tiny sentence or was it completely innocent? 'Fine, as far as I know. And maybe I'd have enjoyed Rollo's party more if—'

'If you and Seb . . .?' Tanya smiled sweetly again.

Maddy refused to rise. '—I'd not had a hangover from hell.'

'You did make rather free with Rollo's wine cellar. Not that the others didn't.'

'Poor Amy slept with me to make sure I didn't come to any harm while I was out of it.'

'Which rather scuppered your plans for the evening, didn't it? Didn't I detect you had hopes for Seb?'

Maddy looked crestfallen. 'I wish.' She shrugged and sent Tanya a rather baleful look.

'Look, Maddy, you really have to get your act together there. Stop being so bourgeois and make a proper play for him yourself. Stop dropping hints and be more obvious. Honestly, if the mountain won't come to Muhammad . . . Besides, you don't know what you're missing out on by faffing about as you are. Seb really is surprisingly good in bed you know. Hung like a horse – trust me.'

Maddy's mouth dropped open. 'What? But what about Rollo . . . aren't you supposed to be . . . You're an item, aren't you?' Maddy finally managed to stutter out.

'Oh really. And what if we are *an item* as you so coyly put it? We're not married yet, and anyway, it's only sex. He doesn't care who I sleep with so why should I care about him and his conquests? Honestly, Maddy, once it was obvious to anyone with half an eye that Rollo was hell-bent on screwing Amy, which he did, and once you put yourself out of the running with Seb, I thought – well, why not?'

Maddy stared at Tanya. 'You bitch,' she snapped, getting off the sofa.

Tanya shrugged and returned to her magazine.

Maddy stamped out of the bar and away from the club and stormed back towards the centre of Oxford, shaking with anger and close to tears. Trying to breathe deeply and banish her turbulent feelings she stormed up towards St Aldate's before turning on to the High and heading for the college. The porter on duty in his lodge wished her a good evening but she didn't hear him. She had other things on her mind: namely what Seb had got up to with Tanya. She made her way up the stairs that led to his rooms. There was a line of light under his door. She'd rehearsed what she had to say to him, she had her argument off pat, and all she had to hope for now was that he was sober and alone.

She thumped on the antique oak planking.

'Yes?'

She opened the door. There was the sod.

'You shagged Tanya at Rollo's,' she railed.

'What?'

'You heard me.'

'Yes, but . . .'

236

'But nothing.'

'But,' said Seb, looking completely bamboozled, 'why not?'

'Because . . . because *I* wanted *you* to sleep with *me*.' There she'd said it.

'You?'

Oh shit . . . He hated her. He was ridiculing her idea. She was small and ugly and a complete joke.

'Why not?' Shit, she shouldn't have asked him that.

'Because you were pissed.'

'I wouldn't have been if you hadn't spent all evening making eyes at Tanya.'

'You hardly looked at me,' said Seb, sounding bewildered. 'How was I to know you fancied me then? I only got the vaguest hint at the ball and you haven't mentioned anything of the sort since. I mean, this is almost the first inkling I've had.'

'Well, I can't help it if you're too thick to see it.'

'And I can't help being a bloke. I don't do psychic, I don't do subtle, I don't get hints, okay? I'm sorry if that destroys your concept of the opposite sex but that's how I am. Take it or leave it.'

'Then I'll leave it,' she stormed before slamming out of his room, banging the door behind her with a ferocious thump.

Another undergrad coming out of his room, muttered, 'temper, temper,' at her.

'And you can fuck off too!'

Back in her own room she threw herself on the bed and sobbed until she thought her heart would break.

15

The day of the Boat Race dawned overcast but dry and Amy, Maddy and Tanya, who had driven up to town in time for the race, which was taking place at teatime, were almost sick with nerves.

The last thing Maddy had planned on was Amy inviting Tanya to join them for the journey up to London but short of telling Amy her real reasons for *not* wanting Tanya in the car, it had all got too complicated and she'd given in. And other than that, she wasn't going to give Tanya the satisfaction of knowing how much her deliberately nasty revelation about Seb had hurt. So she was grinning and bearing it and hoping neither guessed how much she was dying inside.

Apart from the journey up to the Thames it promised to be a jolly day out as Rollo and Dan had got the three girls passes to get in to the University of London Boat Club along with Seb and Angus. Chuck and Mike were going to be following the crew in a launch positioned just behind the umpire's one for the length of the race and would arrive from the water once the result was known. Depending on the outcome, it could be quite a party.

Unlike the girls, Seb and Angus had stayed up in London for the previous week, helping with the training, keeping the crew's spirits up, doing odd jobs for the men, running errands and generally keeping the path smooth for the squad so they could concentrate on their rowing and nothing else.

On the journey up to London Amy and Tanya had discussed the chances of 'their' team, not really noticing that Maddy mostly remained silent, but she was busy concentrating on driving wasn't she? Tanya, in the front seat, had copies of all of the quality papers and had read out the rowing correspondents' assessment of the two teams' chances.

'It looks really doubtful,' announced Tanya morosely as she folded up the *Telegraph* having read the last piece out loud.

'Don't say that,' said Amy. 'Please don't, they've put so much effort in.'

'They have, but all the papers are saying that Oxford are too young, too light, too inexperienced and that Cambridge are better technically. Put all that together and, well . . .' Tanya shrugged. 'The phrase "snowball's chance in hell" springs to mind. Just look at the odds the bookies are offering.'

Amy put her fingers in her ears and sang 'la-la-la' loudly. 'Not listening,' she said.

'You'll see,' said Tanya.

Amy slumped on the back seat, her stomach knotted with nerves and anxiety. And if I'm in this state, what about the crew? She knew that there was no point in telling anyone it was only a race – it had transcended that

239

decades and decades previously. This was Oxford versus Cambridge, this was old rivalry at its greatest, this mattered.

'God knows how the boys are feeling,' muttered Amy, finally voicing her inner feelings as they made their way towards Chiswick where they would be able to see the finish. They'd been told that a big screen TV was available at the University of London Boat Club for them to view the first few miles of the race so they wouldn't be missing out on the action in the early stages.

Once they'd arrived and dumped the car they made their way towards the river. Dozens of people had the same idea, carrying deckchairs, cool boxes and rugs to make their time on the towpath as comfortable as possible. The atmosphere of these crowds was one of good humour and fun, with most people determined to have a good day out whatever the outcome of the race. However, there were other, much more partisan people along the bank, who desperately cared about which eight would prevail.

The three girls pushed their way along the roads that ran behind the houses and businesses that fronted onto the river until they reached the boat club. They made their way past the racks of boats parked on the grass at the front and into the stark, white-painted building where their passes were scrutinised. The place was already frantic with activity with a TV film crew setting up their kit, reporters milling around interviewing anyone who stood still for long enough to be cornered and the friends and relatives of the crew, mostly wearing colours that reflected their allegiance were alternately watching the coverage on the televisions and monitors around the club or glancing at their watches and working out how long till the off.

The minutes till the start seemed to drag interminably. The girls passed the time by earwigging the interviews recorded to go out on the broadcast media, by spotting previous rowing stars who were also hanging around, and by taking it in turns to play endless games of patience on Tanya's iPad. And then the crews made their appearance at the Putney end of the course, the boats were launched into the river, the crews paddled into the murky water in their dark or light blue wellies which they then threw back onto the bank. They then rowed a few hundred metres or so to warm up before they were called to take their place at the stake boats.

Dan wondered if he was actually going to be sick. He'd never felt this nervous before in his life. He tried telling himself that this was only a race, if they didn't win no one was going to die, but frankly he couldn't have felt worse if he'd been in a tumbrel on his way to a guillotine. He could almost hear the clack of knitting needles.

He stared at Rollo's back in the number four seat, and beyond him were the other crew members, the cox sitting there with his hand in the air signalling he wasn't ready for the start while the eight were hard forward on their seats, their oars swept back, the blades buried in the water and then his hand dropped. Dan glanced across. The Cambridge cox lowered his hand.

'Attention, go,' yelled the umpire, as he dropped his red flag and they were off.

Off to an initial, unsustainable forty-seven strokes a minute, a stroke rate that they'd planned and which they were banking on getting them ahead of Cambridge in the first section of the race, but the opposition stayed almost level and they knew they'd have to throttle back before long or they'd burn up before the finish line. But their stamina was the greater and inch by agonising inch they managed to claw their way past the Light Blues, a seat at a time. Cambridge dropped the rate first, giving Oxford yet more of an advantage until, as they approached the Hammersmith Bridge, they were up by almost three-quarters of a length. Their cox gave them the signal to really dig deep and somehow the whole crew found a long, steady, easy rhythm. It was then that, despite the fact that the bookies had Cambridge as the odds-on favourite, they all knew that they had a chance. They began flying over the water, each stroke of their oars was almost technically perfect, and suddenly, their three-quarter-length advantage had morphed into two clear lengths of muddy water between the two boats.

Although Dan concentrated on every fibre of his body producing a perfect rowing stroke every time, his sliding seat swooshed forwards and back, a small corner of his mind allowed him to watch the backs of the Light Blues receding steadily as his team pulled away. They zipped past the Chiswick Steps, pretty much the halfway point of the race and Dan felt elation surge through his body, lifting away the awful agony of the lactic acid collecting in his muscles and replacing it with sheer euphoria. Yes, each monumental haul of his blade still hurt, yes, his thighs still burned and yes, his shoulders felt as if they were being pulled out of their sockets, but how on earth could Cambridge come back from the position they were in now? It couldn't be done and short of sinking or crashing it was in the bag.

The steady voice of the cox coming from a speaker near his feet kept him focused on the job in hand and stopped him from losing concentration.

'Keep it long and powerful. Use your legs. Sit up tall. Drive for the finish.'

Dan used the quiet urging of the cox to keep going. No matter that he was now beyond exhausted, no matter that the end of the race was still two miles away, another eight minutes of shattering physical effort, he, like the rest of the crew, just had to keep it together. He concentrated on his stroke, on the feather, the thrust, all the component parts of each tug and strain and just kept his mind on endless repetition of the dip and pull, forward and back of each stroke. He zoned out the air horns and shouts, applause and whistles coming from the thousands that lined the banks, he zoned out the cold of the chill breeze that scudded over the water and he zoned out the knowledge of how much more of the torture he had to endure before it was all over.

And then he realised they were almost at Barnes Bridge. The end of the race was approaching. It was like someone had fitted him with new batteries and suddenly the rowing seemed easier, the strokes came more fluidly, the boat was lighter to power through the water. So before the feeling went, before the exhaustion, the tiredness and the pain reasserted themselves, Dan shut out everything outside of his rowing and focused once again on every stroke.

Downstream, Cambridge still trailed. They must know the race was lost; they had to put themselves through the same agonies as their opponents but they wouldn't get the spoils at the end. Oxford would be rewarded with applause and champagne, Cambridge would not. Dan didn't want to think about what it would feel like to lose, not after this amount of effort and the preceding months of hard, relentless training, of endless workouts on top of university work, of cold mornings on the river and late nights over books.

Four seconds after the flag dropped to signify the Oxford had won it dropped again for Cambridge but the Dark Blues didn't register the gap. They were collapsed over their blades even though their spirits were soaring sky-high. Euphoria, joy, utter exhaustion, pain, delight all mixed up into one amazing cocktail of feelings as the boat, carried by the momentum of the rowers, slipped into the shadow of Chiswick Bridge.

Their cox beat the water with his hands. 'Brilliant, just fucking brilliant,' he crowed.

The stroke leaned forward and hugged him, congratulating him for inspiring them to pull out the stops when necessary, to keep going for all those miles and encouraging them in ways that were difficult to quantify but which made all the difference at the finish.

They called for three cheers for their brave opposition, which Cambridge returned with a weak response that barely registered even though it was amplified by the arches of Chiswick Bridge. After the cheers the Oxford crew stopped grinning like loons and high-fiving each other and picked up their oars to bring the boat back to the shore and more congratulation from their well-wishers. Cambridge did likewise with their blades but, thought Dan, they must be hoping to slink back with no one noticing. Get the boat out of the water, back on its trailer and slide off so they can forget their defeat as soon as possible.

They got to the shore and clambered out wearily on legs made of rubber. Their heads might be celebrating but their bodies were wrecked.

'Well done, Dan.'

He looked up and saw Amy heading towards him at speed. Before he had a chance to brace himself she had thrown herself at him, her tiny eight-stone frame making his fifteen-stone one rock with the force. He wrapped his arms around her and kissed her hard, then drew back and looked at her properly. He was touched by her expression of real happiness.

Beside them Susie was in Angus's arms and Rollo and Tanya were also hugging. Only Maddy and Seb weren't embracing. That is, until Seb reached out and grabbed her and put his arms around her. 'Come here,' Dan heard him say and was surprised to see tears raining down Maddy's face. Surely their win wasn't worth that amount of emotion – well, not from a spectator at any rate.

He returned his attention to Amy, aware that he was dripping with sweat. Girls might like a nice whiff of masculinity but this was, possibly, a tad too much.

'You were awesome,' said Amy, gazing up at him.

'Thanks. Tough race,' was all he could say. His lungs still ached and his muscles burned and frankly he felt so wobbly he wasn't sure he mightn't fall down and what with the emotion of winning, her kindness and sympathy were almost too much for him. God, he was as bad as Maddy. He turned and walked a few steps away from the group before he made a fool of himself. Some jerk photographer was bound to get a shot of him if he did and it would be up on Twitter before you knew it. He wiped his hand down his face from brow to jaw to clear his thoughts and get rid of his sweat. It also hid him from view for a second while he composed himself.

The rest of the team seemed to have a more impressive recovery rate or maybe they hadn't put quite so much into the race but they were cavorting triumphantly, tossing their cox ceremonially into the water. Dan hoped the poor bugger didn't get Weil's disease as a result.

'Are you all right, Dan?'

Amy had followed him.

He turned. 'Of course. What isn't there to be "all right" about?'

She nodded. 'I know but you look done in.'

Dan nodded. 'I am. It's a killer. Thank God normal races are just two kilometres. I couldn't put my body through that on a regular basis.'

Amy patted his arm, still slick with sweat.

A member of the company that had sponsored the race began to herd the crew for the presentation, TV interviews, and all the hoop-la that went hand in hand with being the victors. The Cambridge crew would be interviewed as well of course but not to the same degree as the Dark Blues. Amy slipped away to join the rest of the happy and cheering Oxford supporters and Dan was swept off to the podium and the presentation. Finally, the shenanigans were over. Their stroke and the Cambridge one had given television interviews, the coaches had done theirs, Oxford had popped champagne corks and sprayed anyone in range, the cup had been presented, kissed and held aloft, the crowds along the towpaths were dispersing, the event was over for another year.

It was only then that Dan was allowed to slip off to find some space of his own. In the relative privacy of the boat-house he slumped onto a bench that ran the length of the changing-room wall. He tried to analyse his feelings but was too tired even to do that. Of course he was happy but there was something deeper going on. Some feeling of satisfaction, of achievement of . . . no, he couldn't nail it. But whatever it was he enjoyed savouring it.

'Dan?'

It was Chuck. The feeling evaporated. What now? 'Yes, Chuck?'

'Well done, great effort. The whole team was amazing.'

'Thanks.'

'Can I have a word?' Without waiting for an answer Chuck sat down on the bench next to Dan.

'Sure.' Dan nodded.

'About next year . . .'

Row in the Boat Race again? Chuck had to be mad. 'No. No way.'

'Yup – and I remember one Steve Redgrave saying something similar after the Olympics in Atlanta.'

'Yeah, but I mean it.'

'So did he – then.'

Dan sighed. 'Anyway, I doubt if I'm going to go on to do a master's so as I'll be leaving St George's in the summer, it's academic. And you obviously don't want to chat about Sir Steve, so what is it?'

'No, I thought I'd chat to you about a possible future rowing legend.'

'Yeah, who?'

Chuck looked him in the eye. 'You. Well, you and Rollo actually. Nathan Bedgrove wants you two to trial for the British team.'

Dan felt a moment of bewilderment. Him? In the British squad? 'No. no way.' It wasn't that he didn't want the opportunity. He was just utterly stunned that it looked as if it was finally coming his way.

Chuck stood over him. 'You'd better believe it. He says he'll come and drag you there himself if you two don't show up voluntarily.'

Dan shook his head. 'No, still doesn't sound right.'

'Dan, I don't fuck about on matters like this. And this is only a trial. I know anyone can enter for it, but for the national coach to say he want you there in person . . .' Chuck shook his head, hardly believing the news himself. 'And he doesn't say that to many rowers, either. Dan, this is serious shit. You've got about six months to prepare and there's no guarantee you'll make the grade – or Rollo, for that matter – but he's been watching your training, and thinks you have potential, *real* potential.'

Dan blew out his cheeks and exhaled slowly. Shit, this had been a day and a half. 'Me and Rollo?'

'So you and Rollo need to row in as many races and regattas as you can until October. I'll make sure the entry fees get picked up so you needn't worry about those. The coach thinks you two are made for each other; let's prove him right.'

Which wasn't what Dan wanted to hear. But still the news wasn't all bad. He began sorting out his kit, pulling on tracksuit bottoms, changing out of his sweat-damp vest for something clean and dry when Rollo appeared.

'So the day's just got better and better,' he said, throwing his own sports bag on the bench.

'Apparently so. Not that I'm banking on success at the trials.'

Rollo sneered. 'You better had. They'll probably have us earmarked for the double sculls so we sink or swim together, remember. So we'd better get out on the river again. Starting again on Monday.'

The prospect of spending hours on the Isis with Rollo did not appeal. Although if he made the squad, rowing with Rollo would be worth it.

16

Amy stood at the top of the stairs and surveyed the scene. The bar at the St George's Boat Club was rocking. Having produced the largest contingent for the eight, plus the assistant coach, the post-race party was being held there. Amy had never seen the bar so packed as all the crew, their partners, supporters, parents, well-wishers and general hangers-on wanted to toast the victors. The noise was headache-inducing as the sound-system blared upbeat, happy music and the crowd raised their voices more and more to be heard over the racket. The place was awash with drink, goodwill and quite a lot of testosterone. The winning eight were out from under the cosh, they'd won, they were virtual gods as far as the Dark Blue supporters' club was concerned, they could let rip and get hammered and not a single person would object tonight.

How the hell, Amy thought, was she going to be able to push her way through the crowd and hook up with Dan? She put her left shoulder down and, like a rugger Blue determined to score a try at Twickenham, she began heading through the bar.

250

'Amy, Amy! Over here.'

That was Maddy's voice she could hear over the racket. She jumped up and down, trying to see over the shoulders of the people all around her. Sometimes, being five foot three in a club where most of the members were giants was a real disadvantage. She headed towards where she thought Maddy was until an arm snaked around her waist and stopped her in her tracks.

'Little Amy,' said Rollo.

Just what she didn't need. 'Hi, Rollo, well done on the victory.'

'Don't I get a congratulatory kiss?'

Oh, what the heck. She stood on tiptoe and planted a smacker on his cheek and reeled from the smell of alcohol. Just how much had he sunk already? Pints and pints and possibly some shots, if she were any judge.

'Call that a kiss?' said Rollo. His grip around her waist tightened as he lifted her bodily off the floor and kissed her hard on the mouth. She felt his tongue trying to prise her lips apart but she clenched her teeth so hard she thought her molars might shatter. He dropped her back onto the floor.

'A bit late to get all frigid, isn't it?'

'I'm not frigid, I just don't like being groped by a drunk,' said Amy. She pulled Rollo's arm off her waist like she was removing an unwelcome octopus and smoothed down her rumpled shirt.

'You still owe me, Jones,' said Rollo with a hint of menace. 'Remember.'

'Yeah? Well, you can whistle.' She pushed through the

251

crowd as hard as she could to get away from him. Bloody man.

She finally found Maddy in a corner with Dan and Seb. 'Hiya,' said Amy. 'How are you feeling now? Recovered?'

'I seriously don't think I've ever felt this knackered,' said Seb. He yawned as if to prove his point and leaned against the wall. 'Don't suppose this is helping much either.' He waved his pint of lager around.

'Knackered?' said Dan. 'Knackered! What on earth have you got to feel knackered about? You weren't even rowing.'

'Hey, the high-grade support you were getting from me and Angus doesn't come without cost, you know. All that rushing around sorting out your kit, all the shouting and hollering, the stress, making sure the girls were looked after . . .' He gave Maddy a squeeze.

Dan yawned too. 'On the other hand, I have a proper excuse to want an early night.' He looked at Amy as he said this. Her insides flipped.

'Hmm,' she said casually. 'I expect you do. Shall we go? I mean is there anything to stop us slipping away?'

'Nothing at all, and anyway, even if there was, I'd rather be with you.'

'Then fuck off,' said Seb, evenly. 'You're only cluttering the place up.'

Dan and Amy didn't need telling twice.

Tanya was annoyed. Rollo seemed hell-bent on getting pissed and he certainly wasn't going to be in any sort of position to give her a celebratory shag tonight. Dan was making sheep's eyes at Amy, and unless she picked up

252

Maddy and chucked her in the river – which was an option – there was no way she'd be able to get her hands on Seb. Which was a bummer as Seb had been so sensational. What on earth would a little mouse like Maddy want with a cock like Seb's? Tanya sighed. Really, life could be so unfair.

Her gaze moved around the room, searching for someone who might be able to satisfy her tonight. But everyone seemed to be in a couple and those who weren't were alone for very good reason. Ugh, no! she thought as she looked at some of the singles. And then she saw Chuck. Hmmm, there's a possibility. And no Hannah clinging onto him like she'd done ever since the ball. Just because Chuck had taken pity on her that once, she now kept hanging about him like some sort of stalker. Except not tonight, thought Tanya, as she turned stalker herself and began tracking her quarry.

'Hi, Chuck,' she said as she got close enough to him to be heard. She put her hand on his arm. 'You must be so thrilled with the result.' She gazed at him, knowing how her full-on stare brought most men to heel. 'And you really ought to take some of the credit. Let me buy you a drink.'

'Honest, Tan, if I took a drink off of everyone who's offered me one tonight I'd be as drunk as a skunk.'

'That's a shame, Chuck, I was really hoping to be able to do something for you.' She gave him a slow, lewd wink.

Chuck's eyes widened fractionally.

'Anything,' breathed Tanya. 'I mean, what's to stop us. We're both single and unattached.'

'Rollo?'

Tanya looked across the room and Chuck followed her gaze. Rollo was almost bouncing off the walls, his eyes unfocused and his gait staggering.

'I see your point,' said Chuck.

'And I wouldn't mind seeing yours.' Tanya slid her hand down to Chuck's groin.

'Look,' he said, loosening the neck of his polo shirt, 'I can't go just yet. Give me another thirty and then I'm all yours.'

'That'd better be a promise.' She gave his crotch a gentle squeeze. 'I'll come and find you. Don't disappear.'

She swanned off, happy that she'd managed to pull.

Rollo knew he was pissed, but hey, why shouldn't a guy celebrate, and anyway, he was only a tiddly bit tiddly. And all he needed now to complete the evening was a bloody good shag and he knew just the girl for that. He wove through the packed bar in search of Tanya. There she was. He grabbed her shoulder and spun her round to face him, not caring that he was interrupting a conversation, not caring that he'd sent half her drink slopping over the edge of her glass.

'You're drunk,' she snapped at him.

Jeez what had got to her? 'And why shouldn't I be? Gorra lot to celebrate,' he slurred.

'Well, go and get more pissed then, but don't do it round me.'

'Come on, Tans, don't be like that.' He stroked her arm.

'And you can stop pawing at me. I'm not a dog.'

For fuck's sake! 'No, you're a bitch.'

Tanya shook her head. 'Don't try and be funny Rollo, it just makes you look pathetic. Now go away and sober up and we can talk in the morning.'

'But I want to talk now. Actually I want to do more than talk.' Surely she knew what he wanted. And how could she refuse him? He'd won the bloody Boat Race, hadn't he? How many girls got to shag someone who'd done that?

'Not tonight.'

'Aw, come on, Tanya.'

'What bit of "no" don't you understand? Go and find someone else to pester. How about little Amy?' she sneered.

Now that's an idea, thought Rollo, the drink having erased the memory of her previous rebuff. He swayed around the bar, trying to find her until Stevie told him that she'd seen Amy grab her coat and leave some fifteen minutes earlier.

So the little minx had gone home had she? Better and better. The walk to St Clem's would sober him up nicely and then Amy's just deserts could be served up any way she liked them.

Swaying and cannoning off walls, doorjambs and the banisters, Rollo left the boathouse and made his way to Amy's.

Maddy gazed at Seb. 'Fancy going on somewhere?' she asked innocently.

'Where have you got in mind?' He yawned prodigiously again.

'My room,' said Maddy. She was emboldened by drink but she'd still just managed to astound herself with her brazenness.

'Oh?'

She nodded. 'Why not?'

'Okay.' Seb waggled his eyebrows at her. 'Sounds like a perfect idea.'

Maddy's heart thundered. She felt deliriously happy. She'd done it, she'd pulled Seb, they were both almost sober, Tanya was nowhere in sight and this was her moment.

'I'll just get my coat,' she told him. 'I'll be back in a sec.'

Maddy floated off to the cloakroom where she'd dumped her thick winter jacket. And while she was in the ladies' she might as well have a pee; she'd only want one on the walk back to college otherwise. High on love and happiness she popped into a cubicle, dropped her trousers and knicks and sat down.

Noooo! No, no, fucking no! She'd come on. Shit. She almost sobbed in frustration. Not tonight. Why? Why her? What had she done that was so wrong to deserve this?

She peed and tidied herself up as best she could, bought a Tampax from the machine and returned to Seb. Maybe some girls, and some blokes, could carry on regardless but she couldn't, not with Seb on their first time.

'Ready?' he said.

Maddy swallowed, misery and embarrassment fighting to be her premier emotion. 'Actually, Seb, could you just walk me back? I'm sorry but I suddenly don't feel very well.'

256

'Oh, Maddy, I'm sorry. Can I get you something? Should we call a cab?'

She wished he'd stop being so concerned and such a gentleman. She brushed away a tear.

'You really aren't well, are you? Come on, I'll get you back and tuck you up.'

'No, Seb. Just get me back, please.'

Maddy wondered if he could hear her heart splintering into a thousand pieces.

Amy and Dan held hands like a pair of secondary school kids and they strolled up the High towards St Clem's.

'I am so thrilled for you, Dan, you have no idea.'

Dan stopped and gazed down at Amy. 'Are you? Because you were an inspiration to me. I wanted to prove to you that I can row – really row.'

'But I know that, I didn't need any more proof. I have such faith in you, Dan.'

'Have you?'

'You know I have.'

'Honestly, Ames, when you're around I feel like I can achieve anything.'

'Really?' She felt a glow build in her with the knowledge that she really meant something to him.

Dan nodded. 'Really.' He kissed her nose then said, 'I still can't believe we did it,' said Dan.

'Well, you should. And by a lot,' she replied. 'You beat them by miles.'

'Do you think . . . ?'

'Do I think what?'

'First the Boat Race and then the national coach telling

me he wants to see me at the national trials . . . you don't think my dream of rowing at the Olympics might be just a step or two closer?'

'The national coach?! You didn't tell me that. When did this happen?'

Dan related what Chuck had told him at the boathouse after the race.

'But that's just wonderful.' Amy stopped walking and gazed up at him. 'I am so thrilled for you. You must be over the moon.'

'I suppose I am. It just all seems a bit surreal.'

Amy ferreted in her bag and pulled out a couple of notes. 'Take this and get a nice bottle of chilled fizz.'

'No . . .'

'Dan, I insist. Really. There's an offie on the Cowley Road, about two minutes from my flat. I'll leave the door on the latch for you and go and find some glasses.'

'Are you sure?'

'Yes. But it's on the understanding I get a very good look at your medal when you've won it. Now quit wasting time. Scram.'

Dan peeled away and Amy skipped over the Magdalene Bridge and to her home. She dropped the snib on the front door then ran up the three flights. She gave her flat a cursory look round. It'd do – except . . . She dragged a clean sheet and duvet cover out from a drawer and quickly changed the bed linen, then she dashed into the bathroom, cleaned her teeth, pulled a brush through her hair, slicked on a bit more mascara and lip gloss and surveyed the result. Like her flat, it'd do.

She'd just fished a pair of half-decent glasses out of a kitchen cupboard when she heard feet pounding up the stairs. She'd left her door on the latch too, so Dan could let himself in.

'I hope this is okay,' he said brandishing a bottle of Moët and pushing the door shut behind him.

'And you think I'm a connoisseur? It's champers, it's cold, it'll be perfect.'

Dan peeled off the foil and the cage and then twisted off the cork. It made a quiet hiss and no more.

'Oh,' said Amy, slightly disappointed that it hadn't made that celebratory pop.

'Sorry, but it is the proper way to do it.'

'Oh, well then, that's all right.'

'And it means you don't waste any,' added Dan as he started to pour. Neatly and economically he filled two glasses.

Amy raised her glass. 'To dreams and ambitions.'

Dan clinked his glass against hers. 'Dreams and ambitions.'

They both drank.

'Come on,' said Amy, 'let's take this to bed. It's been an age – months – since the last time.' She giggled in anticipation as she took his glass and put it on the bedside table next to hers.

'So we can make up for that tonight,' said Dan with a slow-burning smile, undoing the belt on his trousers.

'We so can,' said Amy, unbuttoning her top.

'And we've got all the time in the world.'

Amy whipped off her top and then stretched lan - guorously. 'What a prospect!'

259

Dan pulled his trousers off. Amy couldn't help but notice the bulge in his boxers. Her stomach clenched in divine anticipation. She pulled off her jeans, chucking them in a corner after she'd shoved her phone next to the glasses. Dan snuggled his phone next to hers and five seconds later, both naked, they dived beneath the covers.

They lay facing each other, side-by-side, gazing into each other's eyes, both thinking of what they could do to the other or for the other.

Dan's hand stole under the duvet and rubbed Amy's shoulder.

'Oh Amy,' he said. 'I can't believe how perfect today has been.'

'Me neither.'

'Come here,' said Dan.

Amy needed no further encouragement. She shuffled across the bed and snuggled up to Dan as close as she could. She could hear the slow rhythmic pumping of his heart as she rested her head on his chest while Dan kissed the top of her head. She sighed. This was bliss.

She put her arm over Dan's shoulder and began tracing circles on the smooth skin of his back while he in turn stroked her hair, then as one they turned their faces towards each other and they began to kiss. There was no hurry, no urgency, they could savour and revel in each other, enjoying the moments, the minutes, maybe even the hours. Slowly, gently, their kissing and caresses grew more passionate until neither of them could resist the other any longer.

With Amy on her back, Dan entered her as gently as he knew how, making the most of that ecstatic moment. In unison they moved together, gazing at each other, drawing pleasure from each other as their senses and emotions built.

But then a vague commotion on the ground floor couldn't be ignored as the racket crescendoed. The sound of footsteps pounding up the stairs made them both halt and stare at each other in bewilderment. The door was slammed open.

Dan and Amy flung themselves apart and sat bolt upright. Amy grabbed the duvet to cover herself.

'Rollo!' they said in unison.

Rollo leered drunkenly at them. 'What are you doing here, Dan? No, don't answer that, I think I can guess.' He laughed at his own wisecrack. 'And there was me thinking Amy'd left the door open for me.'

'What the hell are *you* doing here?' yelled Amy.

'Came to give you a good time. Budge over, Dan. My turn now.'

'You shit,' said Amy. 'You've no right.'

Rollo staggered across the floor and flopped into Amy's only armchair. 'Think I have every right. Remember that promise?'

'Shut up, Rollo,' she said.

But he ignored her. 'Enjoying yourself, Dan? She's good, isn't she? You know, I think women are a little bit like chilli peppers: the smaller they are the hotter they come. Tanya being an exception, of course. Waddya think Danny-boy?'

Dan, naked, climbed out of bed. 'I don't know what

your game is but you can just fuck off. Now.' His voice was low and menacing but Rollo was in a booze-filled bubble and oblivious.

'Oh? You don't want to share? I don't mind having sloppy seconds.'

'Shut up,' shouted Amy. 'Stop.'

'Or maybe you want to have a shower first, Amy. Remember the shower?' Rollo turned to Dan. 'She was especially hot in the shower.'

Amy felt as if she was in the middle of some ghastly nightmare where events were out of control, out of reach and escaping out of boxes with 'do not open' written all over them. 'Don't, Rollo. Please.'

Dan turned to her. 'You mean he isn't just boasting. You have . . . with him? I might have known. That bloody house-party.'

Amy knew her face was a dead give-away. She always had been a shit liar.

'You did! Amy.' He looked like a kicked kid – the sort on the NSPCC ads, the ones specifically designed to make viewers cry. Which was exactly what Amy felt like doing. His disappointment in her was tangible.

Amy, scared of what was about to happen, what she was about to lose, lashed out irrationally like a frightened, cornered animal. She turned on Dan and stood the argu-ment on its head. 'Don't blame me for this. If you hadn't left the doors on the latch, this would never have happened.'

'What? What the fuck has me not locking the doors tonight got to do with you shagging Rollo?'

'Because if you'd locked the doors, you'd have never have found out.'

'So that makes it okay, does it? You can shag Tom, Dick and Harry – and Rollo – as long as I don't know. And how many others, Amy?'

'None,' she screamed back at him. 'And anyway, you weren't just shagging Karen, I was told you were dating her. You lied to me, Dan.'

Beside them Rollo was watching the argument rock back and forth like a Wimbledon spectator.

'No, I didn't.'

'That's not what I heard.'

'Then you heard wrong.'

On cue, Dan's phone chirped. Amy picked it up and saw the name of the texter. Karen. She hit 'read'.

'"Finished work, fancy a celebratory shag?" Oh, no?' She threw the phone at Dan.

At least he had the good grace to blush when he'd read it.

'But I'd have said "no". I told you there was never anything between Karen and me.'

'Says you.'

'I don't lie, Amy.'

'Implying?'

'You didn't tell me about, Rollo,' he volleyed back.

'You didn't ask!' she shrieked.

'I shouldn't have to.' Dan shook his head and glared at her. 'You know, I think this was meant to happen. So that I see you for just what you are, Amy Jones.'

He grabbed his clothes and began getting back into them, not looking at Amy, just concentrating on getting dressed and out of her flat as fast as he could. Amy watched in silence, wanting to say something to rewind the last few minutes and knowing it was impossible.

'And don't ring me, Amy. It'll be a waste of your time,' said Dan coldly.

Without looking back or saying goodbye, he carefully and deliberately took the door off the latch and left.

'So where were we?' said Rollo.

Amy turned – she'd almost forgotten his presence. She wanted to cry; everything was ruined. Dan hated her, their perfect ending to a perfect day was in horrid, ugly, sharp slivers like a broken piece of glass and all she was left with was Rollo. Drunk and obnoxious.

'Fuck off, Rollo,' she said wearily.

'Aw, you don't mean that sweetie, do you?'

'I've never meant anything more seriously in my life.' She picked up her phone. 'If you don't go I swear I'm going to call the police and tell them I've got an intruder.'

'Come off it.'

'Just go, please.' She didn't need this, she just wanted to pull the covers over her head and cry and cry. But she wasn't going to give Rollo the satisfaction of knowing how much he'd screwed things up for her and Dan, how much he'd broken her heart.

'Come on, Amy, you know you want me really.' He got up from the chair and approached the bed.

Amy looked up at him, florid, swaying, sweating. Not now, not in a million years. Her weariness vanished. She could do self-pity later, this she had to deal with now. She reached out to the bedpost where her dressing gown was draped and pulled it round herself, tying the belt as tightly as she could before getting out of bed.

She stood as straight and tall as she could and stared

Rollo in the eye as she pushed up the sleeves of her gown. She had had enough.

'Right, where were we?' said Rollo, lurching towards her

'How dare you?' spluttered Amy, stepping back out of his reach and winding up against a wall. 'How dare you come in here and behave like this!'

'Behave like what?' Rollo looked genuinely at a loss.

'Like that. You had no right, absolutely *no right*,' yelled Amy, 'to talk to Dan like that. Or to let him know you and I had sex. It was unfair and uncalled for. It was . . . it was . . . ungentlemanly.'

'Oh, come off it. You're not seriously saying you'd prefer that oik's company to mine?'

'Yes. And frankly I'd prefer a barrel of maggots to your company right now.' She was panting and shaking with rage.

'Oi,' yelled a voice from downstairs, 'keep it down. Some of us are trying to sleep.' A door slammed shut.

Amy glowered at Rollo. 'Now look what you've done,' she hissed.

'God, you're so middle class. Who cares what the neighbours think?'

'I do. I have to live with these people.'

Rollo rolled his eyes. 'Anyway, it's your fault for shouting at me,' he said petulantly.

'It's your fault for barging in uninvited. And now you can barge out again. You're not welcome.'

'You don't mean that.'

Amy glared. 'Rollo, I am *not* going to have sex with you and if you try anything I'll have you for sexual assault.'

'You mean it, don't you?'

'Yes I do, Rollo.'

265

'You could at least give me a coffee first.'

'Why?'

'Because I'm pissed and it's a long walk back to my rooms.'

'That's your own fault for coming here.'

'Please, Ames. If I fell downstairs on my way out, you'd feel guilty.'

'I'd cheer,' she contradicted. But he did look very pissed and he was right: if she threw him out and he *did* do something stupid she'd blame herself for ever.

'Come on,' he pleaded, 'just a mug of instant and then I'll go.'

'One coffee and then you can fuck off.' She stamped into the kitchen and filled the kettle. She was still livid – incan-fucking-descent.

As she waited for the water to boil she chuntered under her breath about Rollo's inexcusable behaviour and how he'd wrecked her chances with Dan and . . . and . . . arrgghh, he was just the bloody limit. She blinked hot, insistent tears back. No, not in front of Rollo. Never.

The kettle clicked off and she spooned the granules into a mug and slopped the water in on top.

'Here you are,' she said stepping back into her bedsit, and then stopped in her tracks. Rollo was out for the count, lying right across her bed.

'Oh for fuck's sake,' she muttered. She went over and tried prodding and poking him, pinching and slapping but he was gone, unconscious, comatose.

Well, she wasn't going to play Florence Nightingale with him. She wasn't going to wake up every hour to make sure he hadn't rolled out of the recovery position like she had with Maddy. Sighing angrily she tipped the redundant coffee down the sink and put the washing-up bowl on the floor beside him. Sprawled sideways as he was, a very large man on her standard double bed, there wasn't even a corner for a kitten, let alone her.

Which left the floor or the armchair for herself. Just how much worse could the day get?

17

Amy was still livid the following day and she crashed around the flat, refusing to tiptoe in deference to the sleeping giant on the bed. It was gone ten o'clock when Rollo groaned and showed signs of life.

'Good, you're awake,' said Amy coldly, banging down a cup of tea on the table beside him. 'I've go things to do and places to be. I don't expect you to be here when I get back.'

'And good morning to you too,' said Rollo, looking hurt and hung-over in equal measure.

'I don't want to talk to you. Just drink your tea and sod off.'

'Please, Amy.'

'Rollo, I've nothing to say to you.' She slipped on her coat and picked up her bag. 'Just make sure you shut the doors properly behind you.'

She banged out of the flat leaving Rollo looking white, shaky and contrite.

At the Magdalene Bridge Amy turned into the botanic gardens. The glasshouses were guaranteed to be warm compared to the early spring chill and at this time of year she was pretty much certain of being able to find a solitary corner where she could sit and grieve for what might have been. Greta Garbo's desire to be alone was nothing in comparison to hers.

She wandered past the lawns and herbaceous borders and headed for the greenhouses. She picked one at random, not interested in what grew within it, and let herself in. A fug of lukewarm, humid air, like a poor quality steam room, enveloped her. To judge by the absolute silence, she was the only one in here. Finding a seat in the corner she sat down and curled her feet up on the bench beside her. Finally, alone, she could let her misery escape. If only . . . if only . . . if only . . . was the recurring mantra as the bitter tears of heart-break rolled down her cheeks. If only she hadn't gone to Rollo's, if only she hadn't let him seduce her, if only she hadn't believe what people had said about Dan and Karen, if only . . .

She was interrupted out of her wretchedness by the trilling of her phone. She took it out of her pocket. Ellie? Well, at least she'd be a sympathetic shoulder and she wouldn't know any of the sordid details about the house party.

'Hiya,' she said trying to disguise her misery with a faux upbeat tone.

'Hi, Ames. Guess what? I saw you yesterday.'

Amy's guilt-trip went into overdrive. God, what had she witnessed? 'Where?'

'On TV, silly, when Oxford won. There, on the slipway.'

'Oh, of course.' The relief made her feel wobbly.

269

'And I thought, bloody hell, how long is it since you and I have had a good old girly get-together? So how about it, Ames? How about you come to Reading or I come up to Oxford and we go out and catch up?'

It was the last thing she felt like right now but what else had she to do at weekends? She had already made her mind up that she was never going back to the boat club; she just couldn't face Dan or the gossip and the whispers. Dan wouldn't say anything, she was pretty sure of that. But Rollo? He'd blab it all over just as soon as he could, making a huge joke over barging in on her and poking fun of the row. No, too awful to contemplate.

'That's a wonderful idea,' she lied. 'God, it's been months.'

'Six, Amy, but who's counting? How are you placed? I mean, when's your next free weekend?'

'They're all free,'

'What about the boat club?'

'Oh,' she said lightly, 'their real physio is better and back to work and now the Boat Race is over . . . well, I'm surplus to requirements.' It was sort of true.

'Oh, of course,' said Ellie accepting the fib at face value. 'If you don't mind coming to a Head next weekend, how about it? It's only in London so we'd still have Friday evening and some of Saturday and if you don't have to be back till Sunday night . . . '

'Next weekend it is,' said Amy. 'I'll text you with my train times.' She felt the veneer of fake chirpiness start to buckle as a wave of unhappiness engulfed her again. 'Look, I'll ring you in the week Ellie, but I've got to go. Meeting someone. Bye.' She severed the connection and shut her eyes as a sob hiccuped and escaped, followed by another, then another . . .

'You all right, miss?' Amy looked up into the kind avuncular eyes of one of the gardeners. That simple, sympathetic question tipped her completely over the brink.

'No,' she bawled as she gave in to her emotions.

Bewildered, the gardener, more used to tending plants than people, sat beside her and patted her hand. 'There, there,' he said at a total loss at what else to offer.

All week Amy threw herself into her work and tried to blot out the awfulness of the weekend just gone. The other physios mentioned that they'd seen her on the TV and asked her about what it was like to be there when Oxford won and Amy was able to tell the truth and say it had been wonderful and no one noticed that she then clammed up and didn't say anything more. On the Wednesday, for only about the second time since she'd started work in the department, she asked if she could join the team in a post-work drink. On Wednesday nights (because on Thursday and Friday it was always rammed) her workmates always went to a relatively local pub for a drink or a bite or both. Previously, because Amy had wanted to get off to the boat club, she'd always cried off. Well, not any more.

The pub was pretty, by the river and surprisingly rural for a place so near Headington and, like most Oxford pubs, had loads of stills from the *Inspector Morse* and *Lewis* TV series on the walls, showing the stars drinking there.

As they waited for their drinks at the bar Amy looked at her co-workers, who were, almost without exception, twenty years or more her senior and worried about their teenaged kids or their aged parents or both. What did she have in common with any of them?

'What's up?' asked Suzanna, her team leader.

'Oh,' said Amy with an attempt at a smile. 'Nothing much.'

'So have you given up that rowing malarkey?'

'It's given me up, really. You know . . . the Boat Race is over . . . ' Would Suzanna know so little about rowing she'd accept that?

'Of course. Still, I expect you must be really glad to have all that extra free time. It must have been a tie.'

'Hmm,' said Amy non-committally, nursing her red wine. And what did she have to do with the free time? Monday evening had been a total bore so she'd filled it with the jobs she usually did on a Tuesday, which had left that evening such a complete blank she'd wound up in bed at nine thirty. She was twenty-two and going to bed at nine thirty! That couldn't be right.

The session dragged on interminably over the course of a couple of hours until everyone went off to cook for their partners or watch soaps or do some other mind-numbing activity that showed Amy her future like a magic mirror. As she dragged herself home on a bus along the Marston Road she made her mind up: she needed to move, to get away from Oxford and start again.

She stepped off the train at Reading station and made her way through the automatic barrier to the main concourse. Ellie was waiting for her, almost jumping with excitement. Despite the dull ache that had gripped her heart for nearly a week, she forced a smile and ran to meet her friend.

'Have you lost weight, Amy?' said Ellie accusingly when she released her from her grip.

Probably, as I haven't felt like eating since Sunday. 'Nah, you've just always had a lousy memory. Anyway, you can't talk.' Ellie looked even more lissom and athletic than ever. 'So, life is suiting you here?'

Ellie nodded and told her it was and they exchanged chit-chat as they walked to Ellie's tiny house that she had managed to buy with considerable help from her parents. It was, according to Ellie, quite a shabby little place but it was handy for the station and even handier for the river.

'So when I have to work in London, the commute is a doddle and when I want to go rowing, it's even easier.'

'How often do you work in London?' asked Amy.

'As little as possible. That development grant from GB Rowing has made such a difference,' responded Ellie. 'But I temp for a few companies to keep my hand in and so I can afford a few little treats. I cover sick leave, that sort of thing. And the sort of HR stuff I do pays quite well, which means I rarely need to do a full week, leaving lots of time for training. It's not perfect but it works until I hit the next level in rowing.'

'Which is?'

'Making the GB Rowing Team at the trials in October.'

'And then?'

'Rowing at Caversham all day every day, training

camps and kissing goodbye to sexual harassment complaints and unfair pay band claims and . . . well, all the HR crap I deal with now.'

They reached the end of Ellie's road and Amy saw two neat rows of Victorian terraced railway workers' cottages stretching away from them. 'These are sweet.'

'On the outside, yes, wait till you see the inside of mine.'

Ellie fished out her key and led Amy to a door with rather tired red paint. She let them in.

'Maria?' she yelled. No answer. 'Not home yet, good.'

'Good?'

'Not the easiest tenant and frankly, I'm glad she's going soon.'

'How soon?'

'Three months, and I can't wait.'

'Um, you got anyone lined up to take her place?' asked Amy innocently.

'Not yet, but I'm not worried. This close to the station and with the rent I'm asking, I can expect a queue around the block. Even if the paint is a bit shabby and the bathroom avocado green.'

That evening the girls went out into Reading centre to enjoy the scene there. Ellie didn't drink as she had the Head the next day but Amy more than made up for her.

Unsurprisingly, after her third red wine, her guard slipped and the story of her split with Dan poured out.

'It was so awful, Ellie.'

'I won't say "I told you so" but anything that involves Rollo is always a shagging disaster.'

274

Amy, raw and still mourning the end of her brief affair with Dan, glared at her. 'Are you trying to be funny?'

'Why, what have I said?'

'"*Shagging* disaster". Because it was.'

Ellie's lip twitched. 'Well, you've got to see the funny side . . .'

'No I haven't. There isn't one.'

'Sure?'

Amy folded her arms stubbornly and then caught sight of Ellie who was really struggling to stay under control. 'Well, maybe as shags went it was a disastrous one.'

'Told you,' said Ellie giggling.

Amy began to laugh too, but then the tears began to fall instead. 'Oh Ellie, I made such a mess of it. I rang Dan on the Monday after and he blanked my call. I tried texting him but he hasn't replied. He hates me.'

'Oh, babes. There's loads of other men out there.'

'But I don't want other men. I want Dan.'

'How do you feel this morning?' asked Ellie, putting her head round the sitting-room door where Amy was sleeping on the sofa-bed. 'Tea?' She proffered a steaming mug.

'Hi Ellie, and thanks,' Amy said as she took the tea. She felt better than she ought given she'd drunk a whole bottle of red on her own. 'I'm still upset about Dan. I honestly think we might have really had something going there.' She shrugged. 'And I was unreasonable, I see that now. But how can I make it up to him, if he won't talk to me?'

'Time's a healer.'

'Maybe.' Amy wasn't convinced as she sipped her tea.

Time hadn't done much in the healing department so far. 'What time do you have to be at your boat club?'

'Ten, then over to Hammersmith for the Head and back here for tea and buns. You can come along or go shopping in Reading.'

'I wouldn't mind coming.' Amy didn't fancy time alone to brood and besides, she missed hanging out with rowers.

'Sure. I'm certain we can find a space in the transport for a littl'un. There'll be a lot of hanging around, though,' said Ellie.

'I know how a Head works,' said Amy. 'I'll take something to read and a thermos. I'll be fine.'

'If you're sure.'

The journey to Hammersmith was straightforward and the scene was almost as manic as it had been for the Fours Head. Ellie's eight got busy sorting out and rigging their boat and then headed to the water to paddle to their allotted marshalling area. Amy stayed in the minibus with her thermos and the local paper she'd grabbed off the table before they'd left. She turned to the jobs pages. Maybe it was a bit early to be doing some serious job-hunting, but if her plan was going to come together – if she was going to take Maria's place as Ellie's tenant – she had to have a job. She could hardly approach Ellie with her idea if she didn't. She knew Ellie well enough to know she'd take Amy in even if she didn't have a job, but what if she couldn't get one? Ellie needed the rent to make the mortgage payments each month.

She read the pages from top to bottom, making notes of all the recruitment agency numbers but there didn't seem to be much for a junior health professional – or even any sort of junior professional. If she wanted to butter baps in Subway she was sorted but it wasn't really what she was after.

It was still too early to make her way to waterside to cheer the girls on so she poured herself a coffee from her thermos and turned to the front page of the *Reading Post*.

The lead story was all about the progress of Chazey Hall, a huge leisure, sport and country club that was nearing completion out near Caversham. Another bloody spa for rich old ladies who want some pampering, thought Amy dismissively but, having nothing better to occupy her, she read the story anyway. When she finished she folded the paper thoughtfully. The complex wasn't what she'd initially thought at all. What they were offering were intense one-to-one coaching sessions, sports facilities for out-of-season team training and various other activities – the rich old ladies weren't going to feel a bit at home there.

And . . . the sorts who *were* going to feel right at home there would probably need the services of a physio from time to time, and it was an easy commute from Ellie's.

Suddenly, Amy felt that the old saw about one door closing and another opening might have a grain of truth in it.

As she put the paper on the dashboard her phone rang.

'Hello, stranger,' said Chuck.

'Hiya.'

'You've deserted us. You haven't been around all week.'

'Hmmm,' said Amy non-committally.

'So what's the problem? You okay or is there something else going on?'

'It got complicated,' said Amy.

'So I hear.'

Amy's face flared. So he knew. She was glad Chuck couldn't see her. 'What did you hear?'

'Rollo, you, Dan.'

Amy couldn't bring herself to ask if he knew all the gory details or just the gist. 'It was a mess.'

'So you've bailed out.'

'Marcus is back, you don't really need me. Chuck, I won't beat about the bush, I need to move on. And I don't care what anyone says, my mind is made up.'

'I understand. But we'll miss you. Tanya's already bitching like a bear with a thorn up its ass that Rollo's seen off one of the best coxes she's ever known.'

'She'll find another cox.'

'Don't put yourself down, Amy, you're good.'

'Maybe. Chuck, I'll come clean with you. I'm already job-hunting for another post, somewhere away from Oxford. I would quite like to stay in the rowing scene but not the St George's one. I want to find another job, another club, start again.'

'I guess,' said Chuck. 'But in a little country like yours, you do know you'll keep running into the same old faces.'

'I know, but there's a difference between running into them now and again and seeing them half the week.'

'If you're determined to go I won't stop you but I'd sure like to take you out to dinner before you do disappear. To show there's no hard feelings – well, not on my part anyway.'

'I'd like that, Chuck.'

'Tonight?'

'I'm away with a friend tonight. A girlfriend,' she added hastily. 'You might even know of her. Ellie Mayhew?'

'I've heard the name. I gather she's got promise.'

'She's trialling in October.'

'So,' said Chuck, 'next Saturday then?'

'That'd be lovely.'

'I'll pick you up from yours around seven. I'd make it later but these early starts on the river are starting to kill me. Getting too old for this.'

'Never,' said Amy.

'See ya on Saturday, babe.'

'Bye, Chuck.'

Amy, feeling much happier because Chuck had that effect on her, disconnected the call, left the bus, and made her way slowly to the riverbank. She might as well soak up the atmosphere as sit on her own, but she barely registered anything as her head was filled with thoughts of how she could secure a job at the new sports centre and how she might persuade Ellie to take her on as a tenant.

18

Amy found dinner with Chuck pleasant and uncomplicated and it was nice, she thought, to go out with a man for once and for there to be nothing else but dinner and good conversation on the agenda. They met at a riverside pub and sat at a table by a French window that looked out across the patio and the river to the island in its middle where a couple of dejected peacocks walked around looking miserable in the light April drizzle.

'I feel like that peacock,' said Chuck, after the waitress had taken their order.

'Why? You getting dripped on or something?' said Amy, checking the ceiling.

'No. I just feel low. I'm going to miss you, kiddo, and that's the truth.'

'Just because I worked for free,' said Amy.

Chuck looked at her sternly. 'It wasn't just that. You were a hard worker and an even better cox.'

'You'll get over it.'

They paused while the bottle of wine Chuck had ordered was brought, opened, tasted and poured.

'Sure I will, but I'd rather not have to. You were ace at motivating Tanya's eight.'

'Tanya's got Hannah and I'm sure they'll be fine without me. Marcus is back and I'm only planning on moving to Reading. It's not like I'm emigrating.'

'So it's all fixed?'

Amy shook her head but told him about the two bits of jigsaw that had fallen so neatly into place the previous weekend. 'But I need to get that job.'

'Have you applied?'

'I have written to them with my CV and asked for the details. I've been promised an application form and I plan to ask you for a reference.'

'Of course. You can count on me. Do you think it'd help matters if I were to write on GB Rowing Team stationery?'

Amy looked doubtful. 'Well, I mean . . . what if they found out you were lying?'

'What? That I've been asked to work for them?'

'But you haven't . . .' Amy checked out Chuck's face. 'Have you?'

Chuck nodded. 'I got a call after the Boat Race. They want a sculling coach.'

'Really?' squealed Amy, launching herself across the table, almost sending two glasses and most of a bottle of wine flying as she gave him a smacking kiss. 'But Chuck, that's fantastic. I am *so* pleased for you.'

'I'm glad. To be honest *I'm* pleased for me. So, if your plans fall through, I wouldn't mind asking Ellie if she'll take me on as a lodger, because I'll be spending a lot of time in Caversham myself.'

'Bugger off,' said Amy good-naturedly. 'Find your own digs.'

Amy duly sent her application off to the sports centre, references were requested and glowing ones sent back – if Chuck and Suzanna were to be believed – and, as April segued into May, Amy asked Ellie if she'd hold off looking for a new tenant as she might need Maria's room. Ellie was delighted and told her she'd cross fingers and light candles to help bring luck.

'Although you don't need it. You ought to be a shoo-in for that job. They're mad if they don't take you.'

Amy carried on at work, keeping her own fingers crossed, and noticing that she'd stopped thinking about Dan *every* free minute and had reduced it to *every other* free minute. And she could do that, she also noticed, without wanting to cry inconsolably, although she did have a monumental wobble the day she saw Dan on the far side of Broad Street and she felt as if someone was salami-slicing her heart but without the benefit of an anaesthetic. She'd cried all the way home, not caring about the odd looks from passers-by.

By mid-May Amy had given up on the job. The bastards didn't even have the courtesy to tell her they'd turned her down flat, she thought, as she mooched around her immaculate bedsit – well, what else did she have to do these days with her spare time but tidy it? As it was the weekend she was considering the possibility of walking up the High and doing a spot of retail therapy instead and wishing she hadn't made such a fuck-up of things and that she could go for a drink at the boat club like old times and hang out for a few hours with the gang.

Her phone rang. Maddy! Had she been reading her mind?

'Hello, what have you been up to? I haven't heard from you for an age. How's Seb?' She got a wail as an answer. 'Oh, Maddy, what's gone wrong now?'

She heard a snuffle down the phone then a sigh like a tornado whistled in her ear. 'It's a long story. Don't suppose you're free for a coffee?'

'Mads, of course I am. Can't think of anything better to do. I'm at a complete loose end.'

'Honest?'

'Honest.'

Twenty minutes later she was in a café near The Turl, a cappuccino and a slice of cake in front of her waiting for her friend. Then Dan walked in. Amy froze. If she'd had a paper with her she'd have hidden behind it, but as it was, she was a rabbit in the middle of the five-lane section of the M25 and a pair of lights on full beam was heading straight for her.

Dan didn't see her as he perused the chalkboard menus, nor as he ordered and paid for a Coke and a tuna roll. It was only when he turned back with his loaded tray and began to look for a seat that he did. Their eyes locked. Amy was about to throw herself across the café at him and try to explain, apologise, beg forgiveness, ask what it would take to make it up to him, but before she could push her chair back, without a trace of emotion he dumped his meal and walked out.

Amy was still trying to dry her tears when Maddy walked in a couple of minutes later.

'I hope that had nothing to do with you,' Amy rounded on her before she'd even sat down.

'What? What have I done?' Maddy was such a picture of uncomprehending, wide-eyed innocence that Amy knew for certain she hadn't engineered that encounter.

'Sorry, Mads,' she apologised, blowing her nose. 'Get your coffee and I'll explain.'

Two minutes later, with Maddy getting around the outside of a latte, Amy told her what had just happened.

'Oh Amy, poor you. You and I are such hopeless cases.'

'So what's happened with Seb?'

Amy thought Maddy was going to cry too, and to judge by the look on the barista's face, so did she.

Maddy leaned forward. 'Amy,' she said with a sniffle, 'it was awful. It was beyond embarrassing.'

'What was?'

'The night after the Boat Race.'

Amy was agog. 'But that was weeks back.'

'I know, but honestly it was so awful I'm not sure I can talk about it even now.'

'Oh Maddy, what on earth could have been that bad? You didn't get pissed again, did you?'

'No. It was worse.'

'Worse? Maddy, you've got to tell me about it now. Besides I might be able to help.'

'You can't, it's too late now,' but Maddy lowered her voice and relayed the whole story about her period choosing exactly the wrong moment to make an appearance. 'And when I got to the door of my room I couldn't even invite him in for a coffee. I just had to pretend I was really poorly and say goodnight. Talk about wasted opportunity. Shagging Seb just isn't meant to happen, Ames. The fates have got it in for me.'

'Oh, Maddy. Why don't you just keep taking the pill? It stops all that rubbish in its tracks.'

'But you can't,' said Maddy, horrified.

'Not for ever, but now and again. When you think you're in with a shot.'

'Really?'

Amy nodded. 'I'm sure a doctor would probably tell you not to but now and again can't do much harm. Promise me, next time you've got a hot date with Seb lined up just keep popping the tablets till you score. Play the fates at their own game and make your own luck. So what's happening now?'

Maddy's face fell again. 'He's got his finals in a matter of weeks so his social life is on complete hold.'

'And his sex life too, I suppose.'

Maddy nodded.

'Didn't you see him over Easter?'

Maddy shook her head. 'He had to go on exercise with his regiment. They're going to Afghanistan so it's essen-tial he does the training. But it also meant he couldn't revise then so he's under even more pressure. Honestly, Amy, he's so stressed out and the last thing I want to do is be a distraction.'

'As long as Tanya isn't one either,' Amy said, drily.

'I don't think so. Last I heard she had a fling with Chuck – at least that's the rumour down at the boat club.'

Amy wondered why that news hurt too. She told herself she was being ridiculous; they were only friends, after all.

The dreary, overcast and blustery early May weather suited her mood. But then, suddenly and unexpectedly, the sun came out and the day was further improved by Amy receiving a call asking her to attend an interview for the job at the sports complex the following day. Maybe life wasn't completely shit after all. And it improved still further the week after when she was told she'd been successful.

She wasn't sure whether to hand her notice in at the JR first or ring Ellie to tell her she had a new tenant. She chose Ellie.

'Fan-bloody-tastic,' crowed Ellie. 'I am so thrilled. When are you planning on moving in?'

'Beginning of June. Is that okay? And I want a proper contract and to pay a proper deposit. I know we're mates but the easiest way for friends to fall out is over money. If we make this all legal and proper we might stay that way.' From the way Ellie agreed, Amy reckoned she'd been hoping she'd say that.

Amy pulled on the handbrake of the van she'd rented to move her kit down to Reading and opened the door. She stretched as she got out and then rang Ellie's doorbell. Ellie was thrilled to see her friend and after hugs, a cup of tea and some excellent teamwork to unload Amy's

286

boxes, Ellie looked at her watch and suggested Amy might like a trip to the boat club.

'What, now?'

'Why not?'

'Because I haven't unpacked, because I need to drop off the van at the rental company.'

'So? That can wait. I want you to meet the girls.'

'But I have, remember? The Hammersmith Head?'

'Yeah, but . . . ' Ellie looked shifty.

'"Yeah, but" what?'

'Yeah but we've got a training session in about an hour. We were wondering if you'd cox.'

'Today?'

Ellie shrugged. 'You've only got to sit there and watch us working. You'll have plenty of energy left for dealing with your van and unpacking.'

It was a nice day, the sun was out and it would be grand to get back onto the water. What the heck? Amy rolled her eyes. 'I suppose.'

'Thanks, Amy, the girls'll be chuffed. Honest.'

At least Ellie hadn't lied about how close the house was to the river and the club. It was just a hop, skip and a jump. Which gave her just enough time to quiz Ellie about why they needed her to cox so soon after her arrival.

Ellie looked shifty again.

Amy stopped in her tracks. 'Ellie Mayhew. If you don't come clean with me, so help me, I'm going right back home.'

'The truth is I've told the girls how good you are and they want to see for themselves. So we've laid on this extra session and haven't told Kimberly.' Ellie started walking again and Amy kept pace with her as she remembered from the Hammersmith Head that Kim was their cox.

'So you want me to go behind her back and try and steal her place.'

'It's not like that.'

'It bloody looks like that from where I am.'

'But Ames, it's Henley soon and we so want to do well. If you cox us . . . well, we're in with a better chance than we've got right now.

'And what does Kimberly have to say about it?'

'Well . . . '

'*Well* you haven't told her?'

'Something like that. But she knows she's rubbish.'

Amy rolled her eyes. 'Really?'

'She ought to,' said Ellie defiantly.

'That isn't the point and you know it.'

Ellie looked downcast. 'But I promised them. And you're here now,' she wheedled.

And they were. There was the clubhouse with the river rolling past in front of it.

She remembered the faces of Ellie's crew but not all the names except for Sian, the stroke, who told her how thrilled they all were that she had decided to give them a shot. Amy didn't enlighten her that she'd been conned.

The boat was already rigged and ready by the water and in less time than it took to adjust her head-mike, Amy found herself in the boat and plugged into the cox-box.

The crew paddled under the Caversham Bridge,

heading downstream towards Slough and Windsor, while Amy tried to commit the crew's names to memory and Sian told her about some of their recent races.

'I just know we're capable of doing better,' she said. 'To be honest, I think Kimberly's heart isn't quite in it. Whether she wants to row herself and resents time spent coxing or whether she's got trouble with her man or whether she just doesn't care, I don't know but there's no fire there. Nothing, not a spark.' Sian looked over her shoulder at Ellie. 'Isn't that right?'

Ellie peered around the back of Sian's head. 'Not a sausage. Honestly, Amy, she just goes through the motions. Compared to how you were when you were coxing me at Bath it's like being coxed by a stick of celery.'

Amy smiled. 'I just hope you haven't built me up too much. I don't want to be a crashing disappointment.'

'You're going to have to go some way to do that,' said Ellie.

Amy got the boat turned and, using the same techniques as she had with Tanya's crew, she sent them back upstream at a pretty punishing rate.

'Come on,' she encouraged as they began to flag. 'Think about your legs. And drive . . . drive . . . . drive. Keep those backs straight. Watch your technique. Twenty strokes till the last piece. Nineteen . . . eighteen . . . seventeen . . . keep it long . . . fifteen . . . ' She checked the cox-box. Not bad. Not record-breaking, but decent enough. As they flew past the one-and-a-half-kilometre point she upped the rate fractionally and instantly the technique began to suffer. She made them focus but some of the crew were obviously too tired. Trying to force the pace was having the same effect as too much throttle in a car: it was the equivalent of wheel-spin but on water. Sian and Ellie were going to be held back by some of this lot unless they could be brought up to standard. That was a coaching problem, not a coxing one, but she couldn't drive the eight as hard as she wanted till it was sorted.

The girls in the third and fifth seats – Caroline and Dannii – were in an especially bad way when they got back to the boathouse and looked ready to pass out or throw up, but Sian was ecstatic.

'Blimey, Amy, Ellie didn't lie. You're a wonder.'

Amy shrugged, self-deprecatingly. 'Just glad to be of help. But I need the day job to live, so I haven't got a clue how much time I'll be able to spend down here.'

'As soon as you know, let us know too, please. If you're happy to help down here then I'm sure we can sort something out.'

'I'll do my best.'

The next day Amy started work at Chazey Hall, the swanky new sports complex on the edge of Caversham. As yet it wasn't open for punters and the aim of the next couple of weeks was for all the workers to become familiar with each other, the site, with the ethos of the place and to act as guinea pigs, trying out all the facilities from the steam rooms to the dining room.

It was vast, Amy discovered. She'd seen a bit of it when she'd attended her interview but being taken around the whole estate was quite mind-boggling. It was designed to offer sports facilities for elite sportspeople who wanted a change of scenery but no break from their training or their lifestyle; and those with too much money and ridiculous amounts of ambition who wanted a magic wand waved over their rubbish tennis or golf skills. Amy and the other two physios who were employed there were to make sure the punters were kept mobile and as active as possible during their stay. With the sort of money they were going to be charged they expected nothing less.

Over the next few days Amy began to bond with Mike and Alastair, the other two physios in the team. With the Hall offering year-round sporting activity from six in the morning to ten at night, they were expected to work shifts so that one of them was always on duty. As long as the shifts were covered and the hours worked by the team were distributed evenly over the month, how it was sorted was their business. Suddenly it seemed to Amy that finding time off to cox might be quite easy. Life seemed to be looking up. Or it *would* be if Dan was still a part of her life. The hurt was still raw.

The recession didn't seem to be affecting the rich and the super-rich, and punters in droves rolled up the gravelled drive in their Rollers and luxury cars as soon as the gates opened in mid-June. The physiotherapy unit was a quantum leap from her little cubbyhole at St George's Boat Club and was large, plush and with state-of-the-art equipment but unlike at St George's where, if she wasn't busy there was always someone to chat to, here quite a lot of her time was spent in mind-numbing boredom. Of course, she did get clients who needed her ministrations, some more demanding than others, and she very quickly discovered that often their level of gratitude was in inverse proportion to their actual sporting prowess. One customer, staying for a week and who pulled his hamstring on day one, was perfectly sweet and was, she discovered later, a former member of the European Ryder Cup team. Yet she subsequently found that another client who was rude, boorish and utterly ungrateful had booked himself in for a week to learn tennis because he wanted to captain the village tennis club and had been horrified to discover that the captain was chosen on ability. He'd obviously thought he could buy the honour – and was now hoping to buy ability instead. As if.

Overall though, Amy loved her job, and with Mike and Alastair very happy to divvy up shifts to accommodate her wish to spend time on the river, it could hardly have suited her better.

'So,' she asked Sian when she was down at the club the week before Henley, 'how's the training going? How are Dannii and Caroline doing?'

'They've improved. Honestly. We've had them on the ergos every day and out on the river as often as has been humanly possible. Ellie's taken out Dannii and I've taken out Caroline and the results are really starting to show.'

'But Henley is almost upon us,' said Amy doubtfully.

'They'll have had seriously intensive training for the best part of a month by the time we get there and I'm not asking to win it. I just don't want us to get knocked out in the first round,' said Sian. 'Honestly, that's all I ask.'

'So who are you drawn against?'

Sian pursed her lips. 'You're not going to like this.'

'Let me guess . . . St George's.'

PART II

19

Henley-on-Thames
July 2011

The cry of 'Amy' at around one hundred decibels and at a pitch that was only marginally lower than an ultra-sonic dog whistle, cut across the polite chit-chat of those queuing to enter the Stewards' Enclosure and caused a number of heads to turn. Those who did look at the source were amused to see a pretty girl in a floral dress racing across the grass to greet another equally pretty girl in a tracksuit.

'Maddy!' the tracksuit-wearer shrieked back and then they met and hugged and jumped up and down and their obvious joy at seeing each other made the onlookers smile.

'Oh my God, oh my God,' screamed Maddy. 'I haven't seen you for weeks and weeks! How are you? You look amazing? Tanned and thinner and everything.'

'It's so good to see you too.' Their mutual excitement was palpable.

'So how's Reading? How's the new job, how are all those Premiership footballers you get to massage?'

'I wish! There *are* some but they know how to warm up and warm down and look after their bodies. It's the fat, florid stockbrokers I mostly get to see.' She grimaced. 'And how are you?'

'Still hankering after Seb, still mostly broke, still rowing badly . . . same old, same old.'

'So when are you going to come and see me? My mate Ellie's got a sofa-bed, we can put you up.'

'Maybe soon.'

'Oh, Mads, do make the effort. I'd come to you but what with the shift work and the rowing it's really tricky for me to get a whole weekend free. Besides, you've not checked out the blokes that Reading has got to offer. You may find someone to take the place of the sainted Seb.'

'Don't be silly, no one could take over from him.'

'And dare I ask . . . have you?'

Maddy sighed and shook her head.

'Maddy?!'

'As soon as he'd done his finals he was whizzed out to his regiment. "Pre-op training," he said. He'd have taken me out to dinner, he said, but he had to go and say goodbye to his folks and with only two days' notice to move there just wasn't time. But I text him and write him letters every day.'

Hardly the same, thought Amy. 'So, you're here to support St George's.'

Maddy nodded. 'And you're coxing the opposition. You know, Tanya has been ranting about that. Spitting feathers doesn't come close. And she's blaming Rollo and Dan for it. I don't suppose Dan gives a flying fuck but I've heard on the grapevine that Rollo isn't getting his oats.'

Amy giggled. 'That won't be going down well. But knowing Rollo he'll be getting it elsewhere.'

'I don't know about that. He and Tanya are living together now. They've got a cottage on the Thames near Wallingford.'

'Lucky old them.' Amy glanced at her watch. 'Look, I've got forty minutes till I need to be ready. Let's find a cold drink and you can fill me in on all the goss.'

Amy bought Maddy a spritzer and herself a Diet Coke and then they sat on the grass near the river and Maddy brought her up to date.

'Rollo hasn't bothered with a job and there's talk at the college that Tanya seems to have decided rowing is more important than her degree and is in danger of being sent down. But I suppose that's okay when you've got a trust fund to fall back on. I hear they're both rowing as much as they can, hoping for selection at the trials.'

'And Angus?'

'He and Susie are living in London now. She's working for some property developer and he's got a placement as a workie on the *Evening Herald*. I hear Susie's supporting him till he gets his break. According to Susie, he's going to be the next Jeremy Paxman. Meantime, he's the *Herald*'s rowing correspondent and is occasionally allowed to file stories on greyhound racing. I tell you, his life is beyond glamorous.'

Amy smiled. 'And Dan?' She hoped she sounded casual but she couldn't suppress the catch in her voice as she said his name out loud.

Either Maddy was tactful or it had passed her by as she gave no clue that she'd heard it when she said, 'Dan's fine, as far as I know. He's got a job at a public school, not a million miles from here, as an assistant housemaster and rowing coach. Starts in September.'

'I bet he'll be good at both. And I bet he'll be really tough on the bullies.'

Maddy nodded. 'He and Rollo are both rowing here, you know that, don't you?'

Amy did. She'd been keeping a weather eye out for them since she'd arrived that morning. Not because she wanted to see them but because she didn't.

'So, you and Dan . . .?' asked Maddy.

Amy shook her head. 'Nothing. I can't bear the idea of ringing him because when he blanks me it's too painful. He doesn't appear to do anything on Facebook; he hasn't updated his page for months. And if I never see Rollo again in my life I'll be perfectly content.'

'I feel a bit like that about Tanya. Especially after that house party. But as it was my fault too . . .' Maddy sighed. 'I just wish I didn't get the feeling that she'll try and muscle in on me and Seb if she ever gets the chance again.'

'You think?'

Maddy nodded. 'She's as good as told me; said he was the best fuck she'd ever had.'

Amy's eyes widened. 'Then he must be fan-bloody-tastic. She's got to be judging out of a field of *thousands*!'

Maddy laughed. 'Probably. Oh, it is good to see you, Ames, you cheer me up no end.'

Amy drained her Coke and checked her watch again. A shadow fell across her wrist and she automatically glanced up.

'Chuck!' She jumped to her feet, sending in her Coke can flying and leapt into his arms.

On the river, only yards away from her, Dan and Rollo sculled past quietly on their way to the start and Dan, trying hard not to look, wondered when he'd get over her.

'Danny-boy, was that our little Amy?' said Rollo over his shoulder as they headed towards Temple Island and the start of their race.

'Who, where?' said Dan pretending indifference and thankful Rollo couldn't see his face.

'On the riverbank, being snogged by Chuck. Ooh, do I see tongues?'

Dan nearly glanced over to the bank but couldn't bring himself to. It was bad enough having Rollo's running commentary but he didn't want to witness it first hand.

'Given that they're both here,' he said carefully, 'it's quite likely they've run into each other.'

'Looked like more than that to me, Danny-boy. Looked to me like your little Amy is now Chuck's little Amy. Lucky Chuck.'

He had no one else to blame but himself if she'd moved on. He'd blanked her calls so why wouldn't she? Just that right now he wished he hadn't as he realised quite how lucky Chuck was to have her. 'Just shut up and row, Rollo,' said Dan wearily. 'That's what we're here to do. And try and focus on the race. I'd rather not get knocked out in the first round like we did last year – remember.'

'We got knocked out in the first round because we got

a crap draw and because you made us sprint for the finish too early.'

'We were knocked out in the first round because we weren't good enough.'

'I think *I* was. Try blaming yourself for once, Danny-boy.'

Danny breathed long and slow. Don't rise, don't rise, he told himself.

Amy decided she had time to watch Dan and Rollo's race before she and the Reading crew had to take to the water for their own heat. She was thrilled when she saw the two boys streak down the river, a length and a half ahead of a pair from Leander. Given the proximity of the finishing line and the distance between the two boats she knew there was no doubt that Dan and Rollo would win their race and said so.

'Unless something goes horribly wrong,' agreed Chuck as they strolled back along the towpath so Amy could meet her crew and prepare for her race. 'And what's more, those two are going to be my responsibility come the fall.'

'You reckon they'll get through the trials?'

'Can't see why not,' said Chuck. 'They looked on fantastic form just there and their results this season are pretty impressive. It makes you wonder just how good they'd be if they stopped trying to bite chunks out of each other and buried the hatchet . . . and not in each other's heads! Now I gotta go, gotta meet a guy. See you later, ladies.' He disappeared into the crowd.

Maddy and Amy continued till they reached the lawn

in front of the boat tent. There was the usual melee of boats being taken down to the water, being brought back, crews assembling and spectators rubbernecking. In the distance a military band was playing a selection of tunes from musicals and Amy wandered through the throng, happy that Dan had won, happy that she'd met Maddy and Chuck and not thinking about anything very much at all.

There, in front of her, were Rollo and Dan, hauling their boat on their shoulders across the grass and into the tent. Dan stared straight at Amy and then looked deliberately away.

Amy felt as if he'd kicked sand at her.

Beside her Maddy saw the brief encounter and sighed. 'Shit, that went well. Not,' she muttered.

'It's hopeless.' Amy walked away before anyone could see the tears.

Maddy stood as close as she could get to the finish line and peered downstream along the river. Hurtling towards her were the St George's women's eight and the Reading women's eight and it looked as if they were neck and neck. Certainly the umpire in the following launch was signalling first to one boat and then the other to keep to their station. He wouldn't bother if there was clear water between them. Maddy jumped up and down with excitement, not knowing who she really wanted to win.

Obviously she had an innate loyalty to her college but her best friend was coxing the Reading boat. Yes, she'd like to see Christina and Stevie do well but that would mean Tanya would too. It would just make the cow even more insufferable. As the boats drew closer it was obvious from the excited shrieks and cheers of the crowd, and from the way that the two competing sets of blades were almost intermeshed, that this was a very close race indeed. Maddy still couldn't quite judge who was winning and the blips from the horn at the finishing line were so close together as to be almost a single note.

The official result was run up the board: Reading by a canvas. Maddy felt ridiculously pleased for her friend. She made her way to the pontoons to meet Amy. When she'd fought her way through to the riverside Tanya and her crew were already lifting their boat out of the water.

'We'd have won that if Amy had been coxing us,' she was telling her crew, her frustration at being pipped at the post clear in her voice. 'They've only got a couple of really good rowers. God, the technique of some of them. It's so unfair she fucked off like she did leaving us with only Hannah. Gah!'

Maddy looked for Hannah, feeling embarrassed on her behalf. The awfulness of being rubbished like that publicly would be pretty hard to take but luckily for Hannah she was already in the boat tent stacking a couple of sweeps. For her own part, Maddy kept a low profile till Tanya had passed, still ranting about Amy leaving the club.

And whose fault is it that she did, thought Maddy. If you and your obnoxious boyfriend kept your appetites under control everyone would be a lot happier. I certainly would, she mentally added, casting a baleful stare at Tanya's retreating back.

Amy's crew reached the landing stage and began to haul their tired bodies onto dry land.

'Well done, well done,' shrieked Maddy.

Amy gave her big grin.

'Who's that?' Sian asked her cox.

'A defector from St George's,' said Amy, adding, 'and an old mate and someone who would support the Taliban before the St George's crew when Tanya is rowing for them.'

Sian stared at Tanya. 'Ah, *that* Tanya. I've never really met her, but I've heard about her on the circuit. Bit of a minx, I hear.'

'A bit?'

'I was being tactful.'

After the crew had showered and changed, Amy, Maddy and the Reading eight wandered along the towpath of the river, partly looking at the rowing action going on beside them and partly looking for somewhere nice to relax and unwind after their race.

'Would you mind,' Amy asked Sian and Ellie, 'if we didn't go anywhere likely to appeal to Dan or Rollo? I'm just not sure I can cope with them right now.'

'Suits me,' said Sian. 'I'm no friend of Rollo's, although I don't know about Dan. Well, nothing except he's a bloody good rower.'

'You know Rollo?' asked Amy.

Sian stopped walking. 'Let's get this straight: I am acquainted with him, nothing more. Okay, girls?'

'Then you're a rarity in rowing,' said Ellie.

'Not you too?' asked Amy agog.

'No, *not* me too. *Nothing* has changed since we ran into him at Henley last year.'

Actually, thought Amy as she quickly scanned over the previous twelve months, almost everything has changed.

They found a riverside bar and Amy got the drinks in. They settled down to sip lemonades and limes and watch the rowing action and discuss their chances in the next round when they were drawn against a crew from Newcastle.

'So this is where you've hidden yourselves,' boomed a familiar Midwest accent.

Amy squinted up, shielding her eyes from the lowering sun in the sky. 'Hey, Chuck. I don't see you for months and then twice in one day.' She was genuinely pleased. Then she noticed Chuck wasn't alone. She looked at Chuck and waited for the introduction. Around her she noticed the other girls had fallen silent.

She checked out Chuck's companion again. There was something about his face that was vaguely familiar. A distant bell was ringing but, no, the name didn't materialise.

'You all know Nathan Bedgrove, don't you?' said Chuck.

All around her everyone nodded. Even Maddy. And Amy had heard of the name but the circumstances around how she had heard of him remained tantalisingly elusive. She shot Maddy a questioning look. Maddy leaned over and whispered, 'He coaches the national squad – ex-Olympic rower.'

'Of course.' Now she could understand why the girls were looking awed and somewhat expectant in equal measure. Surely if someone of that stature had sought them out then it meant that he thought highly of the girls' rowing skills. Which, thought Amy, was perfectly understandable, but then she was biased.

Nathan, 'call me Nate', flopped down on the grass with the crew. Amy shuffled backwards so she didn't obscure any of her crew from his line of sight. Chuck sat next to her.

'That was a terrific win, Ames,' he said. 'Especially considering the calibre of the St George's crew compared to yours.'

'That's not fair, I've got a great crew,' said Amy staunchly.

'Aw, come on, admit it, you've got a couple of weak links there.'

'Maybe, but we can knock them into shape. You wait: next year at Henley we're going to come home with the trophy.'

'I wouldn't bank on that, Amy,' said Chuck.

'Bet?'

'How much?'

'A fiver.'

'How about a grand?'

Amy spluttered. 'Fuck off,' she said amiably. 'You know that's out of my pay grade.'

'Indeed? Well, I am absolutely certain you're not going to be rowing at Henley next year.'

'Really?'

'Really.'

Amy slowly became aware that no one else was talking and everyone was staring at her. She began to blush. What had she said . . . or done?

'Amy,' said Nate, 'I came here today with the specific purpose of watching you cox. I want you to try out for the national women's eight with a view to you being the cox for the Olympics.'

Amy looked about her for the hidden camera. This was a wind-up, right? A joke? Well, she wasn't going to fall for it. 'Yeah, right,' she said, a broad grin across her face.

'Amy,' said Chuck, 'he's serious.'

'And I'm the Archbishop of Canterbury.'

Nate rolled his eyes. 'Amy, I don't joke about things as serious as this.'

'Oh.' Suddenly she began to feel a little foolish. Maybe it wasn't a wind-up.

'Look, I know it's a big ask but I honestly think you've got what it takes. No disrespect to your crew, but on paper there is no way they should have beaten St George's. And okay, you didn't beat them by much but that's not the point. St George's should have creamed that race. And it wasn't as if they weren't trying hard – they were.'

Shit, this Nathan bloke really was serious.

'But my job, my career . . .'

'I know. That's why this is a big ask. There's some money to pay you, of course there is, but I doubt if it'll match what you're earning now. Think about it: how many people in this country would give their eye teeth to wear the Team GB strip, represent their country and have a real chance of getting a gong.'

It was an attractive offer, but . . . he'd asked her to *try out* for the women's eight. That meant there was no guarantee of getting the place. And if she did make the squad, then how much time would she have to dedicate? What would happen to her job? She'd pushed her friendship with Mike and Alastair to the limit recently, getting them to swap shifts and work an extra weekend so she could swan off to Henley and she wouldn't be able to make it up to them if she had to spend another week or so at Caversham to suit Nate.

'I need to think about this,' she told Nate. 'It's a bit of a bolt from the blue, to be honest.'

He nodded. 'I understand. On the plus side the winter training camps are pretty cushy – nice warm locations, great food, good company. On the downside, you will be spending a lot of time with quite a small band of fellow competitors. It can get a bit claustrophobic.'

Amy could imagine. 'When do you need an answer?'

'Soon,' said Nate. 'It just might have escaped your notice but the Olympics are only thirteen months away. Trials are in October, the winter training camp is in January, the final trials for the team are in March; we don't have time to muck around.'

'Okay.' So no pressure then.

'But Amy, I just don't see why this decision is so hard,' harangued Ellie that night in their digs in Henley. Squashed into the sitting room, a sitting room that would have been considered spacious without eight Amazons and their cox crowded into it, Amy felt completely outnumbered.

'Because I might have to give up a job I love, I might not make it, I don't think I'm good enough, GB Rowing already has a cox and—' she stopped. And, assuming Dan is going to make the team, like everyone is saying he will, I can't face being thrown in contact with him again.

'But that's all tosh,' said Sian.

'No it's not. GB Rowing has certainly got a cox.'

'Okay, I'll give you that one but the rest is crap,' said Ellie

'Oh? And Chazey Hall are going to let me swan off for weeks and then welcome me back with open arms?'

'I would think they'd be proud to boast an Olympian on their staff.'

'But that's it . . . I might not make it and then I won't be an Olympian will I, just some random physio with no job.'

'But give it a shot, Amy. I mean, your country needs you,' said Sian.

'Why, when they've already got a perfectly serviceable cox?'

'Oh yes? And did we get a medal in the women's coxed eight event in 2008?

Amy shrugged. 'I don't know.'

'We didn't. We didn't even make the repêchage, didn't get to the final. QED,' said Ellie, crossing her arms and looking smug.

'And there's another thing,' said Amy.

'What?' said Sian and Ellie, in exasperated unison.

'I can't afford it. You know coxes don't get a development grant or anything. If I lose my job I just don't see how I can live.'

Silence fell.

'You need to talk to Nate then,' said Ellie. 'There must be some rabbit, somewhere, they can pull out of a hat. You can't be the first person who needs funding. Maybe the National Lottery . . . or something.' She shrugged and looked at the others, hoping that someone in the room had a better idea than her of what might be available, but to judge by the blank stares, no one else had a clue either.

'Please, Amy,' said Sian and Ellie.

'Maybe,' continued Ellie, 'maybe I'm jumping the gun but if my ergo scores are anything to go by I have a real chance of making the team and I want a medal. Really I do. And I want the best shot I can get, the best teammates and the best cox. That's you, Amy.'

'I'll think about it,' was all she'd promise.

The Reading eight got knocked out of their competition in the semi-finals, which was a great deal further than they should have got in theory, while Dan and Rollo made it to the final on the Sunday and lost there. All in all there were lots of reasons for many of Amy's friends and acquaintances to celebrate at the end of the regatta. As the fireworks lit up the sky over Henley and everyone around Amy was getting happily tipsy, she was still fighting with Nate's offer.

Further down the river Tanya and Rollo were also watching the fireworks.

'Have you heard the rumour?' said Tanya.

'Which one would that be?'

'The one about Amy and Nate Bedgrove?'

'Don't tell me she's got off with *him*?' said Rollo incredulously. 'God, if she has Mrs Bedgrove will have a lot to say about it and from what I've heard she's an utter ball-breaker.'

'Jeez, Rollo, why on earth do you always think that everything is sex-related?'

'Because I like sex.'

'Which is why you're not getting any from me,' Tanya reminded him with a cold stare. 'Not until you're properly sorry for Amy leaving St George's.'

Rollo sighed. 'That's history now. Come on, Tans, you know you want to,' he wheedled. 'How about we rectify things tonight?' He gave her bum a gentle squeeze.

'Anyway,' said Tanya, refusing to be distracted and removing his hand, 'the rumour is that Nate has asked Amy to trial for the Olympic team.'

'Has he now? You always said she was good.'

'Which is why I'm still angry with you, Rollo. But she's turned him down, or that's what the rumour is.'

'She's *what*?'

'You heard,' said Tanya. She shook her head. 'What on earth is the stupid girl playing at?'

'And why should you care?' asked Rollo.

She stared at him in utter disbelief. 'Because I plan to be in that GB eight, with Amy as the cox.'

Rollo looked sceptical. 'You?'

'Why not? I've made up my mind. For the rest of the summer I'm giving up sweeps and taking up sculling seriously. I'm going to the trials and I'm going to succeed.'

'Yes, of course, babe.'

'Don't you dare patronise me, Rollo. I'm going to do it.'

20

The Sunday after Henley, Dan sat in his rooms at Shalford School, his new place of employment, checking out Facebook. Having got the post of rowing coach, he had been told by the Head that he could move in before the end of term to get acquainted with the school and the rest of the staff before the long summer holiday; the Head's rationale being that it would make life easier for him in September when, as well as finding his feet, he would have a bunch of new boys to contend with.

In a week he'd have to pack up again and go off and live with his mother in her tiny terrace near Maidenhead. However he would still have the key to the Shalford boathouse so he'd be able to cycle over to row on a daily basis to keep training. All in all, life was pretty good. Or it would be, he thought, if he had made it up with Amy at Henley. But she'd obviously moved on and it hurt him to think of her and Chuck together. He shouldn't have cut her dead when he saw her, really he shouldn't. He should have taken the opportunity to just try and be friends again. But he'd blown it. He gazed at the pictures taken at Henley – or rather, he was now looking at just one picture from Henley: one of Amy. And he hurt.

A little message in the corner of his screen told him he was being poked . . . by Maddy, he read. He clicked on the dialogue box.

'Hi Dan,' it read.

'Hi Maddy,' he typed back

'I'm bored, what are you doing?'

'Not much.'

'Fancy a drink?'

'If you can come here. Still no wheels except my bike. Ring me and I'll come down and meet you.'

'Thirty mins. See you then.'

Dan closed down the box. That was a bonus. It'd be nice to see Maddy. He hadn't had the chance to talk to her either and he'd rather lost touch with the St George's lot since he'd left in June. And maybe seeing her would take his mind off Amy.

He switched off his computer and shut it down, then gave his room a cursory tidy, pushing some dirty clothes under the bed and washing up a couple of used mugs.

When Maddy arrived she looked around his new quarters with an appreciative eye.

'Nice,' she commented. 'I thought boys' public schools were all into hardship and cold baths.'

'Not these days and never for the staff, I think.' Dan waved a bottle of wine. 'Drink here, drink at the local pub, which?'

'Don't mind. Drinking in's cheaper.'

Dan unscrewed the top and pulled out a couple of mismatched glasses. 'So what do I owe this to?'

'I've been staying in Reading and I thought I'd see if I could drop in on you on the way back to Oxford. It's sort of on the way.'

Dan frowned. 'Er, no it's not.'

'A bit of a detour, then,' she admitted, 'but not that bad.'

Dan poured out the wine and handed Maddy a glass.

'I've been staying with Ellie Mayhew,' continued Maddy.

'How do you know her? I think she used to row for Bath and . . . is it Reading she rows for now?'

Maddy nodded. 'The club Amy coxes for. Remember her? And the person Amy now lodges with.'

Dan looked at her sharply. 'What's your game, Maddy?'

Maddy shook her head and put up her empty hand in a gesture of surrender. 'No games, Dan, honest.'

'Really?'

'Really. I wouldn't play games with you two; it wouldn't be fair. I really did think that I would almost pass Shalford on my way home, and I really did think it'd be nice to see you. We didn't get a chance to chat at Henley.'

'No, well.'

'Although it did feel like you were avoiding us.'

'Us?'

'Me, Amy, Ellie, the rest of the Reading crew.'

'You don't row for Reading.'

'No, but I was hanging out with them. It was them or St George's and Tanya . . . well, she and I aren't best mates.'

'No. Funny that, most women at St George's don't seem to get on with her either.'

'No.' Maddy took a sip of her drink. 'You're still angry with Amy, aren't you?'

'What makes you say that?'

'Because you cut her dead at Henley.'

Dan stared at his drink. 'I shouldn't have.'

'But you did. How long are you going to hold a grudge for?'

He shook his head. 'I'm not, not really.'

'Amy's no more to blame than you are, you know.'

'Me to blame?' Dan looked up sharply. 'What did I do?'

'You and Karen . . . while you were dating Amy.'

Dan shook his head. 'Me and Karen?' He sighed. 'There was never really anything going on there, although Amy thought there was. I told her we were just friends with benefits, and the benefits stopped as soon as I got together with Amy.' He shook his head at the absurdity of it all.

Maddy nodded. 'Might have been because I told her so.'

Dan stared at her. 'You?'

'I honestly thought you were. I told her on the way to Rollo's house party,' she said in a small voice.

Dan rolled his eyes. He knew Amy had thought that he and Karen had had a bit of a thing going at some time, but now it seemed she'd spent all her time at Rollo's thinking that he had actually been properly two-timing her. What a mess.

He sighed again. 'Anyway, it's all too late now.'

'Why?' Maddy was genuinely baffled.

'Because of her and Chuck.'

'What about them?'

'Rollo said they were snogging at Henley.'

Maddy leaned forward, resting her elbows on her knees. 'Dan, Rollo's a shit-stirrer. Amy isn't going with *anyone* at the moment. She told me herself, in person . . .' Maddy didn't add the detail that Amy had speculated that her fanny was about to heal up through lack of use.

'Oh.' Dan stopped as he thought things through. 'Guess I've got some bridges to mend.'

'I guess you have. And I tell you where you could start: Nate Bedgrove has asked Amy to try out as cox for the national women's eight and she's having a wobble. Keeps finding reasons not to do it.'

Dan almost choked on his wine. 'She's *what*?'

'That's what we're all saying. She's been offered this opportunity and she's thinking of turning it down. Dan, she might listen to you because she sure as hell isn't listening to her female friends. She keeps banging on about money and her career, and not realising that this is a chance in a lifetime.'

After Maddy had left, Dan poured himself another glass of wine and sipped it as he wondered what sort of reaction he might get from Amy if he rang her out of the blue. Not good, he thought. He couldn't face phoning her tonight. He'd do it in the morning when he was absolutely sober and had slept on it.

Amy did a double take when she saw the caller ID on her phone. She stared at the name while the phone trilled away in her hand.

Dan? Why now? She was riddled with curiosity but the curiosity was over-ridden by the enduring hurt that had been exacerbated by the way he'd deliberately ignored her at Henley. She couldn't face it. She refused the call and then stared at her phone wondering if he'd been phoning for a reason or if he'd just hit the wrong button. She'd never know.

A couple of minutes later her phone trilled again. Good job she was between clients, she thought, as she checked the ID out again. Caller unknown. Warily she pressed the button to answer it. Was this Dan again, on another phone?

'Hiya,' she said, cautiously.

'Amy? This is Nate.'

'Oh, hi.' Relief whizzed through her.

'I was just wondering . . .' he said diffidently.

'You want an answer, don't you?'

'Amy, the clock is ticking.'

'I know, I know.'

'Do you need more time . . .?'

Five minutes ago she might have answered yes, but that call from Dan had flicked a switch. Stuff the finances, stuff the job and stuff bloody Dan. She wasn't going to put her life on hold just because of him. It might be tricky if they both ended up in the squad but they'd just have to start behaving like grown-ups, anyway, she could ignore him, just like he had her. This opportunity was never, ever, going to come her way a second time. She'd be mad to pass it up. 'Yes. I'll do it,' she said.

'Amy, I love you. I'll send you details of where and when I need you as soon as possible. The main thing will be the winter training camp in Portugal.' He gave her the dates. 'Clear your diary for that because that is pretty non-negotiable. It would be good if you could attend the sessions at the other dates I send you because I will want to see how you interact with the squad, how you motivate them, all that sort of stuff. Okay?'

'Okay. When will I know if I've done enough – or not?'

'The winter training camp.'

When Amy hung up she made her way over to the main building of Chazey Hall and knocked on the manager's door.

'Hello, Amy,' he said jovially. 'How are the walking wounded?'

'Still walking,' she replied with a grin.

'Good, good.' Nick Bradbury rubbed his hand and sat behind his desk. 'So what brings you here?'

Amy told him what she'd just done.

Nick's smile faded. 'You didn't mention this as a possibility when you joined us. Bloody hell, Amy, all you said was that you did a bit of coxing in your spare time. I don't want to split hairs but there's a hell of a difference between that and being an Olympic hopeful. To be honest, Amy, if you'd have levelled with me I might not have given you the job.'

'I know, I know and I was telling you the truth – then. Really,' she pleaded.

Nick stared at her. 'Pull the other one.'

Amy pulled her mobile out. 'Ring this guy.' She pulled up Nate's number. 'He's the Olympic coach. Ask him. He'll tell you that he approached me at Henley and that it was out of the blue.' She shoved the phone on the desk. 'Go on, ask him.'

Nick stared at the phone. 'But why you? Don't get me wrong, I'm sure you're very good but . . .' His incredulity was palpable.

'I know. I'm as baffled as the next person. I guess I can just do it. It's not like ice-skating or swimming when you have to have trained since birth. Coxing is . . . ' she shrugged, '. . . just about the words I use, I guess.'

Nick shook his head and sighed. 'I won't beat about the bush, this is going to make things tricky. Have you told Alastair and Mike?'

'Not yet. But I think for a bit we might be able to work around it. And I can take leave for the winter training camp. If I make the squad it'll be a whole other issue but you've got till January to find someone else.'

Nick looked thoughtful. 'This is tricky. I mean, it'd be quite good for our image to have an Olympic hopeful on the staff. It'd also be quite bad PR if it got out that we'd had to let you go because of it.'

Amy could see that. 'I wouldn't tell anyone if that was what you decided.'

'Thanks, I really appreciate your loyalty but it'd get out, you can bet your bottom dollar. Leave it with me for the time being.'

Amy turned away to go.

'Oh, and congratulations.'

'I haven't made it yet. Save that till January.'

While Amy was at work, Tanya and Rollo were lying in bed, Tanya's skin still glistening with sweat from the energetic and athletic sex they'd both just enjoyed. Her bum cheeks were a little red from the spanking Rollo had administered – because she'd asked him too, just to see what it might be like, and which she'd enjoyed even more than she'd expected. Maybe this was something they could develop even further next time. And Rollo had obviously been turned on by it. He'd got so horny that he'd had to take her in a complete rush the first time. She hadn't been best pleased. 'Ladies first,' she'd told him, but Rollo had made it up to her by diving under the covers and doing amazing things with his tongue until she'd begged him to fuck her properly. And he had, making her orgasm so tremendous that she'd screamed and sobbed and asked him to stop.

'But you like it really,' he'd teased her as he'd pumped relentlessly and she writhed and squirmed as wave after wave of intense pleasure rolled through her. His own shuddering climax finally released her from the exquisite torture before he collapsed on top of her, shaking and panting.

Jeez, thought Tanya, she was going to be bow-legged for a week after that. Not that she'd tell Rollo. Didn't want him getting even more big-headed about his abilities. He was quite cocky enough. Although, she thought naughtily, when it came to being *cocky*, Seb was the man. The memory of Rollo's house party triggered a little spasm of lust.

'You can't want more?' said Rollo noticing that her nipples had suddenly turned from soft pink discs into enticing little peaks. He traced a finger round one of them.

For a second, Tanya was tempted but then she remembered how bruised and sore she felt. No. She slapped his hand away. 'You'd never manage it a third time,' she said.

And Rollo had to agree as he looked down at his floppy penis. 'Anyway, it's time we got down to the club and out on the water.'

As Tanya was getting out of bed her phone buzzed. Idly she picked it up to see who was sending her a message. It was Stevie.

Just heard from Chuck. Amy's going to try for cox after all.

Interesting news indeed. But Tanya was torn. Yes, she thought Amy was the best cox she'd ever encountered but if she and Rollo made it as far as the winter training camp did she really want Amy there as well? She'd be a distraction to Rollo. In Portugal they'd be there to work and she wasn't sure Rollo would focus on his rowing if he thought he had another chance with her.

The pair turned up at their boat club on the Thames about an hour later and strolled into the gym.

'What time do you call this?' said their coach, Alex.

Tanya looked at the clock on the wall pointedly. 'Half ten.'

'Very funny. Still, it's your place in the squad you're playing roulette with.'

'Alex,' said Rollo. 'Whether we start at ten and finish at six or start at six and finish at lunchtime, does it really matter?'

Beside him Tanya was already stretching out various muscle groups and warming up. To get a place in the squad she had to brush up on her sculling skills. It was all right for Rollo. Sculling was his discipline but she was used to sweeps. And the boats used in the trials in Leicester in October were single sculls. She had to get the technique perfect or she wouldn't stand a chance. Her ergo score was good enough to get her through the first round but the second day was out on the water. GB Rowing would make exceptions occasionally for people who really couldn't scull and would allow them to row in pairs but that would mean she'd be at the mercy of another woman's ability – or possible lack of it. Tanya knew she couldn't take that risk. She'd never failed at anything she'd really set her heart on and she wasn't planning to start now.

At the end of their training session even Rollo had noticed how much effort she'd put into it and had commented.

'I've got even more incentive to make the team now,' Tanya replied. 'I heard from Stevie that Amy's changed her mind and agreed to try out for cox.'

Rollo's eyebrows hit his hairline. 'Has she now? Winter training in Portugal with Amy,' he mused.

'Portugal with Amy and me,' corrected Tanya. 'Anyway, we've both got to get there first.'

'But with Amy as an incentive . . .'

Tanya glared at him. Couldn't he, just once, put rowing ahead of screwing?

21

All week Amy had worked extra shifts, partly to get into Alastair and Mike's good books so they might feel more kindly disposed towards her if she left them in the lurch after the winter training camp and partly so she didn't have to work over the weekend because, yet again, she and her eight were on the road. Henley was still a recent memory and yet now they were about to compete in another competition. Amy didn't mind the travel in the minibus too badly – at least she was only five foot three and had plenty of room for her legs but Ellie, Sian and the others spent most of the journey bitching about the problems of being around the six-foot mark. And it didn't help matters that they were all feeling especially tense because this wasn't just any old rowing regatta they were on their way to, this was the British Rowing Championships and they were schlepping all the way to Nottingham for the privilege of taking part. If they progressed they'd be there the full weekend – if they didn't they'd be slinging their hook as soon as they got knocked out.

It was, hopefully, going to be a *long* weekend and Amy

was prepared to be completely shattered by the end of it. She was always busy at the races because if she wasn't on the water coxing, someone from the boat club would need some strapping done, a massage or some stretches to loosen up muscles. She was not only part of the team, she was also part of their support group. When the team relaxed between races that was when she really had to work. She might tell people that she was the dead-weight that sat in the stern of the Reading women's eight but in reality she was a vital member of the whole rowing squad.

And as if it wasn't enough she had the Team GB trials to distract her. Sometimes she wondered when the men in white coats were going to take her away to a nice, comfy padded cell.

She was miles away, thinking about juggling every - thing when she was brought back to the present by the minibus jouncing and jolting over tussocky grass, the boat trailer behind clattering, as the crew arrived at their destination.

Sian slid the side door back and got out, stretching as she did. The others in the crew grumbled about being cramped and stiff and clambered out after her, groaning as their muscles loosened. It might be mid-July but it was nippy outside the minibus with a chill breeze blowing over the open field where all the other crews were parked up. The smell of frying onions wafted towards them from a nearby burger van, reminding all of them that it had been a long time since their very early breakfast.

Amy looked at her watch. 'What time are you boating?' she asked Sian.

'Half one.'

'In which case I would suggest that you all eat something now to give you energy for the race.' She went round to the back of the van and opened the rear door. Tucked behind the back seat was a cool box packed with energy bars and sugary drinks as well as more sustaining food. Under the box were the tents they'd brought to stay in overnight. Even if they got knocked out they didn't want to drive back straight away. A lot of the other teams had elected to stay in local hotels but with the amount of time these girls spent away at regattas they had to find ways of making their chosen sport as affordable as possible – and camping was the obvious option, even if they would have loved having the benefit of a few creature comforts.

Amy handed out the rations. 'And chew properly,' she instructed, sternly. 'You don't need indigestion as well as nerves.'

The girls grinned at her. 'Yes, miss,' some of them chorused. As her crew ate, Amy got busy unhitching the trailer, pulling the kit out of the back of the van and making herself useful. As the girls finished their food they drifted over, one by one, to lend a hand before Amy checked her watch again and suggested they begin to warm up. Obediently the girls began their stretches before going off for a jog around the field.

Amy cast about for other things to do to keep her busy.

'Hello, Amy.'

She froze. She knew that voice. Dan.

She turned slowly and warily, her heart racing, and her knees nearly gave way at the sight of him, tall, muscled and tanned, in his rowing all-in-one. Jesus, he

326

had no right to look so gorgeous when just the sight of him made her feel like a complete nervous wreck. 'Hello,' she said. Was he going to have another go about her and Rollo, only this time in public, in front of witnesses?

He shuffled awkwardly, reminding Amy of a primary school kid up before the Head. Given how he'd blanked her at Henley she was wasn't inclined to cut him any slack.

'I'd like to say it's nice to see you again,' she said.

He took it on the chin. 'I deserved that.'

She wasn't expecting that. She felt a bit wrong-footed.

'I owe you an apology,' he continued.

Several. 'Really?'

'Yeah. I shouldn't have shouted at you about Rollo. And I got the wrong end of the stick at Henley. I thought you and Chuck were an item and . . . and it hurt. I was rude and I'm sorry. Forgive me.'

Oh, that was even more unexpected. A proper olive branch. She grabbed at it. 'We should have shouted at Rollo, not each other. He was the bloody trouble-maker.'

Dan nodded in agreement but the conversation, such as it was, ground to a halt, both of them embarrassed by the memory of their horrible row.

'What brought this on?' said Amy after a pause. 'Why the change of heart?'

'Maddy came to see me. On her way home, after she'd been to stay with you, the weekend after Henley.'

'She didn't tell me.'

'Maybe she thought you'd try and dissuade her.'

'Why? It's a free country. Why would I stop her seeing

you? Just because you and I fell out didn't mean she had to take sides.'

'She came to ask me to help her with something.'

'Oh?'

'Yes,' said Dan. 'She tried to get me to persuade you to take up Nathan Bedgrove's offer.'

'Which I've done.'

'So I hear, and I'm really glad, you'll be brilliant.'

'But I only told him a couple of days ago. Shit, the jungle drums don't half beat fast in this world.'

'You'd better believe it.' Dan paused and looked at her. 'So how've you been?'

Amy shrugged. 'Busy.'

'I've missed you, Amy.'

Amy's heart stuttered, this was what she'd been desperate to hear for ages. 'I've missed you too, Dan.'

'Can we start again?'

Amy didn't need asking twice, she walked over to him and put her arms around his delicious body. 'As long as you promise never to bring it up again?'

'I was stupid, Amy, I won't do it again.'

'Good. In which case, I won't keep reminding you of what a stupid arse you've been for the past few months.' She laid her head on his chest and inhaled his scent. God she'd missed him.

The jeers and catcalls from the eight returning from their jog made them break apart. 'Get a room,' seemed to be the heckle of choice.

'This is impossible,' said Amy, shaking her head. 'We need to talk and this isn't the time or the place.'

'And we've both got things to do, places to be.'

'We need to meet later. How about the clubhouse at seven?' she suggested.

'Perfect.'

Dan loped off and Ellie moved forwards.

So,' she said, 'you and Dan? Back on?'

'Maybe,' said Amy.

'Do you want it to be?'

Amy nodded. 'Yes, I think I do.'

Amy's crew were ecstatic; they'd won. They'd won their event, they were through to the semi-finals on the Sunday without recourse to a repêchage. They could take the rest of the day off, and take it easy. Despite their tiredness, they all set to work getting their tents pitched on the grassy areas around the huge lake, before cracking open some beers which Amy rationed out.

'Just one each, girls. You've got to perform again tomorrow, remember, but you deserve a treat right now.'

Some primeval sixth sense made her aware of some - one standing near her. She swung round.

'Rollo.' Of course he was here. It was a given that if Dan was rowing Rollo would be too.

'You might sound more pleased to see me,' he said petulantly.

'Why? And,' she said glancing at her watch, 'shouldn't you be getting ready to race?'

'In a minute. I wanted to see you.'

'Did you now.' Her voice couldn't have been icier if she'd been licking a glacier.

'Don't be like that.'

'Why not? I've got a long memory, Rollo, and hell will

329

freeze over before I forget that evening after the Boat Race.'

'Oh, come on, Amy, I was pissed. What I did was a bit crass, I admit, but it wasn't the end of the world.'

'It seemed like it to me.'

'You're not telling me that you actually cared that Dan got all narked?'

'What I felt is none of your business, Rollo. Now go away and leave me in peace.'

'Okay, okay,' said Rollo, backing away, his hands held up in surrender. 'But if you're going to be like that, let me tell you you're not the only one with a long memory. I haven't forgotten your promise. Remember the shower? A promise is a promise.'

After Rollo had gone, Amy found that she was shaking.

'And what was all that about?' said Sian.

'Nothing,' mumbled Amy.

'So you and Rollo . . .?'

Amy let out a deep sigh.

'I take it that is a yes.'

Amy nodded.

'So you've made out with the two biggest rivals in rowing?' Sian shook her head. 'Nice one.'

'I know. How dumb am I?'

Sian nodded. 'But given how I've heard Rollo operates, I don't suppose you had much of a chance.'

'It wasn't exactly rape, though.'

'Maybe not, but frankly, I think every woman on the rowing circuit is just longing for the day when Tanya drags him up the aisle so he leaves everyone else in peace. Though, frankly, I doubt whether marriage will slow either of them down. If ever there was a match made in heaven, the marriage of Rollo and Tanya would be it. If only because there'll be two other people in the world who'll be spared being married to either of them.'

Amy chuckled before she said, 'Huh. I can't see any marriage between those two lasting longer than the honeymoon.'

It was Sian's turn to chuckle at that.

The bar was rammed when Amy got there, in plenty of time to meet Dan. She instantly recognised heaps of faces she knew and waved and nodded and smiled. There were even some people she wasn't expecting to meet there. Angus and Susie for a start. She elbowed her way through to them.

'Hiya,' she said as they exchanged air-kisses. 'You're not rowing, are you?'

'No,' said Angus, 'I'm here as a hack.'

'And I'm here as a hanger-on,' added Susie. 'And to catch up on the goss.' She sent Angus off to get Amy a drink. 'So what's this I hear about you and Dan kissing and making up?'

Amy jaw dropped. 'But that was only this morning. Is nothing sacred?'

'No,' said Susie cheerfully. 'But I'm pleased for you, Dan's lovely.'

'Who's lovely?' said Dan from behind.

Amy spun round. 'You know very well who.' She stood on tiptoe and gave him a kiss. 'How was your race?'

'We won.'

'Excellent.' And it was excellent in more ways than one. If they were rowing again they'd have to stay off the booze. She didn't want another encounter with a drunken Rollo – once was quite enough.

One by one the old St George's club gang rocked up. Christina and Stevie, Tanya, and then Rollo, but Amy pointedly ignored him so he ignored her back.

She turned to talk to Susie again. 'Seems odd there's no Maddy or Seb.'

'Maddy's here,' said Susie.

'Is she?'

'She came up on the spur of the moment. I think she was hoping Seb was going to be allowed over to row for the British Army.'

Amy hadn't spotted his name in the programme. 'But he isn't.'

'Don't think they entered a team this year. Too busy in Afghanistan.'

'Which isn't renowned for its boating lakes.'

Angus had just delivered her drink to Amy when she saw Maddy weaving her way through the crowds.

'Over here,' she yelled to her friend.

Maddy's face creased into a smile and she doubled her efforts to get to her destination.

'Amy!' She gave Amy a rib-cracking hug. And then she saw the proximity of Dan to Amy and gave Dan a hug too.

'So my cunning plan worked,' she crowed.

'What plan was that?' asked Amy.

'To get Dan to persuade you to take up Nathan's offer, of course.'

'Er, actually, Dan never spoke to me about that.'

Maddy swivelled and stared at Dan. 'But . . .?'

'Amy blanked my call so I thought that was that,' he explained.

'But then Nate phoned and I realised that I'd been hesitating because of Dan and I thought *fuck it*.'

'Oh, who cares how it all worked out,' said Maddy happily. 'It has, that's all that matters. And best of all, you two are talking to each other again.'

'I expect we'll be doing more than that later,' said Dan with a dirty laugh. Amy gave him an affectionate slap but didn't contradict him.

Across the crowd of friends Rollo sneered at them.

'Piss off,' Dan and Amy said in unison and with vehemence and then they laughed.

'Let's go and find somewhere quiet and away from Rollo,' said Amy.

The pair of them left the bar and ran down the stairs, ignoring the lewd comments that followed them. Outside, the evening was relatively cold compared to the stuffy fug of the packed bar. Amy shivered and Dan took his jersey off and wrapped it around her shoulders.

'I've missed you, Dan.'

Dan stopped and drew her against him. 'And I've missed you, Amy.'

'It's been months.'

'And whose fault is that?'

Amy pressed her index finger against his lips. 'Shhh. No one is going to blame anyone for what happened. Deal?'

Dan nodded. 'Deal.'

'Now what?'

'I think,' said Dan slowly, 'we ought to find a quiet spot somewhere and try and pick up from where we were so rudely interrupted by Rollo back in April.'

'That sounds like the best idea I've heard in ages.'

Amy's crew crossed the finish line a full two lengths clear of their nearest rival. The girls were ecstatic. Sian, the stroke, leaned right forward and threw her arms around Amy.

'We did it, we did it,' she crowed. 'We're the British champions. We're the tops.' Behind her the other seven in the crew were cheering and hollering, despite their exhaustion, despite the agonising pain in their shoulders and thighs. The other crews crossed the finish line in the following few seconds to the sound of little blips from the hooter but they didn't have the elation of winning to buoy them up and they slumped dejectedly over their oars as soon as they could.

Amy was thrilled for her crew, they'd done it, they were the champions, they'd beaten the opposition and, to judge by the reaction of the spectators on the banks, loads of other people were pleased too.

'Dear God, Amy you are such a little star,' Sian said as she almost crushed the life out of her cox. 'You made all the difference.'

Amy was speechless. Partly because Sian wasn't allowing her to catch her breath but partly because she just knew that these female athletes were more than capable of whopping the opposition even if they had a stuffed bear sitting in the cox's seat.

Eventually Sian released her and Amy gulped in air. 'Aw, shucks,' said Amy.

'None of that false modesty, now,' said Sian sternly. 'This is the same crew that rowed at Henley and we weren't tipped to do well there either.'

'So the pundits were wrong.'

'And we're much the same crew as last year and we didn't even get through the repêchage.'

Amy shrugged. 'Luck of the draw,' she offered.

'Luck of the draw, my arse. This crew would walk over molten lava for you, Amy Jones, so busting blood vessels and passing out with exhaustion is just nothing in comparison.'

'You're exaggerating,' said Amy.

'Hell, no. You are one Grade A cox, Amy, and the sooner you come to terms with that the better all round.'

However, before Amy could worry about that they had to get the boat to the shore. There was the exchange of three-cheers between the competing crews – Reading yelling theirs enthusiastically while the others were subdued to the point of being sulky, and then they were by the landing stages and being helped from their craft by enthusiastic supporters and other rowers. There was a frenzy of back-slapping and mutual admiration, the eight women of the crew towering over Amy and dwarfing her with their sheer bulk.

Suddenly, before she got a grasp of what was going on, she felt herself being hoisted into the air and then she was sailing through it, tumbling gently, ten feet out, over the water of the lake until gravity made the result of her journey inevitable and she was plunged into the startlingly cold water.

Spluttering and gasping she came up for air and paddled back to the jetty where the girls pulled her out.

'What was that for?'

'To show our appreciation for what you put us through. We've suffered all weekend. We thought it was about time we got our own back on our very own pint-sized slave driver,' said Sian, handing her a towel.

Amy peeled off her wet top, glad she was wearing a sports bra, and then fumbled with the sodden laces of her soaked trainers before she started to rub her hair and dry her neck and arms. 'Appreciation?' Oh yes, physical abuse always made her feel like she'd got her feet under the table. Her teeth stared to chatter. Thank God they hadn't wanted to have a real go at her.

'Anyway, it was about time you got more than your feet wet. Most of us have spent a fair bit of time in the water one way or another. Only too easy for the boat to sink or capsize.'

Amy hadn't agreed to become a cox because she had an affinity with water. People always told her she swam like a duchess: chin high out of the water, hair kept dry, face unsplashed. Still, she supposed, it was a tradition, only until this minute, she'd believed it was only a Boat Race one. She made a mental note to get the hell out of the way if they ever won any other major competitions.

Friends and well-wishers crowded around the team on the pontoon including Chuck and Nathan.

'Well done, Amy,' said Nathan, pumping her hand. 'Stellar performance.'

'Hey, hey,' said Amy. 'There were nine of us in that boat and I was the only one not rowing.'

'Maybe, but you've just vindicated my faith in you.'

'Well done, babe,' said Dan materialising at her side. 'You and the crew were fantastic.'

'Correction, the crew were fantastic.'

'Never,' said Dan sternly, 'underestimate the importance of the cox to a team.'

'Dan's right,' said Rollo, joining them.

Why did he always turn up like a bad penny?

'So,' said Amy, 'how did you two do?'

'Came third in the double sculls,' said Rollo.

'Beaten by a couple of crews who are serious contenders for the Olympics. They're definitely the ones we've got to beat,' added Dan.

'So, no shame there.'

'Not for me,' said Rollo. 'Although, I don't know what you were thinking of, Amy Jones.'

'What do you mean?'

'Going off with Dan last night. Really, Amy, a girl of your calibre could have your pick of men and yet you seem drawn to the lowest common denominator.'

'Fuck off, Rollo,' said Dan.

Rollo shook his head, sadly. 'Dan, you don't get it, do you. You're not the man for Amy. She could do so much better. I've just got her best interests at heart.'

Amy pushed her way between the two men. 'Will you two stop it,' she yelled, craning her neck to stare up at them.

'Hey, you two, break it up.' Chuck strode towards them. His voice carried across the noise of the chatter and congratulations at the water's edge.

The Reading women's eight stopped high-fiving and hugging each other and turned to look at what had attracted Chuck's attention.

'Keep out of it, Chuck,' said Dan.

'What's going on, Amy?' said Chuck, ignoring Dan.

'Nothing.'

'Yeah, like it looks like it. These two giving you trouble?'

'Rollo is being a pain,' said Dan, before Amy could answer, 'but I can handle it.'

'Oh yes,' said Rollo. 'You and whose army?'

'Don't be more of a fuck-wit than you are already,' said Dan as he lifted Amy out of the way and set her on her feet beside him.

'That's rich coming from you,' snarled Rollo. 'You know you only got your place at Belvedere because your mother played the sympathy card. She was probably shagging the bursar to make sure.'

Dan drew his fist back and Rollo actually flinched before Amy jumped back in between the two men.

'Stop it!' she shrieked. 'Stop it! Stop behaving like pillocks. If you're going to behave like that, then I want nothing to do with either of you.'

Dan looked at her before he stormed away from the scene, the crowd that had gathered around parting to let him through.

'Once an oik, always an oik,' Rollo said.

'Shut up, Rollo,' said Amy. 'Don't think I was

defending you. You're a bastard and you always will be as far as I'm concerned. Don't you ever come near me again.'

'Amy, you don't mean it, you know you don't.'

'Try me.' And with that she gave him a shove with every ounce of strength in her body. Rollo, off guard and off-balance was taken by surprise and, with a wide-eyed yell of disbelief, fell sideways into the lake.

22

Amy, damp, dripping and shoeless, chased through the area around the edge of the rowing lake trying to spot Dan. Under ordinary circumstances, finding a six foot four bloke would be easy but everyone here was huge and Amy was only little. Finally she found him in the car park, angrily strapping the sculls to the boat trailer.

'I should have hit him you know,' he said furiously. 'I would have if you hadn't got in the way.'

'It wouldn't have solved anything. Probably just made more trouble.'

Dan sighed heavily. 'But it would have felt so bloody good.'

Amy's mouth twitched into a smile. 'And I expect there are a lot of other people round about who might have been quite pleased. But you shouldn't have stormed off.'

'Amy, if I'd have hung around I would have lost control, with or without you being in the way.'

'You'd have had to beat me to it.'

Dan shook his head. 'Eh?'

'You missed me pushing Rollo in the lake.'

'You didn't!'

She nodded. 'I truly did. I didn't really mean to, I just gave him a shove, but hey, right result.'

Dan picked her up and swung her round. 'You star.' He gave her a big smacking kiss that deepened into something much more intense. After a few minutes he put her feet on the ground again and Amy leaned against his torso for support.

'Where do we go from here, Dan?' she asked.

'Your place or mine?'

'I don't mean that.' She gave him a playful slap.

'I know. It's going to be tricky. I'm going to be living with my mum for the summer hols and then when I get back to Shalford School I'm going to be a bit restricted.'

'Where does your mum live?'

'Maidenhead.'

'But that's only twenty minutes on the train and there's heaps of them every hour.'

'I suppose. But you work funny hours.'

'Dan, we're grown-ups, we can work things out. If we both want to that is.' She gave him a hard stare. 'You do, don't you?'

'Oh, God, Amy, of course I do.'

'Then that's settled then.' She stood on tiptoe and gave him another kiss.

The summer, such as it was, rolled on and Dan and Amy found that her shifts and his training schedule inter-twined well enough to allow them plenty of time to see each other as well as work and train. Not that Dan's work started properly till September but part of his deal with the school was that over the summer holidays he checked over all the school boats and serviced them ready for the autumn term. In return he was free to use the equipment for his own training and competition purposes.

Amy for her part was mostly only required to be at the Reading club on Saturday mornings to cox the eight as the rest of the week, like Tanya, Dan, Rollo, and anyone else hoping to compete at the October trials, they concentrated on their sculling and fitness.

With the return of the boys to Dan's new school in September Dan had less free time but most days he was left to himself in the boathouse where he could train in the gym or on the water to his heart's content. And if Amy wasn't on shift she'd join him there.

'After all,' she once said as she peeled down Dan's shorts, 'anything that gets your heart pumping and makes you breathless for more than five minutes is good exercise – medical fact.'

'I don't think,' said Dan, pulling off Amy's T-shirt and unclipping her bra, 'they had this in mind.'

'Who cares?'

Weekends were often taken up with competitions but if not Dan managed to come over to Reading and would hang around with Ellie and Amy, sometimes lending a hand with coaching, or sometimes just chilling in the boathouse with other rowers.

'How's the training going?' asked Ellie one sunny autumn afternoon as they stood on the balcony outside the main bar, watching the activity on the water.

'Okay, I think. I'm confident about my ergo score and

I *know* I should be in with a chance . . .' he paused and chewed his lip.

Amy put a reassuring hand on his arm. 'We're all gunning for you, you know that.'

Dan nodded. 'But it almost makes it worse. I feel I won't just be letting myself down if I fail. It's such a big deal. How about you, Ellie?'

'Like you, I know I should be in with a shout but I daren't let myself feel confident although I don't want to get panicky because if I get really uptight I am certain my technique'll go to pot.'

'It's all right for you,' said Dan, turning to Amy, 'there's nothing you can do to improve your performance. You're a natural at inspiring your crews, but Ellie and I can't afford to take our foot off the gas for a second.'

'You'll be so glad when it's over,' said Amy.

Ellie shrugged. 'Only over until the December trials, and then the final ones in the spring. Honestly, Amy, I reckon Dan and I are going to be mental wrecks by that time.'

'It'll be worth it,' said Amy. 'You both know how much you want it.'

'If we get it,' said Dan gloomily.

'Listen to Eeyore, here,' said Amy. 'Just focus on the trials in a few weeks' time and in the meantime I'll cross everything for luck.'

'I don't think you crossing *everything* will help Dan,' said Ellie with a dirty laugh. 'Maybe just stick with crossing your fingers.'

*

343

The up-coming trials in Boston in Lincolnshire didn't just dominate the lives of Dan and Ellie. Every serious rower in the country was training on ergos non-stop, spending hours on the water perfecting their technique and skills, jogging, and doing endless gym work as the weekend designated to sort the wheat from the chaff rolled closer and closer. And then it was upon them.

The testing area for the hopefuls for the British Rowing Team was in a large soulless hall at the sports arena in Boston. There were twenty ergo machines and the test was done in alphabetical order. As there were very few rowers with last names beginning with letters between L and Q, Rollo and Dan were allocated the same time. The rowers all hung around the area nervously warming up before they were called to perform their test. The noise of the seats shooting to and fro and the whirring fans was almost deafening. On the other side of the hall was the area reserved for those cooling down. It didn't help their nerves any to observe that around half of those cooling down were also throwing up into buckets. Whatever else the test was, it wasn't easy – not if you did it properly.

Then it came time for Dan and Rollo to perform the test. They walked forwards to their allotted ergo machines, sat down, set the digital display to time them over two thousand metres and waited for the signal to commence. The temptation to go at it like the proverbial bull at a gate was almost overwhelming but Dan knew that he'd be better going at a rate he could maintain to the end. Better that than to invite cramp or exhaustion before the end of the distance.

But as the distance clicked down on the display, Dan wasn't entirely sure that he hadn't overestimated his ability. Sliding back and forth, his muscles screaming with effort, he watched the numbers decreasing, while he wondered whether he'd run out of steam before he hit the magic zero. He knew he actually had six minutes and ten seconds to 'row' the distance but to do it in less would only help. The start for the race the next day was organised so the fastest set off first to try to negate the need for overtaking. To be in the top twenty – or even ten – could improve his chances of ultimate success. Of course, everyone was here because they shared his desire to make the team – but he wondered if they were quite as hungry as he was. For him making the GB Rowing Team and competing in the Olympics was everything. He spent more time than was healthy dreaming about it, it drove his training schedule, it was his sole focus.

So it didn't matter how much his muscles protested, it didn't matter how much everything hurt, it didn't matter that his lungs were on fire: it was only six minutes of his life and if he got through this he was a giant stride nearer his ultimate goal. Besides, after the Boat Race, what was six minutes?

Dan gritted his teeth and hauled on the handle of the ergo machine, willing his agonised legs to thrust him back at maximum speed. He focused on his technique and ignored everything around him: the other com - petitors, the coaches, the hangers-on – no distractions to interrupt his total concentration.

The distance flicked to zero and Dan slumped forwards, his legs trembling and burning and his arms aching. He gasped for air, feeling physically sick with the effort as his head spun and sweat poured off his face and dripped onto the floor. For a couple of seconds he wondered if he was going to pass out but then the feeling eased. He hauled his feet out of the straps on the foot rests and put them on the ground, resting his head on his knees as he recovered. The noise in the gym diminished as the remaining GB squad hopefuls finished their trials. An official with a clipboard came round taking their times. When he saw Dan's he looked impressed.

'Well done,' he acknowledged as he wrote it down.

Dan noticed that Rollo, next to him, got no such compliment. Inwardly, despite his exhaustion, he crowed.

When he'd recovered a bit he staggered to his feet feeling horribly weak and wobbly. He tottered over to a water cooler, grabbed a plastic cup of ice-cold water and then moved to a bench at the side of the gym and slumped down onto it. He sipped his drink, trying to raise the energy to do some proper stretches to help the cooling off process.

'Hi, Dan.'

He looked up. 'Angus. Hey, great to see you, buddy. You here for the paper?'

'I've pitched a feature for them, about Olympic rowing hopefuls. I'm hoping they'll take it.'

'Good luck.'

'You'd be perfect,' said Angus hopefully.

'For what?' Dan's brain seemed to be working at half speed.

'In the feature.'

'Oh.'

'I'll have to take pictures to illustrate it. It's for their Sunday supplement. You wouldn't mind, would you?'

Dan felt too knackered to say no and then have Angus argue the toss. 'Why not?'

Instantly Angus whipped out a big Pentax digital camera from behind his back and started clicking. Dan knew he looked like shit but also felt too shit to care.

'Do you get paid for this?'

'If they take the feature I will. Generally I don't get much though. You don't when you're on work experience.'

'Still,' said Dan, 'it's a start.'

Angus nodded. 'So, not that I really need to ask, did you make the grade?'

Dan nodded. 'Five minutes fifty-four.'

It was Angus's turn to whistle. 'Not bad. Not bad at all.'

Dan shrugged. 'Well . . .'

'Don't knock it, you know it was excellent.'

Dan began to feel moderately more human. 'So who else are you planning on conning for this article?'

'Tanya, Rollo. I think Christina and Stevie are here. Nate Bedgrove said he'd talk to me.'

'All the old crowd then.'

'It's all about contacts when it comes to covering sport so I might as well make use of the people I know.'

'So Tanya's here trying out or here to support Rollo?'

'Trying out.'

'Is she good enough?' asked Dan.

'Dunno,' said Angus, 'but you know what Tanya's like, once she's set her heart on something.'

'Yeah.' Dan's heart rate had now got down to something approaching normal and his legs had stopped shaking. He began to take more notice of what was going on. During the warm-up he'd been too nervous and wired to think about anything but the up-coming test and he certainly hadn't wanted to talk to anyone but now he realised just about everyone he knew in rowing was hanging around the giant sports hall. Quite a few from St George's were there, and other Oxford rowers as well, plus Ellie and Sian, many of the defeated Cambridge crew and people he'd bumped into at Heads and regattas over the years.

He spotted Ellie Mayhew walking towards him.

'Hiya, Dan.'

'Hi,' he responded. 'How did you do?'

'Well enough to have to row tomorrow. I was hoping to persuade Amy to come up and cheer us all on but she's working this weekend.'

'I know, she rang me and said.'

'Stupid of me – of course she did.'

'She's saving all her holiday entitlement to be able to come out to Portugal and the winter training camp.'

'Do you think we'll make it too?'

Dan shrugged. 'You've got to hold onto the dream, haven't you?'

Ellie nodded. 'But it's such a big one. It matters so much.'

Chuck materialised out of the milling crowd of rowers. 'I saw your time, Dan. Should mean you're rowing early tomorrow. Well done.'

'Thanks.'

'You make sure you eat properly today and get an early night.'

'Chuck, I know.'

'Yeah, of course you do. I just want to see you in the squad.'

'You and me both.'

'You can do it, Dan.'

'Thanks.'

'Okay. Well, see you tomorrow.'

Dan nodded and watched Chuck go off to support other rowers. He knew that having done the test he ought to take it easy until his race the next morning but he was still horribly nervous. And his conversation with Chuck, which should have put him more at ease, had had the reverse effect. He felt even more pressure now; not just from his own ambition but now he felt he had the added responsibility of not letting Chuck down.

So the last thing he felt like doing was resting. He changed out of his rowing kit and into shorts and a T-shirt and loped away from the huge sports complex right out of the town of Boston. He took the long, straight flat road that led out across the fenland, past ploughed fields sowed with winter wheat, past isolated farms, navigating by instinct and the hazy sun that struggled to make its presence felt behind thin flat clouds and which was getting steadily lower and lower in the sky as he covered the miles. He ended up alongside the river again which he followed to the sports arena. By the time he'd got back, all the people he knew at the trials were long gone, but he could catch up with the ones he really wanted to see the next day. In the meantime he'd worked up a huge appetite and he was feeling tired enough to know, despite his nerves, he'd sleep the night through.

He picked his sports bag up from the locker room and made his way back towards Boston and returned to the B & B he was staying in for the weekend. He let himself in and, having showered and changed, he flopped on his bed and dozed intermittently as pictures of unhappy squabbling families, celebrity chefs or banal quizzes were beamed into his room until it was time for one of his landlady's legendary teas.

Mrs Marmaduke knew all about rowers' prodigious appetites and need for carbs. Dan had no doubt there would be cake at teatime to keep him going until supper and then a proper breakfast before the rowing test.

As he left his room his phone chirruped to announce Amy had sent him a text.

Frantic – how did you do?

Carefully he typed back that he had passed the ergo test.

Good luck tomoz xxx

came winging back before he got to the bottom of the stairs.

Dan rather hoped he wouldn't need luck but that skill would be what got him through.

23

It was icy cold, and the sky was only just light, when Dan set off from his digs to get to the Boston Rowing Club. Carrying his sports bag over his shoulder he made his way down the road to the track that ran parallel with the river. As the sky lightened he could see fingers of mist rising off the banks and the water, which was mirror-still. It would be a good day for rowing – perfect conditions – assuming the weather held, which at this time of year wasn't a given.

Although he was early when he got to the club it was mad with activity. There were dozens, maybe hundreds, of single sculls and pairs on racks all over the land around the austere building that was the club itself. Dan picked his way through the chaos to find his trailer and boat. He couldn't see Rollo anywhere – hopefully that meant he hadn't made it through the ergo test, which would give him a better chance to row as a single sculler in the Games.

He busied himself getting his boat ready to go on the water. He checked everything that needed checking, he made sure the seat moved freely, that it was rigged

351

correctly that the hull was clean and polished and that everything was absolutely as the manufacturer had intended.

'You're off at nine,' said Chuck. 'Give yourself plenty of time to get up to the start.'

'I know, I know,' said Dan tersely.

'Hey, I'm only saying.'

'Sorry, Chuck, I'm just stressed.'

'And you won't be the only one who's stressed if fucking Rollo doesn't show up soon.'

So Rollo had made it to this stage. Bugger.

Dan's boat was ready in every respect, as was Dan. He still had a little while before he needed to set off and he was jogging up and down, slapping his arms to keep himself warm in the freezing autumn morning. The briefing was in a few minutes and Rollo still hadn't pitched up. Then, as Dan was beginning to hope that Rollo had completely overslept and would miss the second qualifying session, he arrived in a minicab looking as if he expected the entire session would wait for him rather than start without him.

'Morning,' he said through a yawn.

Chuck shot him a filthy look. 'The briefing is hap - pening in five minutes and you haven't even got your boat sorted.'

'Chill. I'm here. I'm not boating till nine fifteen, what's the panic?'

'The panic,' said Chuck icily, 'is that I told you to be here fifteen minutes ago.'

Rollo shrugged. 'I'm here now.'

He wandered over to his boat on the boat rack and

began to give it a cursory once-over before he was called back to listen to the briefing about the rules of the qualifying session. It was all very straightforward; essentially it was a Head. Slower boats weren't to impede the faster boats, the umpire's decision was final and the times would be announced as soon as possible. Obviously, only the fastest rowers could hope to proceed any further in the process.

Angus, wrapped up in a ski jacket, scarf and fingerless gloves, stood next to Dan.

'How are you feeling?'

'Nervous,' admitted Dan. 'This is important.'

Angus nodded. 'Do you mind if I take some more pics?'

Dan shrugged. 'As long as you don't get in my way.'

Angus laughed. 'Dan, unless I walk on water, there is no way I can get in your way.'

'Yeah, well, you know what I mean.'

The first rowers were called forward and told to get their boats on the water and go up to the start. Dan was amongst this group. In some ways he was grateful – at least his ordeal would be over early, although he'd have longer to wait for his results.

He fetched his blades and carried them to the water's edge and then went back for his boat. It was light enough for him to manhandle it down to the river by himself.

'Here,' said Rollo, as Dan approached the water, 'let me help.'

Dan looked up in surprise as Rollo appeared beside him. 'You feeling okay, Rollo?'

'Just trying to be helpful, Danny-boy, no need for the snide comments.'

There were lots of members of the Boston Rowing Club milling about helping or hindering depending on their age and maturity, and Dan was grateful for Rollo's help, though he wouldn't have admitted it to anyone. It was one thing getting one's boat onto the water single-handedly, it was another thing getting into it and pushing off without help. And anyway, to have Rollo push him off helped to underline the fact that he was boating ahead of Rollo, he was the superior rower and he had the better chance of making the team.

Dan stepped into the centre of his slender craft and sat down. He removed his trainers, shoved his feet into shoes on the footstretcher and secured them, then he passed his trainers to Rollo, who in turn passed Dan his sculls. Dan fitted each into its rigger, closed and secured the gate over the top of the blade and made ready for the off. Rollo, crouching beside him on the bank, tapped Dan's blade.

'Good luck,' he said. 'May the best man win and all that.'

Dan snorted.

'Hey, Dan,' called Angus, from several metres further along the bank. 'Try and look happy, eh?'

Dan forced a smile for Angus. He saw the automatic flash on Angus's camera function, activated by the all-pervading gloom of the morning.

Rollo pushed hard on Dan's starboard rigger, shoving him out into the river far enough for Dan to be able to start paddling his way upstream to the start, five long kilometres away. A procession of boats, of which Dan's was just one, set off; a stream of Olympic hopefuls that would compete this day, most of whom would be disappointed by the end of it, although probably not this lead group. All of these guys had put in seriously impressive times on the ergo and had a track record of wins and places in regattas and races over the previous few seasons.

'He's got a good chance,' said Angus to Rollo.

'Maybe,' said Rollo, refusing to commit himself. 'Assuming his luck holds out.'

'I should think Dan'll rely on technique,' said Angus. 'He's a professional if ever there was one.'

'Maybe,' said Rollo. 'Maybe.'

Dan sculled gently up to the start, keeping his place in the procession, concentrating as always on his stroke: catch, drive, extraction, feather, recovery; catch, drive, extraction, feather, recovery. And again. And again. Again and again. Concentrating on the rhythm, the position of his arms, his elbows, using his legs to drive him forwards and back, keeping his back almost vertical at all stages, trying to be perfect. Despite the sedate pace up to the start the bank swept past with little to distract him. The river was relentlessly straight, the landscape on either side flat. There was the occasional stand of trees on the bank, now and again some sort of waterfowl got startled and raced off across the surface quacking angrily at being disturbed but apart from that nothing. He glanced over his shoulder to see how much further he had to go and saw the first of the scullers in this initial tranche of hopefuls hurtling towards him, followed by another sculler who was closing the gap with each stroke. Dan hauled over towards the bank as close as he dared to make sure the overtaking rower had plenty of space to get past. After the two boats had gone by, still battling for position, the wake caused Dan's tiny craft to rock perilously but he continued steadily on his way: drive, recover, drive, recover . . .

But now boats were racing past him regularly, each rower doing his best to catch the boat in front. The start had to be close. He glanced again. There it was. Instantly he felt his heart rate soar. This was it. This was the race that would matter almost more than any other in his life. Carefully he sculled up to the turning point and made his way back downstream. He shipped his oars, removed his top, which he stowed in the stern and then focused. He focused on his start, on the moment he was told to 'go'. He was ready.

He paddled down towards the start, picking up the rate as he neared the line. He glanced over his shoulder again. Just a matter of yards. The starter called his num - ber and 'go'. This was it, he dug deep to take the start line at full pace and . . . oh fuck . . . his starboard blade flew out of the gate.

The shock of not having a fulcrum for his oar almost unseated Dan and made his boat rock so wildly it came within a few millimetres of shipping water and capsizing. It was astounding he didn't go right over but sheer luck was on his side. For a second Dan panicked but then he pulled himself together, steadied his boat, leaned across and lifted his oar out of the water and plonked it back on the rigger and screwed the gate shut. But it all took time. Precious time.

He'd lost momentum, he'd lost the advantage of a flying start over the line, he'd lost valuable seconds and, in all likelihood, he'd now lost the race. Or at least he'd lost his chance of finishing far enough up the field to go through to the next round of training camps and qualifying races.

Frustration welled up in him like oil rising out of a newly drilled gusher but he forced himself to channel it into aggression. He began rowing again, driving himself to the absolute extreme, his rate nudging forty. At that speed his technique would suffer but he had to risk it. It was now shit or bust.

He blotted out the burn in his calves and thighs, the ache in his shoulders as he watched the distance between him and the following scull, which had been dangerously close, begin to lengthen. He didn't dare glance over his shoulder to see how awful the gap was between him and the boat that had immediately preceded him through the start. It would be too dispiriting to find out just how bad the damage was. And another thing he was blocking out of his mind was just how had the gate opened? He *knew* he'd screwed it tight shut. He always did. He'd never *not* screwed it shut. So why today of all days had he failed? It had never happened before. Had he been distracted at the last minute and not done it? But now was not the moment to rack his brains to try to remember. Absolutely not. If ever there was a time to think about rowing technique it was this moment.

The boat behind him was receding quite markedly

now but Dan knew that he had lost too much time to make it up. But the fat lady wasn't singing just yet, he told himself as he continued to thunder down the remainder of the five-kilometre course. Only three miles, he told himself. Nothing like the four and a quarter of the Boat Race. He could do this, he could keep up this rate. Drive, recover, drive, recover: the rhythm was steady, each stroke as perfect as he could make it as his craft sliced through the water, the blades pulling it along, pushing the water backwards. He swept past the reed beds that signified he wasn't so far from the end. Maybe just a third of the distance left to cover.

Okay, he had to know. He flicked a glance over his shoulder. The sculler in front was in sight – which was something he supposed. Maybe he'd made up some ground. Or maybe the sculler ahead of him wasn't that great. He'd find out soon enough as the line could only be a matter of a few minutes away.

Like the previous day with the ergo test Dan ignored his screaming muscles and burning lungs as he drove as hard as he could for the line. He shot through at a rate that had barely diminished from his initial pace and then collapsed, panting, his chest heaving as the ordeal ended. If he'd felt done in at the end of the Boat Race it was nothing to the way he felt now. He slapped the water with the flat of his blade as a vent to his anger and frustration. Stupid, stupid, stupid. But how on earth could the gate have come undone? He was so sure he'd screwed it shut properly. Of course he had. So how . . .?

When he'd recovered enough to paddle to the shore, Chuck was waiting for him.

'And what the fuck happened to you?' he said, his face hard with anger. 'You should have had that sculler from Newcastle. He's rubbish compared to you.'

Dan told him about the blade.

Chuck exploded. 'You stupid, stupid bastard. Basic stuff that a novice rower shouldn't get wrong let alone someone at your level.'

Dan shipped his blades onto the slipway and levered himself out of his boat. 'Chuck, I know I did the gates up properly.'

The look on Chuck's face expressed his disbelief more eloquently than anything he could have said.

There was no point in arguing. Something had gone wrong, that gate had worked loose and in a single scull there wasn't anyone else to blame.

'You'll just have to hope you scraped in under the wire,' said Chuck. 'But I doubt it.'

Dan sighed. What a fucking awful mess the day had turned out to be.

It got worse when Rollo turned in a perfectly creditable performance. That really would be the icing on the fucking cake if Rollo got to the Olympics and he didn't. Dan kicked at a stone.

Angus was trying to get his story, without antagonising the rowers. Those who had yet to race needed to focus and concentrate and those who already had were jumpy about their results. Having been told to 'sod off' or worse by a number of rowers, Angus had decided to give up on doing the reporter's equivalent of 'cold-calling' possible interviewees and stick with some of the rowers he knew from his Oxford days. He spotted Dan. Perfect, and he knew for a fact he must have finished racing having seen him head off earlier.

'Hi, Dan. Can I have a quick word?'

Dan looked less than enthusiastic but didn't blow him out like others had done. 'Hi, Angus.'

'How did you do?'

Dan shook his head and sighed. 'Badly.'

'You? No.'

Dan recounted a second time the incident at the start.

'What?' said Angus, bewildered. 'But you'd never do anything like that.'

'Well, apparently I did,' said Dan morosely.

'I'm really sorry to hear that. That's a bummer.'

'I suppose there's always 2016, but I wanted 2012 and given the time I lost I don't think that is going to happen. I might as well just pack up and go home right now. I know there's no point in waiting for the score. By the way, if you want to follow a rower, Rollo's probably your man.'

Dan turned and left, leaving Angus wondering just how a rower like Dan could make such an elementary mistake.

24

'You missed the cut by a few seconds,' said Chuck.

Dan took his mobile away from his ear. As little as that? He'd have creamed it if he hadn't had that mishap. How fucking unlucky can you get? 'Yeah, well, a miss is as good as a mile and all that crap.'

He finished packing his bag, zipped it up and carried it downstairs to find Mrs Marmaduke to pay his bill. There was no point in hanging around this place any longer. He didn't want to see Chuck and chew over what might have caused the accident. He certainly didn't want to see Rollo's smug features and the sooner he got back to his rooms at the school the sooner he could put his ambitions and hopes behind him and begin being a proper assistant housemaster to the boys.

He got into the van he'd borrowed from the school with its boat trailer hitched to the back and drove away from Boston. As he headed south he turned over and over in his mind all his preparations for the race. But the trouble with an action that you do automatically and on an almost daily basis is that he could not remember exactly what he'd done once he'd got his boat into the water and climbed in. Had he shut and screwed tight the gate? Surely just the action of slotting his blades into the riggers would have prompted it? He hadn't been distracted – or not then. Angus hadn't started to take pictures until Rollo had been pushing him off.

That was a thought! May be Angus had some shots that would show if he'd forgotten to screw tight the gate. Would it show up in a picture? He knew he was clutching at straws, but at least it might prove that he wasn't a complete tosser. But before he spoke to Angus, he needed to ring Amy. At the next service station, he'd let her know that she might be going to Portugal but he wasn't.

After his phone call to Amy he thought about calling Angus as well but decided he couldn't face talking to anyone else until he'd got back to his rooms at the school. He parked the van up by the boathouse, unloaded his scull and put it away carefully. Then he made his way back to his House and took the back stairs not wanting to meet any of the boys or the House Master who would be bound to ask questions. He could imagine the looks of disappointment, and cries of 'Oh, sir. Bad luck,' and the sympathy the questions about what had gone wrong. That had to be avoided if at all possible.

He slipped unnoticed back to his room at the top of the House, and threw his jacket onto a chair before taking out his phone and dialling Angus. Diffidently he asked Angus if he could check the pictures he'd taken to see if there were any close-ups of his starboard rigger.

'I'll see. Why?'

'I need to be sure that it wasn't my fault. If it was a

362

mechanical problem, if the gate worked itself loose, then I think I'll be able to hack the disappointment better.'

'I'll have a look but it might take me a while. I took hundreds of shots over the weekend, Dan, and I haven't gone through any of them yet. I just snapped away. You know what it's like with a digital camera.'

'But you couldn't have taken that many millions before you took those shots of me this morning. I was one of the first off.'

'I know, Dan, but things are pretty full-on for me. I've got the deadline from hell and a bastard for an editor. I'll see what I can do, though. Promise.'

'Yeah. Fine.' Dan said goodbye and ended the call. 'Don't knock yourself out on my account,' he muttered as he chucked his phone onto a nearby chair, although he knew he was being unreasonable about Angus. He prowled around his room, at a loose end.

Fuck it, he'd go for a run. Once again that day he changed his kit and crept back down the back stairs, managing to avoid human contact, and set off at a steady pace around the school grounds. The sky was almost dark but there was enough of a moon to light his way across the main lawn and down the drive to the sports fields and thence the river.

A light was on in the boathouse. Dan increased his pace and ran to the door almost at a sprint. Who on earth was in there? And, more importantly, what were they doing? As he reached the slipway he stopped running and crept towards the door. As silently as the old hinges allowed he opened the door and looked in. With relief he noticed that the boats were all there, up-turned on their racks, undamaged and safe. He crept past the boats and looked in the gym. Again, that was all okay. The boats and the gym equipment were the only things of value. Upstairs there were just some saggy-baggy arm - chairs, a game of table football and a handful of rather tarnished and ancient silver-plate trophies.

Dan scratched his head. Had he left the lights on then? Was he going mad? First the gate and now the boathouse lights. But it hadn't been dark enough to put the lights on when he got back from Boston.

He crept up the stairs. As he reached to top he saw a few tousled wisps of blonde hair sticking over the back of an armchair. Whoever the intruder was they weren't causing any trouble.

'Excuse me,' he said firmly.

There was a high-pitched shriek as the figure leapt out of the chair. 'Dan! You scared the living daylights out of me. What on earth are you doing creeping about like that?'

'Amy?' He was thrilled to see her and raced across the room to give her a big hug and instantly felt a wave of sympathy transfer itself from her to him. The day was still shit but now Amy was here he felt he could bear it.

'I knew you had to be about somewhere as the door was unlocked, so I thought I'd wait for you here. I thought you might want some cheering up.'

'The door was unlocked?'

Amy nodded as she stared up at him. 'Dan, I am a woman of many talents but passing through locked doors isn't one of them.'

Dan's shoulders drooped. 'I am losing it, Ames. First I don't screw the gate shut and then I don't lock the door.'

Amy gave him another big hug. 'I'm sorry, hon.' She leaned her head on his chest. 'I know how much it meant to you.'

Dan squeezed his eyes tight. He wasn't going to cry but the pain of disappointment and failure was awful. 'No one died,' he said in an attempt to be brave.

'No,' said Amy. 'I came over to see if there was anything I could do to help make it better.'

Nothing was going to make it better but he could think of something that would help him take his mind off it for a bit.

'Well . . .' he said.

His phone rang.

'Don't answer it,' she murmured.

Dan glanced at the caller ID, his thumb hovering over the off button. 'Fuck, it's Angus. This is important.' He hit the answer button. 'Hi, what've you found?'

Amy sat on the arm of the chair and stared mournfully at Dan but he was too interested in the call to notice.

She listened to his half of the conversation, not being able to make head nor tail of it and wishing that she could. All she could tell was that Dan was looking increasingly animated but it wasn't good animated. He was livid. The side of his jaw was working as he clenched and unclenched his teeth and his breathing became quite erratic.

'Yes, email it to me, please. And thanks.'

'Well?' said Amy.

'*Well*, I'm not the complete moron I thought I was. I

might have failed to lock the boathouse but I did shut my gate.' His phone trilled again.

'This'll be it.'

'What?'

But Dan ignored her and stared at the screen on his phone. 'The bastard. The absolute shit. I just don't believe it.' He threw his phone onto the armchair and paced around the boathouse clubroom.

Amy picked up his phone and looked at the picture Angus had emailed him.

'So what's this about?'

Dan span round, his face a mask of rage. 'What's this about? Just look at where that bastard's hand is.'

Amy peered at the picture again. 'So Rollo's got his hand on your rigger?'

'Rollo's undoing the fucking gate.'

'Is he?'

Dan stared at her incredulously. 'Of course he is. Why else would he have his hand there?'

'But you can't see him actually undoing it, can you.'

'You're not defending him are you?'

'No . . . no, I . . . it's just the picture isn't that clear. He could be doing anything including *not* undoing your gate.'

'You *are* defending him. I don't believe it. Why would he have his hand there if he's just pushing me off? And given what happened later it stands to reason.'

'Does it?' Amy was far from convinced.

Dan rounded on her. 'I'm his rival, he hates me, he takes every opportunity to have a go at me. Let's face it, he even shags my girlfriend.'

366

'I wasn't your girlfriend.'

'Oh really? Funny, I didn't see it that way.'

'Oh, for God's sake, that has nothing to do with this.' Amy was starting to lose her temper.

'Why not? You can't say I'm making the facts up about that, like you are about this picture.'

'Oh, fuck off, Dan. I'm not making the facts up but you are completely failing to look at the other side of the argument.'

'There is no other side. He shafted me – just like he shafted you, and he did both to get at me, like he always does.'

Amy was shouting now. 'Why is it that you're always the victim? Why is it that the chip on *your* shoulder is the only one that matters? And it has to be bigger and better than anyone else's? Grow up, Dan. So I slept with him once. It doesn't make me your enemy or mean that I'm defending Rollo, but this picture isn't proof.'

'Isn't it?'

'No, it's not.'

Dan's rage hit a new level, which made him lash out uncontrollably. 'Then you can just sod off. If you're not with me then you're against me.'

'Dan, for fuck's sake, all I'm saying is you should be careful before you start throwing serious accusations around.'

'I know exactly what you're saying. I get the message loud and clear, so, if you're so keen to defend him, why don't you go back to lover boy because I don't want you here.'

Amy's eyes filled with tears but she blinked them back

and shook her head in disbelief at his words. 'I can't believe you're saying this. Getting back with you was a big mistake, I can see that now. You're no better than bloody Rollo. You two deserve each other.' And with that Amy flung herself down the stairs of the boathouse and stormed back to the station.

25

Dan stared after Amy, still shaking with anger. Good riddance. He thought she'd be as angry as he was about Rollo's actions. He couldn't believe she'd stuck up for him. If that was how the wind blew then he was better off without her.

He followed Amy down the stairs and locked up with difficulty as his hands were still trembling with rage. Bloody Rollo – he was the cause of everything bad that had happened in his life. At least now he had proof that the guy was a complete shit. He looked again at the picture. How could Amy say that this wasn't proof positive?

By morning, after a bad night's sleep, Dan had calmed down a bit. Maybe Amy had a point – maybe one picture wasn't incontrovertible proof, although given how events had panned out it ought to be enough to hang Rollo. He texted Angus to see if there were any more shots of him messing with his boat. Sure enough, Angus was able to email him another three pictures. If that wasn't enough to get a guilty verdict nothing was. As soon as Dan had supervised breakfast and had seen the boys in his House off to lessons, he rang Chuck.

'Are you at Caversham?' he asked after they'd exchanged greetings.

'Yes,' said Chuck cautiously.

'I need to see you.'

'If it's about the trial there's nothing I can do,' said Chuck. 'You've just got to take it on the chin.'

'Chuck, I need you to see something. It's important. I wouldn't waste your time if I didn't think it'd make a difference.'

'So what is it?'

'I need to show you something. It's not really the subject of a phone call.'

There was a pause. 'Okay, Dan, if you insist. When can you get here?'

'I can come over this afternoon. Say about three-ish.'

'I'll see you then.'

Dan pedalled the six miles from his school over to the Redgrave Pinsent Lake and made his way to the swanky new boathouse. He ran up the stairs and knocked on Chuck's door.

'This had better be good,' said Chuck as Dan shut the door behind him.

He took off his backpack and reached inside, pulling out his laptop. Amy had been right about the picture on his phone, it was too small to be really clear – not that it excused her attitude in any way – but on the laptop, and with the whole series of shots, he was sure there could be no doubt. Two minutes later Chuck was peering intently at the screen.

Chuck exhaled. 'What a dick.'

'It's not what I want to call him.'

'No, I can imagine.'

Chuck had another close look at the pictures and then took a pen-drive from his desk drawer. He slid it into the USB port and copied them over to it.

'Leave this with me.'

'What are you going to do?'

'Well, first off I'm going to talk to Rollo. After that . . . I suspect it'll be out of my hands.'

Dan longed to hang around and watch the fireworks but he had to get back to the school to supervise prep, which was going to be hugely less entertaining than watching Chuck chew out Rollo.

Rollo parked his car by the lake and levered himself out of the seat. The trouble with being six foot six was that cars were never quite big enough. Even with the seat fully back he still felt as if his knees were up around his ears, even in the new Merc he'd bought. Stretching, he looked at the scene and imagined himself training there. Cool.

Unworried, he wandered into the boathouse and up the stairs.

'Top of the stairs, turn right, third door on the left,' was what Chuck had told him. He knocked.

'Come,' said Chuck.

Rollo strolled in.

'Shut the door.'

For the first time since Chuck's phone call earlier that afternoon Rollo got a feeling that all wasn't entirely right.

Surely this was going to be a pat on the back and well done for getting through the trials? And maybe an offer of extra one-to-one coaching before the training camp?

'Sit.'

Uh-oh. 'Yes, Chuck,' he said brightly to mask the increasing feeling of unease.

'What the fuck were you playing at?' said Chuck.

'I don't get you.'

Chuck swivelled his laptop around. 'Take a look.'

Rollo felt the blood drain right down to his toes. Shit. 'I was helping Dan launch his boat,' he blustered.

'Don't give me that crap,' snarled Chuck. 'Do I look like some sort of dumb-ass?'

Rollo didn't know what to say. Bloody Angus and his bloody camera, he thought.

'Well?' said Chuck. There was a pause while he waited for Rollo's answer. 'I mean, why? Why, for God's sake? Sabotaging your own rowing partner? What were you thinking?'

Good point, Chuck. Rollo himself had no explanation. Except that the opportunity to get one over on Dan had presented itself and he'd taken it. A moment of unthink - ing, blind madness.

'I'll have to tell Nate,' said Chuck.

Rollo nodded. 'I didn't mean to do it.'

Chuck's eyes widened in disbelief.

'What I mean is . . . actually, I don't know what I mean. I didn't think.'

'Then it's about time you *did* start thinking,' snapped Chuck.

'I suppose I thought he'd notice, before it was too late.'

'Really?'

'I don't know.'

'So when you found out that he didn't and he failed the trial, you didn't think to own up?'

'I was ashamed,' admitted Rollo.

'No, you're ashamed *now* because you've been caught. *Then* you thought you'd got away with it. You saw Dan beat himself up and you thought you were home, free.'

Rollo nodded.

'You know, if you weren't such a fucking good rower I'd have you banned from this sport for life before you could say knife.'

Rollo felt sick. How could he have been so stupid? To throw everything away on such a stupid impulse.

'You've got to hope that Nate thinks you're worth keeping. And then you've got to hope even more that Dan doesn't kick up stink. And I wouldn't blame him if he did.' Chuck glared at Rollo. 'Stay there,' he ordered as he unclipped the pen-drive from his computer and stamped out

Rollo slumped in his chair and contemplated a future in rowing that looked bleak. He tried blaming Angus and Dan but he knew that it all came back to him.

Five minutes later Nathan Bedgrove appeared.

'You twat. You *utter* fucking twat.'

Rollo stayed silent.

'Who knows about this?' he asked.

'Us, Angus, Dan . . .' speculated Rollo.

Nathan sighed. 'Leave this with me,' he said. 'Just thank your stars you row as well as you do. Now get out.'

Rollo crept out of the boathouse and returned, shaking, to his car.

Dan was walking through the main hall of the school when the duty prefect stopped him.

'Sir, you've got a visitor. I asked him to wait in the masters' common room.'

'Thanks, Jenkins.'

Dan made his way along the oak-panelled corridor to the cosy, battered sitting room reserved for the staff. He was only vaguely curious. He wasn't expecting a visitor but since his arrival there had been several occasions when a pushy parent or a rep from some rowing outlet had pitched up to talk to him out of the blue. He expected it to be one or the other. He opened the door and peered around.

'Nathan.'

'Evening, Dan. Can you spare me a few minutes?'

Dan nodded. He knew what this was going to be about. A couple of other staff were reading the papers or working on their laptops. Even if they whispered, in the deep silence, every word would be overheard and he didn't think it was a conversation to share with outsiders.

'Let's walk,' said Dan. He led the way back through the school and out into the grounds.

'I imagine you know what this is all about,' said Nathan as they strolled over the big lawn at the front.

Dan nodded.

'So obviously there's a place for you at the next trials in December, if you want it.'

'Thank you,' said Dan. And with a whoosh of relief he

374

realised quite how much he did want another chance.

'But there's a problem.'

'Oh?'

'Rollo.'

That figured. 'Why? Why is Rollo a problem? Surely he should just be sacked.'

'I *should* ban him, yes.'

'So?'

Dan knew there was a 'but' coming. It hung in the air between them along with the smoke from a nearby bonfire.

'But . . . but he's good. And together you and he are sensational.'

Dan stared at Nate. He didn't really expect him to row in the same squad as that bastard after what had happened, did he?

Nathan obviously read his mind. 'I know it's a big ask, Dan.'

'Big?! It's monu-fucking-mental.'

Nate remained silent for a couple of beats. 'This isn't just about you, Dan.'

'No? So, who else did Rollo shit on? Who else are you asking to forgive and forget?'

'It's about the squad, about the country's chances of getting medals, it's about what the public expect, it's about our sponsors and *their* expectations . . .' He looked pleadingly at Dan.

'So you're telling me that the public and our sponsors are expecting me to row with a cheat?'

'No one will know if you don't tell.'

'And why shouldn't I? Or Angus for that matter? Or

375

Amy.' No, Amy wouldn't be a problem would she? She'd be on Rollo's side, cheering for him to be kept in and could be guaranteed to keep her trap shut.

'Because I'm asking. And I'll ask *them* in due course, if it's necessary. If you don't agree then it's irrelevant, but that would be unfortunate and it would piss off our sponsors. Do you know how much we'd lose financially if they walk? Millions.'

'And if I don't agree? Will I still be welcome at the December trials?'

'Of course, Dan, that's a given.'

'Really?'

'You have my word. But let me say just one thing, Dan: if I don't let Rollo stay in the squad, tell me just who do you envisage rowing with in the double sculls?'

Dan stopped and stared at him. 'Maybe I don't want to row in the double sculls.'

It was Nate's turn to stare. 'What?'

'You heard.'

'So what have you got in mind?'

'Single sculls.'

Nate shook his head. 'No chance. You're not good enough, and as I'm coach I can tell you here and now you don't stand a snowball's chance of that seat.'

Dan felt as though Nate had punched him. But that was his burning hope. 'Not good enough?'

'No. Sorry, Dan, but there it is. I'm looking at you for the double sculls or possibly the quad sculls and that's it. Take it or leave it.'

Hobson's choice. Row with Rollo or don't row at all. He needed to know the answer to a question before he made a final decision. 'Is Rollo being considered for anything else?'

'No. I might just consider him for the quad sculls too but it's unlikely.'

So at least Rollo couldn't compete in the single sculls either.

Dan swallowed. 'Okay, it's a deal.'

In response to an emergency text from Ellie, Maddy had jumped into her little car and had hurtled over to Reading from Oxford. It seemed that Amy hadn't stopped crying for twenty-four hours and she needed TLC from her best mates. Brandishing two bottles of wine, Maddy had been welcomed into Ellie's house with open arms and a whispered warning that Amy was in bits and was lying on her bed, sobbing her eyes out.

Instantly Maddy had gone upstairs to see her friend and had insisted that she should come downstairs to get pissed and tell her all about it.

'You've helped me through some bad times,' said Maddy, hauling on Amy's arm to make her sit up. 'It's my turn now to repay the debt.'

'You and Ellie get pissed together,' sobbed Amy. 'You don't want me around, being a wet blanket.'

'Yes we do, and you're not a wet blanket. You've had your heart broken, again, and Ellie and I want to help it heal. I'm not taking no for an answer and if you don't come down I'll get Ellie to drag you down, and you know she could.'

Seeing that she was beaten, Amy grabbed her box of tissues and followed Maddy back to the sitting room

377

where over a glass of wine she gave Maddy a verbatim account of the row. 'And it's Rollo who's to blame *again*,' she wailed.

'But that's awful,' said Maddy. 'I don't believe Dan could be so horrid and say those things. No wonder you're so upset. What a shit!'

Amy snuffled into her tissue, her eyes red, her nose pink and her mascara a disaster.

Ellie leaned over and poured some more wine into Amy's glass as across her sitting room she exchanged a look with Maddy, a look that implied she couldn't believe how Dan had behaved either.

'I just don't see why Dan would lose it like that,' said Maddy.

'He was *utterly* gutted he didn't make it,' said Ellie. 'Maybe Amy just got the fallout because she didn't condemn Rollo out of hand.'

'What is it with Rollo? He's been at the heart of both rows. He's just like some sort of wrecking ball when it comes to Dan and Amy,' said Maddy angrily. 'So, do we know if Dan was right? Did Rollo mess with his gate?'

Amy nodded tearfully. 'He did. If I'd just agreed with Dan none of this would have happened but the picture wasn't clear, really it wasn't.' She gazed imploringly at her friends, willing them to take her side. 'I had this call from Nate yesterday evening, asking me to keep quiet about it all.' She blew her nose again. 'So you don't know anything about this whole business either, understand? Apparently it'd upset the sponsors if they got wind of what Rollo did, given that Nate still wants him in the squad if he makes it through the selection process.'

'You're joking,' said Ellie, stunned.

Amy shook her head. 'That's what Nate told me.' She dabbed her eyes. 'He still wants Dan and Rollo in the double sculls.'

'What?' both girls screeched.

'So Dan doesn't want anything to do with me but is still going to row with Rollo.' Amy dissolved into tears again. 'And if I want cox for Britain I've got to face going to training camp with the pair of them. Ellie, I don't think I can do it.'

'Now you listen to me, Amy,' said Ellie sternly, 'you are *not* to give up on your chances because of that pair of gits. None of this is your fault. So you promise me that you'll go to Portugal because if *I* make it through I want *you* as my cox. My chances of a medal and your decision are linked so you'll have me to answer to if you decide against it.'

Amy nodded submissively. She knew Ellie wasn't a woman to mess with and didn't make idle threats, but even so she wasn't sure she could face spending a fortnight in Dan's company. She knew it would be unutterably heart-breaking.

26

The atmosphere in Chuck's car heading north-east up the highways of Britain to Boston was tense as Dan contemplated his chances of success in the second round of trials. Behind Chuck's car was the trailer with the two single sculls he and Rollo would have to row in the following day. The only decent thing about travelling up with Chuck – apart from the fact that Chuck was a nice guy – was that Rollo had opted to take Tanya up in his Merc. At least he was being spared sharing the journey with the shit.

Dan slumped in the front seat, trying to keep his mind off the imminent test, while also blotting out Chuck's appalling taste in Country and Western music.

Outside the car the frosty, winter countryside sped past, the steel-grey clouds lowered and the wind thrashed the bare branches of the trees. At the sides of the road were piled mounds of oily black slush from an early snowfall and the conditions looked cold and miserable. Dan thought that they were the sort of conditions for inflicting on wannabe members of the SAS or the Marines to see if they were hard enough. But he was going to be enduring them for a sport, for God's sake, something that you did for pleasure – allegedly.

Rowing in this was going to be just horrible. Dan knew he ought to be grateful to be given this chance but it was a chance that came with a hefty price tag: being shackled to Rollo for the next six months. If he was good enough at these trials. But rowing in freezing temperatures on an exposed river on the east side of the country was going to be just about as taxing as the sport could get and he was volunteering to put his body through hours of misery. And it would be even harder than the previous trial. Today it was the same five-kilometre race down the river but this time they'd be competing against the rowers who had already got a place in the squad, not just the hopefuls. The first assessment, back in October, hadn't included the men and women who had just competed in the World Championships. But now everyone was being tested, and naturally the existing squad wanted to keep their seats and the newbies wanted to oust them. No quarter would be given, everyone would be trying their hardest and it was probably going to be the toughest and most important race in Dan's career. Or at least it would be till he got to the Olympics . . . *if* he made it.

The more he thought about it, the more he felt sick with nerves. The people he was going to be competing against – the guys who'd rowed at Bled in the World Championships – had had at least a year of top-class training camps, of specialist nutritionists making sure their diet was as perfect as they could make it and of coaching at a level he could only dream about. Sure,

Chuck had been good while he'd been at St George's but he'd been on his own for three months now, relying on his own drive, his own determination and his own stamina to carry him through.

The one advantage of not being an established member of the GB Rowing Team was that he hadn't spent the last year enjoying cushy training camps in southern Germany, Italy and Portugal where the weather was guaranteed to be pleasant. He'd been training in rain, hail, sleet, snow and wind and had become used to rubbish conditions. Physically, he knew the world-class rowers were as fit as they could be but would they have the mental strength to cope with the absolute shit that the British winter was throwing at them today? All he could hope for was that they might have gone a bit soft.

Chuck drove as smoothly and as carefully as possible given the wretched road conditions but even so the journey seemed to take for ever. They were going to stay overnight with Mrs Marmaduke, which was the only bright spot in an otherwise bleak picture. Her fantastic cooking and wonderful cake made the whole expedition almost bearable – almost, but not quite.

When they finally arrived at the boat club they off-loaded the trailer before going back into Boston to find Mrs Marmaduke, fill their boots with her cooking and get an early night.

The next morning they set off for the river and their race. Dan had forced down a plate of porridge but was now terrified it might make a reappearance as he felt completely screwed up with nerves and adrenalin. They got to the boat club where they could see dozens of other rowers, wrapped up in boots and hoodies, preparing their boats, standing around chatting, sipping mugs of hot tea or chocolate and trying to look nonchalant. One or two rowers were even managing to laugh but Dan knew that everyone was just as tense and worried as he was.

Chuck left them to go off for a briefing and to find out at what time his own two protégés would be expected to boat. In a big gaggle, just along the riverbank from where Dan was standing, were all his old rowing buddies – and Rollo. Unless he wanted to be a sad loner he'd have to try and ignore Rollo's presence. Ellie, Sian and Tanya were huddled together, looking both frozen and fraught as Dan approached them.

'Hi,' said Dan.

'Good to see you here,' said Sian, 'but . . . I don't want to be rude but I didn't think you made the grade last time.'

'I was given a dog's chance. It wasn't my fault, there was problem with my boat – a malfunction,' he said, sticking to the lie that had been agreed with Nathan. 'So, here I am.'

He noticed Ellie giving him a long, cold stare. He wondered how much Amy had told her about their break-up; to judge by her attitude it was quite a lot. He still found it hard to believe that Amy had sided with Rollo, but did Ellie know about that or had Amy given it a different spin?

And talk of the devil, he thought angrily as Rollo joined them. He draped an arm around Tanya's shoulders before giving her a kiss on the cheek. Dan tried to put a lid on his feeling of violent antagonism. How did he have the nerve to even show his face again, given what he'd done? The arrogance . . . But, of course, the sponsors had to be kept happy so here he was. And Dan knew he had to pretend all was hunky-dory.

'So it was the gate that worked loose on its own?' asked Sian.

Dan nodded, not looking at Rollo.

'Shit, I hope that doesn't happen to me,' she said.

'I think you'll be all right. It was just one of those freak things. I don't think it's likely to happen again.' This time he did stare at Rollo. Beside, Rollo doesn't want *your* seats, he added mentally, so you're in no danger.

'Anyway,' said Rollo, obviously intent on changing the subject, 'what do you reckon our chances are?'

'Better than even,' said Ellie confidently. 'Sian and I are British Champions only with sweeps not sculls but even so . . . my ergo score was great, you and Dan got to the finals at Henley this year and from what Tanya's been saying she's been training as hard as any of us. Surely some of us should make it through.'

Rollo shrugged. 'But the opposition we're against today have medalled at the World Championships and have had the benefit of the absolutely best level of training for a whole year, if not more. I call that such an unfair advantage,' he grumbled.

'And they started out exactly where we are now, fighting for their seat against rowers who already had one,' said Ellie. 'Some will be getting too old, too fed up, too jaded to want to go on putting themselves through

384

this. There's bound to be a churn of the squad.'

'Huh. And you don't think they won't all be hanging on for grim death to row at the home Olympics? Get real, Ellie. If more than one of us makes it through I'll be amazed.'

Dan was surprised at Rollo's attitude. Usually he was so arrogant and cocky and just assumed that he would succeed that this expression of doubt seemed totally out of character.

'Cold feet, Rollo?' Dan asked.

'Not really. Obviously I reckon I'll be the one to make it through, given that I did pretty well last time. I just feel a bit sorry for the rest of you. Wasted journey and all that.'

'Thanks a bunch,' said Tanya, shrugging off his arm.

Chuck made a timely reappearance and gave Dan and Rollo their boating times. 'Sorry, Dan,' he said, 'but it looks like you're going to be at the back of the field, given that you didn't get a proper time at the last trial.'

Dan sighed. It was fair enough but he knew he should be quicker than the others right down the field with him so he'd have to do a whole bunch of overtaking. And the fact the Rollo was smirking about his more advantageous position really didn't help. On the plus side, Rollo would have to be on the water long before he did so there was no way Rollo could mess with his scull this time.

It was soon time to get their boats ready. The girls had a bit longer to wait and decided to go off for a gentle jog to loosen up while Chuck went off with Rollo to get his scull on the water. Dan did some stretches and then also went for a short run. By the time he got back Rollo was

385

on his way upstream to the start and it was time for him to get his act together.

Unsurprisingly, by the time he was paddling slowly upstream he'd checked the gates on his riggers a dozen times or more. He was turning into an obsessive-compulsive. He knew in his heart that his blades were secure but he had to keep checking to reassure himself.

The temperature on the water was perishing and he was thankful for his hoodie as he made his way to the start line. He was tempted to try to warm up by rowing at a fast pace but he knew he had to conserve his energy for the five-kilometre dash back. It was a question of balance between keeping himself from freezing or risking exhaustion on the return.

Boats started to hurtle past going back downstream – the race was on. It was difficult to see who was who as they shot past but it was obvious from the uneven gaps between some of the boats that even amongst this first, supposedly fastest group, there was quite a marked difference of ability. All Dan could hope for was that his own ability had been seriously underestimated and that he could put in such a flying time, he'd get picked up for further training.

He came to the top of the course and turned his boat through one hundred and eighty degrees. Now he was heading downstream and ready for his flying start across the line. Once again he checked his gates before he started to pick up the pace. He was well into his rhythm as he swooped across the line and his own race began in earnest. Unlike rowing in lanes where you have an accurate visual gauge as to how you are doing compared to the opposition, this sort of racing needed a great deal more mental strength to pace yourself; not to go too fast for too long at the start, not to take one's foot off the throttle too much in the middle and the ability to really go for it over the last quarter of the race, to row through pain and aches and burn with no reference at all as to how your time compared to all the others.

Dan began to dig into his resources – concentration, stamina, self-belief, technique – as the rhythm of his stroke propelled him down the river. Every twenty or so strokes he allowed himself a glance over his shoulder to see where the boat ahead of him was. He was definitely closing on it and drawing away from the one upstream. He was progressing. Before the first kilometre he'd taken the boat ahead, by the second kilometre he was hunting down the next one. His stroke was still relatively easy, the pain hadn't really kicked in, he had to be in with a chance. But concentrate, he told himself. Don't get cocky; don't lose it.

He kept checking his own technique, thinking about his arms, his shoulders, his legs. He remembered what the cox had told them as they rowed on the Thames in the Boat Race. Sit up tall, use the legs, sharp catches . . . The phrases began to go round in his brain like a mantra, the rhythm and his own instruction induced an almost Zen-like state until a marshal on the riverbank warned him that he was getting too close to another boat. Instantly Dan corrected his course and overtook a third competitor and when he checked over his shoulder again a fourth was within easy reach. He upped his stroke and shot past yet another rower within the next few hundred metres. This had to be good. Looking at the guys he'd already passed and who seemed to be getting further and further away from him he knew he had to be on for a good time for the five-kilometre piece. Surely he was doing enough to earn a place in the squad.

He'd studied this stretch of water endlessly and knew he was about eighty per cent through the race. Just one kilometre to go. Now was the time for the final push. He made sure his stroke stayed long and powerful, he ignored the way his muscles were screaming at him for rest, as he drove for the finish. Another glance, another sculler for the taking, and then the relief as he crossed the line.

Instantly his body collapsed. He'd asked it for every last drop of energy and for the next minute or so he had nothing in the tank, not even enough to head towards the bank. He let the boat drift aimlessly as he collapsed forward onto his knees, resting his head on them as his lungs strained to get enough air to satisfy his pounding heart.

Slowly his body began to recover, the burn in his calf, thigh and shoulder muscles eased, his heart rate slowed and his breathing became less ragged and desperate. He dipped his oars into the water, regained control of his craft and headed back towards the landing stage along with half a dozen other rowers.

Chuck was waiting for him on the shore and behind him was Nathan.

'Fantastic, Dan, just fantastic,' said Chuck. 'How many did you get past?'

'Five.'

'Brilliant. Unless they were ridiculously slow you have to be in with a great chance of a place.'

'And Rollo?'

'Too early to tell. He dropped a place but he was in a tough position to start with.'

Dan could only hope that Rollo hadn't done enough. He knew it was wrong, he knew it was vindictive, but he wanted the place more than anything in the world – and what Rollo had said earlier about the chances that only one of the five friends would make it through had rung true for him.

The hopefuls gathered in the clubhouse to hear the results. The atmosphere was fraught; people were drumming their fingers, legs were jiggling, lips were being chewed, nails gnawed and most of the competitors were silent. Just a few were having muted conversations. All their ambitions and hopes were in the balance. Just one or two of the rowers, those who had medalled in the World Championships, looked vaguely relaxed. They knew they were the most likely of the potential candidates to be selected for the next phase but even they knew they couldn't take their position for granted.

Then Nathan Bedgrove strode in and the tension racked even higher. The low murmur of voices ceased. He made his way to the front of the room. Around him the rowers shifted nervously; this was it.

'Today was all about performance,' he started. 'And I am pleased at how very high the standard was. I find it very encouraging that many of you, training on your own, have put in the effort over weeks and months to get to this level.'

'Oh for fuck's sake, just get on with it,' someone whispered, almost inaudibly.

'And so, as they say on the TV reality shows, in no particular order, the following lightweight men have been selected for further training with the GB Rowing Team.' Nathan began to read out the ten or so names. A few sighs of relief whistled out and a few stunned silences. The assembled men and women clapped when he got to the end. 'And now the lightweight women.' Again the names of the successful were listed to more applause. 'And the women's squad. Ellie Mayhew, Sian Roberts . . .' and then a bunch of names that Dan missed because he was so pleased for his two friends. It was only when Nathan stopped that Dan realised that Tanya's name hadn't been mentioned. He turned and looked at her but she was staring at the floor, blinking rapidly. Poor girl, she had to be gutted. 'And finally the men. Nathan started to read out the twenty-five names that would make up the squad from whom the final rowers would be selected. 'Rollo Lyndon-Forster,' said Nathan after the first half dozen had been listed. On and on the roll-call went, and with each name Dan felt his chances slipping further away. There were plenty of rowers left but only a few places. Dan began to empathise with Tanya.

'And last, but by no means least, Dan Quantick.' Thunderous applause broke out for all the successful participants, chatter and congratulations filled the air, transforming the tension into celebration. A few com - petitors slipped away, their disappointment clear on their faces, as they pushed their way past the successful rowers to find a quiet place where they could let their emotions out and not blight the happy atmosphere.

Dan couldn't move; he was so stunned. Dear God, he'd made it. He was in the squad. He was over yet another hurdle. Dan could barely believe it. Instinctively he reached for his mobile to call Amy and then with a sickening jolt of sadness he swatted the impulse away. He'd call his mum instead; she'd be delighted, but it was Amy who really understood what it meant to him, only now she probably didn't care.

Sian leaned over and patted him on the back.

'Well done,' she said.

'And you!' Dan switched on his happy face again and shoved thoughts of Amy to the far recesses of his mind. 'I thought winning the Boat Race was a good feeling,' he admitted, 'but this . . . this is just as amazing.' Then stupidly he thought he was going to blub but as he looked around the room he realised that if he did he might not be alone. There were a lot of very glittery eyes. Obviously he wasn't the only person finding their achievement overwhelming.

27

Dan's phone rang, waking him up. He was feeling a bit jaded after the celebrations the previous night. He rolled over and picked it up. Maddy.

'Hi Dan. I heard about your success. Congratulations.'

'Thanks.'

'You must be over the moon.'

'I can't even start to tell you. How did you find out?'

'Tanya.'

'Oh. Of course. How is she?'

'A bit hacked off. She's been very pragmatic. She says that she knows she has no one to blame but herself. Not that I care overly.'

'No, I can understand that. But it may cheer you up to know that she's putting on a brave face. I think she's devastated.'

'Maybe.' Maddy still didn't sound sympathetic. 'Anyway, the St George's Boat Club is having a Christmas party and we'd really like you and Rollo to be there. You're our most successful rowers by a long chalk.'

Dan considered the invite. It'd be nice to see the old crowd. He could avoid Rollo, couldn't he? 'Cool.'

'It's on Saturday. Can you make it?'

Dan mentally checked his calendar. 'I'd love to.'

'Excellent.'

The upstairs bar of the boat club was rammed. Dan, who had trudged there from the station carrying his overnight things in a backpack, was trying to force his way through the throng to find Maddy. As he pushed across the room people slapped him on the back, telling him they always knew he had it in him, and how much they'd bet at Ladbrokes on him getting a gold. They had to shout to be heard over the music that was pumping away but the goodwill that was being expressed was blatant.

'So no pressure then,' said Maddy when he got to her. 'All these people relying on you to win medals.'

'I know, it's just mad. This is beginning to make everything hit home about what a big deal it is.'

'You just wait till we get to July. This country is going to be going ape with Olympic fever and they'll be banking on the rowers as much as any of the other competitors to win medals so you had better not let them down.'

Dan rolled his eyes. 'Thanks Maddy, you're a real help.'

Maddy bought him a celebratory drink and as she gave it to him he spotted Amy across the bar. His insides lurched at the sight of her. God, he wished she was standing beside him now. He had so many regrets about what had happened, but he still couldn't shake the sense of betrayal over her support for Rollo, and even though he knew it was irrational, it still hurt.

*

Maddy was sipping her wine when her elbow was nudged.

'Maddy!' The tone was confrontational.

'Hello, Amy.'

'You didn't tell me Dan was going to be here.'

'You didn't ask.'

'I shouldn't have to. You know the situation.'

Maddy looked insouciant.

'You planned this, didn't you?' accused Amy.

'Might have done.'

Amy heaved a sigh. 'I wouldn't have come if you'd told me.'

'Well, that's why I didn't.'

'It's not going to work you know.'

'Amy, you and Dan are made for each other. I had to try.'

'Listen, on Planet Maddy love is all hunky-dory and even though you and Seb haven't got it together, you still love each other and one day it'll be happy-ever-after. However, in Amy World, love lives are shit and when people interfere it just makes everything more shit. Please, Maddy, stop shit-stirring.'

'But I wasn't,' she said, aggrieved.

'Maddy, I shall explain this very slowly and clearly. Dan and Rollo hate each other; I slept with Rollo. I can't undo my past and I can't cope with my mistake always begin there between us like some giant who is playing gooseberry. So I've given up, thrown in the towel, walked away from it. And this is the bit you don't seem to get: I don't want to go back. I can't bear to go through that awful heartache again. You saw what it did to me,

394

Maddy. We've had two awful bust-ups and I don't want to make it three in a row. Got it?'

'Oh Amy.'

Amy held up her hand. 'Don't "oh Amy" me. It's not going to change.'

Angus and Susie were chatting to Christina and Stevie. Dan pushed his way into the group.

'Isn't Amy looking gorgeous?' said Stevie. 'She's lost weight.

'I wouldn't know,' said Dan coldly.

Stevie gave him a look. 'But you and she—'

'It's off again,' said Dan. 'We had a row.'

'Bloody hell,' interrupted Christina, 'not again.'

Stevie said, 'Oh no, poor you,' before adding with a bit of a naughty giggle. 'But if Amy's back on the market I wouldn't say no.'

Christina gave her partner a playful slap. 'Hey, you're mine, remember.'

'I'm just window shopping.' Stevie turned to gaze at Amy wistfully.

'So, what was it this time?' asked Christina, ignoring her partner's provocation.

But Dan couldn't tell her about Rollo cheating and the row it sparked, not without breaking his promise to Nate. 'We're obviously just incompatible.'

Christina shook her head. 'It wasn't how it looked last time I saw you together.'

Dan shrugged. 'Well, we're not now,' he snapped in a tone that didn't invite further comment.

He moved away but Angus followed him.

'Sorry to hear about you and Amy, mate.'

'It's all fucking Rollo's fault.' He explained to Angus, the one person he could confide in, about the row, giving him a description of the exchange between him and Amy in the Shalford boathouse. He'd gone over it in his head often enough to have learned it by heart. 'I can't believe she took Rollo's side,' he finished.

'But to judge what you've just told me, she didn't take his side she just wasn't condemning him out of hand. There is a difference. Dan, my dad's a lawyer, I know this shit. Innocent till proven guilty and all that.'

'Not you too.'

'No,' said Angus, 'not *me too*. And yes, Rollo was as guilty as fuck because he admitted everything to Nate but, from that first picture, as Amy said, you couldn't tell that he actually *was* tampering with your gate, and that was all she was pointing out to you. Maybe if you hadn't been so sore about it all you wouldn't have gone off on one with her, but I guess it's too late now to alter that.'

Dan considered Angus's calm argument and realised with a sickening feeling of regret that he was right. He'd been blind, stupid and a total wanker. 'God, I was out of order with her wasn't I? Shouting at her that she was on Rollo's side. How could I have been so bloody stupid?' He sighed. 'Shit, Angus, no wonder she hates me, she's got every reason to.'

'You want my honest opinion?'

Dan nodded.

'You owe her an apology. A big fat grovelling one, especially for having a go at her for going with Rollo. I

396

mean why did you dig that up again? And it was just the once. Isn't everyone entitled to make one mistake?'

'What do women see in him?' said Dan, genuinely at a loss.

'No idea, except that he's a smooth talker with a big bank account.'

'Amy's not so shallow she'd fall for that.'

'You think? Given how many hearts he's broken in Oxford – and these are all really intelligent girls, remember – I don't think you have to be shallow to fall for Rollo. But what would I know, I'm a bloke.'

Dan sighed. 'I've fucked up here haven't I?'

'Well go and un-fuck it. Go and tell Amy you're sorry, *really* sorry, buy her a drink, take her out to dinner . . . But just do it.'

Dan went to the bar and got himself another drink – Dutch courage. Angus was right: Amy deserved an apology. The trouble was, he wasn't very good at apologies and he knew it. Holding a grudge? He could do that just fine, but backing down? No, not in his skill set. He sipped his drink and stared out of the big window as he thought about it. Behind him the party throbbed and swirled as he prepared a speech.

Angus came up behind him.

'Dan?'

He turned around.

'It's not that difficult – just say "I'm sorry for being a dickhead, please forgive me". That's all that's needed, trust me.'

Dan grinned. 'You're right. Wish me luck, I'm going in.'

*

Amy saw Dan heading towards her. What did he want? She had been surprised at how angry she still was with him. When he'd walked into the bar she'd felt the rage at the injustice of his accusations rise up in her again, almost as strongly as when he'd first made them.

Simmering, she wished she knew about his past – he couldn't be that squeaky clean, surely. There had to be some transgression, some cock-up that she could use as a stick to beat him right back with. And now he wanted to talk to her again but she didn't have to play nice.

'Amy?'

She snorted. 'Yeah.'

'I want to say I'm sorry.'

'Really. Why?'

'Because I am – sorry, that is.'

'No, *why* do you want to tell me that? I think you're mistaking me for someone who gives a fuck. Because I don't.' She swept off. That'll show him. She'd cried herself stupid over him twice now, and she wasn't going to make that mistake a third time. Not worth it. So why were her eyes pricking with tears?

Behind her, Dan watched her go. He couldn't blame her and the way she'd reacted was nothing more than he deserved but he was still devastated. He didn't think that he could rescue this situation, no one could. And the pain that came with the thought that Amy was lost to him for ever was almost physical. The party had lost any sense of fun for him; as soon as was polite he thought he'd say his goodbyes and bugger off.

*

Tanya watched the interaction between Dan and Amy. Oooh, trouble in paradise. She knew from Maddy and boat club gossip that Dan and Amy had broken up, which meant Dan was single again. She considered him – he was a bit of a hunk. Dark and brooding with that hint of danger. He wasn't smooth like Rollo, he was a bit rough around the edges and she could fancy a bit of rough. She wandered over to Dan.

'I know I congratulated you up at Boston but I'm really pleased you made it into the squad.'

'Are you?'

He sounded so moody. Maybe she could take his mind off his bad temper. 'Yes I am. Honest. You've worked bloody hard and you deserve it.' She put her hand on his arm and gazed into his eyes. She noticed his pupils dilate just fractionally. Gotcha. Get him on the rebound, when he's vulnerable, she thought, and he'll be putty. No, putty was the wrong analogy: things were rarely soft and squishy once she got going.

'It's too loud to talk here,' she purred, 'let's find somewhere a bit quieter.' She tugged gently on Dan's arm and he followed her like Mary's little lamb.

She led him downstairs and out onto the riverbank. 'That's better, isn't it?' she said.

'It's quieter,' said Dan, 'and I need some fresh air, it was too hot up there.'

'Maybe a bit chilly out here, though,' said Tanya pressing herself against him. 'But shared body heat and all that.' She gazed up at him and saw him swallow. She reached up slightly and nibbled his ear. 'Come on, Dan,' she whispered into it, 'you know you want to.'

She rubbed the front of his trousers and felt a gratifying response. 'Follow me,' she instructed and led him around the side of the boathouse. She pushed him against the wall and then unzipped his trousers, flipping his wonderfully stiff penis out of his boxers with a deft and practised hand. Then, gazing into Dan's eyes, she sank to her knees.

She was a tad surprised when Dan pushed her in return, catching her off-balance so she toppled backwards and sat down hard on her heels. So he didn't want a blow? Straight to the fuck, was that it?

But then he tucked himself away and zipped up.

'Thanks for the offer, Tanya. And much as I am tempted to score with you, just to get one over on your shit of a boyfriend, you're really not my type.'

And then he stalked off, leaving Tanya stunned and frustrated and very angry in equal measure.

Amy stared out the window and saw Dan and Tanya walk through the big square of light from the clubhouse bar that shone on the hardstanding outside. She watched as Tanya reached up to nibble Dan's ear and then she witnessed them walk together out of sight and into the inky shadows.

How. Fucking. Dare. He? After the accusations he'd levelled at her and now he was going with Tanya? Amy had absolutely no doubt in her mind what the agenda was there. A quickie behind the proverbial bike sheds. Disgusted, she turned away from the window, just in time to miss Dan stalking back to the door, alone.

She couldn't keep up the front that she didn't care any longer so she headed to the loos to seek solitude till she'd pulled herself together. Why did she let the bastard get to her? And when she'd promised herself that he wouldn't.

Maddy saw Dan return to the bar and clocked the look on his face.

'What's with you?'

'Nothing,' he replied with a heavy sigh.

'Doesn't look like nothing from where I am.'

'Tanya's just made a heavy pass at me.'

Maddy snorted. 'So? She makes heavy passes at any man with a pulse.'

Dan shook his head. 'Putting it like that doesn't make it any better. I mean, I know I'm one of a long list, but I've never considered myself to be *only* attractive because I happen to have a pulse.'

'Darling Dan, of course you're more attractive than that, and I am amazed it's taken her so long to get around to you. Frankly I'd have thought she would have had you on her wish list ages ago. If I wasn't so mad-crazy about Seb I wouldn't kick you out of bed.'

Dan laughed. 'You're sweet. Shame Amy doesn't share your opinion.'

'Have you tried to make it up?'

'This evening,' said Dan glumly. 'Total failure. She told me to take a hike in no uncertain terms and using some basic Anglo-Saxon to underline her meaning.'

'She had a go at me too, for not telling her that you were going to be here. She was really cross and said she wouldn't have come if she'd known. I'm really sorry, Dan, but I think you've blown it with her.'

'Unlike what happened between me and Tanya, just now.'

Maddy's eyes widened. 'You didn't let her . . .'

'No, I didn't. But only because I told Tanya . . . well, never mind what I told her, but I think she got the message I wasn't interested. Anyway, I've come back to grab my stuff and say goodbye to you. Thanks for inviting me but given the way things are, I'm not in the mood to enjoy myself and I think I'm only going to put a damper on other people's fun.'

'Oh, Dan, I'm really sorry. Tell you what,' said Maddy. 'Let's go and get a pizza together, have a glass of wine, or two, cry on each other's shoulders about life, love and the universe and then you can walk me back to college. And, no offence, but I do mean *walk me back* I'm not being euphemistic. I imagine you're kipping there tonight too.'

He nodded. 'Got a place on a mate's sofa.' He looked around the party and suddenly felt weary. Stuff trying to say goodbye to his old mates, he was just going to light out with Maddy. 'Get your coat, Mads, you've pulled.'

Dan grabbed his backpack from when he'd stashed it in a corner while Maddy got her coat and then they sped down the stairs.

'Shit,' said Maddy as they hit the final tread. 'My scarf. I must have left it in the bar somewhere. Wait here and I'll be right back.'

Dan leaned against the wall as Maddy raced back to find it. Down here in the hall, the music from the club's

402

stereo system was muted to almost nothing except for the rhythmic boom-boom of the bass speakers which thumped like a heartbeat through the building. Boom-boom and eee-er-eee-er. Something was squeaking in time to the bass. He listened harder. Eee-er-eee-er. And it wasn't the music, it was coming from the gym.

He walked quietly across the floor and listened at the door that led into it. Behind him Maddy clattered back down the stairs, triumphantly waving her scarf. Dan saw she was about to open her mouth and say something so he shushed her.

'What?' she mouthed at him.

Dan beckoned her over. 'Listen,' he whispered.

She cocked an ear. 'Ooh, someone's having a shag in the gym. Who do you think? Rollo?'

'Might be. His sort of style. Angus and Susie? They've got previous.'

'Bet you a fiver it's Rollo.'

'A fiver on Angus.'

'Done.'

They opened the door and peered around it. The eee-er-eee-er got louder.

In the dim light they could make out a couple heavily entwined on one of the benches at the side of the room, the one on top pumping vigorously and the one under - neath, her long brunette hair sweeping the floor, making noises of pleasure and encouragement.

'That's Tanya,' breathed Maddy. She giggled quietly. 'We didn't think of her.' She paused. 'But she was trying to screw you just a few minutes ago. Blimey, that must have been quick work. Or is it Rollo who's shagging her?'

'No. It's some stranger.' Dan let out an uncontrolled snort of laughter and Tanya's eyes snapped open. Above her, her random lover was so carried away, he was oblivious to all other events.

'Fuck off, Dan,' she mouthed.

Dan and Maddy careered out of the boat shed, clutching each other for support as they fell about laughing.

'What is she *like*?' said Maddy. 'She's supposed to be Rollo's bird, she just tried to pull you and now she's shagging some passing bloke.' They began to walk along the path that took them to the city centre.

'Well, that's Tanya for you.'

'I couldn't be like her,' said Maddy. 'I honestly couldn't screw around like that.'

'Seb's a lucky man.'

Maddy shook her head. 'Not yet he isn't.'

Dan stopped in his tracks. 'You're kidding me. Still?'

'I've got to wait till he comes back from Afghanistan now. He should be back just in time for the Olympics. I've even managed to get a couple of tickets to watch the rowing.'

'Shouldn't think he'll want to do that, not with a hot date with you on the cards.'

Maddy smiled. 'We can't stay in bed for all of his leave.'

Dan gave Maddy a squeeze. 'I think if I were Seb I might want to.'

'Awww, Dan. Thanks.'

28

Amy stood on the terrace outside the bar of the hotel and stared at the view of the Portuguese countryside before her. It was a stunning location with the reservoir spread beneath her, sheltered by gently rolling hills and a flawless blue sky above. The winter rains had refreshed the ground and the fields were lush and green, the oranges were ripening in the orchards and the cork oaks were flourishing. She knew it was only January but to her thin English blood, it felt more like May. She breathed deeply – not a whiff of diesel, not a hint of pollution, just freshness with a faint hint of something perfumed or herby. The air was simply delicious.

'It's lovely, isn't it?' Sian had joined her.

'I just can't believe I'm actually here, on the training camp. I was unpacking earlier and I had to pinch myself when I was putting my official GB Rowing shirts in the drawer.'

Sian nodded. 'Me too. Surreal isn't it?'

'I'm just worried that I'll have to hand them back. My place isn't assured, is it? I've got to beat Anna. I feel a bit rubbish about that if I'm honest; she's been the cox for ages and now here I am to try to take it away from her.'

'And how do you think she got her seat, Ames?' said Sian. 'We're all competing against each other all the time.'

'Maybe, but every time I catch sight of her I know that it's me versus her. It's sort of personal.'

'I understand where you're coming from but Nate'll only give you the seat if he thinks you're better. And if you are, don't Ellie and I and the rest deserve the best? It's not just the seat, it's medals too.'

'Okay, you're right. I'll man up.'

Behind them the bar area was filling up as the rest of the sixty or so members of the squad gathered for their official briefing from Nathan which was due to take place in just a few minutes.

'I suppose we'd better get in there and find a seat before they're all gone,' said Amy, moving through the big sliding glass doors. And apart from that consid -eration, she didn't want to get stuck anywhere near Dan. Sian and Amy found a couple of spare chairs at the back and settled down, feeling slightly in awe of some of the super-famous rowers whose company they now shared.

Rollo pulled a chair up and sat down as close to Amy as he could get. 'Hello, gorgeous.' He leered at her. 'What's your room like?'

'Nice, thank you.'

'Fancy showing me?'

'No.'

'I'll show you mine if you show me yours.'

'Grow up, Rollo.'

Across the room Dan was glaring at her. So he thought she was siding with the enemy. As if she would. He ought to know her better than that and, to cover the hurt she felt, she glared back.

'Spoilsport,' said Rollo. 'You're going to get lonely at night. I could keep you company.'

Amy turned to him. 'Rollo, frankly I'd rather have bedbugs keep me company than you.'

'The offer stands.' He patted her knee.

Dan watched but because Amy was making a point of ignoring him she missed the agonised look on his face when Rollo fondled her leg.

The buzz of conversation filled the big airy space as the rowers chatted amongst themselves. The noise died down suddenly as Nate strode in, clipboard in hand. He hauled himself onto the bar and sat there looking at his team.

'Welcome,' he said. 'Some of you have been here before and know the rules and what I expect from you. Others are new to the team and will be feeling a little nervous about your first training camp. However, I do know you're all grown-ups, so you will be treated as such and you're all as dedicated to your rowing as it's possible to be. Let's face it: if you weren't you wouldn't be here.' A small ripple of laughter washed through the room.

'So, the rules are few, but I don't expect any of them to be breached, understand? If they are, you're out of this hotel, out of the squad and on the next plane home. So, no alcohol, no drugs – unless specifically prescribed to you by the team doctor – and no s . . .'

'Sex,' someone heckled.

Nate shook his head. 'No *slacking.*' A big laugh greeted this. 'I wouldn't be so dumb as to try and inflict such a puritanical restriction on you as "no sex" as I know it just wouldn't work.'

'Not with Lyndon-Forster here,' called someone.

'There, you see,' murmured Rollo in Amy's ear, 'it's almost compulsory.'

Amy rolled her eyes.

Nate didn't say a word but grinned broadly. 'The only other rule is that you are not allowed out of the complex. Frankly, I should think that you'll be just too darn tired after each day's training to want to do anything but eat and sleep—'

'—and shag?' asked a hopeful voice, a comment which was greeted with more laughter.

'It's not just me,' said Rollo.

'Shut up,' said Amy with a heavy sigh.

'This is partly for your own safety and partly for security reasons and partly for insurance. All your needs will be catered for here and apart from the village itself down the road, we are in the back of beyond here. There is bugger all out there, trust me.

'I shall pin the training schedules to the noticeboard in the reception, please make a note of when you are boating, when you are supposed to be in the gym or doing road work. You are *not* here to enjoy yourselves,' he said sternly, 'but I hope you do all the same.'

'I for one certainly intend to.' Rollo leered at Amy again but she blanked him

'Any questions?' finished Nate. All the heads in the room shook and a murmur of conversation started up again. 'Dinner is in thirty minutes,' he added. 'You're free to enjoy yourselves till then.'

'Well,' said Sian. 'That all seems very straightforward. I suppose I'd better have a look at what I am expected to do tomorrow and finish unpacking.'

'Me too,' agreed Amy, keen to put space between her and Rollo.

They left some people ordering Cokes or squashes at the bar and joined the majority who were crowding around the big noticeboard by the front desk. They managed to fight their way to a position where they could see their own schedules.

Amy groaned. 'Six thirty breakfast. Sheesh. He was right when he said we weren't here to enjoy ourselves.'

'Early to bed and early to rise . . .' said Sian.

'Makes life as boring as fuck,' said Rollo.

Jeez, couldn't he leave her alone for a minute? 'It's only for a fortnight,' said Amy tartly.

'And as for that business about not being allowed out,' moaned Rollo. 'God, even Belvedere wasn't that restrictive.'

Sian and Amy left Rollo chuntering about stupid bloody rules and went to their rooms to finish unpacking. When they got back to the dining room half an hour later Rollo was still beefing to anyone who would listen that he didn't appreciate being treated like he was still in the Lower Fourth.

'Doesn't he understand how lucky he is to be here?' said Amy to Sian.

'He never will, not in a month of Sundays.'

They went over to the service area to collect their food

from the buffet. The choices were predicable – masses of carbs in the form of pasta and potatoes, lots of vegetables, low-fat proteins like chicken and fish, and a choice of water or fruit juice to drink.

Rollo joked about the fact that he was sure fermented grape juice could be one of his five-a-day but no one laughed.

'It's an act,' said Sian. 'I suspect he's bricking it, like most of us, that he's going to find this fortnight very tough indeed.'

Amy wasn't so sure. She'd seen enough of Rollo's monumental arrogance to suspect that he thought he would waltz through the camp without effort.

They grabbed their food, Amy taking about a quarter as much as Sian, and they went to join Ellie and the others in the women's eight who were already tucking in and discussing excitedly the fact that the next day they would be rowing in a team with some of their idols.

'We've competed against these people in the past, we've seen them win stuff at the World Champs but now we're going to be rowing *with* them. I mean,' said Ellie her eyes shining, 'I mean, it's like *wow*.'

Outside the windows it was already dark and the lights from the hotel gleamed softly on the lake and the moon rose over the hills. Amy ate her supper, and agreed.

Dan watched her animation, her enthusiasm, her easy natural charm and wondered if there was any way he could get her back. He felt bereft without her.

At the end of the sixth day's training, the rowers piled into the hotel beside the reservoir having put away their boats and tidied their kit. They were knackered and hungry, but not cold, something they were all supremely grateful for. The reservoir, tucked in the hills north-east of Lisbon was amazingly sheltered, and the air temperature that day had been a pleasant fifteen degrees. The light was more like that experienced in England in April and the pale blue sky was cloudless so despite the fact that it was effectively midwinter, to the rowers it was like a perfect spring day. Dan, whose training up till then had been almost exclusively on the rivers and lakes of the UK, found having such conditions in the winter a total luxury.

'Hi, Dan,' said a familiar voice behind him as he headed for reception and his room key.

'Angus. What the devil . . .?'

'I've been sent out by the *Herald* to do another piece on the British rowers. They liked the last feature I did and they want more. Now we're into the Olympic year the editors can't get enough stories with some sort of Games angle or hook. Nate's agreed that I can hang out around you guys for the next couple of days.'

'Good for you.'

'Bloody nice hotel,' said Angus appreciatively. 'Glad to see you're not slumming. Susie and I are in a dive in the village. Actually, it's not that bad but it isn't as lush as this place. Just a B & B really.'

'Susie's with you?'

'Yeah. She thought she'd come out with me. We're only here a couple of days and she fancied some winter sun. Trouble is, Nate's being a bit of a git, saying that only authorised people are allowed in the complex and Susie isn't authorised.'

411

'But that's bonkers,' said Dan. 'It isn't as if she isn't one of us. We all know her, for heaven's sakes! Nate knows her.' He got his key and the pair of them started to make their way through the main building and then along the paths that led to the block containing Dan's room.

'I know, but Nate's the boss and they're his rules. Susie's really pissed off, especially as you lot aren't allowed out. She was expecting to have a great time with the girls here and now she's stuck in the village on her own with nothing to do but drink coffee and kick her heels. Anyway, she's enjoying the weather and it's a break.' He sighed. 'Moving on, how is rowing with Rollo? I mean, when you take everything into consideration it's quite a tough ask, making you and him team up again.'

'He's got talent,' said Dan, simply. 'He could help us win medals and that's what it's all about, isn't it?'

'He's got brass neck, no morals and a load of luck. Still doesn't make it right,' grumbled Angus. 'Have you been told which discipline you're being lined up for yet?'

'Definitely sculling, quads or doubles, one or the other.'

'And Rollo?'

'The same.' Dan opened the door of his room. 'Come in. Make us both a cuppa while I make myself presentable.'

Angus got the kettle on, caught him up on some gossip from home regarding the rowing scene there and Dan told Angus how it was at the training camp.

'Don't get me wrong, I know it's a privilege to be here but I'm getting sick of pasta.'

Angus laughed. 'Every meal?'

'It seems like it, although we're spared it at breakfast.'

'And how are you getting on with everyone?'

'Just fine.'

'Even Rollo?'

Dan grimaced. 'We avoid each other as much as possible. And Amy's busy avoiding me. Honestly the way we all move about the room, ducking and diving, it's like some sort of country dance.'

Angus gave a wry laugh. 'But it isn't funny, though, is it?'

Dan shook his head. 'Not really. And because Amy and I aren't an item, Rollo's sniffing around her again. I know I shouldn't let it, but it winds me up. I pissed Amy off so I don't have any rights any more but it's not the point. Angus, I still care about her.'

Angus was clearly embarrassed by the revelation. 'I don't know what to say, old boy.' He shrugged. 'If the grovelling apology didn't work, I honestly don't know where you ought to go next.'

'I was wondering if maybe Susie could drop a hint to her. Tell Amy I'm not all bad, that I am genuinely sorry.'

'But how? I mean she could give her a call, chat on the phone, but she can't meet her here can she what with Nate's rules and everything. I think girls like to do that sort of conversation face to face.'

Dan didn't know so he didn't argue. 'Never mind,' was all he said dejectedly. 'It was just a thought.'

'So is Rollo still trying to shag every woman on the planet?'

'I reckon. He's being more discreet than he used to be but leopards don't change their spots.'

'I'm staggered he has the energy.'

'You know Rollo.'

Dan finished doing up his jeans and slipped a polo shirt over his head, emblazoned with the GB Rowing Team logo.

'I really envy you,' said Angus out of the blue. Dan was puzzled. 'For having the commitment to make the grade.' He pointed at Dan's shirt. 'That's real dedication. I just didn't have the mind-set, I guess, that's why I gave it up. I mean, I still row a bit, mess about on water, but not like I used to when I was trying to get into the Blue Boat. I suppose it was not getting into the Blue Boat that made me quit. I decided, all that effort, all that pain, all that self-sacrifice and then . . . nothing. Well, that's in the past.' He shrugged. 'And hey, I even have a social life now.'

'Lucky you,' said Dan with a certain amount of feeling. 'Having an ambition that is borderline certifiable is probably more of a hindrance than a help in life. I mean, this is all I do at the moment to the exclusion of everything else and what happens when I get too old?'

'Do what you're doing at the moment. Any decent school with a rowing squad will snap you up. And if you got your PGCE – well, an Olympic rower who teaches too . . . the world's your oyster, mate.'

'I'm not an Olympic rower yet, Angus. I'm in the squad. I should make it but it's not a done deal. Injury, not being quite good enough, not improving enough – any or all of those and I'll be out on my ear. There's still a bit of slack in the system; more bums than there are seats.'

Angus shook his head. 'You need more faith in yourself. Now, fancy a pint before dinner?' He stood, ready to leave Dan's room.

'I'd love one but it won't be beer.'

Angus stopped dead in his tracks. 'Now that is dedication. I am in awe.'

'It's the rules. No drugs, no alcohol, no medications of any sort unless they've been checked by the team medics. No risks, no high-jinks . . . no fun, basically!'

'Women?'

'I'm not the guy to ask at the moment.'

Angus shuffled his feet. 'Sorry.'

When they arrived at the bar a dozen or so rowers were already there, downing soft drinks or mineral water. Angus confessed to feeling very self-conscious ordering a local beer.

'Go on,' urged Dan who had just asked for a glass of orange juice. 'It's nice to see someone leading a normal life. I'll enjoy it vicariously. And believe me, after the Games I am going to go on such a bender.'

The barman delivered their drinks and they took them over to a nearby table.

Rollo swaggered in and walked across to stand by them. 'Hello, Angus, old chap. How's life as a hack?'

'Life as a sports journalist,' said Angus emphasising the word 'journalist' just slightly, 'is pretty good. At least I get to drink beer.' He waved his beer glass at Rollo.

Rollo swallowed and a glimmer of envy flickered across his face.

'Beer's not everything,' he said, leaving them to go to the bar. He returned a couple of minutes later with a Diet Coke. 'Cheers.' But his eyes were on Angus's drink as he swigged his own.

Angus quizzed them about their training, their ambitions, their realistic expectations, accepting that some of their answers were guarded.

'Don't want to let the opposition know what we're up to, do we?' drawled Rollo. He notice Angus's glass was empty. 'The other half, old chap? More juice for you, Danny-boy?'

Both men nodded and Rollo went to the bar.

'I thought you said you were avoiding each other,' said Angus, looking at Rollo standing at the bar and waving a twenty-euro note at the barman to gain his attention.

'It's been more of a case of me avoiding him, rather than vice versa. But he is only being chummy because you're here. He probably hopes you'll give him a few column inches.'

Angus laughed. 'That's our Rollo. Always the supremo at self-promo.'

Out of the corner of his eye, Dan saw Rollo take the top half inch off Angus's beer before he carried it over with the other drinks. He thought about saying some - thing but didn't want to start an argument. He was too knackered for that.

Across the bar Amy waggled her fingers at Angus but pointedly didn't come over to talk to him because he was with Dan so he went to join her and her little circle. Naturally she was thrilled to hear Susie was around and then equally hacked off to realise there was no way they could meet.

'If this was Holloway nick I'd at least have visiting rights,' she said. 'That's rubbish that we can't see each other. Maybe we can meet down by the gate. Wave at each other over the barrier like people used to across the Berlin Wall.'

They all laughed but Amy was still annoyed at the unfairness of it and was still grumbling when Sian joined them.

'So, how's it going for the women's eight?' Angus asked her. 'I mean, I assume that's your discipline.'

Sian nodded. 'Good, thanks. All we need to do is get Amy in place as our cox and things'll be even better.'

'You think she's better than Anna?'

'I *know* she's better,' said Sian.

They sipped their drinks as they chatted some more until Angus declared that it was time to go back to Susie and take her out to supper. He returned to Dan and Rollo, who were now sitting together but in silence, to say his goodbyes.

'I think there is some roast suckling pig and a bottle of Vino Verde with our names on them. Sorry to be missing out on the pasta,' he added with a wicked grin.

Angus left the last of his drink on the table as they rose to go and Rollo gathered up the almost empty glasses and returned them to the bar, swigging the last of Angus's beer as he went. Should he mention it, Dan wondered again. In the great scheme of things, did two mouthfuls of stolen beer matter a jot? Dan decided against it.

'I'll see you tomorrow, guys,' Angus said as he left the hotel.

'Wine with a meal,' said Rollo. 'I dream of that.'

'It's only till after the Games,' said Dan. 'Get over it.' Rollo didn't have to be here if he didn't want to be.

The meal was pleasant enough and for a change didn't consist of pasta but was still loaded with protein and carbs to ensure their energy levels and body-building abilities were maintained.

'Just think,' said Rollo. 'Chilled Vino Verde.' He looked at his glass of mineral water in disgust.

'Shut up,' said Dan.

'What I'd give to be able to stroll into the village like Angus.'

'Well, fuck off and do it then,' said Dan, his patience wearing extremely thin. 'Go on, blow your chances.'

Rollo shook his head and assured Dan he was as committed as any of them but Dan wasn't entirely convinced. He knew Rollo too well.

29

Dan was in his room getting ready for bed, brushing his teeth while gazing out of the window over the moonlight reflecting on the lake. Once again he felt a thrill of happiness that he was here in a great hotel, in a lovely setting, with lots of likeminded people and friends for company and learning so much from the fantastic coaching he knew his rowing had achieved a whole new level. Maintaining that level on his return to the UK was going to be a challenge but he now truly knew what he was capable of and the heights he might yet attain.

But anything he might achieve in the future wasn't going to be the same without Amy there to share the pleasure with him. He'd really hoped that once they'd got to Portugal he'd get a chance to try and win her back but the way she constantly ignored him had left him in no doubt that he'd completely and utterly stuffed his chances there. And it hurt.

A movement on the path outside caught his eye. He recognised that gait. It was Rollo. Where was he going? A suspicion formed in Dan's mind. He raced over to his basin, rinsed his mouth, grabbed his key and left his room. The hotel was deserted. Everyone had gone to bed despite it only being nine at night. But in the village, where people siesta'd in the afternoon, the bars and cafés would just be getting into the evening rush.

He sped along the track that led past the apartments around the main hotel complex, the bright moon making it easy to find his way. The barrier at the gate was down but the little security hut was empty. Not that Dan was very concerned that he was also breaking the rules by leaving the complex, he was far more driven by the prospect of catching Rollo red-handed and getting even for the Boston trials. A couple of hundred yards away he could see a dark figure, walking swiftly and with a purpose down the little road that led to the village whose lights were softly glimmering about a mile away.

Dan kept his distance and walked close to the edge of the path so he could blend in with the scrub that flanked it should Rollo turn. But Rollo didn't so much as look behind him as he strode towards his destination. Once they reached the outskirts of the village of Aviz, Dan dropped back a bit further, the streetlights making it difficult to remain inconspicuous. Rollo made his way towards the centre. Obviously, having got a taste for beer and remembering how much he liked it he was determined to have some more. Or that bottle of chilled Vino Verde he'd banged on about.

Ahead, on the skyline, Dan could make out the twin white towers of the little church with its red, pantiled roof, the solid stone tower next to it and the white and red houses of the surrounding streets. More of a village than a town but it had all the essentials for its inhabitants' needs, including a number of watering holes.

Predictably, Rollo didn't bother searching for the nicest or the most convivial bar but went into the first one he came to. Dan loitered for a few minutes before following him in. If he was going to accuse him of having an illicit drink he needed to be sure Rollo had been served with one.

Rollo was at the bar drinking deeply from a glass of the local brew when Dan tapped him on the shoulder. Rollo jumped so violently his beer slopped over his hand. He swung round, his face a mask of guilt.

'Dan!' Then he laughed. 'So you fancied a beer too, did you?'

Dan just stared at him. 'What the hell do you think you're doing? You know the rules.'

'For fuck's sake, don't be such a snivelling little teacher's pet.'

'I'm not. The rules are there for a reason. It's about what's best for the team – and us. Don't you want to win?'

'What, like you do? Get all the glory? Be the toast of the country?'

'Yes,' said Dan simply. 'What's wrong with that?'

'All work and no play, Danny-boy? But considering how dull you are anyway, I don't suppose it'll be noticeable in your case.'

Dan sighed. 'Change the record, Rollo.'

'Look, I just fancied one beer. That's all. It's not a crime.'

'Nate won't see it like that.'

'You're not going to snitch on me are you?' Rollo said with breezy insouciance but Dan knew he was worried.

'Give me a good reason why not?'

'Because I'd get thrown out. It'd wreck my chances.'

'So whose fault would that be? You're letting us *all* down. Why on earth should he keep you in the team when there are others who'd give their eye teeth to be in the squad but can't be because someone who is so arrogant that he believes the rules don't apply to him is keeping them out. And given your track record in cheating, maybe you shouldn't have made it this far.'

'It's just one drink,' said Rollo defensively, ignoring the other jibe.

The barman said something in Portuguese to Dan – obviously asking if he wanted a drink too. Dan shook his head.

'But if I hadn't have pitched up? Admit it: you'd have had another, and another.'

'No.' But Rollo's colour told Dan he was lying.

'If you leave now and come back with me, I swear I'll keep quiet. But if you don't . . .' Dan shook his head. 'I'm making no promises.'

Rollo stared at him. 'You would too, wouldn't you, you bastard.'

Dan nodded. 'I don't owe you anything, quite the reverse, and I may end up rowing with you. It's on the cards, we always get paired in the double sculls—'

'Not that you want it to stay that way. I've heard you want to go it alone. You want the seat in the single scull.'

Dan didn't ask how Rollo knew that had once been his ambition till Nate had told him he wouldn't achieve it this time round. But it was still a dream. And the only person who he'd ever told about it had been Amy. How could she? How could she have told Rollo? Did she hate him *that* much? The quote 'hell hath no fury like a woman scorned' floated across his brain. And he'd certainly scorned Amy, so he supposed he deserved it. But it still hurt.

'That's not going to happen now.'

'But you still want shot of me and if you dob me in it, you'll get your way. But who will you row with then, Danny-boy? I don't think you've thought this through.'

'I don't care and Nate'll find someone else. All I do know is that I'm *not* going to row with anyone who doesn't give it one hundred per cent. I want a medal and I'm going to do everything in my power to get one. And if that means getting rid of someone who is jeopardising my chances, then I will. It's up to you, Rollo. Your call. But don't think I won't tell Nate, because I will.' Dan turned and walked towards the door of the bar. In a mirror on the wall by the window he watched Rollo glance at his beer and then push it onto the bar.

'Wait,' he said. 'I'm coming.'

They walked out of the village in silence. Dan could feel the anger radiating off Rollo. He didn't dare say anything, afraid it might be misconstrued as being smug.

They were nearing the roundabout at the edge of the town when Rollo muttered, 'I'm sorry.'

'I beg your pardon?' Dan stopped in his tracks.

'You heard me,' he said.

'Yeah. I just wasn't expecting an apology. I didn't ask for one.'

'No, but you're right.'

'You feeling okay?'

423

'Very funny.'

'So what made you do it? What made you think it would be a good idea to try and sneak a drink?' They began walking again.

'It's all very well being strong-minded when everyone else is but when Angus came along and had that beer I could smell it, I could taste it. I wanted it.'

'But it's only for another few months. Is it really worth ruining it all just for the sake of a beer? I don't get it.'

'Maybe I shouldn't be here. Maybe I don't have the mind-set.'

'That's what Angus said earlier. He said he recognised he didn't have the dedication to make the grade. That's why he gave up the struggle to get there.'

'I've never *not* achieved, my dad saw to that.'

'I'm not with you.'

'My dad doesn't do failure. If he thinks failure might be on the cards he throws money at the problem till the possibility goes away. Or he throws money at an opportunity to ensure it succeeds from the start. When I was at prep school and I was about to go to Belvedere, because he wanted me to play rugby for the school, he got me private coaching so I'd be the stand-out player of my year from the get-go. Then he decided he wanted me on the rowing squad so I got coached for that. All the way through school I spent my holidays having private coaching to make sure I was in the squad or in the first fifteen or even captain of sport, and then I had maths and English coaching just to make sure I got a place at Oxford.'

'Which all happened.'

'Yeah. My father never left anything to chance.'

'But you made the Blue Boat. That's one hell of an achievement.' Dan sensed Rollo shaking his head, as if he was denying it. Dan didn't understand. 'Well, you did. No one can deny you that.'

'I think they would if they knew,' said Rollo quietly. 'Do you know just how much money my dad gave to the boat club?'

For the second time in as many minutes Dan stopped dead in his tracks. 'No!'

'I don't know if it made any difference but before the final selection was made Chuck told me it was a toss-up between me and Angus. My dad just did his best to make sure the coin came down the right way up.'

Dan thought about what Angus had said to him only a matter of a couple of hours before. But maybe Rollo would have got the seat anyway. And maybe Angus didn't have the mind-set. But even so it was a very uncomfortable piece of knowledge. He put it to the back of his mind for the time being.

'But you're here because you made it through the trials.'

Rollo nodded again. 'But I'm not completely sure I want to be. I'm here because I couldn't face how my father would react if I hadn't. I thought if I could get through the trials it would all get easier, but it hasn't. It's getting harder and harder and I'm hating it. I've never really done self-sacrifice. All my life I've had it pretty cushy and suddenly I'm expected to toe the line on everything. Dan, I'm finding it so hard,' Rollo admitted.

'Then give it up.' They'd reached the edge of the hotel

complex. Almost all the bedrooms were in darkness. There were lights shining from the reception and some security lights blazed but it was obvious that the vast majority of its guests were asleep. The two men tramped along the path that led towards their block of rooms.

'Let's go and sit by the lake,' said Rollo, so they carried on past their front door. Once by the reservoir, they found a bench and stared at the silver ribbon of moonlight that streaked the black water like a parting through a head of ebony hair. 'I can't give it up,' he said.

'You could. You just go to Nate and say you'd rather someone else has your seat.'

'But you see, even though I'm hating it, hating the self-sacrifice, hating the restrictions, hating the training regime, I've suddenly realised that if I do row at the Games and we do get a medal, then I'll know that it's something I've achieved for myself and not because of my father's millions. It'll somehow vindicate the seat I had in the Blue Boat – the seat I wasn't sure I deserved. I think for the first time in my life I'll feel really proud of myself.'

'But you nearly blew it tonight.'

'I know. I don't know what came over me. I have no idea why I suddenly had this absolute total craving to go and get pissed. I mean, I've got pissed loads of times but it's never been a taboo before. I never thought I'd say this, Dan, but I owe you for that.'

'Blimey,' said Dan, blowing out his cheeks. 'I followed you to get the evidence to drop you right in it; I didn't plan on it ending like this.'

Rollo laughed. 'At least this time you haven't hit me because I've been a complete pillock.'

'No. I suppose I owe you an apology for that in return.'

'No, I deserved it. I've been a shit.'

Dan nodded. 'You really have.' He wondered momentarily about taking Rollo to task over Amy but he could hardly blame Rollo for his own, staggeringly crass behaviour.

Rollo nodded. 'I'm sorry but I was so envious of you.'

'What the fuck? You? Envious of me? The poor boy whose mum was the school dinner lady?'

'You mother was always so proud of you. I could see it in her eyes every time she saw you in the dining hall.'

'Come off it, Rollo, I'll have to get the tissues out in a minute.'

'No, really. Because Dad had thrown so much money at my education anything I did was just a return on his investment. At the end of the day, I was just a walking balance sheet. Profit and loss – that was all that I ever represented to him.'

'So you picked on me to make yourself feel better. And did it?'

'There's no denying it did at the time. Or I thought it did. Looking back I'm pretty ashamed. So while I'm at it I'd better apologise for that too.'

Dan stood up and held out his hand. 'Accepted. And let's call it quits, eh?'

The two men shook on it, then Dan yawned and glanced at his watch. 'Shit a brick, it's gone ten. I'll be dead in the morning.'

The pair walked back towards the hotel. 'Thanks again,' said Rollo.

Dan shrugged. 'Glad to have been of service.' He took his key out of his pocket and went into his room. On the plus side, he thought, Rollo wasn't his enemy any more. On the minus side Amy was – and how. Any pleasure he might have gleaned from the rapprochement with Rollo was completely wiped out by the knowledge that Amy hated him as much as she did. How could he have been such a total wanker to lose her?

30

Sian and Amy met at the breakfast buffet. Sian had a plate laden with several rashers of bacon, eggs, fried bread and beans while Amy had a glass of juice and a slice of toast on her tray.

'Sleep well?' said Sian.

'Like a log, thanks. I have no right to be as tired as I am. I don't do half of what you guys do.'

'You're pretty busy. There in the gym, encouraging us to keep going, out on the water with us, always finding ways to motivate us all.'

'No more than Anna does.'

Sian shrugged. She didn't think Anna was a patch on Amy in that department and she knew from some of the things the others in the eight had said that they didn't either but it wasn't down to them. The final decision rested with Nate and it had yet to be made.

'So what have you got on your schedule today?' asked Sian.

'Not a lot. Anna's out with you lot to do her time trials so I'm pretty free. Complete loose end, actually. Which is great as I can spend the whole morning brooding about my time trial tomorrow with nothing to take my mind off it. Nate's pretty much told us that the result will determine who gets the seat.'

'No pressure then.'

'No, none at all.' Amy grimaced as she felt a little rustle of butterfly wings in her stomach at the thought of what lay ahead.

'Still, a morning off,' said Sian with feeling as she contemplated her own training schedule of gym work, two two-thousand-metre pieces with Anna coxing, two coaching sessions with Chuck and a five-mile run. 'What are you going to do?'

'Dunno. I seem to have run out of books, I've read most of the mags in the lounge and the weather today isn't really nice enough just to sunbathe.'

'It *is* January,' pointed out Sian although they both knew that so far they'd been spoilt with warm tem - peratures and blue skies. Today it was breezy and there was a definite nip in the air.

'Don't you worry about me. I'll find something to amuse myself for the day.'

'You'd better hope that Rollo isn't at a loose end too.'

Amy shuddered. 'Just because I *once* made that mistake . . .'

'So twice shy.'

Amy nodded with feeling. 'Never again.'

Amy kicked around the hotel for a couple of hours, doing a few bits of washing, sorting her kit out, writing a postcard to her mum and dad and then the boredom really took hold. She thought of going to the lounge and watching the news on the satellite TV, or making a cup of tea, or going for a walk or even going down to the lakeside and watching the rowing action but that meant she might run into Dan. Every time she caught sight of him she felt as if acid was dripping directly into her heart and because the pain was so intense she avoided him completely. She knew she looked like a sulky cow by refusing to make eye contact with him but it was the only way she could cope.

Her phone trilled. Susie.

'Hi, babe,' she said.

'Hi, Ames. Are you busy? I've just had a call from Angus and he says you're at a bit of a loose end today, so what are you up to?'

'Nothing. Angus is right; I've sort of got the day off.'

'Really? So you're bored too.'

'Totally.'

'I wish I hadn't come over to Portugal with Angus. I thought I'd be allowed into the hotel. If I was, you and I could have had a good time today.'

'Nate's really strict.'

'And you're not allowed out, Angus says.'

'No, although I can't see why. He says it's for security and insurance but, honestly, how dodgy would it be to just go for a walk down the road?'

'Why not, Ames? I mean, why not come over to the village? It's not like you're one of the rowers.'

Amy thought about it. She was sick of mooching round the hotel doing nothing and no one need know.

'Okay, Susie, why not?'

'I'll meet you in the square in front of the church. You

431

can't miss the church, there's only one and you can see it from everywhere. Fifteen minutes?'

'It's a date.'

Amy skipped back to her room, grabbed a jacket and some euros and slipped out of the hotel. As she neared the barrier she left the tarmacked drive and took to the scrubby undergrowth that flanked the manicured verges. She walked past the barrier and the security hut and the guard who was reading a battered paperback and smoking a cigarette and turned onto the track that led to the village.

'Susie,' she squealed as she saw her friend across the paved square outside the little church. She ran the last few yards. 'It's so good to see you. What a surprise.'

'And you. Let's find a bar and a coffee. I'm chilly.'

The two girls walked to a nearby café and found a table in the window where they could watch village life while they chatted. Amy ordered a Coke and a bowl of ice cream while Susie asked for a coffee and a locally made pastry.

'I feel like I'm bunking off,' said Amy.

'You are.'

'But of all the things I could do, meeting a girlfriend for elevenses is hardly a crime.'

'No, of course it isn't. Just don't get caught going back.'

'No chance. The chap on the barrier is the doziest security guard I've ever seen. I reckon the entire Red Army could march up the drive and he wouldn't notice.'

'So what's the training camp like?' asked Susie.

Amy told her a little of what went on, nothing specific, nothing Nate could possibly take offence to.

432

'And how's Rollo?' asked Susie.

'The same. Still being a letch, still sniffing around anything in a skirt, still being obnoxious and arrogant . . . oh, and that reminds me, did you hear from Maddy that Tanya shagged a virtual stranger in the gym the night of that party after the second Boston trials? What a slapper, eh?' Amy presumed she must have done that right after she'd shagged Dan round the back of the boat shed. But she couldn't tell Susie that bit, not without making herself miserable.

Susie laughed, spluttering crumbs across the table. 'What would we do without Rollo and Tanya to keep us entertained?'

Amy agreed.

'So what about you and Dan?'

Amy shook her head. 'I'm not talking about that.'

'You should. You know Dan told Angus that he's still got feelings for you?'

'Oh yes? Jealousy about me and Rollo being the primary one I should imagine.'

'No. Dan's really upset, he told Angus as much. And you know how those public-school types never reveal their feelings.'

'Never reveal their feelings? Suse, Dan revealed his to me in no uncertain terms after the Boston trial. It was horrible. I told Maddy and I'll tell you: Dan and I are finished. We both need to move on so please just let us.'

'I guess that's me told.'

'Sorry,' said Amy, 'but that's how it is.' She finished her ice cream, licking her spoon and scraping out the bowl. 'Yum,' she said as she pushed her plate away from her.

She glanced at her watch. 'I hate to be a party pooper, Susie but I need to get back soon. It'll be lunch in half an hour and I don't want to be missed.'

'No, you go. I'll get the bill.'

'You sure?'

'Yes, call it an apology for dragging Dan into the conversation. You scoot. And I think Angus is going to be around this afternoon, so we're probably going to do a bit of sightseeing. Maybe go to Lisbon.'

'Lucky old you. All I've seen of Portugal is what we saw from the coach windows on the transfer from the airport.'

'You need to come here on a holiday when this is all over, the beaches are lovely – so I'm told.'

'Fat chance of seeing them this trip though.'

Amy slipped back unnoticed and joined the others in the lunch queue as though nothing had happened. She'd made Susie swear not to tell Angus the pair had met and as far as Amy was concerned her little moment of skiving was a safe secret.

After lunch she went down to the gym to help the rowers keep motivated and energised with words of encouragement. They always appreciated her presence because she had a knack of getting them to do the extra rep, the extra push, the extra couple of minutes, making their session just that fraction more productive than they'd have achieved on their own.

After she'd finished helping out in the gym, the weather had picked up and, knowing that Dan was out doing road work around the complex, she went down to the lake to watch the rowing. The women's eight was doing a second trial. She watched the boat skim across the water and she tried to judge if the crew was doing better with Anna than they'd ever done with her. But it was impossible to tell without a stopwatch. She judged the rate was about thirty-six or thirty-seven but could she get the crew to squeeze more out of their performance? Could she get them to knock a second or two off their time with Anna? They looked good – but then so they should. This was the national crew, eight women at the top of their game who had now been training together for a week – and in the case of four of the crew, since the Olympics in Beijing. It was only Ellie and Sian and two others who were new to the squad. Oh, and herself if she was good enough.

That thought reminded her that it would be her time trials tomorrow and she suddenly felt her guts gripe. Bloody butterflies – only this time these ones weren't just butterflies. These were great vultures. But this is the Big One, she told herself. This is shit or bust. And talking of shit . . . she suddenly had a desperate urge for the loo.

She raced back to her room and got to her bathroom just in time as the squits hit and her bowels turned to water.

After she'd finished, she sat on the bog for a few seconds feeling quite shaky. Jesus Christ, if she was this nervous before a time trial, what the hell was she going to be like before a race at the Olympics? Maybe, if she was going to be this nervous, there might be something she'd be allowed to take to calm her down. She hoped to goodness there was some sort of medical cork she'd be allowed. She wouldn't want to be out on the water if she was hit by another such event.

Amy lay on her bed and tried to relax. It was only a time trial. If she failed, Anna would be cox. It wouldn't be the end of the world, she told herself. She just wished her guts would be as rational about it as her head and stop churning.

By suppertime she was feeling slightly calmer and not so shaky and she risked taking herself off to the dining room. The trouble was, when she was confronted by the mounds and mounds of steaming platters her appetite deserted her. She picked at some tuna bake and salad, eating almost nothing of what was on her plate, more just rearranging it, and hoped that no one would ask why she was off her food. She really didn't want to have to own up to the fact that she was literally shitting herself at the prospect of her own personal test the next day. What a wuss that would make her. However, as all the rowers were used to her eating like a bird no one really paid any attention.

After supper, while other rowers went to the sitting room to chat or discuss their training, Amy felt a wave of exhaustion wash over her. She yawned hugely, thinking that the stress of her time trial the next day had to be getting to her. She went to bed hoping that after a good night's sleep she would wake refreshed, raring to go and more relaxed.

She awoke in the middle of the night and knew in the instant she became conscious that she was about to be violently sick. Gulping, she raced into her bathroom, snapping on the light as she ran. She was about to lean over the lav when she realised that she wasn't just feeling nauseous. She grabbed the plastic waste bin as she sat on the toilet and for the next five minutes she didn't know how it was possible to lose so much bodily waste so continuously and not be turned inside out. The awful retching and griping ceased eventually and, shivering and shaking, Amy hauled herself off the loo, rinsed out the bin and switched on the shower. She slumped in the corner of the shower stall as the hot water washed over her until she felt vaguely clean. Feeling wasted and shaky she managed to stand upright and turn the taps off again. Her head swam as she sipped some water and then crept back to bed. She lay under the covers trying to get warm again as, despite the hot shower, she was chilled to the bone.

This wasn't nerves, she knew. She remembered the ice cream she'd eaten with Susie. The shits had started in the afternoon, so if it had been something wrong with the food at lunch others would have been taken ill too. It stood to reason that it had to be the only thing that she'd eaten and no one else had. Twice more in the night she was violently sick, and each time all she brought up was the water she'd sipped. And yet, despite the fact that she was just vomiting a tablespoon of water, her body seemed to be making her sick up her ankles as well. Her stomach ached, her diaphragm felt as if a herd of elephants had used it as a trampoline, and her throat burned. She couldn't remember ever feeling so awful before in her life.

By the time her alarm went off at six she felt as if she done several rounds with a prizefighter before being pushed through a mangle. Never in her life had she felt so battered or so wrung out. And she couldn't ask for help or sympathy because if she did it was bound to emerge that she didn't have a 'bug' picked up somewhere. And when she dragged herself to the dining room for breakfast, feeling bone-weary and still wiped-out, it was obvious it was just her. Her theory that the ice cream was the culprit was right; everyone else was a picture of health and vitality, so there was no way she could ask Nate to give her a day's grace before her own trial, because she had broken one of his cardinal rules. But if she kept quiet she might just perform well enough to win a place at the Olympics. Amy knew she had no choice.

31

Amy pretended that she was eating a proper breakfast but again, no one really noticed. No one except Ellie.

'Are you all right?' she asked.

'Fine,' she said, forcing her face into a smile and praying she didn't still smell of sick.

'You look a bit pale.'

'Oh, you know. Big day.'

'You sure that's all it is?' Ellie peered at her really closely. 'You look pretty peaky to me. You sickening for something?'

'Me? Nah! Fit as a fiddle.'

'Good, because we really need you to do well with this trial today. Obviously we'll all do our best for you too. But we so want you to beat Anna's time.'

Great. Even more pressure.

Amy trudged down to the lakeside, wearing a hoodie because she still felt shivery despite the fact it was a glorious day and the temperature was warm. The girls were too busy getting the boat ready to notice how quiet she was and it was only when she was sitting opposite Sian, the stroke, that she was quizzed again.

'Bloody hell, Ames, you're going to fry in that top.' Then she looked at her friend more closely. 'Are you all right? You're a bloody funny colour.'

'Just nerves,' said Amy gulping slightly as she felt her stomach heave at the motion of the water beneath the boat.

Sian gave her a hard stare. 'Okay, if you say so, but you don't normally get nervous.'

'I don't normally do time trials for the Olympics,' Amy snapped back.

They paddled up to the point that designated the start of the two-kilometre piece back down the lake. With each surge of the boat as the girls drove it forward Amy felt her gorge rise. This was torment and they were only paddling. What would it be like on the return when they were pelting back at full speed? She wouldn't allow herself to think about it – but the feeling of nausea dominated everything to the exclusion of all else.

'Amy,' said Sian. 'You really do look awful. Are you going to be sick?'

It was the last straw. She leaned over the boat and hurled. When she'd finished the girls in the boat looked shocked and concerned. Chuck and Nate in their launch puttered over.

'What's the matter, Amy?' said Chuck and once again she lied about her nerves, causing Chuck and Nathan to exchange worried glances.

'I'm fine,' she reassured everyone, taking a swig out of her water bottle to rinse her mouth. She spat the water into the lake, not wanting to swallow it and risk having it boomerang back like everything else that had passed her lips in the past twelve hours.

'You're not preggers, are you?' asked Sian.

'No, I'm bloody not.' For a second her indignation subsumed her nausea. 'It's just bloody nerves, okay.'

'Okay,' called Chuck, through a loud hailer. 'Standard procedure, I'll give you a start and I want you to head to the finish in your best time.'

Amy got her crew settled, the girls crouched forwards in their sliding seats, their sweeps in the water ready for the first drive. Down the lake Amy could see the pontoon that represented the finishing line. She prayed she could hold it together for the six minutes it would take to get there.

'Attention, go.' And they were off. Surge, dip, surge, dip . . . it was awful. Amy began to encourage her crew with all the skill she had while ignoring the urge to vomit. She checked the cox-box at her feet. What was she thinking of? The rate was only thirty-five. She called a rhythm, got the pace up to where it ought to have been and then got the crew focused on their technique. But when she re-checked the rate it had fallen again. Her concentration was shot to bits, she was hopeless and the harder she tried the worse it seemed to get.

When they crossed the line she could see from the box that they'd put in a shit time and it was entirely her fault. The crew had nothing to do with that performance; it was all down to her.

'Amy?' said Sian. 'What gives? Are you throwing this? Do you want Anna to beat you to the Olympics? If so, you're going the right way about it.'

441

Amy could feel her eyes filling up. No, she wanted to yell. No, I want this as much as the next person but I've sabotaged my own chances and I can't admit it to anyone.

The atmosphere amongst Amy's coterie of friends in the bar that evening was subdued.

'So I've asked Nate if I can fly home tomorrow,' said Amy on the brink of tears again.

'Oh, Ames, surely you can stay till the end,' said Ellie.

'I really don't want to. And I've got a day job, remember.'

'But you were so good right up until today, I just don't understand it,' said Sian.

'You're better than Anna,' said Ellie, 'really you are. Our time in yesterday's trial wasn't that good. You've got a faster time out of the Reading eight than Anna got out of us. This is ridiculous. You ought to ask Nate to give you another go. Besides, I don't think you were well. Are you sure it was just nerves?'

Amy thought about owning up but the idea of a bollocking from Nate on top of everything else was too much to bear. And anyway, it wouldn't change anything; she would still be out of the squad, only it would be a dismissal for breaking the rules instead of for being crap. Either way she was stuffed.

Dan's heart ached for Amy but there was nothing he could do to comfort her and if he tried he knew he'd just make it worse.

Amy's flight landed at Heathrow and as she made her

way through the airport to continue her journey back to Reading she was assaulted by the 2012 Olympic logo everywhere she looked. Every advert, every billboard seemed to belong to an official sponsor of the Games, mocking her with what she was going to be missing out on. As she sat on the rattly Piccadilly-line train she'd never felt more miserable in her life.

She let herself in to Ellie's house a couple of hours later and with the door safely shut behind her she allowed her emotions to flood out. Lying on the sofa, she howled and howled. Eventually her sobs died away. She knew feeling sorry for herself wasn't going to solve anything but there was something cathartic about such a release of emotion. Feeling more clear-headed she took her kit to her room and unpacked. She'd left her GB Rowing T-shirts on her bed back at the hotel so she didn't have those to remind her of her failure but there was plenty of other stuff in her case that twisted the knife. But she was cried-out so she gathered up the dirty clothes and bundled them in the washing machine before sitting back on the sofa and ringing her mum.

'Hello, sweetie,' said her mum. 'I wasn't expecting to hear from you for another few days. How did you get on?'

'That's the thing, Mum, I came home early because I didn't make the grade.'

There was a small pause before her mother said brightly, 'Oh dear, I am sorry. But never mind, there'll be other opportunities.'

'I don't think so, Mum. I've decided to give up on the rowing. I need to think about my career.'

'That's a shame but if that's what you think is for the best.'

'I do, Mum.'

'So how was Portugal?'

Amy told her, leaving out the details of her grisly episode following her illicit ice cream.

'Anyway, I'd better ring off now. I need to contact work and see if they want me back in.'

She didn't need to ring work, of course, she was on leave for another few days but she could feel the tears starting to well again and she couldn't face breaking down with her mother listening. The sympathy and the maternal clucking and concern would just make everything so much worse.

Amy spent the next day loafing around the little house on her own, trying to avoid thinking about the Olympics and rowing and what her friends were doing. In the end she gave in and took herself up to Chazey Hall just to relieve the monotony. She knocked on Nick Bradbury's office door and waited a couple of seconds till he called her in.

Yet again she had to explain her early return and try and put a brave face on it, only this time she owned up to breaking the rules.

'You stupid twat,' said Nick evenly.

'I know,' said Amy, relieved to have told the truth to someone.

'I mean, ice cream of all things. It was probably left over from last summer. Everyone knows how dodgy it can be.'

'Everyone but me, apparently.'

'So what are you going to do now?'

'Keep working for you. I'm sacking the rowing lark, so I can work my fair share of the weekend shifts from here on in. I won't need scads of time off in July and August and Mike and Alastair won't need to keep covering for me.'

'Obviously I'm pleased about that but I'm also really disappointed on your behalf.'

'Don't, Nick, I'm only just holding it together.'

'But what about all your rowing buddies?'

'What about them?'

'Well, won't Reading Rowing Club still want you?'

'Tough. Nick, when I was asked to try for the national squad I honestly thought I wouldn't care that much if I didn't succeed. There was another cox in the frame and it was a case of may the best woman win and all that.' She gave Nick a weak smile. 'But when I didn't . . .' Amy blew out her cheeks and forced the rising sob back down into her chest. 'When I didn't, I realised that I wanted this more than anything I'd ever wanted. That it was the most enormous deal and I'd fucked up monumentally. All by myself. I can't bear the thought of going through that again and I know that if I continue to cox I won't be able to put it behind me. Clean break – that's what's needed.'

'And your housemate? She's a rower, isn't she?'

Amy nodded. 'I know. Convincing her that I'm serious about this is going to be tricky. Maybe I'll need to move out.'

'That's a bit drastic, isn't it?'

'I'm joking.' She hoped.

They arranged that Amy could start work again the

next day and Nick promised to send her her shift pattern for the next few weeks.

At least, thought Amy as she made her way back to her house, she had something else to occupy herself now, and she wouldn't be sitting around moping and feeling sorry for herself.

32

It took a while for the others at the training camp to notice the sea-change between Rollo and Dan. It only became really apparent to all and sundry a couple of days later when they were all milling around on the jetty. Dan had stripped off his tracksuit and dumped it on the ground ready to start his next training session on the water with Rollo. Beside them, on the flat calm lake, was their boat, waiting from them to step in. Nate was giving the two men a final briefing about how he wanted them to attack the two-thousand piece they were about to row.

'Given that the Kiwis rowed six-ten at the World Championships we have to expect that the predicted gold medal time for 2012 is going to be faster. The World record is still six-three and has stood for two years. You've got to aim for that. Which means I want you to aim at one minute thirty seconds for the first, second and last of each of the five-hundred-metre pieces. You can slacken off a little in the third but remember the more you do, the more you have to make up at the end. To be in with a chance of a medal at Dorney you have to be looking at getting PBs now. Understand?'

Dan and Rollo looked at each other and shrugged. 'We'll give it our best shot, Nate,' said Dan while Rollo nodded in agreement.

Nate turned to go and talk to the men's coxless fours crew, and not particularly looking where he was going, caught his foot on Dan's pile of clothes. He lost his footing and began to fall, but Dan, with lightning reactions, jumped forward, shot out a hand and caught him, but in doing so managed to kick his own clothes, clean off the landing stage and into the water.

'Fuck,' he said, as he watched the thick fleecy cotton start to sink. He let go of Nate and knelt down on the wooden planking to grab his kit. He managed to haul out his bottoms but the top had already sunk.

Rollo, kicking off his trainers, ran back along the jetty to where it joined the slipway and waded out into the water.

'Don't bother, Rollo,' said Dan. 'I'll do it.'

'No, you stay put. I need you to mark the place it fell in,' said Rollo as he continued wading out, the water passing his knees and then his thighs as he drew level with where Dan was still standing on the jetty.

'It must be around here somewhere,' he said to Dan, as he felt around in the soft, slimy mud with his feet.

'Don't bother,' yelled Dan. 'It's only a fleece.'

But at that moment Rollo cried out and fell backwards in a flurry of expletives and splashes. 'Fuck, fuck, fuck,' he yelled as he surfaced, spluttering and thrashed his way towards the shore, his gait ungainly and stumbling.

'What's up, mate?' called Dan running along the jetty to meet him. Rollo threw himself onto the edge of the jetty and examined the sole of his foot.

'I trod on something really sharp,' he said. 'It bloody hurt.'

'Let me look,' said Dan, genuinely concerned.

Rollo stretched his leg out so Dan could see what the problem was. Nate came running up too. 'How bad?' he asked.

'It's a cut. I don't think it's too deep,' said Dan peering at the damage. A trickle of blood seeped from the wound and ran down Rollo's foot where it dripped off his toes. 'But God knows what's in that mud down there. I should think a tetanus jab and antiseptic cream for starters. I'll take him back to the hotel and get the medic on it.'

It was only after the pair left that the other rowers looked at each other in bewilderment.

'Fuck me,' said Ellie, 'what is it with those two?'

'Maybe they've been repressing their real feelings all these years. I mean, you know what boys' boarding schools are like,' Sian said with a smirk.

Ellie stared at Sian and shook her head slowly. 'What a load of bollocks. But something's going on there after all these years of the pair of them being barely on speaking terms.'

The training that morning continued. The women's eight went out on the water with Anna as cox. Nate and Chuck watched from a following launch, both of them using their years of experience and expertise to assess the performance of these elite women.

'It's not good enough, Chuck,' said Nate.

'It's ragged, I agree.'

To the untrained eye the girls seemed to be rowing in

perfect unison, their sweeps dipping in and out of the water with a beautiful rhythm, which, viewed from the stern, resembled the beating wings of a bird. But Nate and Chuck could see an extra splash here and there, a shower of droplets which meant a less-than-perfect stroke, they noted a blade entering the water a fraction later than the other seven or exiting a fraction earlier. It was the sort of error that meant nothing on a training run but under stress, in a race, might mean a sudden catastrophic loss of technique ending up with the rower catching a crab and causing mayhem for the rest of the eight. And over and above that the eight seemed . . . lacklustre. Nate couldn't put his finger on it but there was something not quite right about the crew as an entity. And the more he watched as they powered down the lake the more uneasy he grew.

The women finished their training session and paddled back to the shore. Once they had their boat out of the water, their sweeps hanging on the racks and their kit organised for the next session, Nate drew Sian to one side.

'How's it going?' he asked.

'Terrific,' she said brightly.

'Let's walk,' said Nate, steering Sian away from the path that led up to the hotel and onto the one that led around the lake. 'There's something not right,' he said. 'I can see it in your performance – not just yours but the whole crew's.'

'We're all trying our best,' said Sian, defensively.

'I don't doubt it but that doesn't address the problem, does it?'

450

Sian stopped. 'Nate, can I level with you?'

'I wish you would. So what is it? You girls fighting over boys? A clash of personality? What?'

'It's Anna.'

'Yeah?'

'She's rubbish. We'd be so much better if it was Amy in charge of us.'

'But Anna was better than Amy on the day.'

'Amy was ill.'

'She said it was nerves. Which makes her even more of a liability. If she was nervous at a trial how is she going to be at Dorney Lake with a mob of British supporters baying for medals?'

'She wasn't nervous. She lied,' insisted Sian. 'She coxed us at the British Championships, there was pressure there and she was ice cold. I don't know what was wrong with her but she wasn't well, I'm sure of it.'

'Sian, I know Amy's your friend, I know you like being coxed by her, but on the day Anna was the better cox. I'm sorry you don't like the decision but you're going to have to accept it.'

Sian shook her head. 'Then we're not going to win. Best you tell the British public that because we'll be lucky to even make the finals.'

'Don't be defeatist.'

'I'm being a *realist*,' said Sian. 'Our world ranking is sixth. I know we could be second or even first. Nate, you've only got to look at the talent in our crew, at the PBs the girls score on the ergos, to know how good we could be. But we're not. We know we're not and it's making the crew anxious.'

451

'I'm sorry, but you can't have Amy to cox you. I'm not going to change my mind so you're going to have to work with what you've got. You're stroke, you tell Anna what you need. Talk to her.'

'Nate I have, trust me I have. And I may be stroke but Anna's been coxing for Britain for years now. As far as she is concerned, I'm the jumped-up newbie. I should fit with her way of doing things, not vice versa.'

Nate stared out across the lake and rubbed his chin. 'Anna is a very good cox, you know.'

'Yes, but we don't need *very good*, we need *excellent*.' And with that Sian strode off towards her room and a rest before the next gruelling session.

When Amy got home from work on the Friday she could tell from the cases in the hall that Ellie was back from Portugal. Even though it had only been a few days since she'd last seen her friend she was pleased to have company in the house once again. And, of course, if Ellie was back then she'd have to level with her sooner rather than later about her decision to quit rowing but she'd cross that bridge another day.

Excitedly she called out her housemate's name.

'I'm in the kitchen,' called back Ellie.

Amy squealed with happiness as she ran through the little sitting room to the shabby kitchen. She hugged Ellie.

'So?' she said.

'So, Nate's confirmed Sian and I are definitely in the squad, we've got a couple of qualifying races and test events to get through before the actual Olympics but

452

short of total disaster we'll be at the Games.'

'That's brilliant.' Amy was genuinely pleased for her friend.

'It's not,' said Ellie. 'We've got a shit cox. Honestly, Amy, when we rowed with you at your time trial it was like watching match fixing at work. It was as if you didn't want the place. What the fuck was going on?'

'Nothing, Ellie.' Amy's good mood evaporated. 'Nothing, so can we drop it?'

Elli stared at her with narrowed eyes, patently disbelieving her friend. 'On a lighter note,' she said, 'Dan and Rollo have buried the hatchet.'

'Dan and Rollo? That's just not possible.'

'They may not be quite at the best-friends-forever stage but they're not at each other's throats any more.'

'I don't believe it! And until I see it with my own eyes, which seems unlikely now, I never will.'

Amy moved over to the counter and began filling the kettle while she pondered this news. It just didn't compute. The animosity between Dan and Rollo seemed far too ingrained for it to just disappear and then there was the fact that Dan had gone with Tanya. Surely he would have only done that to get back at Rollo. Anyway, it didn't matter what was going on with that lot; she wouldn't be seeing them ever again – except maybe on the TV when they rowed for their country.

The confrontation with Ellie, when Amy told her she was never coxing again, not even for the Reading eight, wasn't quite as bad as she had anticipated. Naturally Ellie was disappointed but when Amy had broken down and cried when she explained just how gutted she'd been to lose her place Ellie hadn't the heart to browbeat her any more.

'Think how you'd have felt if it had been you,' sniffled Amy. 'And I know I haven't worked for my seat like you have for yours, but it was still awful. And as it all came on the back of splitting up with Dan . . . Ellie, I don't want to be a part of the rowing world any more.'

'I reckon Dan regrets what happened between you and him,' said Ellie gently.

'Oh yeah? Susie said as much too but what if I told you that he's screwed Tanya since we split? I don't care why but he did, so he can't feel too many regrets, can he?'

'No! Dan and Tanya? He wouldn't touch her with a four-foot pole.'

'I saw them, Ellie.'

'Oh. Really, when?'

'At a party at St George's, last December.'

Ellie chewed on this information for a second or two. 'But it doesn't mean he's not still holding a candle for you. I saw the way he was always watching you in Portugal. Amy, if Dan doesn't still love you I'll eat my hat. Just because you had an epic row doesn't mean he's going to hold a grudge for ever. For God's sake, he's even made up with Rollo.' She sounded exasperated.

'Says you, but I don't think you understand just how much he hates me. He hates me for going with Rollo, he hates me for not believing Rollo was a cheat, and he hates me for telling him to fuck off when he tried to apologise at Christmas – just before he went off with Tanya. And if he *was* watching me at the training camp he was just

454

checking out where I was so he could keep away from me.'

Ellie tried to tell her she was wrong but Amy was having none of it.

33

It was a few weeks later. Spring was really beginning to make a show and the daffs blooming in Ellie's little front garden made it look almost pretty. Amy was basking in the warm sun that streamed through the front window. She was sitting quietly on the shabby sofa in Ellie's sitting room, happily immersed in a property relocation show while also fiddling around on Facebook and playing an occasional game of spider patience when she heard the front door open. She checked her watch. Bit early for Ellie to be back from training wasn't it?

'Hi,' she called.

'Hello,' said Sian.

Sian? What the hell?

'Long time no see,' said Sian.

Amy nodded.

'I borrowed Ellie's key,' said Sian, putting it on the mantelpiece. 'She said you were around this afternoon so I thought – if the mountain won't come to Muhammad . . . And it was a nice day to cycle over from the training lake, so I decided why not look up my old mate Amy.'

'Lovely,' said Amy as she switched of the TV with the

remote. She knew from the tone of Sian's voice that this wasn't going to be just a social call.

'So, how've you been?' Sian flopped into one of the battered armchairs.

'Okay. You?'

'Busy, training hard, knackered most of the time, no free time to call my own.' She stared pointedly at the spider patience game on the laptop. 'Unlike some. Daytime TV and computer games?'

'So what? It's not illegal the last time I checked.'

'You used to have things to do which meant you weren't a couch potato.'

'That's not fair.'

Sian put her hands up. 'All right, I'll take that back. Maybe I'm just jealous.' She grinned at Amy and Amy backed off too.

'Want a cuppa?'

'Thought you'd never offer.'

Amy got up and went to the kitchen, followed by Sian.

'So what brings you here?' said Amy as she filled the kettle. Although she was sure it'd be something to do with rowing.

'I want you back as cox.'

Amy shook her head.

'Please, Amy. I'm sure if you agree I could get Nate to change his mind.'

'But what about Anna? Doesn't she get a vote in this?'

'She's not a patch on you. Ellie and I both knew it at the training camp and honestly, things in the crew are going from bad to worse. Our times aren't improving like they should which is making the girls anxious, which is affecting their technique, which is making the times worse. Amy, we *need* you.'

The kettle boiled and Amy began to pour the water. 'But she did better than me in Portugal. Remember, my time trial was total shit, so that's that. That's how it works.'

'But that doesn't make her the best. And we both know it wasn't nerves that you were suffering from. No,' Sian held up her hand. 'Don't lie again and tell me it was because I'm not stupid, Amy. Why the fuck didn't you tell Nate you were ill? I just don't understand it.'

Amy got the milk out of the fridge and sloshed it into the two mugs. Sian might as well know the truth – after all it wasn't going to make any difference to anything at this juncture.

'Okay, I *was* ill – food poisoning.'

'What? How? We all ate the same.'

'I didn't. Not the day before my trial. I sloped off and met Susie in the village and I ate an ice cream.'

Sian rolled her eyes and shook her head. 'You complete pillock.'

As if she didn't know. 'Thank you, Sian for that blinding assessment. And yes, I was.'

'But why didn't you cough to Nathan?'

'Why do you think? He'd have put me on the next flight for breaking his rules. I was stuffed either way, Sian. Lose–lose rather than win–win.'

'Oh, Amy.' Sian's voice was laden with sympathy.

Amy shook her head. She was still feeling raw and if Sian was kind and sympathetic she might just cry all over again. 'Don't. Don't imagine for a second I don't have regrets every single day. I want to put it all behind me, and so that's why I don't want to have anything to do with rowing any more, okay? I need a clean break or I'm going to end up having a total breakdown. Really.' She handed Sian her tea and the pair moved back into the sitting room. 'And you've got Anna and you've still got a few months before the big day.'

'But as it stands, I can't see us getting a medal.'

'And if I coxed, you still wouldn't. I'm not *that* good. I don't have a magic wand.' Amy took a slurp of her tea and then put her mug on the arm of her chair.

'But you do. And Ellie thinks so, too.'

'I'm going to watch you on TV and I'll cheer you on like crazy but that's as far as it goes.'

'You won't be there?'

'I haven't got a ticket.'

'No?' Sian blew her cheeks out.

'I rather hoped I wouldn't need one – have a free pass and all that. Fucked that up too, didn't I?'

'You're a hopeless case, Amy Jones.'

'It does seem like it. But you'll do fine, I'm sure you'll get a gong. I've got every faith in you.'

'The world rankings don't lie, Amy. We're sixth. We might get to the finals at a push but that's it. There are national squads who are streets ahead of us.'

'So that's even more reason why you ought to stick with Anna. If I came on board it would just be disruptive.'

'No,' insisted Sian with increasing frustration. 'You don't get it. We're sixth because we need a better cox.'

'Bollocks.'

Sian glared at her. 'Forget it, then. I really thought you'd want to do this, not for me and Ellie but for your country. Now I see that I was wasting my time.' She got up and headed for the front door.

'Don't be like this, Sian.'

'Why shouldn't I?' She was getting shrill. 'My over-riding ambition, the thing I've worked towards for years and years is to get an Olympic medal. This is going to be my very best shot, and in front of our home crowd. And I don't think it's going to happen without you, and you're refusing to help. Well, thanks a bunch, Amy Jones.'

And with that she slammed out of the house.

That went well, thought Amy as she slumped on the sofa. Another one of my rowing friends who hates me. At this rate I'll have them all alienated in a year or so.

Spring segued effortlessly into summer and Olympic fever began to grip the country. Everything seemed to be Olympic-related. Every Olympic sponsor was bom - barding the country with adverts which proclaimed their proud association with the event. No news bulletin seemed to be complete without at least one Olympic-related story, the Olympic rings on public buildings proliferated like bacterial cultures on Petri dishes and the country was divided into two: those who were completely hyped-up and excited about the prospect and those who wanted to escape from the whole shebang and never hear the words 'London 2012' again.

Amy tried as hard as she could to ignore it all but it was impossible, especially working, as she was, at a sports complex. All the papers were left lying around turned to the sports pages, all the TVs were tuned to Sky Sports, the one topic of conversation was the chances of Britain's Olympic hopefuls and the countdown bore down on the population with all the subtlety of an out-of-control juggernaut. But over and above everything was the fact that she was living with Ellie who was completely focused on and stressed out by those two weeks in midsummer and could rarely speak of anything that wasn't Olympics or rowing-related

Amy was at work, easing a client's shoulder muscles, when her phone vibrated silently on the counter beside her. She checked the ID. Maddy. Idly she wondered what Maddy wanted and promised herself that she'd ring her friend back as soon as she was free.

It was half an hour later that she was able to do so. The phone rang twice before it was picked up. Maddy was completely distraught.

'Hello, Amy,' she gulped.

'Maddy, what's the matter?' asked Amy.

'It's . . . it's . . . it's . . . S-s-s-eb.'

Amy's heart stopped. Oh God – had he been injured or killed by the Taliban? Poor, poor Maddy. 'Oh Maddy, sweetie, what's happened to him? How bad is it?'

'He's . . .he's . . . he's had his end of tour date moved,' she wailed.

'What? Is that all?' Amy's heart resumed its rhythm.

Maddy's sobs ceased abruptly. 'What do you mean "is that all"?'

'I thought something terrible had happened.'

'It *is* terrible!'

461

'Of course,' Amy back-pedalled. 'But I thought he'd been injured or something.'

'Oh.' Amy could hear Maddy blowing her nose. 'Oh, yes that would be really, really terrible.' She hiccuped before saying, 'But the thing is he won't be around to come to the Olympic rowing with me.'

'Oh, that's such a bummer.'

'And I had a hotel booked in Windsor and everything. Of course I've cancelled the hotel but I don't want to go to the rowing on my own. Don't suppose you'd come with me?'

'Oh.'

'Please.'

'I don't know, Mads.'

'Look a gift horse in the mouth, why don't you.'

'I am really touched by your offer.'

'Yeah, sounds like it.'

'I just don't want to run into Dan.'

'For God's sake, Amy, there'll be no chance of that. He's competing, you'll be in the stands. The closest you're going to get to him will be when he whizzes past on the water and when that happens I expect he'll have other things on his mind than looking out for ex-girlfriends.'

Harsh but true. 'I suppose. Oh, all right then.'

'Ace. I'll email you the details. And can I stay at yours? We can catch the train to Maidenhead and then pick up the shuttle buses to get there.'

'Sounds like a plan.'

In her lunch hour, having got the date and other details

through from Maddy, she wandered across to Nick Bradbury's office to ask for that day off.

'And I thought you didn't want to have anything to do with rowing ever again.'

'I know but this is just watching and I'd probably be doing that anyway, just not actually at the venue.'

'And you won't regret that you're not taking part?'

Amy shrugged. 'I very probably will but it's a situation I can't change and I'm going to feel the same even if I'm just watching it on the box.'

But as the days sped by, Amy got more and more despondent about her missed opportunity. And the more fed up she got, the less she wanted to be at Dorney Lake. She even considered ringing Maddy and cancelling, but she couldn't quite bring herself to let down her friend when she was already so disappointed about Seb's change of dates. Also, if she was being honest with herself, she was desperate to see Dan row. He might never want her back, but she couldn't stop caring about him, no matter what she told anyone else.

34

'Oooh, isn't this exciting,' said Maddy as she squeezed herself and her case in through the front door of Ellie and Amy's house. 'I've been looking forward to this for weeks.'

Amy put on an expression that she hoped indicated that she had been too, because she hadn't. Apart from her own apprehensions about meeting her old rowing buddies, Ellie, until she'd moved out to the Olympic Rowing Village, had been almost impossible to live with. She'd bitched about Anna while throwing Amy dark looks, she'd been snappy and jumpy and when she wasn't being obnoxious, which really wasn't like her, she'd been in tears, which wasn't like her either. And if Amy had asked her how the training was going it was the wrong subject.

'How do you fucking think, with that moron, Anna, in charge?' had been a typical response.

But if Amy hadn't asked that was wrong too. Sometimes Amy had felt like asking Nick if she could move into the staff quarters at Chazey Hall and let Ellie stew on her own. But she was too fond of Ellie to have done that. Who would have run the house, bought the food and kept the laundry under control if not her, because Ellie certainly hadn't had the time and even if she had, she was too darn knackered.

'I've put you in Ellie's room now she's over at Royal Holloway with the rest of the squad,' Amy told Maddy as she led her up the narrow stairs. She pushed open the door to the bright room at the front of the house. Maddy dumped her case on the bed and looked around her at Ellie's taste in décor, which consisted mostly of rowing memorabilia.

'How is she?'

'She's fine,' lied Amy. 'Although I haven't heard from her since she moved over to Egham. I watched them on the TV on Sunday though.'

'They were lucky to scrape through the heats, weren't they?'

'I was on the edge of my seat. I really thought they'd blown it.'

'Maybe if you'd been coxing . . .'

But Amy had shoved her fingers in her ears and was going 'la-la-la' at the top of her voice. 'Not listening, Maddy.'

'All right, I won't mention it again.'

'Good. Did you watch the other races?'

Maddy nodded. 'Of course. I was glued to the box all morning.'

'They all seem to be doing okay, don't they? Although I hear on the grapevine that Rollo's being a complete bear. According to Susie, Tanya's at her wits' end with him.'

465

'I can't find it in me to care. Serves Tanya right for all the misery *she's* caused.'

'That's a bit harsh, Maddy.'

Maddy shrugged. 'I might have got over her and Seb, but I haven't forgiven her. Anyway, let's forget about her. Isn't it fantastic that Rollo and Dan are through to the finals, and we'll be there to watch them? How magic is that?'

Amy turned away and refolded a towel. She felt tears welling up again. When she'd watched the race that had got the two men through to the finals she had burst with pride on his behalf and then sobbed her heart out that she wasn't sharing Dan's obvious happiness with him. She should have been around to give him hugs and kisses and instead there was this horrible barrier between them and no chance of it being dismantled.

Maddy mistook Amy's silence for something else. 'Oh, Amy, you don't still hate him do you?'

'No,' she admitted sadly. 'But I hate the hurt he's caused me. It's awful, Maddy. Why can't I get over him and move on? I need to accept that I've made a complete fuck-up of that bit of my life—'

'Amy, I don't think you have. Dan and I went for a pizza after that party at St George's . . .'

Amy held her hand up. 'Please, Maddy, stop. Please, no more Dan, okay?'

Maddy sighed. She could see how close Amy was to tears and didn't want to make things worse. 'If you say so.'

'You unpack, I'll make tea,' Amy called over her shoulder as she fled downstairs.

By the time Maddy joined her in the kitchen she'd pulled herself together again and was busy making the picnic for the next day.

'Blimey, how much food?'

'It's going to be a long day and God knows how long it'll take to get away from the lake at the end. I don't want us to go hungry.'

'Fat chance of that,' said Maddy as she eyed the mounds of tuna sandwiches, the pork pie, baby quiches, oranges, bottles of water and iced buns.

'And we're going to have to get up bloody early to make sure we don't miss anything. I reckon we need to catch a train to Maidenhead at around six thirty, so we can have some of this for breakfast.'

'If you say so.'

'And we're going to need sunscreen and hats if it stays as hot as this.'

'The forecast says the weather is due to break.'

'Not great for us spectators,' Amy observed.

'But good for the rowers. They don't want to be sweating their nuts off.'

Amy had to agree, the heat was oppressive and while the spectators and the armchair pundits agreed that this was to be preferred to teeming rain it was tough for some of the competitors. Even as she was thinking this there was a distant rumble of thunder.

'And maybe we should pack brollies and wellies too.'

Dan awoke and was instantly assailed with apprehension and nerves that bordered on blind terror. He opened his eyes and stared at the early morning light shining through the curtains of his small student study-bedroom at Royal Holloway College. The building he was accommodated in was a perfectly ordinary modern campus building like ones found at universities the length and breadth of the country but the main university building was something else again. It didn't have the quiet beauty of the Cotswold-stone colleges of Oxford but what it lacked in dignity, history and age it certainly made up for it with flamboyance and size.

Five stories of ornate red-brick Victorian gothic complete with cloisters, turrets, decorative chimneys, domes and spires, it was like some vast, mad French chateau. And, if nothing else, it had impressed the visiting rowing teams who hadn't expected anything quite as grandiose as a backdrop for their time at the Olympics. What with that and the ancient royal grandeur of Windsor town, the castle and Eton College, it was game, set and match to the British just on venue choice alone. It had to be said that the GB Rowing Team had all felt slightly smug at being able to boast that this was the norm as far as they were concerned and that they were now so blasé about such surroundings they barely noticed them. Meanwhile the visiting crews all went mad snapping anything and everything and exclaiming over the history of their surroundings and speculating whether Her Majesty was watching the rowing from Windsor Castle battlements.

Dan leaned out of his bed and twitched back the corner of his curtain. The sky was pale blue and the air crystal clear. Gone was the haze which had beset the country for the last few days; the thunderstorms that had rolled around the south-east the previous evening had done the job of washing the oppressive heatwave away and replacing it with something fresher and cooler but still fine and dry. If he'd ordered perfect weather from Harrods itself, nothing more appropriate could have been delivered for the finals of his race today. Was this propitious? No, he mustn't think like this. He and Rollo would only win if they deserved to, luck wasn't going to come into it.

Glancing at his bedside clock he realised that, despite the early hour, it was time to be up and moving. He leapt out of bed, pulled on his jogging bottoms and a T-shirt and let himself out of his hall of residence. After a few minutes of stretches he set off at a steady lope for a three-mile jog before breakfast, nothing too strenuous but something to get the blood circulating and the heart ticking over. At first he was pretty much alone in the extensive grounds but as he ran, more and more toned, bronzed athletes appeared and also started to pound the paths and roads around the campus. By the time he'd finished, the tracks around the buildings were so crowded it was more like the rush-hour on the nearby A30 than a centre of academic studies.

Dan returned to his room, his heart thumping and he was sure it was more with dread, nerves and worry about the impending final than from his recent exertion.

There was a quiet knock at his door.

'Come in,' he called.

Rollo stuck his head around it, also glistening with a light sheen of sweat from an early work-out. 'How you feeling, buddy?' he asked.

'Shit. You?'

Rollo nodded. 'The same.' He paused and gazed out at the view from Dan's window, then, 'What if we cock up?'

'Don't. We won't, we can't think like that. We know we can do it.'

Rollo nodded but he didn't look convinced.

'On paper,' added Dan, 'we've got the bronze licked. We might even do better.'

'On paper,' Rollo agreed, but he still sounded glum.

'I need to shower and then have breakfast,' said Dan, glancing again at his clock.

'When does the transport leave?' said Rollo.

'Seven thirty.'

Rollo inhaled slowly. 'God, all these years of training and now the whole thing is just a few hours away. Scary, isn't it?'

'Scary doesn't come close.'

Rollo sloped off, leaving Dan to shower and get into some fresh clothes. He'd wait till he'd eaten before putting on his Olympic uniform; it'd be Sod's Law he'd get his breakfast down his front if he put it on now.

The two men met again in the huge refectory. Despite the numbers of athletes there picking up bowls of porridge and plates of eggs and toast, there was an almost total silence. They weren't the only people with finals that day and those that weren't facing finals were competing in semi-finals. Those crews who had already been eliminated but who hadn't yet gone home were sitting with their national teams to give them moral support and would be cheering them on at the lake later that morning, but the tension was such that even they were silent.

The GB women's eight joined Dan and Rollo as they listlessly spooned their porridge. Even Anna looked white with worry.

'You all right?' Dan asked Sian.

She shook her head. 'I know it's a great achievement to have made the finals,' she said quietly, 'but I just want so much more.'

'We all do,' said Dan. 'But this isn't primary school sports day where everyone gets a prize.'

'And the press have built us up so the public are expecting the works.'

Dan nodded. He didn't mention it was worse for him and Rollo. All the sports pages had tipped them to medal, while the girls had been considered very lucky to get as far as they had. And if none of them made it onto the podium no doubt there would be questions asked. The public had had high expectations of the British Rowing Team ever since Sir Steve had first won gold at Los Angeles in 1984 in the coxed four. Of course it wasn't just Sir Steve who had fired this level of expectation; others had won gold, others had won more than one gold, and now the British public had come to think of rowing, along with a couple of other sports, like cycling and sailing, as the Events Most Likely To Deliver. The cyclists, the sailors and the rowers were all the ones expected to win fistfuls of precious metals and if they didn't the public would want to know why.

And Dan and Rollo were hideously aware of it.

Breakfast finished, they went back to their rooms to change into their official Olympic uniforms, pack their lycra all-in-ones into their sports bags along with any other kit – towels, books, MP3 players and the like – and then head for the transport which was scheduled to take them from Egham to the Eton College boating lake at Dorney.

Dan made his way back to the coach park along with dozens of others from other national rowing teams, also dressed in their smart official blazers, shirts and ties. There was still hardly a word being said as the teams found their allocated transport, stowed their kit and clambered on board.

'Shit or bust,' muttered Dan as he sat in his seat. 'Shit or bust.'

The women's eight had agreed to meet outside their block and walk together to their coach, which was leaving a little later, their race being scheduled for an hour after than Dan's and Rollo's. Like the boys they were excited and nervous, apprehensive, keyed-up and plain old shit-scared. Adrenalin was pumping even though it was still some hours before they took to the water and, even though they hadn't yet got to the stage of being com - pletely focused on what was to come, they were still wrapped up in thoughts about the start, their stroke, the opposition, their chances and the outcome.

Sian was just checking that her Olympic uniform was perfectly pressed and her sports bag contained every - thing she'd need for the morning's racing when her phone rang. It was her mother wanting to wish her luck. As Sian chatted, trying to give her mother the impression that she was taking this momentous day in her stride and that all she cared about was taking part and not winning

– as if! – she grabbed her kit and left her room. As she went down the main stairs of the hall of residence, talking to her mother, she could see Anna waiting in the lobby and through the glass doors, some of the others in the crew, standing around in the sunshine.

Later, Sian wasn't absolutely sure what happened next but it seemed that Anna, seeing her stroke encumbered with mobile in one hand and sports bag in the other went to open the inner door for Sian. Whether she tripped over her own sports bag or her feet Sian couldn't say but one second her cox was reaching for the door handle and the next she was cannoning off the plate glass.

Sian killed the call and dropped her bag as she rushed forward to help but Anna was out for the count, blood streaming from her scalp.

35

'What's the hold-up?' said Dan irritably to Rollo, the tension of the day's events getting to him. 'And where the hell is Nate?'

Rollo shrugged. 'Like I'm suddenly telepathic.'

A couple of seats in front someone had a text message come through. 'Fucking hell,' said Chuck.

'What's up?' asked Rollo.

'It's Anna; she's just given herself a bang on the head. Tripped over something and cannoned off a glass door. Nate said we're to go to the lake without him. He'll be along as soon as he's got Anna sorted.'

'That's doesn't sound too clever,' said Dan.

'I'm sure she'll be fine,' said Rollo. 'She's a tough cookie and, let's face it, she's only got to cox. Now if it was one of the rowers it'd be a different story but all she's got to do is sit and steer.'

Which they both knew was a complete understatement but it was a comforting thought nonetheless.

The two men settled back in their seats as the coach driver started the huge engine and slowly pulled away from the college and headed for the A30. They put Anna out of their minds; they had their own race to worry about.

At the girls' accommodation the women's eight stood around Anna, towering over her as she sat on the coir mat by the front door with her back against a wall.

'I'm all right,' complained Anna, although she looked far from it. She was holding a wad of lint to her head and her face was streaked with blood. Her shirt was also bright red and there was blood on the mat too.

'Let me be the judge of that,' said Nate. He gently removed the pad and had a look at the injury. Blood had almost soaked through the white material and there was more blood clotted in her hair but the bleeding, despite it being a nasty wound, had slowed right down.

Sian arrived back at the scene with an ice-pack which Nathan took from her and placed gently on Anna's head.

He looked into her eyes. 'How do you feel. Any dizziness? Nausea?'

'I've got a bit of a headache,' she admitted.

'Not surprised,' muttered Sian. 'You really whacked that door.'

'Double vision?' asked Nate.

'No, honest. Just give me a painkiller, if I can have one without jeopardising a dope test, and I'll be fine.'

Nate looked at her. 'I want the doctor to check you over.'

Anna shook her head, dislodging the ice-pack. She picked it up off the floor and slapped it back on again. 'It looks worse than it is. Isn't that the way with head wounds? Lots of blood and gore however small the cut?'

Nate removed the ice-pack and had another look at the gash. And the lump under it – which was quite impressive.

'I think you ought to have it seen to, all the same. It may need a stitch or two.'

'No,' Anna almost shouted. 'No, if that happens I might miss the race.'

'Or the doctor might say you're not fit to race,' said Sian, sounding worried.

Nate glanced at Sian and then stared at Anna. 'Are you sure you're okay? I want you to tell me honestly if you are sure that you don't need to see a doctor.'

'I'm sure. Honest. Look, it was a stupid accident, but it looks much worse than it was and I'm going to be fine. And if we don't all get on the bus we're going to be late.' Anna was already trying to struggle to her feet.

Nate pushed her back down onto the floor and took her pulse.

'Normal?' asked Anna after thirty seconds had elapsed.

'Just about. And you're sure you don't feel dizzy and your vision is fine?'

'Yes, really. I'm fine. How many ways and times do I have to say it to convince you?' She stared at Nate, pleadingly. 'Honest, now let's just stop faffing around and get over to Dorney.'

The shuttle bus dropped Maddy and Amy off on the track that ran along beside the lake. There was parking for the competitors, officials and the disabled but everyone else was expected to arrive by shuttle buses from the main local transport hubs. And they were arriving in droves, bringing with them streams of spectators.

Amy enjoyed the freshness of the morning as they walked along the coaching path towards the grandstands at the far end of the lake. In the distance she could see the slightly curved front of the main boathouse with its terraces, crew room and big sign proclaiming 'Eton College' proudly across the front, which was now joined by the Olympic rings and the London 2012 logo. To the right of it was the main race control centre and finish tower and across the other side of the dyke, which ran the length of the lake, was the canal which allowed competing boats to proceed to the start without impeding those already racing. For a school boating lake this one certainly took some beating.

Despite the fact that they'd arrived pretty early the crowds were already building up and the excitement was growing. Almost everyone had come armed with rugs and picnic hampers. Some had binoculars slung around their necks and there were a plethora of swanky cameras with huge lenses and mono-pods. As they walked the first of the competitors' coaches began to drive slowly down the road that led to the car park at the boathouse end of the lake. Some of the rowers waved to the pedestrians and managed to raise a smile but far more looked dead-eyed with nerves. Amy searched for Dan and the others. She tried to kid herself she was looking for any familiar face but her eyes only raked the male competitors.

'I'm going to text Ellie and Sian and wish them luck,' she told Maddy when the last of the coaches had driven to the boathouse.

'Tell them I'm going to be rooting for them too,' said Maddy.

Amy pinged off the message.

'Thanks, we'll need it,' the text came pinging back seconds later.

'They wouldn't if you were with them,' muttered Maddy almost inaudibly. Amy chose to ignore the comment.

They walked on following the signs that directed them towards their stand. As they were mounting the steps to their seats they heard their names being shrieked. There, already settled, were Tanya, Christina, Stevie and Susie. The girls fell on each other's necks.

'Oh my God, this is going to be such a party,' said Susie.

'Where's Angus?'

'Press box,' said Susie. 'The lucky bastard's been here every day to watch. Haven't you been following him in the *Herald*?'

'Not every day,' she admitted a bit guiltily, 'but I've read quite a few of his articles.' And other reporters' ones in the *Times*, the *Telegraph*, the *Mail* . . . Anything she could get her hands on to read about her friends and their progress.

'You haven't read every one,' Susie said with a grin. 'How could you? Angus's reports are much better than any of the other papers' stuff. Not that I'm biased or anything.'

'So how does Angus rate their chances? I mean, I know how supportive of the squad he is in print, but privately?'

478

'Whose chances? Dan's and Rollo's? Angus think they might squeeze bronze.'

Which made sense because Amy knew what the qualifying times had been for the eight finalists in Dan and Rollo's event and she knew that if the crews all performed as they had in the qualifying rounds then Dan and Rollo might not make the podium. She'd watched and re-watched the races enough times to have all the facts and figures at her fingertips. Whichever way she cut the figures, although the pair had cruised through their heat with no need to row in the repêchage because their draw had been easy, their times were way down on the Australian, French and German teams – but then they'd had to fight much tougher, more competitive races. And then, to cap it all, they had only just qualified for the finals in the semis held on the Tuesday. They might have been keeping their powder dry for the final but equally it could be all they were capable of.

And she had to ask, 'And the women's eight?'

'Of course,' said Susie. 'You've got a vested interest in that boat, haven't you?'

'Not any more,' said Amy wearily.

'Angus doesn't think they're going to medal. Not unless something amazing happens. But hey, they're finalists so that's pretty good going.'

But Amy knew that for Ellie and Sian it really wasn't enough.

Amy and Maddy reached their allocated seating and settled themselves down. Around them the crowds were chatting in a multitude of languages, most of which Amy couldn't even start to guess at. However the atmosphere was like one huge international street party with people tucking into snacks and thermoses of cold drinks, checking their programmes, indulging in unashamed people-watching and celeb-spotting. Giant screens projected images of the crowds intercut with stats about the various crews and commentary about the races to come, the venue and interesting facts and figures about rowing at the Olympics over the years.

'Look,' said a loud American (or possibly Canadian – Amy couldn't differentiate), 'there's that Steve Redgrave fella.'

At the mention of the famous rower's name heads turned to check out the screen and then craned to see if they could spot him for real.

'And isn't that Hugh Grant?' said another voice.

The heads swivelled back to the screen again. Amy stared too. Well, if it wasn't it was his doppelganger, she decided.

Along to their right there was activity down by the boating pontoons as the coxed fours from a variety of nations carried their boats to the water and launched them. A smattering of applause greeted this although previously the crowd had also applauded a swan taking off from the lake and the arrival of a busload of officials. The crews got into their boats and began making their way down to the start, rowing at a leisurely pace ready for their start time, still some time off.

Amy checked her programme; it seemed as if there would be one event every twenty minutes. Just an hour now before Dan was due to race and nearly two hours before the women's eights. A sudden burst of nerves clutched at her stomach. Sheesh, if she was nervous, what was it like for the crews?

The cameras panned across the spectators and suddenly Amy saw her face in the centre of the giant screen, twenty-foot high, looking fraught and chewing her lip. She felt her face flood with colour at the embarrassment at the exposure.

'Ooh look,' said Maddy. 'I hope you're not bunking off work because if you are you've been caught red-handed.'

36

Dan, in the men's changing rooms, saw the image along with millions of other viewers around the world, and felt his heart miss a beat. He'd asked Maddy to keep him informed about what Amy was doing, although each update was torture, but he needed to know if he still might have a chance with her. Maddy kept assuring him that Amy wasn't dating anyone else and, as far as she could judge, didn't appear to even want to. But on the other hand, Maddy also admitted that she hadn't been able to convince Amy that Dan still had feelings for her. 'She absolutely refuses to believe anything I tell her; won't even listen. It's hopeless,' was her assessment but Dan refused to give up.

Maybe if he won today, maybe it would mean he could win her back too. He knew it was a ridiculous thought but somehow it made him even more determined to get gold.

Across the corridor, Sian, Ellie and the women's crew were in their changing room. Sian sat on the bench at the side of the room feeling sick. She shut her eyes, willing the wave of nausea to roll past without actually breaking. She swallowed and the ringing in her ears abated somewhat. She breathed slowly and deeply a few more times and then risked opening her eyes. Ellie was staring at her, looking worried.

'You all right?' she asked.

'Yeah, fine,' lied Sian trying to sound bright and chipper.

'I'm glad one of us is. Look at me.' Ellie held her hand out and it trembled like an aspen leaf. 'I can't imagine how we'll manage to carry our boat down to the lake. I'm not even sure my legs are going to carry me, let alone the boat as well, my knees are knocking like crazy.'

Sian nodded. 'I don't think I've ever been this nervous. It makes the first day of finals look like a doddle in comparison – and I was cacking myself over them at the time. But it wasn't as bad as this.'

Ellie nodded. 'Me too.' The pair of them looked around their fellow rowers and no one appeared relaxed or comfortable. Even Anna was sugar-white.

'How's the head?' asked Sian.

'A bit sore,' she admitted. 'But I'm fine, honest,' she said a little too brightly, her eyes a little too glittery, her smile a little too forced.

Sian stared at her. She really didn't look right at all. There was something very odd about her eyes.

'Are you sure you're all right?' she asked again.

'I just feel a bit dizzy, that's all.'

Well, that made sense, given her appearance. Then suddenly Anna leaned forward, heaved, and vomit splattered the floor at her feet.

A few of the girls in the changing room made quiet sounds of disgust but mostly the reaction was one of deep sympathy. Ellie zipped off to find either someone who might be able to clean up the mess or a mop and bucket so she could do it herself.

While Ellie was off in search of cleaning materials or an official who might organise the chore for her, Sian was comforting Anna.

'Hey, hon, we all feel ghastly. It's nerves.'

But Anna's response was to lean over again and vomit some more. Then she slowly slumped sideways on the bench in a dead faint.

'Shit,' said Sian, as she noticed Anna's breathing was shallow and her colour worse. This wasn't nerves; this was something else entirely.

'Someone get a medic here fast,' she called. 'And ring Nate.'

Sian lifted Anna off the bench easily, carried her away from the mess on the floor and laid the cox gently on a nearby treatment table. She patted Anna's hand and murmured consolingly about help being on the way, more to comfort herself than for Anna's benefit. Anna was out for the count.

Nate crashed into the room, followed by a couple of Olympic officials.

'What's up?' he said as he arrived on the scene.

'She was sick, then she passed out. I thought it was nerves to start with . . .'

Nate lifted up an eyelid and looked at Anna's pupils, then checked her pulse.

'Call an ambulance,' he instructed one of the officials.

'You're right, this isn't nerves, this is the head injury.'

Dan and Rollo were getting their boat to the landing stage when they heard the wail of the ambulance siren. They both looked at each other.

'Probably some spectator getting too much sun,' Dan joked.

'Or some fat knacker having a heart attack because they've had to walk a mile or so from the coach drop-off point.'

They carried on towards the lake, where they flipped the boat over and dropped it gently onto the water. For the second time that day they checked everything to make sure their boat was in the most perfect working order that it could be.

Behind them the ambulance screeched to a halt in front of the boathouse. Dan and Rollo exchanged slightly more worried stares.

'Oo-er,' said Rollo.

'Maybe the pressure's got to one of the rowers,' said Dan, only this time in a less jokey way.

The ambulance crew grabbed some kit from their vehicle and dashed into the building. Outside the boathouse the press and camera crews began to gather and a commentator began speculating on what the emergency might be. Shots of the blue flashing light filled the big screen and the BBC's sports reporter was floundering around in front of millions of viewers with a breaking story and not a jot of information.

One of the lightweight double scullers, a pleasant chap called Miles, whose semi-finals would immediately follow on from Dan and Rollo's final, brought their sculls from the boat shed and laid them carefully beside their boat.

'Good luck, gents,' he said.

'Thanks,' said Dan. Then he added, 'So what's the emergency?'

'Dunno. Want me to find out?'

Rollo nodded. 'There's a good chap. I'm rather hoping it's one of the Kraut scullers taken poorly. Now wouldn't that be good.' He rubbed his hands in anticipation that his prediction would be proved right.

Dan had a horrible feeling that such a display of schadenfreude might come back and bite them on the bum.

Miles obligingly loped off to the boathouse to try and get the low-down on whatever was happening. Knots of rowers were gathered on the hardstanding at the front of the building, all obviously discussing what was going on. He went up to some acquaintances from the Canadian team.

'What's happening?' he asked.

'It's one of the women. The paramedics went into the women's changing room like bats out of hell.'

'Doesn't sound good.'

There was a general murmuring of agreement that it didn't. Miles hung around with the other rowers until he saw the ambulance crew exiting the building pushing the trolley. The patient's face was covered with an oxygen mask but it was obvious which team she was from; her GB Rowing Team strip was visible to all.

Instantly shots of Anna appeared on the giant screens,

although she was unidentifiable and the BBC's commentator went berserk speculating on what might be wrong. Somehow she must have got hold of some information as she was able to inform the watching public that one of the members of the GB women's squad had suffered a minor accident earlier that day resulting in a head injury but she was unable to name which one it was. The spectators around the lake, especially those rooting for the British, exchanged worried glances, Dan and Rollo included.

Miles, now seriously concerned about the team, raced into the boathouse and to the women's changing room. There he found the GB Women's Eight shocked and tearful. Nate was prowling around, blaming himself for Anna's condition.

'I should have insisted she went to hospital first thing,' he was muttering as Miles arrived, skidding to a stop on the recently mopped floor.

'Don't beat yourself up,' said Sian. 'You weren't to know she'd develop such problems.'

'What's the matter?' asked Miles.

'The paramedics think Anna's got a blood clot on the brain,' Sian explained. 'She banged her head this morning.'

'Shit.'

'I know. And I'm trying think how awful it is for Anna and her parents but instead, all I can think about is that we haven't got a cox so that's us not rowing. Does that make me a dreadful person?'

Miles took Sian's hand. 'No, it makes you human. Nothing that's happened to Anna is your fault and yet

487

her accident has had massive repercussions on you. God, what a shitty mess.'

Sian nodded, her eyes welling with tears. 'I suppose there's 2016.'

'Yeah. But it's no consolation for today, is it.'

Sadly, Sian shook her head.

Miles took himself away, leaving the girls to mourn their lost chance. He returned to the pontoon and relayed the grim news to Dan and Rollo.

'What a lousy stroke of luck,' said Rollo.

Dan bit back a comment that maybe if Rollo hadn't wished their opposition ill, events might have been different. Of course, Sian hadn't wanted Anna as a cox . . .

She'd wanted Amy . . .

And Amy was here . . .

Dan turned and legged it to the boathouse, ignoring Rollo's yells wanting to know where the fuck he thought he was going as they were due to race in twenty minutes.

Dan burst into the girls' changing room. 'Nate, Nate. Find the race officials,' he demanded.

'Why? Don't tell me you've got a problem too. I've got as much as I can handle right now.'

'Amy's here. Amy's spectating. I saw her on the big screen just now. She can cox.'

Nate's jaw dropped. 'Amy?'

'Yes, but you'll need to talk to the race officials.'

'Yes, yes, of course. Get hold of her. Get her to haul her arse over here. I'll fix the change of crew.' He turned round to the huddle of women who were consoling each other over their broken dreams. Succinctly he told them

488

to get themselves ready to race and why everything had changed again.

'Amy? Amy! I don't believe this,' shrieked Sian, jumping up and down.

'Just remember, it's not a given. She may not make the weight, the race officials might not allow it, she might be high on drugs for all we know . . .'

'Amy? Don't be daft,' said Sian with a broad grin, her mood having completely changed.

Dan fished his phone out and called Maddy. He wasn't going to risk wasting time on calling Amy – she mightn't answer once she saw who it was.

'Maddy, are you sitting with Amy?'

'Yes, why on earth . . . ?'

'No time to explain. Tell her to meet Nathan at the race control building now. Tell her not to argue, just to do it. The women's eight need her.'

Dan rang off and Maddy turned to Amy to relay the message. 'It sounds really vital that you go.'

'No,' she said. 'Mads, whatever it is I can't do it.'

Susie came vaulting up to Amy from where she was sitting. 'Amy, Angus has just told me that Anna's been hauled off to hospital. If you don't step up and take her place, our women's eight can't race.'

'But I can't. I haven't coxed since January, I'll be awful.'

'Then you go and tell Ellie and Sian and the others that you won't. Go on, if you're going to let them down that you've got to tell them in person and not take the coward's way out,' said Susie.

'You couldn't be so mean as to not give them a shot,'

said Maddy. 'They're your friends. You know what this means to them – it's the Olympic final and you're their only hope.'

'But I'll make a fool of myself and them.'

'Better being thought fools than not competing at all, I'd say.'

'I can't,' said Amy suddenly feeling terrified.

'You've got to,' said Maddy. She grabbed Amy's hand. 'Come on.'

Susie grabbed her other hand and between them they dragged her to the race control building. Nathan was waiting for them.

'Thank God you're here,' he said. 'Come with me.' And he swept her inside.

Maddy blew her cheeks out. 'Blimey. What a drama.'

37

While Nathan was explaining to the race officials about what had happened and how he planned to solve the problem, Dan returned to Rollo who was looking at his watch angrily.

'What the fuck was all that about, because as a preparation for the race of our lives, it was completely shite.'

'I'll explain. Let's just get to the start first, though.'

The two men paddled up towards the start, trailing the other boats heading for the beginning of the race by some minutes. En route he gave Rollo the bare facts.

'Fucking hell,' said Rollo. Then he added, 'Bit of luck Amy being here.'

Dan didn't answer because he was thinking about Amy. Maybe now she was a competitor and not a spectator he'd get a chance to talk to her. So much damage had been done and so much needed unpicking. Maybe, like Amy being around to cox, it was serendipitous. He had to hope so.

Down at the boathouse end of the lake the crowd was doing its collective nut for the medal ceremony for the previous final – the lightweight men's coxless fours. As expected, the Aussies had won but Britain had got the silver, which was great, but the nation wanted to see gold for the GB rowers and so far it hadn't happened. Two finals out of fourteen completed and only a silver so far; Dan and Rollo felt the weight of the nation's expectations for a gold in this event as they made their way the two kilometres to the start.

As they rowed, the banks were lined with partisan supporters who applauded them loudly, whooping and cheering and waving Union flags. If Dan and Rollo hadn't been so chock-full of nerves it would have been uplifting but instead all it did was make them feel more worried about delivering. And, as Rollo had so rightly pointed out, their mental preparation for the race had been completely shite.

Amy could hear the Australian national anthem being played to celebrate that country's gold medal in the lightweight men's fours and knew it signalled that it was almost time for Dan's race. And she was going to miss it. Instead, she was taking part in an intense briefing from Sian and Nate about their race and their planned strategy. Someone had managed to scrounge a strip from one of the lightweight women, which fitted where it touched – which was hardly anywhere. Compared to the rest of the crew she looked like a sack of spuds but it couldn't be helped and she didn't care; she had a lot of other stuff to worry about over the next half hour or so. God, why on earth had she agreed to do this? She was so going to make a mess of it and let the crew, the whole squad and the nation down. She felt sick at the thought of it.

'Go over the race plan again,' she said, a frown of worry creasing her brow.

'Look,' said Nate, 'stop stressing.' He gave her a hug. 'Rely on your instincts. They were good enough to make the Reading ladies British champions.'

'But they were an amazing crew,' said Amy miserably.

'And this is an even better crew,' said Sian. 'If you don't do this we have *no* chance. At least with you in the stern we have something to cling to. Besides, I always wanted you over Anna, didn't I, Nate?'

Nate nodded. 'But we've got you in the end.'

'But not a good way of doing it.' Amy shook her head. 'This is Anna's gig not mine.'

Dan stared past the back of Rollo's head at the man lying on his stomach, holding the stern of their scull against the start. They were in lane three, although the draw wasn't so important as it was, say, on the Thames for the Boat Race. No bends, no currents, no advantage; this was just a straight sprint to the line. The tension and the knotting in his stomach were almost unbearable and yet in about six minutes it was all going to be over. Just six minutes. Nervously he checked the gates on the riggers again.

The starter raised his flag.

This was it.

'Attention, go!' A plip, the lights turned green and they were racing.

'Drive,' said Rollo. 'Drive.'

Their start was good, better than the French beside them. They were a canvas up after just two strokes.

Dan concentrated on the length of his stroke, matching Rollo's rate of thirty-seven strokes per minute perfectly. In training and in other competitions they'd always managed to keep this rate going long enough to get ahead of the field allowing them the luxury of easing off in the third five-hundred-metre piece. But this was the Olympics, there were medals at stake and no one was going to give any quarter.

'It's only pain,' Dan told himself, gritting his teeth as the lactate began to build up in his thighs. He glanced right and left. They were well ahead of the French who were having a terrible race and the Slovenians were also trailing them, which put them in fourth. Behind them were the umpires' launches making sure none of the race rules were infringed along the length of the course. He looked over his shoulder at the rest of the opposition and noticed that the others weren't so far ahead. Catchable.

He followed Rollo's stroke exactly. Technically, he knew their rowing was as near to perfect as was possible. If Nate was watching he'd be proud but Dan suspected he was still sorting out the mess caused by Anna's accident.

Out of the corner of his eye he could see the stern of the German boat starting to appear next to them. They were catching them. If they took them they'd move from fourth into the medals. But he couldn't think of that, he had to concentrate on the rowing.

Catch, drive, extract, recover. Catch, drive, extract,

recover. Legs, body, shoulders, arms. He concentrated on keeping all the important power-generators in perfect harmony, trying to ignore the increasing burn in his thighs and shoulders as the pain built up inexorably.

The Germans began to fade badly, their morale taking a dip as the two Brits swept past them. The cheers erupted on the banks and in the grandstands. The flag wavers went berserk but there was still a whole kilometre to go and if they wanted any sort of a chance of a better medal they couldn't give themselves the luxury of dropping the rate.

Dan and Rollo powered on as Dan grabbed another glance. The Australians and the New Zealanders were level pegging just about four metres up. Might they be so engrossed in their own battle Rollo and Dan could squeeze past? Realistically he knew there wasn't a chance of that happening. This wasn't like running where you could sneak up behind the opposition without them being aware. In rowing the competitors could see exactly who was behind them and trying to catch them.

On the coaching path the bikes of the performance directors and coaches kept pace with them, advice being shouted, encouragement given, which was all but drowned by the shrieks and yells of the home crowd willing Dan and Rollo on. Centimetre by centimetre they began to gain on the other two crews. Both pairs had gone off like the clappers, Antipodean rivalry driving them into a separate competition from the Olympic one, but their rate wasn't sustainable. It became apparent both pairs were starting to flag but would their mental stamina keep them going just long enough to prevent Dan and

Rollo winning more than bronze?

Dan glanced backwards again – three metres now and the Australians and New Zealanders were still neck and neck. And they were nearing the end of the third piece, the final five hundred metres was coming up. Did he and Rollo have anything left in the tank? And if they went now would it be too early? Memories of the last time he and Rollo had raced Aussies flashed into his mind – it had been at Henley two years previously and they'd got it fractionally wrong and had lost. He really didn't want a repeat today.

The crowd seemed to think they could do it. The roar as they began to approach the last section managed to drown out the sound of a jet, just out of Heathrow, thundering overhead.

'Come on,' said Dan. 'Draw, draw.' Forwards, back, dip in, lift out, push, recover, on and on they went, their boat slicing through the mirror-calm water leaving the scar of the wake in its path.

Their rate upped to thirty-eight. Would it be enough, would the other two crews respond? The pain in his legs was becoming unbearable, his lungs felt as if they were going to explode but it was only ninety seconds more of agony. That was all, then it would be over.

Dan glanced again, the gap was closing but so was the gap between the three crews and the finish. Would they do it? The crowd roared more, the crowd was going mental: if sheer goodwill could win the race then he and Rollo had the gold medal in the bag.

They pushed on, conscious of not letting the expectations of their supporters down. The sterns of both the oppositions' boats crept into his peripheral vision. Two hundred metres to go. Then Dan was level with both the stern scullers. One hundred metres.

Nip and tuck and still they inched forwards until the three boats in line abreast hurtled the last metres to the line. When it came to the crunch it might all depend on which crew was actually on the drive of the stroke as they crossed it, giving them that extra thrust, that difference between first and second.

The plips came so quickly together it almost sounded as one note.

Dan collapsed forward across his sculls onto his knees. He'd done his best. His chest hurt so much, his heart was pounding so hard he felt beyond ill. He gulped air in and his head swam. Rollo leaned over the side of the boat and threw up, and the other crews were no better. With a monumental effort Dan managed to summon enough energy to lift his head to look at the scoreboard. Had they done enough?

First, lane three, Quantick and Lyndon-Forster.

The crowd went wild but Dan and Rollo could only manage weak smiles.

'Well done, buddy,' gasped Rollo

'Nice one, mate,' responded Dan, before he collapsed back over his blades again.

After the gloom of Anna's accident, the atmosphere around the GB Women's Eight lifted with the boys' success. Several of the girls were on cycling machines, pedalling with minimal resistance to keep their leg muscles warm while they watched the race on the screens. The last seconds had been so close and so tense that it was only when it had finished that Amy realised she'd been holding her breath. But Dan had done it. He'd done it with Rollo and now there were close-up shots of the pair standing on the pontoons hugging each other like lovers. Honestly, the way they were looking at each other, Amy wouldn't have been surprised if they snogged.

And she felt so thrilled for them. It was a wonderful result and she thought she was going to burst with happiness for Dan. A feeling that was ruined when she realised he would never know how much his win meant to her.

Along with the rest of the teams rowing that day they crowded out of the boathouse towards the podium to watch the medals ceremony which took place just a short while later. There on the top step of the podium, gold medals gleaming around their necks were Dan and Rollo, the Union flag was the one raised to the British national anthem, and Amy found herself sobbing at the emotion of it all. He'd done it, against the odds, he'd done it and she couldn't have been more proud. She searched the grandstand for Maddy who was hugging Tanya and Susie. Christina and Stevie were jumping up and down and everyone was deliriously happy.

Once again she saw her face, tears streaming down her cheeks on the big screen. Hastily she swept them away.

But not before Dan saw them too.

38

Sian clapped her on the shoulder. 'Right then, Ames. No more enjoying ourselves. Time to get our shit together and go racing.'

Amy's stomach flipped. This was it.

She turned away from the podium while the cameras clicked madly at the two home-grown medallists, and pundits and commentators elbowed their way towards the men to get interviews, and followed Sian to the boathouse. Four of the girls picked their eight off the rack while Amy, Ellie and three others followed with the sweeps.

Behind them the cheers went up again as the first semi-final for the lightweight men's double sculls took place with Miles and his rowing partner securing a place of their own in their event final.

The girls began to paddle towards the start line and once again the partisan crowd yelled words of encourage - ment to them as they made their way there. Amy plugged her mike into the cox-box and reminded her crew about the importance of their technique, their posture, keeping their backs straight and other minor points. She knew they didn't need this information but she wanted to keep them focused on their rowing while not thinking too hard about the occasion and thus getting freaked out by it. They'd all rowed at big competitions before but nothing with quite the pressure of this one. Everything about this was massive – the number of crews, the size of the stands, the media coverage, the fiercely partisan support – even the crowds came in Olympic quantities.

'I know I'm teaching you to suck eggs,' said Amy as she finished her calm pre-race pep-talk, 'but this shit is important.' She saw Sian grin at her. They came to the top of the lake and Amy gave directions for the stroke and bow sides to help her steer the long boat into position in their lane. Number three. Dan and Rollo's lane – was this propitious? Dear God, she hoped so. She really didn't want them to just be making up the numbers in the final which was, disappointingly, how the press had rated them. This race was so important to Sian and the others and their hopes and ambitions.

Behind her an official grabbed the stern and clamped the boat against the jetty. She smiled at her crew and put her hand in the air to signal they weren't quite ready to start.

'Gates checked?' Eight heads nodded. 'Are we all ready?' More nods. 'Blades in the water, ready for the drive.' The girls got into position.

She lowered her arm. Over the next few seconds the other coxes did likewise. As each arm came down, so Amy's heart rate went up a notch.

'Attention, go.' Plip

They were off.

'Draw, draw,' called Amy to set the initial rate at thirty-six. She let the girls settle into the rhythm. 'You're doing well,' she encouraged. She glanced left and right. The six boats were pretty level with nothing much to chose between the crews. Maybe the Canadians and the Americans had a slight edge but nothing much to brag about at this stage of the game.

'Keep the catch clean,' she advised as she watched her crew's sweeps dip in and out of the water in perfect unison. Whatever else, this crew worked beautifully as a team.

'Okay, let's think about legs. On one, on two, on three, legs for ten . . . nine . . . eight . . .' She wanted the girls to concentrate on the drive, to put as much power as possible into propelling the boat through the water. 'Five . . . four . . . three . . .' It was working; they'd gained several metres against the Dutch boat in the next lane without increasing the rate. 'Let's go again, legs for ten, on one, on two, on three,' and for a second time she did the countdown. The Dutch boat was behind them but the field was more spaced out now and the Americans and the Canadians were ahead by a length. In between were the Romanians and the Chinese.

'Ladies, you are sensational. But keep the rate, and draw . . . draw . . .' she said in time to the thunk and clunk of the sweeps in the riggers and the seats sliding back and forth.

Next ahead were the Romanians, winners of the gold in 2004 and bronze in 2008 and a hot team. But they weren't looking so hot today, thought Amy, watching their technique. There was a lot of splashing compared to her ladies. Their catch wasn't nearly as clean. The blades weren't angled exactly right. They could take them, or at least, they should be able to.

She looked at Sian and raised her thumb asking her if she thought it wise to raise the rate. Amy wasn't rowing, she didn't know what the pain threshold was, she didn't know how exhausted they might feel. She needed input from Sian before she took a decision. Sian nodded.

'Rate to thirty-seven,' she said into her head-mike. 'Draw . . . draw . . .' She said imperceptibly faster than before. She checked the box. Bang on thirty-seven, said the digital dial. She gave herself a pat on the back, she hadn't lost the knack. They were creeping up on the Romanians but they were responding and although her women had gained some distance they had more to do to pass them, unless the Romanians made a mistake. Ha, as if.

As she had that thought, the Romanian number three seat missed the catch, her legs were unexpectedly driving the blade against fresh air and not against the resistance of the water. She toppled over backwards, fouling the stroke of the number two seat. Amy's crew cruised past as the opposition fought to sort themselves out and pick up their momentum again. Fourth. One more place and the girls would be in the medals. But ahead the race was on between the Chinese, Americans and Canadians. Could they catch up and join in? The distance between them and the Chinese wasn't great, maybe a length. It was possible.

'Come on, ladies,' she said, 'we're halfway and we're looking good. Keep it tight, keep it tidy and draw . . .

draw.' She pushed the rate up half a stroke. They were definitely coming back at the Asian team.

They were drawing alongside the first of the main grandstands now and the noise was deafening. The shouts and cheers were enormous and rolled across the lake like an artillery barrage. No wonder Dan and Rollo had been inspired.

'Don't let the supporters down. Let's dig deep. Only minutes to go. You can do it.'

The Canadians and the Americans must have thought the cheering was for them and in their delusion they responded. But the British women were equally inspired and began to push again. The gap narrowed and by the time they got to the five-hundred-metre mark they were level with the Chinese.

'Ninety seconds,' said Amy, 'just ninety. Give me everything for just ninety.'

The girls' faces were contorted with pain from the effort. Their strip was soaked in sweat and their hair clumped in damp tendrils on their foreheads but they pushed again.

'We lead by a canvas. Hold this and we're in the medals,' said Amy. She looked at the cox-box. 'Forty seconds. No time to go at all now. And draw . . . draw . . .'

The girls rowed like demons, holding their minute lead against the Chinese. Over the bombardment of cheers and shouts Amy heard the faint double plip of the two North American teams crossing the line.

'Go . . . go . . . keep it up,' she encouraged. She glanced sideways, the Chinese were pulling back. 'Six seconds. Legs. Three strokes.'

Plip, plip. Great Britain bronze, the Chinese fourth and nothing.

They hadn't won but no one had expected them to medal so the euphoria was crazy. Sian was sobbing and laughing, Ellie was splashing water at anyone within range, the crowd was making the sky ring with cheers and Amy was so shocked by the achievement she felt quite odd. Drained, completely numb and then the realisation of what they'd achieved kicked in and she felt tears of relief and happiness pour down her face.

Sian leaned forward and hugged her. 'You little beauty, you did it. You got us medals. Yee-haa!' she shrieked, almost deafening Amy.

'No, you did it. It was you brilliant, wonderful, lovely ladies,' she snuffled, searching for a tissue she was sure she didn't have. She gave up and blew her nose on the hem of her shirt.

Sian shook her head as she too wiped her eyes and sniffed. 'We'd been written off, remember. "Lucky to be in the final", the press said. You so deserve this medal, Amy Jones. Your parents are going to be so proud of you.'

'Shit, Mum and Dad. It all happened so suddenly I didn't ring them to tell them I was competing. Fuck. They're going to kill me. They just thought I was coming here to do a little bit of loafing around, watching fit men in lycra.' She burst out laughing. 'God, my one moment of glory in my life, my fifteen minutes of fame and I completely balls it up.'

'Ring them and tell them to watch the medals' ceremony. At least you can salvage something.'

When they finally paddled back to the pontoons the cheers and whoops that went up were heartfelt and genuine but Amy hung back, still shy about her part in the proceedings and still feeling guilty that it had been her coxing the boat and not Anna. In the hiatus of congratulations she slipped to one side to talk to Nate.

'How's Anna?'

'They think she's going to be okay. It was a clot on her brain and she's had emergency surgery. They won't know for sure till she comes round but the initial indications are all positive.' He smiled at her. 'Well done. Sian was so right about you. I should have given you another go. And you should have told me you were ill.'

Amy 'fessed up to the truth about the ice cream. 'So now you see why I couldn't.'

'Jesus, Amy, you were such a prat.'

Pillock, prat, twat – yup: whichever name was used by others it was already one she'd used on herself.

'I wouldn't call you that,' said a voice she recognised. She spun round. 'Dan!'

39

'Amy,' he said.

He gazed at her imploringly. Maybe she ought to have listened to Ellie and Maddy's insistence that she should give him a chance, maybe she oughtn't to have been so rude when he tried to apologise at that Christmas party. They ought to talk, after all it couldn't make the situation any worse. But then she felt a hand tugging at her shirt. She turned away from Dan to see a race official waiting to speak to her.

'Miss Jones, I need to ask you to provide a specimen for a dope test.'

'Now?'

'Please.' The official summoned a female steward forward. 'Please accompany Miss Jones and make sure her specimen is delivered to the doping team.'

Thoughts about talking to Dan fled as Amy's heart leapt into her mouth. The officials thought she might have been doping? Her face must have reflected her fears.

'It's just routine, Miss Jones, and because of the nature of your sudden participation in the Games.'

Relief flooded over her. Of course, but then other doubts assailed her. Supposing she had taken something unwittingly that was banned? The team would be stripped of their medals. The ignominy. The humiliation. But she had to have this test, she had no choice and she just had to hope all would be well.

She turned back to tell Dan to wait, that she'd be back in a few minutes but he'd already gone. She could see another official leading him over to the media centre. Of course the British press wanted to talk to him; he and Rollo were national heroes. It was just a shame that it had ruined her chances of having a conversation too.

She allowed herself to be led away to the loos where she filled the little pot, handed it back to the steward who placed it in an envelope, saw it labelled and taken to whoever had the lovely job of examining it.

When she returned to her team, ready for the medals ceremony, there was still no sign of Dan and she was assailed by doubts again. Perhaps she'd misinterpreted the situation because, surely, if he still had feelings for her he'd be here to see her get her gong. Even if the world's press did want to talk to him wouldn't they understand if he asked for a few minutes' grace to watch the medal ceremony? Despite the euphoria she'd felt only minutes previously, it was now crushed by the weight of disappointment.

Amy was swamped by her teammates as the medals presentation commenced and she put on a brave face and a big smile. The cheers rang out for the Canadians and the Americans but then erupted at double the volume when the British women's eight, who dwarfed their cox, all stepped up onto the podium to be presented with their medals by Sir Steve Redgrave. As the Canadian anthem played, Amy knew she ought to be remembering every moment of this, soaking up the atmosphere and committing her emotions to memory but instead, now the podium had given her a slight height advantage, she was using the opportunity to search the cheering crowd for Dan's face. She spotted Angus, Tanya, and the others but no Dan. She blinked back the tears.

'It's quite an emotional moment, isn't it,' Sian whispered to her.

Amy just nodded. It was, but for all the wrong reasons.

The medal ceremony was over and the girls were marshalled by Olympic officials and swept off for their round of interviews. The BBC, Sky Sports, the national papers, the foreign press, CBC, NBC, CNN all wanted to hear about the accident and the 'plucky stand-in', as Amy was now labelled. The 'plucky stand-in', however, was embarrassed to be so feted and felt a complete fraud. What she really wanted was to get back with her other mates, to say nothing of trying to find Dan, but instead she seemed to be on some mad loop where she was answering the same questions time and time again. 'What did it feel like when you got the call?' 'What does it feel like to have a medal?' 'Why weren't you picked to cox from the start?' . . . and so on. And all the time she had to smile and look happy, when inside she was crying as her chances of any reconciliation with Dan seemed to be slipping away.

Finally the crew were free to do as they wished. As a

body they moved towards the stands to join their co-rowers, friends and families who had cheered them on so enthusiastically. Amy smiled – this was the best day of her life, right?

Maddy was waiting for her, jumping up and down and squealing with happiness.

'That was so brilliant. I nearly peed myself with the excitement of it all!'

'Nice one, Ames,' said Tanya, clapping her on the shoulder.

Susie gave her a huge hug. 'What a star you are. Angus texted me and said he'll get hold of you later. He felt you'd had enough of being asked the same questions endlessly.'

'It was a bit repetitive,' admitted Amy. 'Although quite surreal. It wasn't how I thought the day was going to pan out when I got up this morning. And talking of getting up this morning, that was hours and hours ago and I'm famished.'

Maddy ran to get the picnic basket and passed a plastic box full of sandwiches around. The large amount of food that Maddy and Amy had prepared the previous night suddenly didn't seem quite so much now it was being shared. Just as well, Amy thought, there were no men present also wanting to eat. So where were Dan and Rollo?

As casually as she could she said, 'The boys not here? I was hoping to get to see their gold medals.'

'No, they've been whisked off to the main Olympic TV studios over at Stratford. Sue Barker wants an interview with them,' said Tanya.

Amy's heart plummeted. That was that then. If they'd been driven right across London there was no way they'd be coming back to the lake today. It stood to reason they'd go straight back to Egham and the Village. Her chance to make up with Dan had gone.

As they ate they watched the last of the races until, as they were getting ready to leave the lake, there on the giant screen were Dan and Rollo being interviewed by the BBC's premier sports presenter.

'God, look at those two,' said Tanya. 'Light and dark, how hot are they? I mean, I know I've had Rollo a million times, but I'm suddenly feeling horny again.'

Christina threw a sausage roll at her. 'Ugh, stop being disgusting. Anyway, I doubt you'd be in with a chance, the way Rollo's eyeing up Sue.'

Amy couldn't help giggling at that. Rollo was definitely flirting heavily with Sue Barker, he kept using her name and putting his hand on her arm in a very familiar manner, but it didn't seem to be having any effect on the presenter. At the end of the interview, Rollo leant over and gave her a massive kiss on the cheek. Amy looked at Dan's face, he looked amused and apologetic at the same time, and grabbing Rollo's arm, he dragged him offscreen.

Everyone was laughing, but suddenly Amy felt a bit flat. All the excitement, all the media attention had fizzled out for the time being; there were other medals being celebrated, other stories being covered and, although Amy and the crew had been warned they'd have more interviews to come, for now they were off the hook.

'So what now?' she asked.

510

'Back to the Village for us,' said Sian. 'When all the rowing's over we're planning on having a mega-party over at the training lake and you must come to that. No excuses now – it's on your doorstep after all. But tonight I think we're all too knackered to do much. Besides, it would be so unfair for any of us to get wrecked when the rest of the squad still have races to compete in. But just wait till Saturday evening! Woo-hoo!' and she punched the air.

As the shuttle buses began to roll into the venue again and the crowds began to drift off, Ellie and Sian hugged Amy before they left to catch their own coach back to the Olympic Village and reiterated that they expected to see her at the party in two days' time and if she didn't turn up they'd personally drag her there. Susie went to find Angus to see if he was free to leave and Christina and Stevie also said their goodbyes.

'So what now?' asked Maddy.

'I don't know,' said Amy as they gathered up their belongings and made their way towards the pick-up point. 'Home and bath, I suppose. Then watch today's highlights on the box because I can't remember much about the race.'

'Seems a bit rubbish. If nothing else you and I should crack open a bottle of something or even go out. Won't there be a gang of your rowing buddies at the Reading club celebrating Ellie's medal? We could go there.'

'They're not really my rowing buddies any more though are they? I haven't been there for months.'

'I bet they'd forget that detail in a heartbeat if you walked in.'

'They might not – I didn't renew my membership.'

Maddy rolled her eyes. 'Don't you want to celebrate?'

Amy thought about it. Did she? She fingered the heavy bronze medal. 'I know I ought to and I am thrilled we got a medal but it really hasn't sunk in yet. Maybe in a day or two it'll seem real. Anyway, there's that party on Saturday to look forward to.'

'I suppose.' Maddy didn't sound completely convinced.

'And I feel shattered. It's been a mad day.'

'But you can't just sit at home and do nothing, not today of all days.' Maddy's phone buzzed. 'Hang on a sec,' she told Amy. She looked at the screen puzzled, not recognising the caller ID. 'Hi,' she said. The scream that followed nearly perforated Amy's eardrums and made dogs in Maidenhead sit up and take notice. 'Seb!'

From the half of the conversation that Amy could hear it appeared that Seb had managed to hitch an earlier flight back home and was ringing Maddy from a pay phone at Brize Norton where he'd landed a few minutes earlier. If Maddy was available could they meet at Oxford station later that day?

'Available? Seb, you stupid git, there's never been anyone more available than me in the history of the human race.' She disconnected. 'Oh Amy, isn't this wonderful?' Maddy's eyes were shining with happiness. 'You don't mind do you, about going out tonight? I mean, he's back and he wants to see me before he goes home to his folks. He's even managed to book a room at the Randolph for two nights. I'm so happy, Amy. This is it.'

'No, of course I don't mind, you numpty. You must go and see him. Let's get home as soon as we can, you can pick up your case and we'll have you at Oxford station in time for tea.'

'And a shag,' crowed Maddy.

And I can stay home and be Norma No-Mates, thought Amy. But she mustn't rain on Maddy's parade, that wouldn't be fair.

Maddy had whirled out of the house, promising that she'd arrange a knees-up for Amy another time and apologising for leaving Amy on her own, and Amy had shooed her through the door with a bright smile and reassurances that an evening on her own was exactly what she wanted after a tough day.

'You sure?' said Maddy, suddenly assailed by doubts.

'Of course,' answered Amy, wishing Maddy would just bugger off before the mask cracked.

Once the door was shut, the anti-climax hit Amy like a right hook. Maybe she'd protested a bit too much that she didn't deserve her medal, which still hung around her neck. She fingered it thoughtfully and then took it off. By rights it was Anna's – poor woman. She wandered into the sitting room and hung the medal on the mantelpiece, kicked a pile of old newspapers off the sofa and onto the floor and then flopped down in their place.

A wave of self-pity swept over her but she battened it down. She had no right at all to feel miserable. Just because Maddy was finally getting it together with her bloke, just because she was on her own, just because Dan hadn't been there to see her get her medal . . . She wondered what he wanted to talk to her about. It

513

couldn't have been anything that important or he'd have made more of an effort to see her.

Desultorily she switched on the TV and immersed herself in the rest of the day's Olympic action. Coverage flicked between archery and beach volleyball, between hockey and swimming and between these events there were endless reruns of the action at the rowing lake, her team's bronze race, interviews with her and her eight and also recordings of the interview with Dan and Rollo after their success. And every time she saw pictures of Dan her heart broke a little more.

The clock ticked on, and Amy thought about Maddy and what she might be getting up to with Seb. She didn't think about the details, obviously, but the idea that Maddy was lying, at last, in the arms of the man she loved, just served to make Amy feel even lower. She should be out celebrating she should be feeling on top of the world and yet she felt shit.

Fuck it, she might be on her own, but there was a bottle of wine in the fridge and she was going to open it. She heaved herself off the sofa and tramped into the little kitchen. She was just rummaging for the corkscrew when the doorbell rang.

She really wasn't in the mood for visitors. Sighing, she put the bottle and the corkscrew down and went to open it.

What the fuck? On the doorstep were a group of about five people, a mike on a boom, a large camera and a stack of big black boxes.

'I'm sorry,' said Amy, completely nonplussed. 'Can I help?'

'Amy Jones?'

She nodded and frowned.

'BBC *South Today*,' said a glossy woman in a sharp suit. She held out her hand as she said, 'We would have rung but we only had your mobile number and you didn't answer. Someone at GB Rowing gave us your address.'

They did, did they? And why hadn't she answered her mobile? Duh, because it was in her bag, which was now at the bottom of the picnic basket with all sorts of rubbish piled on top of it.

'So what can I do for you?' Although she could guess. Her fifteen minutes of fame was going on a bit.

'I'm Miranda Bridge.' She grinned toothily at Amy, expecting to be recognised. Her smiled faded a bit when Amy gave no sign of doing so. 'We're hoping you'll agree to a quick interview. As a local celebrity and the big sports news story of the day we're hoping to you'll say yes. We're aiming to get it on the local news programme tonight so if you're happy we need to hurry a bit.'

'Tonight?'

Miranda nodded. 'We've just got about two hours till the programme goes out so we're bang up against it.' She edged nearer the door.

'Here?' Amy thought about the state of the house. It was liveable but that was all. Tidying hadn't been top of her priority list for a while.

Miranda nodded. Two of the guys with her picked up a couple of the big equipment boxes and Amy felt she had no choice but to say yes. She opened the door and

515

the team lumbered into the house. She followed them to find Miranda standing in the middle of the sitting room staring at the newspapers on the floor, a couple of used plates and mugs on the table and the layer of dust over most of the surfaces.

Swiftly Amy picked up the old papers, stacked up the crockery and shoved the lot in the kitchen. When she got back thirty seconds later the camera crew had taken over and were setting up lights, shifting the furniture and unravelling cables.

'Any chance of a cuppa?' said one. 'White with two.'

In a daze Amy took the orders for hot drinks and went into the kitchen again to make the tea. On her return with five steaming mugs, the lights were up and lit, bouncing sunshine into corners that generally stayed in the shadows and highlighting cobwebs festooning the cornices and the ceiling like something out of a horror movie. Ashamed of the public exposure of her poor housekeeping she handed round the mugs silently before returning to stand by the door. Four men and a pre-senter meant the little sitting room was full. Thankfully, having turned on all the lights to check they worked, they were turned off again till they would be needed for real. The webs merged into the shadows but they all knew they were there.

'This your medal?' said Miranda, taking it off the mantelpiece. 'Put it on, for the camera.' She handed it to Amy while keeping an eye on the webs as if she expected something to drop out of them. Then she plumped up the cushions of the sofa and sat down. She patted the sofa seat next to her. 'We normally interview face-to-face for the cutaway shots but we haven't really got time for that today. But I'm sure we can get some useful footage anyway.'

Amy plonked herself down next to Miranda while her retinue continued to set up.

'I'm just going to ask you some basic questions first – what you had for breakfast, that sort of thing – to check the levels and then we'll begin. Don't worry if you make a mistake, it can all be ironed out in the edits.'

Amy was tempted to tell her that she'd just done about fifteen interviews in a row and knew how the system worked but was still too stunned by this sudden invasion into her home to be bothered.

And so the interview began. Same old, same old, thought Amy as she repeated the answers to questions similar in every way to the ones she'd answered at the media centre at Dorney. Miranda, she could tell, was a professional, and it all moved along slickly, till the doorbell rang.

'Fuck,' Miranda snapped, angered by the interruption. 'You didn't mention you were expecting anyone.'

'Because I'm not,' Amy snapped back. It had been a long day, she wanted to chill with a glass of wine, the Olympic highlights and then have an early night and now she had a houseful of strangers and, to cap it all, another bloody visitor. She got to her feet.

'What are you doing?' said Miranda.

'Answering the door, what does it look like?'

'The continuity will be wrecked now. We'll have to start again.'

Amy didn't bother to answer. It wasn't her problem, she thought as she picked her way past several tripods and over yards of cable that snaked across the carpet to every available socket.

She opened the door.

It was Dan.

40

Dan gazed at her for a second before saying, 'Maddy said you were home alone.'

God, she was so lovely, how could he have been so stupid as to let her go?

'I'm not,' confessed Amy.

Dan felt a whoosh of disappointment. He was too late, Amy had found another friend – or maybe friends – to spend the evening with and his chance of having a quiet talk with her and trying to make up had, once again, been snatched away.

A man's voice boomed from the sitting room. 'Amy, baby, you going to be long only my equipment's going to overheat.'

Dan stared at her in disbelief. So it was a friend, a man and it sounded as though he'd *really* interrupted something. Maddy must have been mistaken about Amy's barren love life.

'Sorry, I didn't mean to interrupt anything,' he floundered, embarrassed and devastated. It had taken him so much courage to come and see Amy, goaded by a series of texts and finally a call from Maddy as she travelled to see Seb.

'She's all alone, go to her. I saw her watching your interview with Sue Barker. She thought I wasn't but, Dan, if that girl isn't still in love with you, I'll never ever sleep with Seb, so help me.' And so here he was and it was too late, someone else was busy congratulating her – and how.

'Amy,' called the man again. A florid, balding head peered around the sitting-room door.

What the fuck? This guy was old enough to be her dad – possibly her granddad. 'Amy?' questioned Dan, unable to help himself.

Amy looked over her shoulder. 'I'll be with you in a minute.' She sounded cross and impatient. The head disappeared. And then the light levels on the ground floor altered beyond belief. Some incredibly powerful lamp had just been switched off.

'Amy,' called another voice, a woman's this time. 'Amy, we can't hang about. Either bring your visitor in or get rid of them.'

Amy looked thunderous. 'Fucking TV crew,' she muttered. 'Dan, you'd better come in

'TV crew? So that bloke . . . wasn't . . .?'

'Wasn't what?'

Dan shuffled his feet uncomfortably as he stepped over the threshold. 'Sorry,' he grinned. 'It was when he said he was getting overheated . . .'

'His TV lights, Dan. You didn't think that he and I were . . .' Amy stopped. 'Him?!' She giggled. 'I might be desperate these days but even I've got standards.'

'Amy!' roared the female voice.

Dan found himself being dragged into the sitting room and saw the TV equipment and the crew.

'Who's this?' said the toothy female on the sofa.

Amy performed the introductions and instantly Miranda's attitude changed. 'Dan Quantick. Oh my,' she purred, batting her eyelashes and smiling even more toothily. Dan thought she looked like a horse trying to eat an apple through wire netting. 'You're not a local are you, by chance? We'd love to include you in the interview too – the local heroine and our very own gold medallist.'

'My mum lives in Maidenhead,' offered Dan.

'Fab. Change of plan, boys,' she said to her crew, her tone of voice changing totally. 'Let's set this up for a double interview.' She turned to Dan, 'You don't mind do you?'

'Not really,' said Dan.

'You've got your medal with you?' she asked.

Dan pulled it from his pocket.

'Put it on, there's a love. The punters will want to see it.' She turned back to her crew. 'We need to rearrange this room,' she commanded. 'Can you two make your - selves scarce while we do it? But stay close.' She glanced at her watch. 'Come on, lads, if we're going to make tonight's news we have to hustle.' She herded Dan and Amy towards the kitchen and gave the room a dis - paraging look as she took in the chaos left from making the picnic, before she returned to crack the whip on her technicians.

Amy pulled two chairs out from under the table and offered one to Dan. They were about to sit on them when the florid balding guy entered, picked the seats up and took them back to the sitting room. From the other room came the sounds of heavy furniture being shifted around and the increasingly strident and urgent commands from Miranda.

'Let's go into the garden,' said Amy. 'There's a bench out there somewhere if the undergrowth hasn't taken it over.'

Dan followed her out and they sat on the ancient teak bench in a patch of bright, late afternoon sun.

'I haven't had a chance to congratulate you on your medal,' said Amy. She ran her finger over the shiny metal lying on Dan's chest. 'I know how much you wanted it. You must be so pleased.'

'I am. And you must have done a fantastic job too today. Your crew were written off by everyone as medallists.'

'Then everyone was wrong.'

'Amy, Sian and Ellie had written *themselves* off. They knew their chances were zero. You really pulled that one out of the bag. But I haven't come round to chat about medals,' said Dan.

'No?'

'No. Amy, I know last time I tried to apologise you told me to fuck off but will you hear me out this time?' Dan watched with relief as Amy nodded slowly. 'I was a git. I said some horrid hurtful things and made some terrible accusations.'

'You did.'

'I was out of order.'

'You were.'

'And then, when we were in Portugal you wouldn't

even look at me and I couldn't bear the thought that you hated me that much.'

'Dan, I couldn't look at you because every time I did I thought I might cry. And then I made a bollocks of my trial and what with one thing and another I gave up on rowing.'

'Until today.'

She nodded.

'You, at the lake, it was meant to be, Amy. I think the gods of love or St Valentine or whoever got so utterly pissed off that we couldn't get it together again that they engineered it.'

Amy grinned. 'I never had you down for such a romantic, Dan. I've been such a dumb-arse haven't I?'

Neither of them noticed the cameraman with his camera come to the back door to tell them Miranda was ready for them again. Nor did they notice him hitch it onto his shoulder and press the record button as they moved together to kiss. He filmed for thirty seconds before stepping back, making a huge clatter in the kitchen before re-emerging

Dan and Amy were both sitting decorously, side-by-side but both looking undeniably smug and rather pink as he told them they were ready to record and could they come back in.

They were ushered into the sitting room again which had been completely rearranged. There was a hurried, whispered discussion between the cameraman and Miranda while Dan and Amy had light meters thrust under their chins and they went through the rigmarole of having sound levels checked.

Miranda opened her briefcase and pulled out some papers. 'Just a formality – release forms. She brandished the papers and a pen at them. 'You're just signing to say we can use any images we record. Nothing sinister, honest.'

Dan felt he was looking at the smile on the face of a crocodile but signed anyway. After all, they were only going to be filmed answering questions.

At Oxford station Maddy crashed through the ticket barrier, dropped her suitcase in the middle of the concourse and with sobs and squeals threw herself into the arms of a tanned but tired-looking soldier. Even the hardest heart of the most jaded traveller was touched by this joyous reunion.

'Seb, oh Seb,' she sobbed into his dusty camouflage jacket.

Seb picked her up off her feet and rained kisses down on her face. 'Maddy, sweetheart,' he murmured. Around them passers-by smiled at their tangible happiness. Then Seb bent his mouth to Maddy's and they kissed long and slow and appreciative wolf-whistles and applause rang around the bland station.

'Come on,' said Seb, quietly to Maddy as they broke apart. 'I don't mind kissing in front of an audience, but I think what I have in mind next would be better done in private.'

Maddy gazed up at him adoringly. 'Oh Seb, I can't believe you're finally back, that you're here and we're . . .' She stopped, blushing. 'Anyway, I can't wait.'

Seb picked up his huge army bergen and Maddy

retraced her footsteps to where her discarded case lay and then, hand in hand, they went to find a cab to take them to their hotel.

By the time they'd been shown to their room, Maddy was shaking with nerves and anticipation. She hadn't felt like this since the day she'd lost her virginity and even that had been a slightly more relaxed and blurry experience due to a certain amount of alcohol. But now it was with Seb. He was going to see her naked and it was both the most delicious thought and the most scary. Supposing he thought she was fat? Or too pale? She wished his arrival hadn't been so unexpected, she hadn't had time to shave and moisturise and slap on the fake tan . . . And he was so tanned and fit and buff . . .

Assailed by doubts, Maddy's confidence in herself was at rock bottom by the time the member of the hotel staff had dropped off her case, shown them the room's amenities and then backed out discreetly.

'I have dreamed about this moment,' said Seb. 'Every night, when I was watch-keeping in our base, I'd look at the moon and stars and wonder if you were looking at them too.' He took her in his arms and hugged her. 'And did I tell you how much your letters meant to me? Sometimes, it was so awful out there, your descriptions of normal life back here were all that kept me going.'

'Oh Seb. I am so glad they made a difference.'

'And I'm sorry I didn't write back as often as I should have but whenever there was any down-time you were right there in my thoughts. I imagined this moment, you know. You and I, finally together.'

He began to undo the buttons on her top. Maddy put

her hands up to undo the zip on his combat jacket but found they were trembling.

Seb took one and kissed her fingers. 'You're shaking.'

Maddy nodded, feeling a little sheepish.

'I'll be gentle with you I promise.'

'I know you will,' she whispered back.

Slowly, tantalisingly, they undressed each other until they were both naked. Maddy shivered but not because she was cold. She looked at Seb's magnificent cock and remembered Tanya's comment about him being the best fuck ever. With a crunch of lust she now understood why.

'Come on,' she said, moving towards the vast king-size bed. She pulled back the covers and snuggled down into the crisp, smooth bed linen. Seb followed her and then drew her against him. She inhaled the smell of his skin as her hands caressed the skin on his back and her lips kissed his neck, his shoulders, his chest. Against her thigh she could feel Seb's erection growing and moved her hand down to grasp it.

'Jeez, Maddy,' said Seb. 'I think I'm going to explode in a minute. Do you know how long it's been for me?'

'I can't wait either,' said Maddy. 'God, Seb I've wanted you for so bloody long. Ever since I first saw you I haven't been able to get you out of my head. And every time I thought I might be in with a chance . . . Well, we're here together now.' She rubbed her thumb across of the tip of his penis and Seb sighed in ecstasy.

'Maddy, sweetie, if you keep doing things like that to me, it's going to all go horribly wrong again.' He rolled away from her and Maddy heard the rustle of a packet being opened. He rolled back. 'If you're ready . . . And I promise, when we do this again we'll take it all so slowly, honest, my love, but forgive me this once for being beyond impatient.'

'Seb,' breathed Maddy. 'I have never been readier in my life. I've been waiting for bloody ages too, remember. And we have two whole days to do it again and again and again.'

She lay back as Seb knelt over her and then positioned himself. With one long, smooth thrust he was within her and Maddy felt an explosion of happiness and ecstasy burst inside.

'You okay, sweetie?' he asked her tenderly.

'Wonderful,' she replied, smiling up at him lazily.

Gently he began to move as they gazed into each other's eyes. The rhythm and the intensity built until Maddy, with a stifled whimper, felt the start of her orgasm roll through her. The wave of heat washed back and forth and Seb pressed his mouth on hers as she felt him spasm and shudder too.

She clung to him, tears of happiness pricking at her eyes, as Seb kissed her and murmured his thanks in her ear.

'Sssh,' she said as she stroked his hair. 'It was wonderful for me too.'

'It was too quick,' said Seb.

'It won't be next time,' Maddy promised naughtily.

They lay together, entwined in each other's arms as the sun sank lower in the sky.

Seb's tummy rumbled. 'Sorry,' he apologised once more. 'But I haven't eaten since last night.'

'Seb!'

'It was a long flight and I couldn't be bothered to grab anything when we landed. I was just focused on getting to you.'

'Seb, honey. Then we must find you some dinner soon. Room service?'

Seb mulled it over. 'I think I'd like to go out somewhere. Would you mind terribly but it's all quite novel to see normal life carrying on.'

'Whatever you want is fine with me.' Maddy stretched in bed languorously. 'And after dinner . . .'

'After dinner we've got the whole night ahead of us.' Seb stole a glance at the bedside clock. 'Half six. I'm going to have a shower, then let's go and find a drink and something nice to eat.'

'I'll have a shower after you.'

Seb jumped out of bed and Maddy picked up the remote and idly flicked on the TV. The local news had just started on the BBC. She watched the presenter give a rundown of the top stories in the area and then . . .

'And we have two new local sporting stars. Dan Quantick from Maidenhead and Amy Jones the plucky stand-in . . .'

'Seb,' screeched Maddy. 'Seb!'

He came racing out of the bathroom. 'Maddy? What's the matter?'

Maddy was bouncing up and down on the bed. 'Look!' She waved the remote at the screen. 'Look who's on TV. And they're together.' She hugged herself. Had her friends finally kissed and made up? She did hope so, she wanted them to be as happy as she was. Everyone in the world ought to be as happy as she was right now.

As it became obvious that other stories were to be covered first, Seb turned off the shower and then returned to their bed to watch the programme.

'And finally,' said the presenter after they'd been bored rigid by news items about village fetes, a house fire, restoration work on a canal and a protest against a proposed out-of-town supermarket, 'to the sports news. And over to Miranda Bridge in Reading.'

Maddy squealed as the screen showed a picture of Dan and Amy sitting side-by-side in what might have been Amy's sitting room but which had obviously had a fairly drastic makeover – and not for the better.

The interview began and the pair answered the questions that Amy had told her she'd been answering all day: 'How did it feel to get a medal? How much training have you put in? Was it a terrific shock to find you weren't just a spectator? What are your plans for the next Olympics?' And Amy and Dan answered them as the cameras zoomed in on their medals and then out again to their cheerful faces.

'So,' said Miranda as she wrapped up the interview, 'you're not making plans for 2016. How about other plans?'

Amy shook her head. 'Honestly, I can't think beyond the next few days. Today has been mad.'

'And you, Dan?'

'Me?' he said sounding surprised. 'I just think I want to have a beer or two and celebrate with my rowing buddies.'

'And anything else to celebrate?' asked Miranda, archly.

Amy and Dan looked perplexed.

The interior scene faded and on screen came the shot of Amy and Dan kissing in the garden. Miranda had done a voiceover for it. 'We'll keep you posted as to whether I need to buy a hat. And back to the studio.'

'Oh my God,' squealed Maddy. 'At last. At fucking last.'

Seb smiled at her. 'Isn't that brilliant. I am so pleased those two have got back together. When I got your updates in your letters I really despaired that they would.' He smiled at her. 'You know we were about to go out to dinner?'

'Yes?'

'Actually, I think room service might be a better idea.' He winked. 'I think I've got my second wind.'

Maddy looked at him in amazement. 'What, again? Already? Oh wow!'

41

Amy, her arm linked firmly through Dan's as if she never planned to let him go, was sipping champagne and gazing around at all their rowing friends, the GB Rowing Team, their other friends and relations, Chuck, Nate, and the huge clubroom at the top of the Sherriff boathouse at the Redgrave Pinsent Rowing Lake was packed to the gunnels. The noise was epic, the music thumped and the atmosphere was buzzing. Beside them stood Rollo and Tanya and Seb and Maddy.

It was the first time Amy, or most people for that matter, had seen Dan and Rollo in close proximity when there weren't sparks of antagonism flying about and, hard as it was to believe, Dan and Rollo really did seem to be best mates now. One day, vowed Amy to herself, she was going to find out what had happened but for now she was far more interested in her own relationship with Dan than she was about him and Rollo.

Rollo lifted up the full bottle of Roederer champagne that he was carrying. 'More, anyone?'

There was a chorus of yes pleases. He topped up their glasses expertly, not a drop spilt.

'I think we ought to have a toast. To us,' he said, raising his glass. 'And British rowing.'

'To us and British rowing,' the others chorused as they chinked glasses.

'I still feel a fraud,' said Amy

'Why on earth?' said Tanya.

Dan shook his head. 'You've got *every* right to be here. Honest.'

'I know that's what you all tell me but it really, *really* should have been Anna in that boat and it's really her medal not mine. Poor kid can't even be at this party. I hear they're keeping her in for another week.'

Dan shook his head. 'Anna's accident was nothing to do with you and if I've said it once I've said it a dozen times, Sian's convinced they only got the bronze because you coxed.'

'Sian's delusional. They'd have rowed just as hard for Anna. The crowd was inspirational and none of those eight would have given any less than they did, if it had been Anna in the stern.'

'Don't put yourself down like that.'

'Look, I love you for what you say but . . .'

'Do you?'

'What?'

'Love me?' asked Dan bluntly.

God, the man must be blind if he had to ask her a question like that.

She nodded. 'Yes, Dan Quantick, I love you. I love you to bits.'

'I love you too, Ames.'

And for the second time in just a few days the pair shared a very public kiss.

THE POWER OF READING

Outrageous Fortune

Lulu Taylor

'A brilliantly told old-school bonk-saga – hard to find nowadays.'
5 stars, *Heat*

Rich Girl
Daisy Dangerfield has been born to a life of pampered luxury. The apple of her father's eye, she is groomed by him to take over the family's property empire while she spends his money and socialises to her heart's content.

Poor Girl
Chanelle Hughes has never had anything. Dragged up by an alcoholic mother on a run-down council estate, all she's ever wanted was to escape.

But which is which?
When their lives are turned upside-down, their fortunes, too, change utterly. And while daisy is devastated by her new circumstances, Chanelle decides she'll do anything to get the security she craves.

Born on the same day, two girls whose lives could not be more different, find that they have more in common than they could ever have imagined.

'This thrilling tale of money, deceit and love is indulgently escapist.'
5 stars, *Closer*

arrow books